About the Author

Nikki Anne Ellison has been writing stories and books since she was nine years old. She graduated as an English major, creative writing emphasis, from Brigham Young University. Her hobbies include cooking, hiking, swimming, and reading. She wants to live in paradise with her family. Nikki is a member of The Church of Jesus Christ of Latter-day Saints.

Find her online at nikkianneellison.com.

Five Months to Freedom

Nikki Anne Ellison

Five Months to Freedom

Olympia Publishers
London

www.olympiapublishers.com
OLYMPIA PAPERBACK EDITION

Copyright © Nikki Anne Ellison 2023

The right of Nikki Anne Ellison to be identified as author of
this work has been asserted in accordance with sections 77 and 78 of the
Copyright, Designs and Patents Act 1988.

All Rights Reserved

No reproduction, copy or transmission of this publication
may be made without written permission.
No paragraph of this publication may be reproduced,
copied or transmitted save with the written permission of the publisher, or in
accordance with the provisions
of the Copyright Act 1956 (as amended).

Any person who commits any unauthorised act in relation to
this publication may be liable to criminal
prosecution and civil claims for damage.

A CIP catalogue record for this title is
available from the British Library.

ISBN, 978-1-80074-721-0

This is a work of fiction.
Names, characters, places and incidents originate from the writer's imagination.
Any resemblance to actual persons, living or dead, is purely coincidental.

First Published in 2023

**Olympia Publishers
Tallis House
2 Tallis Street
London
EC4Y 0AB**

Printed in Great Britain

Dedication

For Mumzshy, for reading it first, and for teaching me to love the sea.

Chapter One

The loud gong sounded over the slave compounds, startling Tahira from sleep. She groaned into her blanket, unwilling to get up. But when the woman next to her kicked her, Tahira dragged herself out of her cot. Still rubbing her eyes, she joined one of the lines waiting for the four buckets the compound used for relieving oneself. There was a time when she had been responsible for emptying the buckets, a job she was glad to have far behind her.

Tahira finished her turn with a bucket and walked back to her cot. Now that she had stepped away from the crush of women she had enough elbow room to untie her braid. Her long hair was so tangled she couldn't do much more with it than smooth it down and re-braid it. Satisfied, Tahira reached underneath her cot and retrieved the satchel she was allowed to carry to work, a satchel filled with salves and herbs for healing injured slaves. She slung it over her shoulder, pulling from inside it the jar of salve that she had developed after months of trial and error: a salve that helped save her hands from cracking, bleeding, and becoming old before her time. She rubbed a generous amount on her hands, so that they looked like they'd been coated in mucus.

Once finished she stretched her arms above her head, listening to her back popping after another restless night. Then she scratched around her arms, stomach, and legs, where her coarse shift was starting to get uncomfortably tight; she'd grown a lot since she'd gotten that shift, and she knew she would need a new one soon. But she also knew the rule, slaves could only get a new shift when their old one fell off.

As she scratched her arms, her fingers ran over the scar of a letter on her right shoulder. She hated it. For though it meant she belonged to Gall, the most powerful Master in Typeg—a fact that made most slaves feel proud and important—Tahira hated that she belonged to anyone.

Five Masters held all the power and all the slaves in Typeg. It was common knowledge that all the masters were ruthless, but none more so than Gall. Each Master marked his slaves so as to be able to distinguish them, whether by a knife, a brand, or a band of metal. Unlike the other Masters, Gall personally made his mark on all his slaves, either when they were born or when he bought them, a large letter carved into their right shoulders with a hot knife. The scar never faded.

A taskmaster unlocked the compound door from the outside and the women filed out, trying not to look too tired. Tahira followed the woman in front of her, breathing in the early morning air that never lost its stale smell.

Just outside the compound door stood a little dry well. It always made Tahira smile, for it reminded her of Old Joche, the former healer, under whom she had trained for seven years. But when Old Joche had died the year before, the master had given Tahira an impossible task of healing, banishing her to the compounds when she inevitably failed, but promising her the healer's position when she grew older. Tahira still chafed at that unfairness. The only thing that helped her keep her temper was the fact she was allowed her small satchel, so that she might still ply her healing trade.

As the slaves made their way through the labyrinth of identical straw-thatched stone compound buildings to the food compound for their morning meal, they heard the sound of horse's hooves coming toward them from up the road. In the gray early light Tahira couldn't see much more than a shadow. The slaves around her all stopped to watch.

Soon the shadow shaped into a horse-drawn cart, open at the top, with sides high enough that they couldn't see inside. Two taskmasters stood in the front, one holding the reins, the other a whip. As the cart neared, the second taskmaster raised the whip threateningly, and Tahira and the others drew well back.

The arrival of new slaves wasn't an uncommon occurrence; lately a cart had come with new slaves every other day. Tahira sighed quietly at the thought of all the ruined lives each cart represented.

The cart came to a halt in the cleared space. The taskmaster with the whip vaulted over the side and walked to the back, where he unlatched the door and swung it open.

"Out!" he shouted.

After a moment, six men and one woman climbed out. They were dressed in the brown slave shifts, and everything about them was unkempt. The men looked dejected but the woman looked terrified.

Tahira could see the masters' marks on their bodies: two men had brands on their cheeks, another had a huge hoop through one ear; one man's nostrils had been slit and a huge cut ran across his forehead; and the last two men had still-steaming brands burning on their bare chests. The woman had a bandage on her right shoulder through which they could see the bloody outline of a letter.

"They start work today!" the taskmaster shouted, pointing his whip at the new arrivals.

He climbed into the cart and it moved off. There was silence as the cart's sounds disappeared, and all eyes were on the seven new arrivals, who stood cowering under the scrutiny, nursing their wounds.

"We'll take the woman," said Neph, a woman from Tahira's compound. She stepped forward and held her hand out to the new woman. After staring at Neph's proffered hand for several long moments the woman took it. Men from three different compounds scooped up the other six new arrivals.

Neph and the new woman stood behind Tahira in the line to receive food.

"What's your name?" Neph asked.

The woman didn't answer. Tahira looked over her shoulder in time to see the woman shaking her head. Tahira returned her gaze forward and immediately felt sorry for her; she was going to have a hard day.

***

Tahira straightened and wiped her arm across her face as she searched for more crops to pick. There, under a cluster of leaves, were more of the long green plants she was supposed to be gathering. Before a taskmaster could whip her for inactivity, she dove back into work, her satchel heavy against her back.

This was the third day in a row she'd been working in the farming field. This was by far the easiest field to work in, and Tahira was grateful for the reprieve, for she'd worked nearly ten days in the temple field before this.

Slaves worked where the masters wanted them, whether in the cities serving the citizenry, or in the fields. The fields were three kinds of labor: farming, building cities, or building temples and tombs. Slaves could also have a trade, such as healer, midwife, weaver, or cook. Tahira had already been trained to be both healer and midwife, but here she was in the fields, working until the master deemed her worthy to be the healer.

Younger slaves rotated between the three fields. If they were lucky enough to show an affinity for one by the time they reached a certain age, they were given a permanent placement in that field. Tahira, as the under-healer, was not to be given a permanent field placement. But she worked her best in whichever field she was in, hoping to be returned to Old Joche's house that much sooner.

Out of the corner of her eye Tahira saw a taskmaster standing two rows of crops away from her, watching. She'd become accustomed over the last year to having a taskmaster watching her, but she never felt comfortable. She ducked her head further and kept working. After a while the taskmaster moved on and Tahira breathed in relief. But from the sounds of struggle coming from the row on her left, she knew the new woman to the compounds was having a much harder time.

While keeping her hands moving, Tahira turned her head and saw the woman kneeling in the dirt, sobbing as she combed her fingers through the leafy crop in front of her. She seemed at a loss for what to do. Tahira reached across the row and tapped the woman's wrist sharply to get her attention.

"You need to pick the ripe crops," Tahira whispered, not daring to look around for a taskmaster in case one appeared. "Look for the green ones longer than your finger. If they're shorter than that, or yellow, leave them to grow."

The woman turned her tear-stained face to Tahira and tried to smile.

A sharp sting fell hard across Tahira's back and she had to bite her lip against a scream, for she knew from personal experience that screaming only led to more whipping.

"Get back to work!" the taskmaster behind her shouted, pulling his whip back.

Gasping slightly at the pain, Tahira kept working. Beside her, the woman continued to kneel in the dirt, unsure. The taskmaster whipped her once and moved on. Tahira gingerly snaked her hand to her back and felt blood under a new tear in her shift.

Another scar. She didn't know how many she had now, but she was sure it was a great many. And though she'd made a salve for healing scars, like her salve for saving her hands, most of the time the scar had begun to set by the time she could apply it, meaning the scar became permanent.

But she would be whipped again if it meant helping a fellow slave.

***

By the time the taskmasters locked the compound door that evening, the new woman was nearly in hysterics. Neph tried to calm her down enough to sleep, but she hadn't been successful. The newcomer sat on Neph's cot, her arms wrapped around herself, rocking. Before the candles were blown out Neph grabbed her blanket and curled up on the dirt floor, letting the woman have her cot for the night.

"But remember," Neph said, a warning in her voice. "Only for tonight. Tomorrow you're on the floor until a cot opens up for you."

Tahira curled up on her cot, three or four spots away from the rocking woman. She wondered what this woman's story was, why she was so afraid, what she could do to help.

Later that night, Tahira was woken up by screaming. She sat bolt upright, a nightmare still swirling in her head. She blinked several times before she realized she was awake, and a few moments more before she realized that she wasn't the one screaming; it was the newcomer.

Tahira got to her feet and groped her way in the dark towards the woman. As she neared, she heard a slap, followed by Neph's sharp words of quiet. Tahira found Neph's shoulder and put her hand on it.

"It's all right, Neph, I'll take her," she whispered.

She heard Neph's sigh of relief. Tahira took one of the woman's trembling and sweat-soaked hands and led her through the maze of sleeping women, a path she knew well in the pitch-dark compound, to the door.

Though the taskmasters locked the door every night, they didn't know that this lock was broken. Only a few women in the compound knew this, and Tahira was one of them. She pushed the door open and got them outside before the woman had time to gasp in surprise. She led her a few paces from the door to the dry well.

"Sit down, you'll be all right," Tahira said. In the light of the full moon, which was very bright after the darkness of the compound, Tahira and the woman sat in silence. Gradually, her sobs subsided and she took a deep breath, looking skyward.

"I never thought I'd want to see the stars again," she said, her voice hoarse. "But after today, I've never been so glad to see them."

"Why is that?" Tahira asked.

"Because the stars are constant," the woman said. "They make sense when nothing else does."

"Why didn't you want to see them?" Tahira asked. She didn't look at the woman, hoping to show that she didn't expect an answer.

"I was brought on a pirate ship," the woman said. "They kidnapped me from my home and brought me here."

"What's a pirate?"

The woman gave Tahira a skeptical look. "I'm surprised you haven't heard of them. You look old enough to have been brought here by one."

Tahira shook her head. "I was born here."

"Well, pirates are men who sail in ships," the woman said. "They're bandits, thieves. They're horrible people."

"I'm sorry you were with them," Tahira said, sympathetic, though not quite understanding pirates. But she wanted the woman to keep talking, for her own sake, if not for Tahira's. The only thing Tahira had to look forward to was when the slaves were shut in the compounds for the night. On days when the work hadn't been too hard, the women in Tahira's compound lit their candles and told each other stories: about how they were brought to Typeg, about their lives before slavery, about the men they had loved, and the families they had lost. They told folk stories from their home countries, sang songs, and danced. Having never known any other world but the slavery of Typeg, Tahira was hungry for these nights, and the glimpses of other worlds she was given.

"They kept me in the hold of the ship and only let me out on deck at night," the woman said after a pause. "And I thought the stars were mocking me. That's why I thought I'd never want to see them again."

"Were you having a nightmare about them?" Tahira asked. "The pirates, I mean?"

The woman nodded. Tahira put her hand on the woman's shoulder.

"My name is Tahira," she said. "I would welcome you to the slave compound, but there's nothing very welcoming here, I'm afraid. The work is hard, and we get sick all the time. But we do tell stories at night sometimes."

The woman turned and looked at Tahira. "Why are you telling me this?"

Tahira smiled. "I'm trying to make you smile and tell you the truth at the same time."

"Well, it's working," the woman said. She finally smiled. "My name is Mary."

"Well, Mary, are you ready to go back to sleep?" Tahira asked.

Mary's smile faded. "I have nightmares every time I sleep, Tahira," she said. "I can't sleep."

"You need to, Mary," Tahira said. "You need your strength. You don't want to feel what happens when the taskmasters don't think you're working well enough." She paused, then smiled again. "I know just the thing. Stay here and I'll be right back."

Mary looked confused, but stayed seated. Tahira got up and ran along the dirt paths between the compounds, staying to the shadowed side lest she be spotted and killed by patrolling taskmasters, until she reached the two long rows of slave houses. While most slaves lived in the compounds, certain slaves were allowed to live in houses: those who were married, children under sixteen, and those with trades.

Tahira found the healer's house, knocked once, and entered.

The healer didn't look very friendly as he staggered out of his cot to meet her. But when he saw who she was by the dim light of his candle, his cragged face split in a grin.

"I'm sorry to wake you, Amra," Tahira said, bestowing a quick hug on his ancient shoulders. "I have a new friend who's having trouble sleeping, and I need something for her."

"I'd 'ave thought ye'd have it in yer bag," Amra said, this speech clumsy around his toothless gums.

"My satchel is for healing injuries, not for sleep," Tahira said, smiling at him. The old man had been a fixture in Old Joche's house during Tahira's seven years there, for it had been his job to tend to the herb garden, stir the potions, grind up roots, and help carry injured slaves. He had always been fond of Tahira, and she returned his fondness with relish. When Old Joche died Amra was made the healer, with Tahira as his apprentice, though she was far more knowledgeable about healing than him.

"Well, ye know yer way aroun'," Amra said, shuffling back to his cot. "I canna wait until yer the healer again. I don' know what I'm doin'."

Tahira bustled about the house, gathering the herb and tonic she needed. Almost nothing in the house had changed in the year since she'd been sent away; she almost expected Old Joche to come shuffling from the fire, having just finished mixing up a new tonic, and now wanting to teach Tahira how to cook biscuits. Tahira smiled as she looked around. She had been happy here.

Once she gathered what she needed for Mary, she waved to Amra, and ran back to her compound.

"What did you get?" Mary asked as Tahira joined her.

Tahira opened her hands. "Drink a little of this tonic every night," she said. "Just a little, now. It will help you sleep." She held up the other hand, which was full of dried leaves and little white-and-yellow flowers. "After you take the tonic, put one of these in your mouth and suck on it. It'll help calm you, keep the nightmares away."

Mary looked from Tahira's hands to her face a few times. "Will they really?"

"It's been known to work," Tahira said. "These are the best things I can give you."

Mary took the tonic and leaves. "How do you know this?"

Tahira gave a little shrug. "I was trained as a healer before I was brought to the compounds."

"Why didn't you stay?"

"The master put me here," Tahira said. She had tried, but she wasn't able to keep all the disappointment out of her voice. Mary seemed to have heard it, for she put her hand on Tahira's shoulder. Tahira gave her a weak smile.

She opened the compound door and the two stole inside silently. Tahira kept one hand on Mary's left shoulder while her eyes adjusted to the darkness before she led Mary to her own cot, which she knew Mary needed more than she did. Tahira curled up on the floor.

Chapter Two

The next evening, after the taskmasters had locked the door following the evening meal, the women lit their candles and started telling stories. The women around Mary coaxed her into telling her story, and after a while, she admitted she had been brought to Typeg on a pirate ship. Immediately four other women crowded around, all claiming to have been brought by pirates themselves. Tahira had never heard these women's stories before, and so listened attentively to them when they told their stories.

Tahira had heard many stories in the last year, had heard about many different parts of the world so very different from Typeg's desert. But something about the stories about pirates, sailing in something called ships on something called the ocean, excited Tahira; this was a world she'd never heard of before.

One night the woman named Rol described the ocean as being a huge expanse of blue water under a clear blue sky. Tahira could only imagine something as big as the biggest field, which was so big Tahira couldn't see across it when she stood at one end. Rol assured her that the ocean was much bigger, and Tahira got a headache when she tried to imagine it. A blue sky was hardest for Tahira to imagine, as the sky above Typeg was rarely blue, but either cloudy and gray or hazy and yellow.

If Tahira had thought the ocean was difficult to imagine, she found ships nigh to impossible to see. The woman named Dot told her another night that a small ship, like the one she had been on, was so tall that it would take nearly six compound buildings stacked on top of each other to match the height. Bigger ships were even taller than that. The compound buildings were almost twice as tall as Tahira. She just couldn't imagine the height of six stacked on top of each other, even when she looked at the compounds in the light of day. Not even Master Gall's house on the edge of the temple field was that tall.

When Tahira asked one night what ships looked like, Dot cupped her hands as though to hold water between them. She told Tahira this was the rough shape of ships, and they floated on the water. Rol and Mary then poked their fingers into Dot's palms, signifying something they called masts, which were like giant sticks, and it was the masts that were so tall. Some ships had two masts, others had three. On the masts, Dot told Tahira, were giant pieces of canvas called sails. The sails caught the wind and made the ship move forward.

Tahira started getting a headache again at the thought. But though she still didn't understand, having never seen anything like what the women were describing in their pirate stories, Tahira was fascinated. If ever she got out of Typeg, she would want to go on a ship, to see the ocean, to see the blue sky, to see the sails and how they caught the wind.

The five Pirate Women—as Tahira privately called them—told their stories only every so often on a story evening, so it was months before Tahira heard all their stories.

Mary told hers first, as hers was freshest. She had been fishing with her father in the ocean when they saw other sailors stranded in their boat. She and her father had sailed over to help, but they didn't realize until it was too late that these other sailors were pirates, who had only been pretending to be in trouble. When Mary's boat pulled up alongside them, the pirates had killed her father and taken her captive. Mary had been one of twelve prisoners on the pirate ship, all kept belowdecks except for one hour at night, when they were brought topside. On their arrival in Typeg, Mary and six of the men were sold at the slave market and brought to the compounds; Mary didn't know what happened to the other five.

Mary's life before the pirates took her seemed idyllic to Tahira. She'd lived in a beautiful cottage near the ocean on a green field full of flowers and gardens. She'd had two younger brothers and a baby sister. There was a man who wanted to marry her, a man she loved, a man who tended sheep and who always smiled. Mary always smiled herself when she talked about him, though she never mentioned his name. Tahira thought it was because she wanted to keep her memory of him a secret, something kind and warm to remember during the long days working in the fields.

Rol told her tale on the next story evening. She'd lived with her mother on a beautiful island. This island—a spot of land floating in the ocean, as she described it to Tahira—was a haven for pirates. As such, Rol knew more about pirates than any of the other Pirate Women; she knew what drinks they liked, what phrases they used, and rattled off all the curse words she'd learned from a lifetime of living among them. Tahira covered her ears after the first few. Rol had grown up hearing the pirates' stories of adventure and of other lands. And finally, she grew tired of her beautiful island and wanted to travel. She booked passage on a pirate ship with some of her friends, said goodbye to her mother, and set sail. But on the voyage, she'd inadvertently offended the captain and some of his officers by refusing to dine with them. As punishment they had stranded her on the deck during a storm, hoping she would get washed overboard. But she'd survived by lashing herself to a barrel in the waist (Tahira was too entranced by the story to ask what that meant), much to the fury of the pirate captain. Instead of honoring their agreement of taking Rol to the continent, the captain had sailed for Typeg and sold Rol into slavery.

Bitterness threatened to engulf Rol at that point, and it was only when Dot patted her shoulder that Rol recalled herself. She then talked about her island, how it looked like a giant turtle from far away, how the green hills rose toward the center, how the wharf was lined with stores and taverns, and how the quay held dozens of wooden stalls where people sold goods they'd made. Rol's mother had one of those stalls, and she sold clothing she had made or bartered from the pirates. Rol used to help her, and now wished more than anything that she had been contented to stay on her island.

Lores told her story next, a few story evenings later. She'd come from an inland country rich in spices, bright colors, and lots of dancing and songs. Her family had owned cattle, and was very wealthy. Lores spent her turn that first story evening talking about her home: the festivals, the ranchers, the feasts, the whirling skirts and big hats of the dancers, the savory soups and peppers, the hot sun baking the earth.

It was only at the next story evening that Tahira heard Lores's experience with pirates. Lores had gone with her family on a merchant ship to sell some of their cattle to a neighboring country, a journey that would be easier on sea than on land. They were en route when pirates attacked their ship. Lores was immediately grabbed and thrown into the brig of the pirate ship, so she never knew what became of her family. After a few days of being in the dark brig the pirates brought her up on deck and tied her to a mast, so they would have something pretty to look at while they worked. Lores had nearly died exposed to the elements like that. But the worst part for her was watching the pirates. Tahira could tell Lores was being discreet, but still, Lores's account of the pirates' brutalities, drunken brawls, and tortures made Tahira feel sick.

The last two Pirate Women to tell their stories, Dot and a woman named

Tel, had been on the same ship together. Neither of them mentioned their lives before, only to say that they had run away from home when they were young. Even when Tahira asked them in private, they wouldn't tell her any more. When they had run away both of them had disguised themselves as boys and stole away aboard a pirate ship. Thinking both women were boys, the pirates put them to work, teaching them how to reef and hand, run up the rigging, bring powder during battles, and even cook.

Tahira had no idea what they were talking about. Dot explained that the rigging on a ship was the ropes holding the masts to the ship, as well as the ropes holding the sails to the masts. Pirates and other sailors pulled on the ropes to make the sails move. Reefing and handing were words used to describe how the rigging was moved around. As for powder, Tel explained it was a special black powder that made fire, and it was used for cannons. All ships had cannons, which were big metal weapons used for attacking other ships. Tahira was still confused.

Tel told many stories about swinging in the rigging. She said that she was the fastest one of the ship's boys, and could run from the deck to the crosstrees faster than anyone. Tahira pictured again the height of six compound buildings stacked atop each other, and imagined Tel climbing up that high faster than anyone else, with only ropes to hold onto. The very thought made Tahira feel dizzy. And yet it excited her; inexplicably she wanted to try it. To be up that high felt to Tahira akin to touching the sky. And if the sky really was as blue as Rol had said, then Tahira wanted that much more to be closer to it, to feel its warmth and breathe its fresh air.

Dot and Tel had lived like boys on the pirate ship for years before it became painfully obvious that they were women. At that point, the pirates, enraged by their deception, sold them to a passing slaver ship, which was a special kind of ship used for transporting slaves from one place to another. It was the slaver who brought them to Typeg.

After hearing all the stories from the Pirate Women, Tahira lay on her back in her cot, her mind turning over all she had learned about pirates and the ocean. She reflected, then, that it wasn't the pirate stories that fed her hunger to be away from Typeg, it was the stories of the ocean. She knew, now, that pirates were dangerous men, dangerous and angry and more likely to hurt than to help. She knew that if she ever met with a pirate she would be in serious trouble; even Lores's discreet stories told her that much.

But the ocean… That was a different thing entirely. It spoke of happiness to Tahira, and another word she couldn't name, but knew it to mean she was away from Typeg forever. What was that word?

***

Several months after Mary arrived, she became sick. Though she was sleeping better, thanks to Tahira's tonic and the little flowers, Mary was constantly exhausted. Rol and Lores had to practically carry Mary to and from the fields every day, and Mary was frequently beaten by taskmasters for inactivity. Then Mary stopped eating, claiming she wasn't hungry. Tahira had helped Old Joche heal slaves who'd stopped eating, but the sicknesses that caused that condition were so varied that Tahira didn't know what to do. Until she could learn more about Mary's sickness, Tahira nearly forced Mary to eat at every meal. Still, Mary's body lost weight until her bones were nearly poking through her skin.

Tahira became seriously alarmed now, but the taskmasters weren't; they still required Mary to work, despite Tahira's many protests that Mary was too sick to work and needed to be taken to the healer. Mary continued as best she could, but she was often bent double with pain in her stomach, and she moved slowly, saying her shoulders and knees hurt. It wasn't until Mary collapsed in the middle of the planting field and then lost control of all her fluids that the taskmasters finally allowed Tahira to take Mary to see Amra.

Tahira shared her choicest words about the taskmasters with Amra as they worked to save Mary. Though Tahira could see that there was nothing they could do to save her, Tahira wasn't ready to give up yet. The other Pirate Women—Lores, Tel, Rol, and Dot—came to the healer's house that night, asking what they could do to help. The taskmasters would allow Tahira, as the under-healer, to stay with Mary during the day. But that meant that Tahira got no rest, as she stayed with Mary during the night too. The Pirate Women suggested that each of them take turns spending the night with Mary, which would allow Tahira to rest.

Tahira was grateful, for the Pirate Women did this without a taskmaster's permission. Somehow, they were never caught.

For two weeks the five women and Amra worked to save Mary. They gave her tonics to swallow and rubbed soothing salves on her shoulders and knees. They fed her as often as they could, which grew less and less often as Mary descended into a delirium, and was often asleep for days at a time. When she was awake, Mary was often angry, and yelled at her caretakers. But Tahira, at least, knew that Mary's irritation stemmed from a sickness she had no cure for, and it was easy to be patient with her invalid.

Tahira had never worked so hard to save a slave from dying. But she knew it would all end eventually. She, Lores, Rol, Dot, and Tel were gathered around Mary's cot when she looked at them all one more time, and then died. Amra let the women cry their grief before gently lifting Mary's wasted body into his ancient arms and carried her away to where she would be buried.

***

In the months after Mary's death, Tahira became closer to Lores, Tel, Rol, and Dot than ever before. They spent the evenings together, ate together, and walked to their assigned fields together. Tahira felt like hugging each woman every day, for the loss of Mary had made her feel lonelier than she'd thought possible.

It seemed that all the women in the compound felt the death of Mary in some way, if only because it had been a long time since someone had died. As such, the next several story evenings were spent in singing songs, rather than telling stories, for many seemed to feel that singing was the best way to commemorate the dead.

Tahira had heard many songs in her nearly two years in the compound, but she had never tried to sing the songs herself. She did so now, for Mary had liked to sing. Tahira discovered that she liked to sing, too, and Rol was impressed with her voice.

Ever afterward Tahira quietly hummed the songs she'd learned while she worked in the fields, to help pass the time. She never hummed loud enough to be discovered by the taskmasters, for she knew that any slave caught singing was given ten cruel lashes.

But as careful as Tahira was, other slaves heard her. A few started humming songs of their own. Tahira listened and soon picked up their tunes, but she didn't know what they were until she shared them with Lores and Dot.

"Those are slave songs," Lores said. Tahira raised a questioning eyebrow.

"Slaves wrote them," Dot said. "In the words are hidden messages. Here, listen."

She sang one of the songs Tahira had hummed. To Tahira, the words sounded nice, telling a story of walking along the banks of a river. She told Dot as much when Dot finished singing.

Lores chuckled and shook her head. "No, dear, it's a story of slaves running away, escaping down the river. Have you seen the river?"

"It's to the west of here," Tel said, pointing. "It's the largest river in the world. It leads out to the ocean."

"The ocean?" Tahira said, excitement stirring in her chest. It had been a long time since she'd thought about the ocean, and that strange sense of happiness it brought her.

"I came up the river when the pirates brought me," Rol said. "It's wide enough for ships to sail right up it."

Tahira nodded, impressed, for she had accepted, even if she couldn't quite visualize, how big ships were. "What's at the end of the river?"

Lores shrugged. "Freedom. It doesn't matter what else."

Tahira looked around at the four women surrounding her. "Freedom?" she said. "Is that where you're not here in Typeg anymore?"

She asked it innocently, and the other four women felt it at once. They crowded around her as quickly as if she had just called for help.

"Goodness, yes!" Lores said, hugging Tahira tightly, as if she was a lost child. "I didn't realize you didn't know what freedom is."

"We should have figured, though; she was born here," Tel said.

Tahira thought about freedom. Freedom. That must be what the thought of the ocean felt like. Like freedom.

"I don't understand freedom," Tahira said, pulling away from Lores. "Not in the way you do, anyway. But I realize now that I've dreamed of it for a while."

"Of course you have," Tel said, making a sympathetic noise.

Lores leaned closer to Tahira with a serious expression. "Freedom is being able to decide for yourself," she whispered. "Freedom is being your own Master. There is no one to tell you what to do, and there is no one to beat you if you do it wrong."

"Freedom is never having to work for someone else," Rol said. "Not in this way, I mean. Out there in freedom you work for whomever you want. And when you have freedom, no one can make you do anything you don't want to."

"We've had our fair share of being made to do unwanted things," Dot said. "You've heard about a lot of them."

"But imagine being able to do what *you* wanted," Tel said. She took a deep breath and closed her eyes, a faraway look on her face. For the first time since Tahira had known her, she looked happy.

Lores took Tahira's hand and squeezed it. "There's a slave song you need to know," she said. "I'll teach it to you."

Chapter Three

When Tahira was a small child she lived with her parents in the slave houses. Her parents were fair-skinned, like her, and Tahira remembered her mother having bright hair, the color of the sunset. She liked to run her fingers through it in the evenings when her parents came home from the fields. Her father was strong, and could hold her high above his head with one hand. Tahira remembered him as being very quiet, but he had a nice smile.

As Tahira was too young to work in the fields, and the taskmasters would never let her parents stay home with her, she spent her days with Shipra and Pula, the spinster midwives to the slaves. They were both black-haired and aged before their time, but they loved Tahira. She cleaned their house, listened to their stories, and indirectly trained to be a midwife.

But when Tahira was a little older, both her parents and the midwives were sold to different Masters and sent to work in the cities for the citizenry. Tahira thought she would go with her parents, but Master Gall had different plans for her. She was to stay behind.

Though she knew, even at such a young age, that it was wrong to show tears to a taskmaster—for doing so could bring punishment—Tahira couldn't help but shed them as she watched her parents being taken away in a cart. A few days later she watched as Shipra and Pula were taken away too.

Watching that, resentment against Master Gall started to grow in her heart.

The next morning, two taskmasters led Tahira down the long row of slave houses to the healer's house.

"You will live with Old Joche," said one taskmaster, a young man with white hair. "The master has decreed that you will learn to be a healer."

"But who will be the midwife?" Tahira asked. Then she gasped, her hands flying over her mouth. She had forgotten that slaves do not ask questions of taskmasters.

The other taskmaster scowled. "The masters will find a new one," he said.

Tahira stood frozen, not understanding why he had answered instead of beating her. The white-haired taskmaster pushed her into the healer's house and closed the door. She stood blinking for a few moments, her eyes adjusting to the darker interior.

In the dim light she heard a chuckle. "I've never heard anyone ask a question and not receive a punishment," a woman's voice said. "You have pluck, my girl, just like I did at your age. I think you and I will be great friends."

Tahira blinked and the room came into focus. Everywhere she looked she saw tables, each one spread out with growing plants, lit candles, bowls, clear tubes of liquid, smoking bottles, and old parchment. Seated at one of the tables near the back of the house was the woman who had spoken. Tahira wound her way carefully through the tables to stand in front of her.

"My name is Tahira," she said.

"I know, my dear," the woman said. She put down the herbs she was holding and turned on her stool to face Tahira, brushing her hands on her apron.

Tahira smiled at the kind face that looked too young to be given the title of "old". Old Joche had blue eyes and dark braided hair. Her hands were strong and dry and dyed nearly every color. She stood straight and tall, but walked with a slight limp.

Old Joche had taught Tahira everything she knew about healing before she let Tahira try it herself. In the years to come, Tahira was grateful for that, for ever afterward she always knew what caused an illness or injury, and why the healing remedy would work.

***

A few years passed; the two seasons of Typeg, the Hot Time and the Cold Time, following each other with usual slowness. And still Tahira was not allowed to become the healer, even though Amra was now almost too old to heal anyone.

But Tahira was grateful she was still allowed to carry her satchel, loaded with necessary healing ingredients, to the fields where she worked, helping where she could. Often a taskmaster would pull her from her work to help a slave who had been too injured to come to her. Mostly, though, the slaves sought her out.

One such slave was Mo, an overseer of slaves, under the direction of taskmasters. Tahira couldn't help but remember the first time she had met him as she straightened out his bent finger.

It had been during the brutal Hot Time several years ago, just as she was entering womanhood. Taskmasters had dragged Mo, mostly unconscious, into Old Joche's house and placed him on a cot.

"Heal him, Old Joche," said one taskmaster. "We need him in the fields."

Old Joche nodded and the taskmasters left, slamming the door so hard that some bottles rattled. She lifted Mo into the center of the cot and arranged his limbs comfortably. She then looked at Tahira.

"Child, I need your help," she said, her voice urgent. "You're going to help me heal and learn at the same time. You need to be quick."

"Yes, Joche," Tahira said. She wiped her hands down the front of her shift and trotted over to Mo's cot. Excitement pumped through her at the opportunity to do more than watch. She knelt next to Mo and put her hand on his forehead like she'd seen Old Joche do.

"Feel that skin, dear?" Old Joche said. "It's cold, but he's been out in the sun."

"What's wrong with him?"

"He has too much sun. Many slaves get this illness during the Hot Time."

"Will he get better?"

"Yes, but we have to work fast," Old Joche said. Tahira hopped to her feet and followed Old Joche out the back door of the house to the little yard where their well stood. "Draw as much water as you can," Old Joche said, pointing to the pile of buckets by the door. "And bring in some of those rags. We need to cool Mo down."

Old Joche disappeared back into the house, and Tahira set to work. The well was only a few paces away, yet by the tenth bucket, Tahira was almost too tired to lift any more. With difficulty she started carrying the buckets into the house, both tired hands wrapped around the handle. Why was Amra working at the faraway herb garden today?

"Wet those rags and get them over here!" Old Joche called.

Tahira returned to the yard and scooped up the pile of rags. She dunked them into a bucket, hastily squeezed them out, and brought them dripping to the cot. Old Joche took them and spread them out all over Mo's body.

"Now get that plate and fan him," Old Joche said. "Stand over his face. Yes, like that. Use both hands to hold the plate. Good."

"My arms are tired," Tahira said.

"I know, child," Old Joche said gently. "But when you're trying to save someone's life you can't think of your own discomfort. Do you understand?"

Tahira closed her eyes and nodded. She let Old Joche's words sink into her, tasting them in her mind. As she did so, the soreness in her arms lessened. "I understand," she said, opening her eyes again to find Old Joche smiling at her.

Old Joche turned her attention to Mo. While Tahira kept fanning, Old Joche re-wetted the rags and replaced them, then filled a waterskin. She opened Mo's mouth and carefully poured in some water. Mo swallowed, and Old Joche gave him water a few more times. "Now, there's more to do. Mo will die if we don't cool him down. You understand?"

Tahira looked down at Mo and got a shock, where a moment before his dark-tanned skin had been dry, he was now sweating; the muscles in his arms and shoulders were visibly cramping; his eyes were darting madly beneath their lids.

"This came because of too much sun?" she asked.

Old Joche nodded. She picked up a full bucket and slowly poured it over Mo's body. The water sloshed onto the stone floor, and Tahira was grateful as some cold drops splashed her. Old Joche repeated the action with two more buckets before returning to the wet rags.

"This would work better if we had a stream," Old Joche said. She sat down with one hand on her back as though it pained her. "A stream would be a constant flow of cold water that would cool him, and it wouldn't be hard on my poor back."

"What is the cold water doing?" Tahira asked.

"Mo has a lot of heat in him from the sun," Old Joche said. "The cold water is taking the extra heat out of his body. Once it's out, he should wake up. All right, stop fanning and help me give him a drink."

For a very long time Tahira and Old Joche worked. They fanned Mo, gave him water to drink, poured water over his body, and covered him in wet rags. Tahira's arms and back ached from drawing more water from the well and carrying it into the house. Working made her even hotter, and they propped both doors open in hopes of a cross-breeze.

But finally, as the sun was setting, Mo opened his eyes.

Now, all these years later, Mo seemed to remember Tahira. He smiled at her as she yanked his bent finger into a mostly-straight position and bound it to the finger next to it with a strip of ripped fabric.

"You have all of Joche's kindness," Mo said. "Thank you."

***

During the last three years in the slave compounds, Tahira became used to the idea that slaves came and went quite regularly; some were sold to other Masters and moved to other compounds or into the cities, some were set free (or so she was told), and some died. New slaves coming into her compound had either been recently sold, or had arrived in Typeg as slaves.

After the loss of Mary, Tahira didn't think she could cope with losing her other friends too. But slavery had taught her that life was cruel. And that year she had to watch most of her friends being taken away.

Rol and Dot were sold to other Masters and sent to the cities. The mark Master Gall had given Rol when she'd arrived with the pirates was canceled by a cruel knife slice through the letter, and she was given a huge hoop through one ear. Dot's ear hoop was ripped out, and she was given a brand under her collarbone, the mark of her new Master.

Tahira and the Pirate Women huddled together in the compound the night before Rol and Dot were to be taken to the cities. They talked quietly together and cried, knowing they would likely never see each other again.

Not even a month later, Tel was killed in a rockslide in the temple field. The taskmasters didn't even bother to dig out her body, no matter how much Tahira screamed and dug at the rocks. With bleeding hands, she barely felt the taskmasters' whips as they flogged her for getting out of line. But she felt the pain as Amra worked on her injuries.

Somber and saddened by their losses, Tahira and Lores, the only two left of the original six friends, bonded together closer than ever. During the next Cold Time they shared a cot for warmth. Not for the first time in her three years in the compound, Tahira wished there was a fireplace.

This Cold Time was the coldest anyone could remember, so cold that many slaves froze to death or died from sickness. Soon the compound was more empty than full. But it allowed the survivors to share out the blankets to try and stay warm.

The taskmasters were unusually ruthless, whipping slaves for even minor offenses. Workloads doubled or even tripled, as did the number of injuries. Between the extra work and helping the injured, Tahira got very little rest. Soon, she too became ill.

Her body ached down to her marrow, so painful at times that it was impossible to get comfortable, and she was alternately racked with shivers and sweating. She slept fitfully at best, sometimes flailing about, so that Lores had to move one cot over to keep from being bruised. When Tahira was awake, she often couldn't open her eyes because they felt so heavy and swollen. Her throat was dry and sore so she couldn't talk.

Lores took Tahira to see Amra and then faithfully did everything he said to do, including talking to her. Tahira spent the days in a haze, surrounded by the stench of her compound, sometimes hearing Lores's voice. The pains and sickness in her body were almost too much for her mind to take, and the many hours she had to spend alone in the quiet didn't help. She understood then, in a way she never had before, the value of talking to the sick; something she had learned in principle, if not in practice, from Old Joche.

After a while Tahira noticed that she heard Lores's voice more than she used to. At the same time, she could at last feel the pain slowly receding. As the sickness began to leave her body and mind, she realized why Lores was talking more,

Lores was also sick.

As soon as this realization hit her, Tahira willed her body to heal faster. She couldn't bear the thought of Lores continuing to care for her when she was also sick. Finally, Tahira was able to open her eyes. She rubbed them with her fists to clear the gumming around them, then sat up, ignoring her swimming head and shaking body.

Lores lay on the cot next to her, her forehead beaded with sweat, and a faltering smile on her face. She broke off in the middle of a pirate story and reached out a hand to Tahira.

"You're better," she said, her voice hoarse.

"And you're sick," Tahira said. She took Lores's hand with one of hers and put her other hand on Lores's warm forehead. "How do you feel?"

Lores lay on her back and closed her eyes. Tahira reached for the supplies from Amra. Though still recovering, though her own body was still racked with pains and shivers from time to time, Tahira turned her efforts to making Lores better. She told midwifing stories she'd learned from Shipra, funny anecdotes she'd heard from Pula, told stories about her father's strength and her mother's hair, and taught Lores all of Old Joche's cooking tips.

But Lores soon became sicker than Tahira was prepared to heal. Lores fell asleep one morning and Tahira couldn't wake her up. Worried, she staggered to the door of the compound and called for the taskmasters.

"She needs to be taken to the healer," she said.

Wordlessly the taskmasters picked Lores up and carried her up the dirt path to the healer's house. Tahira followed them so she could tell Amra what Lores needed. The taskmasters laid Lores inside then left, barring Tahira from entering. She knew she couldn't contradict them.

"She has a sleeping fever, Amra," she called between their shoulders. Amra nodded and closed the door.

Tahira meant to drop behind the taskmasters and return to her compound, but they kept her in front of them, marching her toward the fields. She didn't understand why, and dread flickered inside her. Finally, she chanced a questioning glance at one of them.

"If you're well enough to walk to the healer's house, you're well enough to work," he said, not looking at her.

The dread settled on her shoulders and she drew her arms around herself as she started shivering. She knew that she wasn't well enough to work, but she also knew it was no use to argue. She swallowed her sigh and worked as well as her body would allow. But before the sun had reached its zenith she collapsed with sickness and exhaustion.

A taskmaster approached her as she huddled on her hands and knees.

"Please, sir," she said. She closed her eyes and waited for the whip to come down. But it never did. Instead, the taskmaster grabbed her arm and pulled her roughly to her feet.

"Get out of here," he growled, pushing her toward the gate into the field. "Don't come back until you can stand."

Tahira wondered at his kindness. She staggered out of the field and made her long way back. She had meant to go be with Lores, but her body was too tired. She collapsed onto her cot in the compound and pulled her blankets up to her chin. She closed her eyes and slept for two days.

Chapter Four

When Tahira awoke, she knew she wasn't in any danger from her sickness any more. She could tell her recovery would take time, but she took small comfort that she would recover at all; many times, slaves with her sickness never recovered.

That's when she remembered Lores.

Tahira waited impatiently until the taskmasters unlocked the compound door, explained where she was going, and sped as quickly as her weak body would allow along the frosty dirt paths to Amra's house. But she could see at once that she was too late.

Amra was waiting outside his house, as though he knew she would come. He held out his arms to her as she approached and enfolded her in them, whispering softly to her that Lores had died the previous night, peacefully and calmly.

"I saved 'er body fer ye te see," he said, looking into her face as she fought back tears. "Go ahead."

Tahira stepped into the house and saw Lores lying on her cot, her hands folded over her chest. She looked more beautiful than Tahira had ever seen her in life, and Tahira finally cried at that unfairness; Lores's life was stolen from her by those pirates, and she never got it back. She would never see her home country of spices and a hot sun again. Tahira had seen many deaths before, but Lores's affected her worse than anyone else's had, even Mary's.

After thinking about this for a few hours, Tahira realized why:, Lores's death meant that Tahira was alone, for the first time in her life.

Tahira spent the day in Amra's warm house, sitting by Lores, letting Amra take care of her. He fed her, gently washed her body, put a salve on some open sores on her back, and rubbed her feet.

But Tahira felt numb. She had never been alone before. She didn't know what to do. She didn't know how she could go on. But go on she must.

When she returned to the compound that night, she found that it was full of women, all fighting for space. As Tahira sat on her old cot, which the woman Neph had saved for her, she learned what had happened: the Cold Time had been so bad that nearly half the slave force had died. All five Masters were going to be bringing in new slaves, all newly purchased to replace the dead ones. Tahira had been sick so long that the Cold Time was nearly over, and when it was, the new slaves would be arriving. Space needed to be made for them, and so the surviving slaves were shuffled around in the compound buildings to make room.

There were so many women packed into the compound that for the first time in months it was warm that night.

A few days later Tahira was well enough to return to work in the fields. But she did so with a heavy heart. Mentally, she named everyone who had died or been sold and sent away, including those who had died in childbirth or under Old Joche's care, even those whose deaths she would rather forget.

Despair threatened to overwhelm her as she thought about those she'd lost; the number seemed so much higher than she'd realized. And it seemed to her all of a sudden that all the masters expected their slaves to do was to die. Then they could get more slaves. Tahira must have greatly disappointed Master Gall by not dying of that sickness. Perhaps he would punish her for it. Or maybe he had taken all her friends away as the punishment. Maybe *he* was Death.

Tahira took a shuddering breath and gripped her head with her dirt-and-salve-covered hands. She breathed as deeply as she could, but to her own ears she sounded like she was gasping.

Most of her life she had resented the master. First for taking her parents, then for taking Shipra and Pula, then for making her fail her healing task, then for taking the healer's trade from her. Now he had taken all her friends. Him and the Cold Time. They were one and the same in Tahira's mind now.

A taskmaster's whip tapped her shoulder and Tahira yelped in fright, cowering against the ground, her hands still gripping her head.

"If you're still not well, under-healer, perhaps you'd best be getting back to the compound," the taskmaster said. Then he strode off.

Tahira looked up and watched him walk away. Her breathing had evened slightly and she was no longer gasping. Her head felt clear and no longer muddled with thoughts of the master and Death. She touched her shoulder where the whip had tapped her. She'd almost never seen an act of mercy from a taskmaster before, and here she'd had two, close together.

Deciding not to take it for granted, Tahira gripped the strap of her satchel with both hands and ran back to the compound.

By the time she arrived she was out of breath again, but she was thinking even clearer. Her mind was still muddled from her fever, she decided. Fever and grief. Tahira sat on the edge of her cot, determined not to go crazy, not to let her feelings overwhelm her, not to let the master win.

But she was still alone. She had still lost so many. How was a person to go on when they had no one? She shook her head and chided herself. Many slaves in the compound had never had anyone. She knew she had been lucky in her friends in the last three years. She mustn't feel sorry for herself now.

***

Within a few weeks the new slaves began to arrive, delivered daily in carts to the compounds by the taskmasters. They were of every color, every age, nearly every variety of physicality. There seemed to be hundreds of them, each marked by their Master, and in various states of grief or anger at their new situation. The taskmasters assigned them to compounds, many times separating loved ones. Tahira's compound, though nearly overflowing, received four new slaves.

One was a woman who had been crippled on her voyage. The taskmasters dragged her into the compound and dumped her on the floor. The woman was crying, looking around for a friend, her hand over the bloody letter of Master Gall cut into her shoulder. Tahira went over to her and took her hand.

"My name is Tahira," she said. "What's yours?"

The woman's big eyes seemed to bulge out of her dark-brown face. She stared at Tahira for several long moments, as though trying to understand what had been said. Finally, she grasped Tahira's hand with surprising strength.

"Walk I can't," she said. Her voice was raspy and so heavily accented that Tahira had to concentrate very hard to understand her. "My legs hurt. Chains my legs on tight. Feel nothing. Walk can't."

"You're going to be all right," Tahira said in her best Old Joche impression. And though the woman seemed to calm down at her tone, Tahira herself felt fearful for this woman, for she knew the brutal life she would have to endure.

Tahira patted the woman's hand. "Come, let's get you some place to sleep."

"A bed get in I can't," the woman said.

"That's all right," Tahira said. She got into a crouch and put her arms around the woman's torso. "There's a spot on the floor next to me. I'm going to lift you up now."

Though the woman was much bigger than her, Tahira lifted her upright and draped her across her back. Slowly Tahira moved through the compound to her cot and gently eased the woman onto the floor beside it. She stroked the woman's face and smiled, hoping these gestures would do more for her than spoken language could. The woman's big eyes travelled around the compound, taking in everything.

"My name Aney," the woman said. "I stolen. My family I stolen from them, brought here. Why I here? Why me? What do I do?"

"Most of us here were stolen too," Tahira said. "We do the best we can."

Tahira wished she could give Aney promises, empty though they would be, that she would be able to go home. But Tahira had always believed in telling the truth. With a rueful smile, Tahira handed Aney her extra blanket and lay down to sleep.

As Tahira knew the taskmasters would not tolerate Aney's inability to work, she racked her mind for something for Aney to do so she wouldn't be punished. Finally, Tahira learned that Aney used to weave.

With no small amount of trepidation, Tahira went to the slave weaver—the man in charge of providing slaves with new shifts when the old ones fell off their bodies. The man was very good at what he did, but he was known for his short temper, and he jealously guarded his trade. Tahira had an idea to ask him if Aney could work as his under-weaver, helping him with the vast amount of work he now had with all the new slaves. She didn't have much hope, as the extra work might make his short temper even shorter.

She was surprised, therefore, when she found him in a reasonable frame of mind. She explained, choosing her words very carefully, that a new slave had arrived who could help him with his work. This new slave probably wasn't as good as he was—she could benefit from his knowledge—but could she help the weaver with his work, make it easier for him, so that he got more rest?

The weaver stared at Tahira for a minute, thinking. And finally, with barely a word, he pointed Tahira to a pile of woven squares of coarse shift fabric that would need to be sewn into shifts. Tahira grabbed the pile, hastily gave her thanks, and ran from the weaver's house before he could change his mind.

Aney was delighted with the work, and faithfully sewed the squares of fabric into shifts. When she ran out of squares, Tahira returned the finished shifts to the weaver and asked for his approval. He was obviously reluctantly impressed, but gave Tahira more squares for Aney. A few weeks later he came to their compound and met Aney himself, and the two talked for a long time.

Tahira thought that the angry man was finally thawing out. The next week the weaver came to visit Aney again, this time with some extra food; it seemed his Master was so pleased with how much work he was getting done that he rewarded the weaver with extra rations. The weaver explained to Aney that the rations were rightfully hers. That was the first time Tahira saw Aney smile.

Aney worked by herself all day, but she saved some of her work to do in the evenings, when the other women returned to the compound. She worked by the light of the candles while the women had story evenings, contributing very little to the conversation, but always giving the women a smile when they complimented her work.

On the nights when the women were too tired for stories, Tahira sat by Aney and watched her work, learning how to sew in the process. In return, Tahira taught Aney about healing, and suggested some things they could try to help Aney's legs.

For the first time since Lores had died Tahira didn't feel so alone any more. The despair she had felt only a short time ago slowly dissipated in the wake of Aney's cheerfully sad smiles, her nimble fingers, and her tired patience at being a permanent cripple.

***

If Tahira were a pessimist, she would have expected something bad to happen after so much happiness. But since she was a happy person by nature, she was dismayed to hear that they had been betrayed. And though the betrayal affected only a few, it rocked through the slave population, who had an unspoken agreement of not telling on one another.

A few months after Aney arrived, the taskmasters learned that she spent her days in the compound doing work for the slave weaver. And as Aney wasn't an under-weaver by trade, her work was not permitted. But while Tahira had thought it was a simple and easily-fixed transgression, the taskmasters had other plans.

They alerted Master Gall.

The first the compound heard of his coming was just after the evening meal, before the door was locked. Neph was standing in the doorway when she froze.

"Taskmasters are coming," she hissed over her shoulder.

The entire compound quietened, for something in her tone said that something was different about taskmasters coming this night. Tahira hurried over to Aney to help her gather up and hide her sewing materials. They had just finished when the taskmasters pushed Neph aside and entered the compound, the Master among them.

For her entire life Tahira had heard about her Master: that he was powerful and wonderful and took care of the slaves, that he always did what was just, despite the rumor that he was the most ruthless of the Masters. She had her own opinions about him, of course, and her resentment of him still resided in her heart.

Slaves rarely saw the Masters. But now her entire compound saw Master Gall as he threw off his brown cloak and emerged from the group of taskmasters.

Master Gall seemed to be made of gold; nearly every stitch of his clothing was gold, down to his rings. It was hard to look at anything else, so bright was his clothing in the candlelight. He sniffed and held a white handkerchief to his nose, looking over it at the congregated women with barely-disguised disdain.

As one the women in the compound stood and bowed, staying bowed until the Master chose to release them.

All except Aney.

"You," Master Gall said. He pointed lazily at Aney and lowered his handkerchief. "You do not stand."

"I'm sorry," Aney said in a small voice, her head bowed. "Stand I can't."

"Then you are the one I have heard about," the Master said. He glanced over his shoulder and two taskmasters broke off from the others and flanked him. "Search her things. Find her work."

Aney tried to cover where she and Tahira had hidden the sewing, but the taskmasters found it in seconds. They handed the sewing to the Master and resumed their places behind him.

"You may stand. I want you all to hear this," the Master said. He spoke quietly, but every ear heard. "I have heard tales that a woman in this compound has taken up work as the under-weaver, against my express wishes. I didn't want to believe it, for who would betray my trust like that? I need every woman to do the job she is given. That is the only way Typeg can function. But for you to take up work on your own goes against what I wish, Aney."

Tahira felt the room stiffen. Slaves were anonymous to the taskmasters, and Tahira thought they were anonymous to the Masters too. But Master Gall knew Aney's name. Who else's might he know?

"Why have you done this?" the Master asked. His voice was still soft but Tahira could hear the malice and the hostility behind it. He waved the sewing lightly.

Aney looked up at the Master. For a second Tahira feared that Aney would blame her for the forbidden work, as it had been her idea. But then Aney set her jaw, and Tahira knew this soft-spoken woman would bear the brunt herself; Tahira couldn't help but admire the bravery of the anger in Aney's face.

"Legs, mine hurt," Aney said. "Can't walk, can't stand. Can't work fields. Help you I want, so sewing picked up. Good job I do."

"Undoubtedly," the Master said, stroking the sewing with one hand. He looked at it for a beat longer, then tore the whole stack in half.

Tahira wasn't alone in crying aloud in anguish over all Aney's hard work.

The Master threw the ruined sewing to the ground and darted forward, grabbing Aney unkindly. He dragged her out of the compound, shouting and calling her names.

The taskmasters followed him outside, but none of them stopped Tahira from leading the women after them. None of the other women dared to interfere, but Tahira felt several women restraining her as she unconsciously leaned toward Aney to help her.

In the dirt by the well, Master Gall bore down on Aney, hitting and kicking her, oblivious to her screams. His golden clothes glittered in the dying sunlight as he methodically beat Aney until she lay crumpled on the ground, crying.

Finally, the Master turned to the taskmasters, his bloodied hands clasped, his voice soft, as though nothing had happened.

"This slave is of no further use to me," he said. "Take her out into the city and leave her in the streets."

Flanked by four taskmasters, the Master walked away. The remaining taskmasters converged on Aney, dragging her to her feet to haul her away.

"No!" Tahira screamed.

Vaguely, she saw the Master pause and start to turn. But the women around her bundled her back into the compound. They pinned her to her cot as she screamed and thrashed, trying to get to Aney, to help her, to stop the taskmasters, to hit the Master as he had hit Aney. Neph had to sit on Tahira to keep her down.

Tahira's resentment against the Master blossomed into a hatred for him, a hatred she knew was justified. For all she'd heard about him being just and caring, she now knew with absolute certainty that he was not. She now knew that he really was the most ruthless of the Masters, for who else would personally carve his letter into new-born baby slaves? Who else would beat a slave nearly to death with his own bare hands? Who else, after these and other atrocities, would then be so calm about it?

Tahira's screams eventually subsided into inconsolable sobs. She stuffed her blanket into her mouth so she wouldn't disturb the others while they tried to sleep, but she knew they were just as awake as she. None of them had seen anything so cruel as that, not even the oldest among them.

Around her, she heard the women talking in the dark.

"I'm surprised the Master didn't kill her," one whispered. "I heard that if slaves don't behave well, he kills them."

"Or sells them," said another.

"But he prefers killing," said a third woman. "I heard he can kill someone with one hand. And that he likes it!"

"He could have taken her to his mansion. I heard he takes women to his mansion for a few days."

"Hush now, you know that's only rumor!"

"But what about him knowing Aney's name?" asked a timid voice.

"Does he know all our names?"

No one had an answer, and to Tahira's relief the women finally fell silent.

Once again Tahira was alone, with no friends around her. She felt pain as much for herself as she did for Aney, despite all her attempts to not feel sorry for herself. She tried to be happy, but this latest blow was just too much. After losing so many people, she felt a part of herself close off.

Chapter Five

The next year Tahira was given a permanent field placement. The news devastated her, for it meant that she was no longer going to become the healer. Something she had done or said had angered the Master, and he had once again taken her trade from her. Tahira suspected he was angry at her for daring to speak out against him about Aney, and this was how he was punishing her.

If Tahira was right, then the Master could not have chosen a better punishment. She was sent to work in the temple-building field, which was more or less a miles-long rock quarry with steep, bowl-like sides. This field was considered to be the worst of the three, the one where the most people were hurt or killed. Master Gall's Mansion sat upon a tall hill overlooking the temple field. Some slaves said the Master watched them from the windows. Tahira didn't know or care if that was true.

The pain at now losing her trade burned through the numbness her heart had acquired in the last year in the wake of losing Aney, and her hatred of the Master grew.

The work in the temple field was brutal, divided up between several groups of slaves: carvers, carriers, chiselers, builders, and cleaners. Carvers dug rocks out of the sides of the field. Carriers brought the rocks to the chiselers, who shaped the rocks into usable shapes. The carriers then took the rocks to the builders, who moved, carried, stacked, and placed them into temple walls or layers for tombs. Between these jobs were the cleaners, who picked up after the carvers, or greased stones with animal fat for the builders to easily move them.

Tahira was given the job of a carrier, moving rocks from the carvers to the chiselers, or from the chiselers to the builders. Most of the rocks were too big for her to carry alone, so she had to coordinate with other carriers on how to best move the rocks in the quickest way possible. The carriers were the ones who were whipped most often, as their jobs required the most speed. Tahira needed help with her wounds as much as she gave it to others.

For though she was no longer going to be the healer, Tahira was still allowed to carry her satchel of healing supplies. She didn't understand the inconsistency of this, but she quickly realized that she could make this work to her advantage; she could defy the Master and still heal people.

She was now too exhausted to participate in any story evenings the compound had, preferring instead to go to sleep right after the evening meal. No one bothered her, for each woman in the compound was too wrapped up in her own cares to notice the pain and heartbreak of a quiet young woman.

The last few years had robbed Tahira of more than her friends; they had robbed her of her interest in hearing about other places, they had robbed her of the dream of seeing ships and the ocean, and they had robbed her of her desire for freedom. Each day was nothing but drudgery. Despair was her constant companion. Pain, both emotional and physical, had sapped her natural happiness from her, leaving behind a shell of her former self. She began to believe she had no one and nothing to believe in, no one for her to help, and no one to help her.

***

The next several months were dark for Tahira; she rarely had a reason to smile, and had little to look forward to. But still, there was something inside her that refused to give up, refused to let go of all the love, warmth, and happiness that she had cultivated her whole life. It might have gone dormant, but it was still there. And the moment Tahira heard humming in the fields for the first time in years, something inside her awoke.

The humming was coming from one of the slaves near her. She listened to the song, while still going about her work, for it sounded familiar, and she finally realized it was a slave song.

Tahira smiled a little; she hadn't heard that song since Lores had taught it to her. The bright pain she had once felt at thinking about Lores had dimmed to a bittersweet memory. Tahira smiled again, her muscles almost unused to the sensation now. But she felt hope coming back into her heart, the hope and accompanying happiness that had been absent for so long. As her heart lifted, the rocks she carried seemed to get lighter too.

Quietly, Tahira joined in with the humming. While surreptitiously looking around for listening taskmasters, she finally located the other hummer: it was Neph. They nodded to each other and kept working.

That evening in the compound, Tahira found Neph and sat next to her. "Thank you for humming that song," she said. "I haven't felt hope in so long." She paused, but Neph said nothing. "Why were you humming?"

"I was despairing," Neph said in her bland way. "Whenever I do, I hum. Slave songs are hope for slaves, after all."

Tahira took Neph's hand. It felt good to have human contact again, to take care of someone. "I'm sorry you were despairing. Is there something I can do for you?"

Neph gave a small smile. "You needn't feel sorry for me," she said. "I was just feeling sorry for myself. You've lost everyone you've ever cared about. If anyone has a right to despair, it's you. And yet here you are, taking care of me."

Tahira didn't know what to say. She squeezed Neph's hand. "Would you like to sing the song together now?" she asked after a while.

Neph nodded, and she and Tahira started to sing. The women around them joined in, until everyone in the compound was singing.

The women applauded when the song was over, the mood considerably lighter than it usually was. Tahira wiped tears from her eyes as everyone else started talking happily with each other. A few of them started a story evening.

Hope was surging in Tahira's chest once more; just singing that song, and indulging in the sweet memories she always attached to it, had swept away the darkness she'd lived in for over a year. She remembered again her dream of seeing ships and the ocean. She remembered her desire for freedom.

Neph smiled at her.

"That's my favorite song," Tahira said.

"Why?" Neph asked.

"I think it's because the last verse talks about leaving, finally being free," Tahira said. "Does the song have a name? When Lores and Dot taught me the slave songs, they didn't tell me what any of them were called."

"That's because slave songs don't really have names," Neph said. "But we can call that one 'Set Me Free', since that's the first line of the chorus."

Tahira nodded. "I like it."

***

The Hot Time was ruthless that year; it was so hot that everyone had difficulty focusing on their work. The air was constantly filled with screams as slaves and even taskmasters made mistakes and got hurt. Tahira spent more of her time running places with her satchel than in working with the stones. It suited her, for the stones scraped her salve from her hands, and so they started looking cracked and worn, her fingers swollen and her fingernails broken. Though it was such a small thing, Tahira mourned the loss of her beautiful hands after all her years of hard work.

Tahira stood in line one day, waiting her turn to receive a stone from a carver. Behind her was a taskmaster, his whip in one hand, wiping his forehead with his other arm. She wanted to hum to pass the time, but she didn't dare. Tahira sighed and looked up.

The steep sides of the field were pocked with boulders, some bigger than others, that the carvers would one day have to dig out for the builders to use. As long as Tahira had worked in the fields the boulders had been there, not falling, silent reminders of the constant work the slaves always had.

But just as Tahira looked up, she saw one of the boulders tremble, and fall.

And it was heading toward the taskmaster behind her.

Tahira had no time to think.

"Look out!" she screamed. She turned around and pushed the taskmaster with all her considerable strength. Surprised, the taskmaster very nearly flew backward and landed hard on his side. Tahira overbalanced and fell to the ground just as the boulder landed next to her.

"You fool!" the taskmaster shouted, jumping to his feet. He unraveled his whip and advanced on Tahira. "You know better than to attack a taskmaster!"

"Mercy," Tahira gasped. She had a sharp pain in her right ankle, and her satchel was pinned underneath the boulder. She was trapped. She could see the taskmaster's feet coming closer and she kept her head down, hoping he wouldn't whip her too badly as she lay crumpled at his feet.

The taskmaster brought his whip down hard on Tahira. She screamed involuntarily as it lashed her from her knee all the way to her shoulder. The pain in her ankle spiked. The taskmaster brought the whip back again.

"Hold it!" another taskmaster yelled. Tahira heard his feet running up. She kept her eyes closed against the pain, braced for another lash that did not come. "She saved your life!"

Silence.

"She did?"

"Yes. That boulder would have crushed you."

Silence again.

No slaves came to her aid, for they knew better than to interfere with taskmasters' business. But she thought she heard one or two sympathetic women waiting patiently to help her.

A rough male hand came down on her shoulder and she flinched.

"Come on." It was the taskmaster she had saved. She raised her head and looked up at him. All his anger was gone, replaced, strangely, by a look of apology. He held out his hands to her, his whip on the ground. She took his hands and he gently raised her to her feet. She felt the strap of her satchel break but didn't mind it as her ankle exploded in pain. She screamed out and staggered backward into the boulder.

"What is it?" both taskmasters asked at the same time, and Tahira just registered, with something between alarm and curiosity, that both men sounded concerned. She had never seen taskmasters behave this way to a slave before.

"My ankle," she gasped. Unconsciously, she reached out her hand for support, and was surprised when one of the taskmasters took her arm. Balancing on one foot she reached down and felt her injured ankle. It was painful and swollen, but she couldn't feel a broken bone. Heat and the pain were making her delirious as she struggled to stay upright.

"What needs to be done?" the taskmaster asked.

Tahira took several deep breaths. Her head was starting to spin. Panic was rising in her chest. "I'll need some herbs and a bandage and I can't walk on it." She pulled her hand away from the taskmaster and reached to her satchel to open it, only to find it was gone, crushed under the boulder behind her. She turned her wild gaze to the taskmasters. "My satchel is gone, I can't do it myself. I'm sorry!"

She was vaguely aware that her thoughts were disjointed, but she couldn't help them. She had never been this close to a taskmaster before, never had one touch her with his hands, never seen one—let alone two—actually concerned about a slave, and she was worried about what that might mean. She needed to get to Amra's house, but she could barely stand.

"It's all right," said the taskmaster she'd saved. In one motion he scooped Tahira up in his arms and carried her toward the entrance into the field.

"Where are you taking me?" Tahira asked. She tried to turn around to maybe see Neph, to ask her for help. But the movement jarred her ankle and she cried out. The panic rose more.

The taskmaster climbed up the path to the top of the bowl, his breathing hard and fast as he climbed, and Tahira focused on his breaths to help calm her own.

She couldn't believe she had just saved a taskmaster's life. After years of despising them for what they did to her, she had saved one in a moment. Now she was being carried out of the field, unable to defend herself because of her ankle.

What was going to happen to her now? She could hear the taskmaster talking to her, but she couldn't quite focus on his words; she was too scared she was going to be sent away for being unable to work. Or worse—that she'd be taken to the Master.

But instead, the taskmaster carried her to the healer's house. While Tahira sat silently, the taskmaster explained what had happened. Amra bent over Tahira's ankle then peered into her face.

"Shock," she heard him say. He wrapped her ankle carefully in the herbs and bandage she would have done herself, then turned to mix up a tonic. He gave it to the taskmaster and bowed.

The taskmaster handed the tonic to Tahira then picked her up again. He carried her all the way to her cot in the compound and placed her on it.

"The healer said to take that tonic and go to sleep," he said. He paused. "Thank you."

He left the compound, closing the door behind him. Tahira wished she hadn't been brought inside; the heat had permeated into the compound, making it hotter inside than outside. The smells were far worse now than in the evening, making her feel nauseated.

Tahira lit a candle and sat still for several long minutes, her mind running over everything that had happened. Finally, she calmed down, and she took a deep breath, shaking her head. She balled up her blanket and put it at the end of her cot. Carefully, she lay down, putting her injured ankle on top of the blanket, moving it around until it was comfortable, ignoring the stabs of pain. At last, she drank the tonic, feeling very quickly its pain-numbing coolness penetrating her body before she fell asleep.

***

Tahira woke to the early-morning sounds of the other women rising. Her ankle was still painful but her panic was gone. She lay still, following the movement of several women with her eyes, wondering if she would be allowed to rest today.

Suddenly the door opened and a taskmaster walked in. It was too early for the door to be unlocked, and taskmasters almost never entered the compound, especially alone. Ignoring the women squatting over the buckets in the corners, he looked around until he found Tahira. As he got nearer, Tahira recognized him as the taskmaster she had saved. She pushed herself into a sitting position, her injured foot still on the cot.

"I have some things for you," he said. He held up a long stick. "This is from the healer. It's a crutch to help you walk. You will be expected to work, though you will not be a carrier until you heal."

Tahira took the crutch and the taskmaster then held up a small piece of brown fabric.

"This is from Master Gall," he said.

"I don't want it," Tahira said automatically. It was the first time since she was a child that she had talked back to a taskmaster. Surprisingly, she wasn't appalled at that.

The taskmaster raised an eyebrow. "You did an honorable thing, saving my life," he said. "The Master would like to reward you. Do you know what this is?" He unfolded the fabric to show Tahira an armband with a gold seal sewn onto it. She shook her head. "When a slave exceeds what is expected of him, he is rewarded with an armband, each a different color depending on what the extra work was. When you get a certain number or color of armbands, you have the right to ask for a job inside."

"What does that mean?" Tahira asked.

"It means that you will be a personal slave to a Master or to someone in his household," the taskmaster said. He grabbed her right hand and slipped the armband around her wrist. "This is your first armband. Work well and you will receive a second."

Tahira stared at the armband for a second, then looked up at the taskmaster. She expected him to look angry, but again he did not. She wanted to ask him something, even though questions were forbidden. On the other hand, she had talked back to him and he hadn't punished her. She decided to push her luck one more time.

"Why…" she asked, and then her courage failed.

The taskmaster raised his eyebrows. "Why did I help you?" he asked. Tahira nodded. "Because last year I was injured in the field, and you healed me. Now, we're even."

He said it blandly, like he didn't care, and Tahira could see by his face that he really didn't. Any concern she had seen in him the day before was gone. He was a taskmaster again, uncaring as he did his job. Tahira bowed her head.

The taskmaster left the compound. In his wake every woman stood stunned, having heard the entire exchange. Those who were friendly with Tahira knelt around her, inspecting the armband. No one in the compound had seen one up close, though a few knew about them.

"This is a real mark of respect, Tahira," Neph said, tapping the gold seal.

Tahira scowled. "The last thing I want is to be noticed by the Master," she said. "Remember what he did to Aney?"

Neph sobered at once, and Tahira felt bad for slapping away Neph's offered congratulation. She put her hand on Neph's shoulder.

"I'm sorry," she said. Neph smiled to show all was forgiven. Tahira hobbled carefully to her feet, the crutch under her arm, and joined the line leaving the compound.

***

While Tahira's ankle healed, she worked with the temple field water carriers—slaves who'd managed to reach an old age and couldn't do any other work. The water carriers filled large waterskins from a well at the top of the bowl of the temple field, and took the brown water to the slaves working below. It was difficult work drawing water from such a deep well while standing on one foot, but Tahira knew it was easier for her than for the old slaves. And at least for now, she wasn't getting whipped.

The band on her wrist kept distracting her and she longed to tear it off, for it had come from the man she hated. But after a few days she learned to ignore it.

A taskmaster came to Tahira every few days to check on her healing ankle, to make sure she wasn't lying about her inability to work. After a couple weeks, Tahira's ankle was healed enough for her to walk without the aid of her crutch, though she still couldn't walk well enough to resume her work as a carrier.

One day, Tahira filled all the waterskins of the water carriers, talking quietly with each one, and they shuffled carefully down the steep slope into the field. Her work done for a while, Tahira walked to the edge of the bowl and looked down.

For the past several months the slaves had been carving three tall conjoined statues while it lay on the ground. This morning was the day they were going to stand it up, after which they would move it to the front of the tomb to which it belonged. Because of the dangerous nature of the move, the taskmasters were clearing out every slave who wasn't strong enough for the task, moving them up the sides of the bowl to the top where they were allowed to rest.

The remainder of the slaves stood side-by-side in three lines, their bare chests gleaming in the sun, the marks from their Masters clearly visible. Each line held onto a long metal bar attached to one of the statues by chains. One taskmaster remained in the bottom of the bowl to direct the slaves. He raised his whip and brought it down with a crack. As one, the three lines of slaves started pulling at their bars.

Tahira watched with fascination as the statues slowly started to rise off the ground. Dark shapes on the far side of the statues told her more slaves were on the other side, steadying the statues as they rose.

The statues were halfway up when Tahira noticed something was wrong. She tore her gaze from the fascination and saw the error: the three lines weren't pulling evenly.

The line on the far left was pulling much faster than the other two, causing the statues to start to twist. The far-right side seemed to have barely moved.

Tahira heard a snapping. The taskmaster in charge hadn't seen the problem.

Hundreds of slaves could die if the statues fell.

Tahira didn't hesitate.

"Stop!" she screamed. She ran as fast as she could down the side of the bowl, ignoring the pain in her half-healed ankle as she ran. "Stop! They're going to die!"

The taskmaster turned as she ran down to him, and didn't help her as she stumbled and fell in a heap on her hands and knees at his feet.

"They're pulling unevenly," she panted out, pushing herself up on her bleeding knees, too much in a hurry to care that she was once again talking back to a taskmaster. "The left side is pulling too fast, they'll break the statues. The right side is behind."

The taskmaster looked angrily at her. But the intensity in her face made him look at where she was pointing. She watched his expression change from anger to horrified realization.

He cracked his whip and started shouting, running toward the far-left line. They immediately stopped pulling. The taskmaster ran past the middle line to the far-right line, where his yelling and cracking whip encouraged them to pull faster. When the three lines were pulling evenly again, the taskmaster repeated his command to pull and the three lines moved forward, this time as one unit. Within minutes, the statues were standing and secured. They were an impressive, if very intimidating, sight, each representing a long-dead Master.

Tahira remained sitting in the rocks and dust as the taskmaster approached her.

"I missed something," he said, his voice haughty. "I don't miss anything."

Tahira lowered her head.

"I'm glad you noticed." His voice was so low Tahira could have imagined he'd said it.

As she struggled to her feet, she heard a group of people approaching from up the hill. She glanced up as she stood, then sat back down again, her head bowed.

Master Gall was bearing down on her.

"Do you know what you did?" he asked, his voice soft but terrible. Tahira didn't answer. "You made sure the statues went up. You made sure I wasn't put behind schedule. Bring her."

Tahira's heart nearly stopped in fear. What was the Master going to do with her?

Two taskmasters grabbed Tahira's arms and hauled her to her feet. They supported her as she limped along, her eyes dazzled by the Master's golden clothing in front of her.

Tahira was made to follow the Master to the top of the bowl, and then the distance across flat ground to his Mansion. Tahira had seen the Mansion as it reposed on its hill above the temple field, but she had never been this close. It rose four floors up from the ground, a beautiful building of white stone arches and pillars. Tahira saw curtains of fine white fabric draped out of some of the windows.

It was immediately cooler when they crossed the threshold. Tahira gasped at how much heat was suddenly gone from her body and she shivered once.

But her shivering from cold quickly turned into shivering from fear. For once again she was terrified about what the Master would do to her. Though she hated him, she was also afraid of him, afraid of the power he held over her life, and how quickly and callously he could take her life away.

As such Tahira hardly noticed where they turned or where they went straight. She barely noticed the beauty around her, in the paintings and furniture, in the wall draperies, in the white marble floors. Finally, the Master reached the end of a long room and sat down in a chair that was so large it could have seated several people. On his left was an open window draped in white fabric. Dimly Tahira could hear the whips of taskmasters and assumed the window directly overlooked the temple field.

The taskmasters pushed her down to the floor and she obeyed their force, kneeling on her bleeding knees with her hands clasped and head bowed. The Master was silent for a long time, but Tahira could feel his eyes on her, and she was uncomfortable. Finally, Master Gall spoke,

"I see you have a brown armband," he said. "And now, for what you have done today, I will present you with another."

He snapped his fingers. A taskmaster approached Tahira and pulled her left arm away from her body. Roughly he pushed on a dark green armband to fit snugly around her upper arm. Tahira looked at it but she didn't know what it meant.

"This is a special privilege," the Master said, as though he'd read her mind. "Not many of my slaves receive a second armband. Indeed, most do not receive the first. But in a matter of weeks, you have done acts to receive and even deserve two."

Tahira remained silent. She could hear a menace below his voice, a threat. Though she wanted to ask questions she didn't dare speak; she had seen what he had done to Aney.

"Do you know what you can do with two armbands, Tahira?" the Master asked, and Tahira involuntarily flinched; so the master knew her name too. "Usually, a slave cannot demand this until he has five. But when he carries my green band, he can demand what he wants now. Speak freely."

Tahira still couldn't help but feel this was some kind of trap. After years of never hearing of these bands, she suddenly had two. Something didn't feel quite right. There was hostility in his voice, in his bearing, under his treatment of her that made her want to run from the Mansion. But she couldn't put her finger on what it was. She felt trapped.

"I understand that I may now ask to be a personal slave," she said quietly.

"Yes," the Master said. Tahira imagined his voice as belonging to a poisonous animal. "You may choose your new Master. Whom would you like to serve?"

She knew he wanted her to serve him, but she wouldn't be that close to him, not if she could help it. He had asked her whom she would like to serve. That question she could answer.

"Please, Master, I wish to serve the healer," Tahira said. She nearly whispered it, hoping that if the Master disapproved of her request, he could pretend he didn't hear, and not punish her.

But Master Gall did hear her. "No, I don't think so," he said, his voice sneering. "You lost the privilege of being the next healer when you defied me over my just treatment of Aney."

Tahira swallowed hard. So she had been right about why she received a permanent field placement. Once again, her heart grieved at the loss of the healing trade. There was but one avenue left to her, the one the Master had been corralling her into since he had her dragged here.

"Then," she said, her voice quivering against her will, "I don't know whom to serve, Master. I only know the slaves."

"Good answer," the Master said after a pause, his voice no longer sneering. "If you had been too eager with a name, I would have worried." He paused again. Tahira started to sweat under his gaze. "As it turns out, my daughter would like a personal slave. Would you consider asking her?"

Tahira knew it would be unwise to refuse. She nodded.

"Call Alycia," the Master said. Someone ran away. "Rise, slave."

Tahira stood up, chafing at being addressed thus. She surreptitiously took a step back as she balanced between her feet.

The Master rose from his chair and approached her. "My daughter will be here shortly," he said. "You are to tell her why you would be a good slave. Answer any questions she asks. If she accepts you, then you will live here in the Mansion. You will not return to the compounds."

For the first time since entering the Mansion, hope rose in her chest; she wasn't going to be punished or killed.

"But if my daughter does not accept you, you will have one more chance to become a personal slave," the Master said. "If you fail again, you will die."

Tahira ducked her head, ostensibly to acknowledge his words, but really to hide her renewed terror from him. This was going be harder than she thought. She looked up in time to see him leave the room, though his taskmasters remained, standing silently around her.

Then she heard clicking footsteps coming from behind her. Tahira turned around to see Master Gall's daughter, Alycia.

Chapter Six

Mistress Alycia walked with the kind of confidence Tahira had only seen in the Master. She was a little taller than Tahira, seemed to be the same age, and wore a flowing blue dress. Her long blonde hair fell to her waist and curled at the ends, and her blue eyes and sweet pink mouth were both smiling a little.

Alycia stopped a few feet away and looked expectantly at Tahira, her nose up in the air. Tahira bowed her head. She did not really know what to say.

"Please, Mistress, consider me to be your slave," Tahira said. "I have been a slave all my life. I am strong, but I am also gentle. I was trained as a midwife, should you need it later in life, and I am a healer. I learned how to sew. I find solutions to problems quickly. I know how to sing, and I learn fast."

She stopped, not knowing what else to say. She kept her eyes and chin down, hoping. She did not want to fail and have to work for Master Gall.

Mistress Alycia took a step forward and lifted Tahira's chin with one finger. "Do you know how to play the game Jack Dogs?" she asked.

"No," Tahira said, her eyes still down. "But I will gladly play it with you."

Mistress Alycia dropped her hand and laughed lightly. "What's your name?"

"Tahira."

"Then, Tahira, you are my slave," Mistress Alycia said.

Tahira finally looked up to find Mistress Alycia smiling at her. Tahira couldn't bring herself to return the smile, for something inside her still rankled at the idea of belonging to someone. She vaguely wondered if she would get a new mark as if for a new Master.

Mistress Alycia raised her hand and snapped her fingers. The door behind her opened and two older women in plain clean dresses scurried in.

"Give Tahira a bath and dress her as my personal slave," Mistress Alycia said.

She gave Tahira one more smile and left the room. The two women took Tahira's hands and led her out of the room and down many stairs to the bottom level of the Mansion. Tahira saw many identical doors surrounding her, but the two women knew where they were going, confidently opening one of the doors and leading her through.

The room inside had a smooth stone floor and walls and felt very cold. On the right side of the room was a long table, covered in piles of fabric. In the room's center was a basin tall enough for Tahira to sit up in, and long enough for her to almost straighten her legs once she was sitting. Three men were inside the room, finishing filling the basin by pouring buckets of water into it. They looked up when Tahira and the other women came in and nodded once before leaving the room with their empty buckets.

"Take off your clothes," one of the women said.

Tahira stared at them. She had never removed her shift in front of strangers and she crossed her arms instinctually. With impatient noises, the two women pulled Tahira's arms down and started ripping off her shift.

"Wait!" Tahira said.

The older woman slapped her, hard.

The younger one sighed. "This is a bath, girl," she said. "We're going to put you in that basin and wash all the dirt off of you."

Tahira meant to ask another question, but with one final tug the two women removed her shift and pulled her toward the basin. Tahira felt very awkward with both women looking at her.

She climbed into the basin, and the cool water felt comforting against her skin. She had a moment to appreciate it while the women got ready to clean her. They pulled out rectangular bars of what they called soap and rubbed them onto long sticks with bristles at one end, raising up bubbles. Once done, they turned their attentions to Tahira and started scrubbing her.

They pushed the bristles of their sticks hard into her skin as they worked the bubbly soap through the years of dirt and sweat. Soon the water in the basin was dark gray. The two women, whom Tahira finally realized were house slaves, pulled her to her feet and continued scrubbing. They weren't gentle or careful as they cleaned every inch of her, and Tahira felt more exposed than ever. But every time she made even the tiniest sound of protest, they either slapped her or pinched her very hard. Tahira bit her lip against making noises.

By the time the women finished scrubbing, Tahira's skin was tingling and the water had turned black.

"I've never seen such a dirty body," the older woman said.

"She was a field slave," the younger woman said. "Of course she's going to be filthy."

"This won't do," the older woman said, pointing at the water. "I can't work with this."

"It's not her fault she's so dirty," the younger woman said.

"So whose fault is it?" the older woman asked. "It certainly isn't *mine*."

She grabbed Tahira's arm and pulled her roughly out of the basin. Tahira staggered on her ankle and the woman pushed her upright. She went over to the door and knocked on it.

Tahira felt stung. She crossed her arms to try and cover herself—against their scrutiny, and the older woman's words. But then she gave a yelp as the door opened and the three men walked in again, each carrying three bucks in his large strong hands. The two women pulled Tahira into a corner. The men, thankfully, paid no mind to Tahira standing completely exposed in the corner, but she kept her eyes on them all the same.

The men opened a hole in the stone floor and tipped the basin over onto its side. Black water poured out of the basin and into the hole. Once the basin was empty the men stood it up, covered the hole, and filled the basin with water again.

While the men were working, the two women pulled out thin metal tools that had been curved into right angles, with which they scraped Tahira's tender skin in long, fluid motions. Tahira was astounded to see even more dirt and scum coming away.

The men finished refilling the basin and left the room. The two women pulled Tahira over to it and helped her climb back in. They picked up their long brushes again and Tahira bit her lip so she wouldn't make a sound. But the pain of their scrubbing her tender skin a second time made it difficult to keep quiet.

In a shorter time than she thought they put their brushes down. But then they surprised her by pushing her under the water until her hair was thoroughly wet. Tahira sat gasping in the basin while both women reached for bottles and poured the contents into their hands. Then they started scrubbing at her hair at the same time, both women pushing and pulling her hair simultaneously so that Tahira cried out more than once. Each time she did they slapped her. Tahira, her face stinging, finally managed to subdue her cries.

The women stopped scrubbing her hair, and Tahira took a deep breath of relief. But then the women pushed her under the water again. One woman held her down while the other scrubbed at her hair yet again. Tahira started to panic as her lungs burned from lack of air. She tried to sit up but the woman resisted her. Tahira's panic spiked.

Just when Tahira thought she might drown, the women pulled her to her feet. Gasping and choking, Tahira felt herself being yanked roughly out of the basin. Soft fabric was wrapped around her and she grasped at it, pulling it tight around her so that she was finally covered again.

"It's a towel, girl, don't be so surprised," the younger woman said.

She tugged it out of Tahira's hands and rubbed it over Tahira's body. The older woman rubbed another towel through Tahira's hair. When she was dry, the two women combed painfully through her hair with combs made of shell, pulling away handfuls of loose hair. Tahira was alarmed at how much hair she was losing, and her alarm must have shown, because the younger woman said, "It's normal to lose so much hair on your first bath. You won't lose so much hair again. You still have plenty."

When they were done, the women led Tahira, her scalp prickling uncomfortably, to the long table on the other side of the room.

"You've never dressed like a house slave, so here's what you're going to wear for the rest of your life," the younger woman said, putting her hand on the piles of fabric, which Tahira just realized were clothes.

The women started dressing Tahira. As they did so, they taught her what each piece of clothing was. Tahira had never worn so many clothes before, and they all felt strange. The dress, clean but plain, pinched her muscular arms and fell to her ankles, much longer than her shift had been. All the underclothes itched, and the slippers kept sliding off her feet. Lastly, the women put the brown and green armbands back on her arms. Tahira tried not to shudder at feeling them again.

"Now, go down the corridor, girl. You need your bands," said the older woman.

"My what?" Tahira asked.

The older woman slapped her again. "I should have thought by now you'd learn to keep quiet," she snapped. "You need your house slave bands." She raised her dress so Tahira could see her ankles, and the thick iron bands that encircled each of them.

Tahira didn't know what to say. The two women led her out of the room and down the hall to one of the other identical doors. Inside the small, dark, and very hot room, they found a large man laboring with metal over a fire. He looked up at their entrance.

"New house slave," the older woman said. "Hurry, the Mistress is waiting."

The man grunted. He beckoned Tahira to him, then lifted her dress so he could wrap his fingers around her ankles, measuring them. He reached to a table by his fire and picked up two semicircular bands that Tahira could see had some kind of locking mechanism on one of their ends. The man bent over and fitted them around one of her ankles; with two loud clicks he locked them. Then he repeated the action with two more semicircular bands around her other ankle.

The bands were heavy, and clinked lightly against the floor. Walking was suddenly very difficult, especially on her half-healed ankle. Tahira focused on walking as the older woman pulled her along, vaguely listening as the woman explained that at one time house slaves had only one band, but soon their legs were so malformed they couldn't walk. Tahira was lucky, the woman said, to have two bands; that way she would still be able to walk in twenty years.

The woman led Tahira up through the Mansion, to the wing furthest from the fields. On the third or fourth level the woman stopped Tahira outside a curtained doorway. Tahira nodded to her and pushed through the curtain.

Mistress Alycia's room was large and had a constant breeze wafting through it, owing to one wall being an open arched window. Through it Tahira could see that the sun was just setting. Comfortable-looking furniture was littered around the floor, including two beds. Mistress Alycia was sitting on one of the lounge chairs, her legs stretched out in front of her, sewing on a small embroidery frame.

Tahira hurried across the polished-stone floor as fast as her slippers would allow and bowed to Mistress Alycia.

"Oh my, look at you!" Mistress Alycia said. Tahira straightened up. Mistress Alycia had put her frame aside and was staring at her in amazement. "Tahira, you're beautiful."

Tahira blushed. "I don't think so, Mistress."

"Then that's because you've never seen yourself," Mistress Alycia said. She stood up and went to one of the many tables around the room. On it was a piece of glass attached to a handle, something Mistress Alycia called a mirror. She brought it over to Tahira.

Tahira took the mirror as carefully as it were a baby, tilted it upward, and saw herself for the first time. She stared, hardly believing that she actually was beautiful. Mistress Alycia looked at the reflection then up at her.

"This is the first time you've seen yourself, isn't it?" she asked.

Tahira nodded and handed the mirror back. "I'm sorry, Mistress, but what color is my hair?" she asked. "It's not blonde like yours, but it's also not brown."

"No, there's a lot of gold among the brown," Mistress Alycia said, running her fingers through Tahira's hair. "I've never seen hair that color here before. It's beautiful."

Tahira started to smile, but then stopped herself; smiling and talking with a Master wasn't allowed, so she thought doing the same with a Mistress wasn't allowed either. She clasped her hands in front of her and bowed her head, reminding herself that Mistress Alycia was her Mistress, and not a friend.

***

As Mistress Alycia's personal slave, Tahira was to be her constant companion, to sit with her, talk with her, hold her embroidery hoop while she changed threads, brush her hair, and occasionally help her dress. She spent much of her time playing Jack Dogs, a simple game comprised of moving sticks around on a flat board, and Tahira mastered it after only a few games.

As the weeks passed, Tahira realized how childlike and almost childish Mistress Alycia was; her greatest pleasures seemed to come from activities Tahira found boring and unfulfilling, and her conversation was often circular, as though she had nothing else to say. Mistress Alycia's life was devoid of hardship or challenges, though full of etiquette and protocols. No one seemed able to refuse her, and she did not seem to notice that. Even Master Gall seemed kind and indulging when she asked for something.

Mistress Alycia was kind and sweet to everyone, and never once did she make Tahira feel worthless.

Being a personal slave was certainly much easier than being in the fields, and Tahira was grateful for the change. She was grateful to be clean for the first time in her life, to not be beaten, to be allowed rest. She was grateful to have food three times a day instead of two, and she could feel her body getting stronger in a way it never had been before.

Yet she still longed for something more. Life as a personal slave was dull, and very, very lonely. Tahira could not talk to Mistress Alycia as she had talked to her friends in the slave compound. And the other house slaves seemed to hate Tahira, resenting her, perhaps, for being a field slave who was promoted to their hallowed ranks, instead of one of them becoming Mistress Alycia's personal slave. Whenever Tahira joined the other house slaves they acted as if she wasn't there. She had no one to talk to.

Tahira hadn't forgotten her dream of seeing the ocean and ships, hadn't forgotten her longing to be free. But how could she now? While she was a field slave there was a chance, no matter how slim, that she could be sold away from Typeg. But now that she was a personal slave, there was no chance she would ever leave.

Perhaps her own conclusions were false, and her chances of leaving Typeg were non-existent wherever she was. But Tahira felt more trapped here in the Master's Mansion than she ever had in the slave compound.

Chapter Seven

A scream woke Tahira in the middle of the night. She bolted out of her bed and staggered sleepily across the room to where Mistress Alycia was thrashing and screaming in her sleep. Tahira grabbed her wrists and held her tight to keep her from injuring either one of them.

"Mistress, Mistress!" Tahira shouted. "Wake up!"

Mistress Alycia's eyes flew open and she stopped screaming. She sat up, panting, and threw her arms around Tahira's neck.

"It was just a nightmare," Tahira said. She patted Mistress Alycia gently and rocked her as she sobbed into her shoulder. When her sobs had subsided a little, she pulled away. Tahira reached over to the bedside table and turned up the flame on the lamp. "Do you want to tell me about it, Mistress?"

Mistress Alycia sniffed and wiped her eyes on the blanket. "No," she said in a whimper. She started trembling, her eyes darting wildly around the room. Tahira remained quiet. Mistress Alycia looked at the lamp, staring into the flame as though it would save her. And after a few minutes the fear left her eyes and she let out a long breath.

"I want to tell you something, Tahira," she said at last. "Why I really wanted a personal slave." She paused. "I really wanted a friend."

Tahira opened her mouth but no sound came out.

Mistress Alycia grasped Tahira's hands. "I have no friends," she said. "You know I go nowhere, I talk to no one. But you. I wanted a personal slave to have someone to talk to."

"But you shouldn't have to compel someone to be a friend," Tahira said. She said it, but she didn't regret it. Still, it didn't seem appropriate to say to her Mistress. She lowered her head. "I'm sorry. I shouldn't have said that."

"No, it's all right," Mistress Alycia said, though she looked hurt. She squeezed Tahira's hands. "I want you to speak freely. I don't want you to be afraid of saying anything. Treat me like any other friend you've ever had. Can you do that?"

Tahira nodded and smiled. "I can, Mistress."

Mistress Alycia laughed. "That's the first thing that can go," she said. "You can stop calling me Mistress."

***

Tahira was more than willing to be friends with Alycia. But it seemed that Alycia was incapable of having a friend. For no matter how open Tahira was, no matter how she stayed quiet so Alycia could talk, or asked her questions that would lead to Alycia opening her heart in return, she never did. In fact, the only thing that really changed in their relationship was that Tahira acted less like a slave. Alycia made it clear, through subtly raising her nose and looking disdainful, that she did not want to hear about Tahira's life as a slave. It saddened Tahira's heart, but she kept her hand of friendship extended; perhaps Alycia just didn't know how to have a friend, and she would learn in time.

One of the topics that Alycia repeatedly brought up was her future ownership of her father's slaves. Tahira felt uncomfortable discussing such things with Alycia, for Alycia seemed to see the slaves as nothing more than animals or property. It was times like these where Tahira knew Alycia had no idea how to have a friend, and the only time Alycia showed a lack of tact.

One morning while Tahira brushed and styled Alycia's hair, Alycia brought up the topic again. "I could never be the master my father is," she said, tracing her finger idly around her mirror's frame. "I don't know how to manage so many slaves and taskmasters, and so many projects at once. It's hard for me to imagine doing all that myself. When my father dies, I will inherit all his slaves. Well, my husband and I will. Assuming I'm married by then, of course."

Tahira paused the brush, holding her tongue against the tirade she longed to say. She stopped herself because she didn't want to hurt Alycia's feelings, nor did she want to destroy Alycia's view of the world in one blow. She kept brushing Alycia's hair.

"Tell me, Tahira," Alycia said, turning in her chair to face Tahira. "Do you think I'll be a good slave owner?"

Tahira sighed. Choosing her words carefully she said, "Alycia, you see the slaves as things you will one day own. I don't think anyone can be a good slave owner if they don't see the slaves as people."

Alycia's expression fell from hopeful happiness to a disdainful pout, and she turned her back on Tahira again. Tahira dropped her eyes and continued working on Alycia's hair in the silence. She didn't regret her words, but she knew that she'd probably hurt Alycia's feelings, no matter how she tried not to.

After a few uncomfortably quiet minutes, Alycia let out a slow breath. "I never saw it that way before, Tahira," she said. Her tone was guarded but diplomatic.

"I know," Tahira said. "But I think you will be a good Mistress, just so long as you are kind to the slaves."

Alycia stood up and faced Tahira. She looked sad. "How am I doing so far?"

Tahira couldn't help but laugh a little. "I have never been treated so kindly before," she said, holding out her hand for Alycia to take.

Alycia bypassed Tahira's hand and hugged her. "Thank you, Tahira," she said with a little laugh of her own. "I'm off to meet with Father. Enjoy your rest while I'm gone."

Tahira liked the times when Alycia went to visit her father. Since Master Gall didn't like her coming along, Tahira stayed in Alycia's room. She used this time to lie down and rest, for the dullness of being a personal slave was somehow just as draining as being a field slave. Tahira never told Alycia this, however; she always just told Alycia that she slept badly.

But this day, Tahira had just fallen asleep when she heard heavy footfalls coming toward Alycia's room. She opened her eyes just in time to see two large taskmasters before they grabbed her and dragged her out of the room.

Tahira didn't dare question them, though she had to bite her tongue to prevent herself from speaking; something about their expressions terrified her. The taskmasters pulled her along the hallways and staircases until they reached the Master's council room, where Tahira had been taken when she first was brought to the Mansion.

The Master was sitting in his huge chair, talking with Alycia as she sat in a smaller chair next to him. As Tahira entered with the taskmasters, however, his expression changed from polite interest to anger.

"Is this the one?" Master Gall asked.

"Yes," Alycia said. She looked confused. "She's the only personal slave

I have, Father, you know that."

"Yes, but one personal slave with a mind of her own is one too many," the Master said. He slowly stood up from his chair, his hand reaching toward one of the many taskmasters around the room, who handed him a multi-tailed whip. Tahira shuddered. "Alycia, there is only one thing to do with upstart slaves. I think you know what it is?"

Alycia stiffened in her seat, her eyes on the whip. "No, Father, I don't. You're not going to hurt her, are you?"

The Master turned his gaze to Tahira, his eyes alight with hate. Tahira dropped her gaze so she wouldn't be seen as challenging, but she longed to spit at him. The Master made another gesture and the taskmasters threw Tahira roughly to the floor. She bit her lip against a gasp of pain as her knees cracked against the marble.

"Of course I'm not going to hurt her," the Master said. "I'm going to show her what happens when she has opinions. And watch carefully, Alycia. You will be expected to do this the next time your slave steps out of place."

Tahira heard a whistle in the air and knew exactly what was going to happen. But that didn't stop her screaming as the whip raked hard across her back.

She had been whipped many times in her life, but never by a multi-tailed whip, and never so many times.

Again, and again, and again, and again the Master brought the whip down onto her back. After only a few lashes Tahira felt her dress rip away so that the whip landed on her bare back. Through her tears she saw her own blood sprinkling all around her on the white floor. Once she glanced up at Alycia, hoping she would say something. But Alycia sat on the edge of her chair, her hands curled around the arms, staring in horror.

The whipping went on so long Tahira could no longer cry out. She wondered how the Master wasn't tired yet. She wondered if she was even still alive.

"Stop!" Alycia screamed.

The whip came down one last time across Tahira's back. And then it finally stopped.

Tahira lay flat on the floor, in too much pain to even breathe; her breaths came shallowly as her vision started to darken. Numbness started to dull out the worst of the pain. But she knew her back would take a very long time to heal.

"Has your slave been punished enough, Alycia?" Master Gall asked. His voice sounded far away.

"Why did you whip her for so long?" Alycia asked. Her voice sounded even further away.

"I thought you wanted me to keep punishing her," Master Gall said. "Why else would you have kept quiet?"

Alycia paused. "I see. You were waiting for me to tell you when to stop punishing her. I'm sorry, Father, I didn't understand the rules."

"And now you do," the Master said. "You will be the one to do this the next time your slave speaks out of place. Punish her for as long as you deem necessary, then let her go."

"But Father, she's so hurt, she couldn't possibly do her work," Alycia said. Tahira vaguely heard Alycia walking closer.

"Would you have her killed, then?" the Master asked. "No? Well, then let her heal as long as you are willing to be without her, and then put her back to work. She's your slave, Alycia. Take her away."

Tahira was grateful that the numbness had spread over most of her body by now. She hardly felt it as the taskmasters lifted her from the floor by her arms. She hardly felt it as she was dragged out of the council room, her feet and iron bands scraping heavily against the floor and the stairs.

By the time the taskmasters had carried her down to the bottom of the Mansion, where she had her baths, and where the other house slaves lived, Tahira was nearly unconscious. She felt them lay her face down on a bed.

Cold hands touched her arms and face and she could barely focus on two women who were fussing around her — the same women who had given her her first bath, the ones who treated her the worst of all the house slaves.

"I've never seen injuries so bad before," said the younger one.

"I have, but I don't know how to heal them," said the older one. She looked at Tahira with something like kindness. "What do you need, girl?"

Tahira shook her head minutely; every time she had tried to speak in this woman's presence, she had been slapped. She couldn't take more pain, not now. But the woman looked so kind and sincere as she stroked Tahira's forehead that Tahira thought she might chance giving an answer.

"Healer," she said, her voice hoarse from screaming, her words halting. "I need lavender, aloe, and papaya. Keep my back clean with warm water. Bandages. Use horsetail first on the worst wounds." Her vision was blacking over worse now, and sounds were starting to retreat from her ears. But she could still hear the two women fussing quietly over her, repeating her instructions. "If the healer has poppy sap, bring it. Elderberries will work if he doesn't."

Before Tahira could say anything else, her vision blacked over completely.

The days passed in a haze and Tahira was barely awake for them. She felt the two women changing her bandaging often and listened to them as they told her in whispers how brave she was to defy the Master and the Mistress. She smiled weakly at Alycia when she came to visit, apologizing that Tahira was so wounded. Tahira healed slowly. But finally, her back healed enough for her to return to work.

***

Some months later, Master Gall decided that Alycia would marry. Alycia told Tahira that she was excited for marriage, but had no intention of leaving the Mansion to meet anyone. And so, the Master brought suitors to the Mansion.

"I don't really mind an arranged marriage," Alycia said as Tahira readied her for meeting with her first suitor. She picked up her mirror and gazed at her reflection as Tahira twisted braids into a kind of nest on the top her head. "Arranged marriages have always been part of a Master's life. Keep all the money and slaves in one family, you know. I never thought I would marry any other way. Besides, what other way is there?"

"Choosing who to marry," Tahira said, her blood simmering a little at Alycia's still-flippant approach to slaves. "That's how we do it. Some of them love each other, and some of them don't."

"Strange," Alycia said, laying down the mirror again. "To marry because you love someone. Is that what you want, Tahira?"

Tahira shook her head. "I haven't thought about it."

They fell silent for a while. Tahira finished Alycia's hair, then brushed powders on her face to color it.

Over the next several weeks Alycia met with all four of her suitors, who were the sons of the other four Masters. At first, she met with them individually, then with two or even three at a time. Tahira, as Alycia's personal slave, had to be in attendance, standing almost invisibly against the wall. She listened to their conversations, saw how the suitors stared at Alycia and at her. After only minutes with each of them, Tahira realized that they were all vain, greedy young men with eyes only on Alycia's inheritance, and, it seemed, Tahira's body.

"Who do you think I should marry?" Alycia asked after a few weeks. Her face was full of excitement and anticipation. Her eyes sparkled, and Tahira realized that Alycia was caught up in the idea of love. Perhaps she really did love one of her suitors, but Tahira wanted nothing to do with any of them.

"What do you think?" Tahira asked.

Alycia stared at her. "I want to hear your opinion first."

Tahira shook her head. "No, I don't think so. This is your decision."

Alycia leaned forward, her expression serious. "Tahira, I won't turn you in to my father again," she said. "I didn't realize that's what I was doing." She reached out her hand and Tahira took it. "I won't ever whip you. I won't hurt my friend."

Tahira nodded, feeling for the first time that she and Alycia really were friends. "Thank you, Alycia. What do *you* think about your suitors?"

Alycia smiled and leaned back in her lounging chair. With a romantic sigh in her voice, she described the merits of each of her suitors. She seemed to prefer Dunca Tephen the most, the one Tahira thought the most selfish and power-hungry of them all. She kept her opinion to herself, however, and a few days later Alycia accepted Dunca's proposal of marriage.

"What do you think of him?" Alycia asked Tahira as she admired the ring Dunca had given her.

"I don't think he loves you. If you wanted love in your marriage, he isn't the one," Tahira said before she could check herself. Her breath caught in her chest as she realized how blunt she'd been; she usually tried not to be so with Alycia, for fear of hurting her feelings and her childlike view of the world. She turned and faced Alycia. "I'm sorry, Alycia, I didn't mean that so badly."

Alycia stared at Tahira, her elation fading from her face. Slowly her nose rose into the air, a sure sign she was rejecting Tahira's words. Tahira was used to Alycia dismissing her. She wasn't even angry; to be able to state her opinion at all was unheard of.

"Thank you, Tahira," Alycia said at last. "But I've accepted Dunca. I'm going to marry him."

***

A few days later Alycia sat in her armchair with an instrument in her lap. It had a thick U-shaped frame with a bar across the top. Five thin strings ran from that bar down to the scoop of the U, attached to the bar by five tiny knobs. Alycia ran her fingers over the strings, releasing a sweet, light sound.

"Tahira, will you sing me a song?" Alycia asked. "My lyre and I are ready."

Tahira looked up from the pile of clothes she was folding. She had seen Alycia's instrument before, but this was the first time in nearly a year that Tahira had seen it in use. She didn't even know what it was called until that moment.

"Yes, but all I know are some sea shanties, folksongs from other countries, and slave songs," she said.

Alycia looked confused. "Slave songs?"

"Yes," Tahira said. "They're songs written by slaves. They're actually dangerous for us. If they're heard by the taskmasters, we could be severely punished."

"Why?"

"Because slave songs are about our wish to be free," Tahira said after a pause. "Taskmasters and Masters don't want us wanting freedom."

Alycia shook her head as though batting away a fly. "That's ridiculous."

Tahira opened her mouth to point out that Alycia, as her father's inheritor, would probably soon feel otherwise, but decided against it. "You wanted me to sing," she said instead.

"I do," Alycia said. She ran her fingers once more across the lyre's strings. "Maybe I can figure out how to play your song, and we can do it together."

"That would be lovely," Tahira said. "Slave songs don't really have names, but Neph and I named it Set Me Free. This is my favorite song."

And Tahira sang,

We toil along both day and night,
    Our own end not in sight.
    Our Masters' pleasure—we must serve them, 'till we are through,

With no hope that we will be free.

Set me free, set me free to a life where I may breathe,
    Set me free to pursue my own goals.
    Set me free, set me free from the life of this oppression,
    Tuned by hardship and omission, with a creed of no compassion.
    Set me free.

For as long as we remember,
    We have been serving Masters.
    But we know that we are not
    Meant just to serve with no reward.

Set me free, set me free to a life where I may breathe,
    Set me free to pursue my own goals.
    Set me free, set me free from the life of this oppression,
    Tuned by hardship and omission, with a creed of no compassion.
    Set me free.

One day soon we'll leave this bondage.
    One day soon we'll be our own people.
    Then we'll dance and play and sing aloud, We, at last, are free.

Set me free, set me free to a life where I may breathe,
    Set me free to pursue my own goals.
    Set me free, set me free from the life of this oppression,
    Tuned by hardship and omission, with a creed of no compassion.
    Set me free.

Alycia was crying by the time Tahira finished singing. She held the lyre to her chest and stared at Tahira as thought seeing her for the first time.

    "Tahira," she finally whispered. "What is it like in the compounds?"

    "It's much worse than the lives of your house slaves," Tahira said. "You saw me when I first arrived."

    "I need to learn this song," Alycia said. She put the lyre on its little stand by her chair and sat on the floor knee-to-knee with Tahira. "Teach me, please."

The rest of the afternoon they worked together, Tahira teaching Alycia the words and Alycia dutifully reciting them until she could sing the whole song by herself. Then she turned to the lyre, plucking out the melody until she didn't need any correction.

Tahira lay down on her back and stretched her arms above her head. She fell asleep to the sounds of Alycia elaborating on the song's tune, glad that for once Alycia had wanted to hear the truth.

Chapter Eight

Tahira noticed that a profound change had come over Alycia as the Hot Time came again. She was more withdrawn, more serious. She laughed still, but she hardly giggled. When Dunca came to visit she didn't fawn over him as she once did. Tahira finally asked Alycia what had come over her.

"I've had my eyes opened, Tahira," she said. "Finally. That slave song opened my eyes in a way nothing else has. It showed me what's really going on."

"Well, that song isn't everything," Tahira said gently.

"Then tell me more!" Alycia grabbed Tahira's hand. "Tell me what your life was like."

Tahira gently extricated her hand from Alycia's painful grip. She hoped, but didn't believe, Alycia to be sincere. "I've tried to tell you what my life was like, Alycia. You haven't wanted to hear it."

"I'm sorry for that, I really am," Alycia said. "I want to hear it now. In my twenty-four years I never truly realized slaves were people." She paused. "Take me to the compounds."

"No," Tahira said. Her refusal shocked even her. She blinked.

"Why?" Alycia asked. She looked hurt, but she also looked more open to Tahira than she ever had before. "Why not go and see it?"

"You won't like it," Tahira said. "I know you, Alycia. Once we set foot in the compounds, you'll want to pretend that nothing bad is going on. You'll come home thinking again that slaves are your property."

Tahira knew what she had said was harsh, and it was the bluntest she'd ever been with Alycia. But it was also the truth. During the last year she had kept her heart open to Alycia, but time and again Alycia had pushed her away. Tahira's heart was sore from the effort.

"I wish that wasn't true," Alycia said after a while. "But it is." She sighed and rested her head on Tahira's shoulder. "But I still want to see the compounds."

"Why?" Tahira asked, taking Alycia's hand.

Alycia took a deep breath. "Tahira, you told me once that I could be a good Mistress, if I saw the slaves as people, if I took care of them, if I was kind to them," she said. "I think I can do that best by freeing them."

Tahira froze. She asked Alycia to repeat herself, which she did.

"Alycia, I'm afraid that will be impossible," Tahira said slowly. "Master Gall won't let them go lightly."

"*I* could do it," Alycia said, sitting up and waving away Tahira's warning. "I could set the slaves free when I take over. But why wait? I could do it now."

Tahira opened her mouth to argue but decided against it. She had learned that Alycia could not be pushed away from an opinion she had decided.

"Very well, Alycia," Tahira said. "I'll take you to the compounds." She put her hands on Alycia's shoulders in an attempt to calm her excitement. "But I have a warning. You are going to smell and see things you'll wish you hadn't. You're going to see how impossible it will be to free the slaves. I don't want you going to the compounds thinking this will be easy."

As it was, the walk to the compounds the next morning was almost too much for Alycia.

"I haven't ever walked this much," she said, failing to keep a whine out of her voice.

"It's only a mile," Tahira said. She took Alycia's hand and pulled her along. "It's much farther than that to the fields."

"But my father… can see one of the fields… from his chamber room," Alycia panted.

"That one is closer, yes, but the other two fields are further away," Tahira said.

She had almost forgotten how the compounds looked, how they felt, and she reproached herself for her neglect. She looked around, remembering the smells, the people. She kept walking until they arrived at the dry well outside her old compound. She hadn't forgotten this at all.

"This is the compound where I lived," she told Alycia.

Rubbing a stitch in her side, Alycia went to the door and slowly opened it. She held her nose as she peered inside at the dark interior.

"Where did you sleep?" she asked.

"On one of those cots, or on the floor," Tahira said. "Sometimes I had a blanket, and sometimes I didn't."

Alycia turned around and stared at Tahira. "But what about during the

Cold—"

"Tahira?"

The call came from up the dirt road. Tahira turned at the familiar voice, and her heart leapt to see Neph running toward her.

"Neph!" Tahira shouted, running to meet her old friend. The two embraced for a long time, tears running down both their faces.

"I'm so glad to see you," Neph said. She took Tahira's face in her hands. "Look at you, you're so beautiful under all the dirt. I always knew you were."

"Thank you, Neph," Tahira said. "You look wonderful. I'm so glad you're still alive." Behind her she heard Alycia scoff in confused disbelief.

"Yes, I survived the last Cold Time," Neph said. "I have so much to tell you."

"Tell me," Tahira said. "Are you ill? Why aren't you in the field?"

Neph smiled. "Do you remember Nor?"

"Yes, I met him once, years ago," Tahira said after a moment's pause. "I helped heal his friend once. He had black hair, right? What about him?"

"He and I are married now," Neph said. Her smile widened. She looked happier than Tahira had ever seen her. "I am now with child."

"What?" Tahira said. She automatically put her hand on Neph's belly and felt the baby dancing. "That's wonderful. Were you just seeing the midwives?" Neph nodded. "But how can you work in the temple field? You could lose the baby."

Neph laughed. "There's the midwife in you coming out," she said. "I've been moved to the farming field until the baby comes."

Tahira nodded in relief. "It's strange, no matter how horrible the Masters want our lives, they want a woman to deliver her baby."

Alycia scoffed again.

Neph didn't seem to notice. She nodded then grabbed Tahira's hands and shook them, her expression suddenly worried. "I'd heard you'd been made a house slave. But why are you back? Have you been dismissed?"

Tahira shook her head and turned toward Alycia, who had been watching them with her nose slightly raised, as Tahira feared it would be. "Neph, this is Alycia, the Master's daughter. She is my Mistress."

Neph looked surprised, then bowed her head to Alycia.

"Neph, I want to free the slaves," Alycia said, visibly wrinkling her nose at Neph's smell.

Neph froze then looked at Tahira with her eyebrows raised. Tahira nodded, indicating Neph could speak.

"Mistress, I imagine that would be difficult," Neph said. She bit the inside of her cheek and Tahira could tell Neph was holding back her words in the Mistress's presence.

"Perhaps, but I'm starting to get an idea how to do it," Alycia said.

She raised her nose and Tahira braced herself for Alycia's dismissal of all she was seeing. But instead, Alycia lowered her nose again and looked around. Neph and Tahira kept silent.

"Could you take me to one of the fields?" Alycia asked after a while.

Neph gasped a little and Tahira raised her eyebrows. "The fields?"

"Yes," Alycia said. Her face and voice were so firm, Tahira didn't question her again.

Together the three women made their way through the dirt roads, past more compound buildings, the smell of slavery all around them. Alycia raised her hands to her face several times to block out the smell, and it seemed to take a considerable amount of self-control to lower them again. At last, they reached the well at the top of the temple field, in the shadow of the Mansion. The old slaves waiting for water bowed their heads to Alycia.

Alycia stopped walking. "Wait here, please," she said softly to Tahira. "I want to see this for myself."

Tahira watched as Alycia approached the well and asked for a drink from one of the slaves. She talked to them for a few minutes, then moved toward the top of the bowl.

"What is she doing?" Neph asked.

"I'm not sure," Tahira said. "She's working on seeing us as people, something she's been taught not to do. Over the last year I've tried to tell her what our lives are like yet she's never listened. Until now. She suddenly decided that she was going to become a kind Mistress and free the slaves."

"What changed?" Neph asked.

"I sang Set Me Free for her," Tahira said. "That one's always been my favorite."

"Yes, it has," Neph said.

The two lapsed into silence and watched Alycia. She stood at the top of the bowl, staring down. One hand was on her stomach, and every few minutes she swayed a little, like she was going to be sick. Tahira knew what she was seeing. And though it pained her to watch Alycia, she knew no other way would have gotten Alycia to see the truth.

A breeze kicked up, cooling the sweat on Tahira's forehead. She closed her eyes against the sun, listening to the all-too-familiar sounds echoing up from the field.

"I must go," Neph whispered. She squeezed Tahira's hand and walked her way toward the farming field.

Tahira walked up slowly behind Alycia. Her breath caught in her chest as she looked down into the bowl for the first time in a year. The statues she had helped, in part, to raise had been added to the front of a new tomb, which was now almost finished. And distantly, down the field, she could see another statue being built on the ground.

Tahira started when Alycia reached out and took her hand. "Tahira," she said slowly. "I know how to free the slaves."

***

But whatever her plan was, Alycia never got the chance to put it into action.

Master Gall found out that Alycia intended to free the slaves. When he did, his shouts of rage at what she had been planning echoed through the Mansion. Alycia cowered in her chair in her room at the sound.

"I've never heard him so angry," she said. "He's never gotten angry with me. How did he find out?"

"It doesn't matter," Tahira said, though she was wondering the same thing. "He's far kinder to you than to anyone else. He won't punish you."

Through the curtained door they heard footsteps running toward them. In moments a house slave stood in the room, announcing the Master wanted to see his daughter and her slave.

They entered the Master's chamber room, where he was pacing in front of his chair between the window overlooking the temple field and the wall opposite. He held a paper in his hand, a letter, Tahira suspected, that had betrayed them.

Though how that had come about she was at a loss to guess. Who had known about Alycia's secret plan? How many times had she voiced aloud her desires to free the slaves? Who had heard her, and, more importantly, who had then betrayed them?

Alycia came to a stop in front of her father with Tahira standing several steps behind her.

"You wanted me, Father?" Alycia asked, the most diplomatic Tahira had ever seen her.

"My dear Alycia," the Master said, his voice calm while the rest of him raged. "I've just had some disturbing news."

"What is it, Father?" Alycia asked, her voice innocent.

The Master waved the paper in his hand. "I've heard a report that you are planning to free my slaves," he said. His gaze bore into Alycia. "Is this true?"

Alycia took a deep breath. "It is, Father," she said softly. She looked the Master in the eye. "The best way to be a good Mistress is to treat the slaves with kindness."

"I see," the Master said after a lengthy pause. His voice sounded like poison. Tahira shuddered, and the Master's eyes darted to her.

"Alycia, has your slave been talking out of place again?" he snapped. "Is that why you planned to do this?"

Alycia glanced back at Tahira. "No, Father. This was all my idea. She has told me about her life in the fields, at my request. And I realized that the way to have slaves is to treat them with kindness. Slaves work better if they love you."

Tahira's skin crawled at the words coming out of Alycia's mouth, and even more so at the realization that Alycia believed what she was saying. Tahira had thought Alycia planned to free the slaves because she saw the evils of slavery. But that wasn't it at all; Alycia planned to free them because she believed they would love her if she was kind.

How Alycia had misunderstood Tahira's words!

"I'm sorry that you feel this way, my dear," the Master said. He tapped Alycia lightly on the head with the letter and smiled. "But slaves who love you don't work better. In fact, they don't work at all, because they know you love them no matter what they do. No, it is best that the slaves fear you."

Alycia opened her mouth to respond, then closed it again. Her nose rose in the air, and for a moment Tahira wondered if Alycia was going to talk back. But instead, she lowered her nose again and remained silent.

"Alycia, I am very disappointed in you," the Master said.

Alycia bowed her head. "I am sorry for that," she said. "I meant no disrespect."

"No, I suppose not," the Master said, scratching his chin with the letter.

He looked long and hard at Alycia. "What you need is time to get your mind right, to understand what it is I do here. Perhaps you were planning on freeing the slaves because you yourself want to be free? Have you been unhappy here, my dear?"

"Of course not, Father," Alycia said. "How could I be? You've given me everything."

The Master snapped his fingers. "That's it, then," he said. "You are happy, but I never let you go explore the world. You want your freedom to do that now. That's why you want to free the slaves."

Against the rules, Tahira raised her head, shocked. But she dropped it again quickly, before the Master noticed.

"But don't worry, Alycia, I can fix this," the Master said. "I can arrange for you to leave here and see the world. You could take your slave with you, if you want. Or you could leave her here."

Tahira's heart froze at the prospect of being left behind with Master Gall. But Alycia shook her head.

"No, Father, she comes with me," she said.

"Very well," the Master said. He snapped his fingers again and a taskmaster ran out of the room. "I'll send you off in two days. Go and see the world for a while before coming home. I'll inform Dunca of the delay to your wedding."

***

Back in Alycia's room, Alycia packed her bags with almost manic energy. Tahira didn't know what to say. She felt like Alycia had betrayed her, though she knew that wasn't true, exactly.

"I think I said some terrible things back there," Alycia said after a long time, her voice soft, defeated. "But sometimes it's easier to let him have his way than to argue."

She turned her face to Tahira and Tahira was alarmed at the wild expression on Alycia's face. She had only seen that expression after one of Alycia's nightmares.

Tahira stood up and hugged Alycia, trying to comfort her. After a moment Alycia patted her arm. "I wish I had never thought of freeing the slaves," she said in a quiet voice. "This wouldn't have happened if I hadn't."

Tahira stepped away, horrified. It wasn't bad enough to learn that Alycia had thought freeing the slaves would mean she'd be loved as a kind mistress; now Tahira must learn that Alycia's heart hadn't really been in freeing the slaves at all. Just when Tahira thought Alycia might finally be sincere, she proved that she wasn't. Tahira fought hard not to sob aloud; she'd hoped so much to have a real friend in Alycia, to have Alycia see the world as it really was, not in the same childlike way she'd been raised to see it.

Alycia, oblivious, shook herself, her expression clearing. "Where do you think my father will send us?"

"I couldn't say," Tahira said, her voice choked. She returned to packing.

"My father's never been this generous before," Alycia said, her voice becoming faraway.

Tahira bit the inside of her cheek to stop herself from saying too much. But Alycia saw. "What?" she asked, a snap in her voice.

"I have not had good experiences with the Master," Tahira said, her eyes on her moving hands. "I have learned that he keeps only part of his word. I was just wondering what part of his word he will keep."

Alycia's nose rose in the air again and Tahira kept quiet. Their friendship over the last year had been tenuous, and now it was threatening to break. Tahira had never felt more like a worthless slave than she did right then as she waited for Alycia's answer.

"If my father never intends for me to return home, I might be happy with that," Alycia said at last.

Tahira nodded, but that wasn't what she meant. She was wondering if the Master was sending them away to see the world at all. He could be sending them away, yes, but to what? She knew he had some positive feelings for Alycia. But he had beat Aney for not doing the work she was assigned. He had taken Tahira's healing trade away for an honest mistake. He had whipped her nearly half to death for having an opinion. What might he do to someone who planned to free his slaves?

Tahira packed faster to keep her mind off the terrible possibilities.

Chapter Nine

The next day, the Master announced that he would be sending Alycia off in a ship, with a merchant friend of his, Captain Mills, to take care of her.

Despite the dread of wondering what the Master was really sending them away to do, Tahira couldn't help but feel excited; she would finally get to see ships. She would finally get to see the ocean. She hid her excitement in front of Alycia, however, for she knew she could never satisfactorily explain why she longed to see these things.

Years before, during the story evenings in the compound when Tahira had first heard the stories of Mary, Lores, Rol, Tel, and Dot, she had tried to imagine everything she was being told about: she had tried to imagine ships as tall as six stacked compound buildings; she had tried to imagine big pieces of canvas tied to tall sticks that somehow caught the wind and made the ship move; she had tried to imagine a vast and endless expanse of flat ocean; she had tried to imagine a blue ocean under a blue sky; she had tried to imagine a river big enough to allow these monstrously huge ships to sail on.

But none of her imagining could have prepared her for seeing the real things.

She couldn't help herself as she climbed out of the carriage at the docks near the river; she stopped and stared.

The sky above her was blue, actually blue. She had seen blue eyes, but never a blue sky before, and she couldn't understand how it could be blue here when it was gray or yellow over the compounds and the fields. White clouds puffed through the sky, borne on the wind she could feel from the hill overlooking the dock and the river. Her gaze traveled down from the sky to the river itself. Rol had been right; it was huge, so wide Tahira could just barely see the bank on the opposite side. Tahira had seen water in a bucket when the sun glinted off it, so she knew that light danced on the water. But she had never seen sun dancing off water to this magnitude. The early morning sun bouncing on the river's agitated surface glittered so brightly she had to shade her eyes against it. And unlike water in a bucket, which was usually brown, the water of the river was blue. If the ocean was anything like this river, she could see immediately why the Pirate Women had loved it.

"Tahira!" Alycia's voice sounded impatient.

Tahira started; she had forgotten both that Alycia was there, and that she still had a duty to perform as Alycia's slave.

"I'm sorry," Tahira said, hastily following Alycia as she walked to the left down a gentle slope to the docks. In the distance Tahira could see the river widen into an even larger expanse of blue. She put her hand over her mouth to hide her gasp at seeing a glimpse of the ocean for the first time.

Behind her walked Gius, the red-nosed swarthy servant Master Gall had sent with them, and two house slaves, carrying their baggage.

As the group reached the bottom of the slope and entered the dockyard, Tahira tore her eyes from the sky and the river and saw the ships themselves. She had to remind herself to keep walking, and to not stop and stare.

The ships were even bigger than she had ever imagined them to be. The masts were more like trees than sticks, and they all had smaller trees tied perpendicular to them, on which were the rolled-up canvas sails. Ropes were everywhere, some straight and tight, others looping and loose. The bodies of the ships were taller and wider than Dot's cupped hands had ever indicated, and Tahira felt a little frightened looking up at them. Men were running all over the decks of all the dozens of ships, and some were up on the masts, tying the sails down. There were men on the docks next to the ships, carrying bags and boxes up narrow planks of wood and onto the ships.

Tahira felt a hand pushing on her back and turned to see Gius's impatient face hovering uncomfortably close to hers. He moved past Tahira and put his pushing hand on Alycia's back too.

"What?" Alycia snapped, shaking off his hand. "Are we in a hurry?"

"The tide is going out soon," Gius said, squinting at Alycia. "The captain wants to get under way."

"Fine," Alycia said. But for all her snappishness, Tahira saw nervousness in her face. She stepped forward and hooked her arm with Alycia's. Alycia gave her a small smile.

As they neared the ships, Tahira felt tiny next to their rocking bulks. The docks became crowded here, and Tahira couldn't help but bump into the sailors. All were big-shouldered burly men that would have been at home in the temple or city fields. Their grizzled and weathered features reminded Tahira of the slaves she knew, though these sailors didn't look as good-tempered as many of the slaves she'd known. The sailors carried boxes, casks, barrels, even animals on their broad shoulders, backs, or under their arms, pushing roughly past each other to get to their ships.

The smell of the docks was a new experience for Tahira too; the smells of sweat and unwashed bodies she knew, but the smell of salt and rot she did not.

"Which ship is it?" Alycia asked Gius, her nose wrinkled in disgust.

"All in good time," Gius said.

They kept walking, threading their way between laden sailors who gave them either angry or interested glances. They passed ships and boats of all sizes, all alive with sailors and passengers and even slaves. Tahira's heart ached to see them in chains.

Finally, Gius stopped in front of the biggest ship. The narrow plank was down on the dock, but the sailors all seemed to be on the ship. A square barrel-shaped man stood up on the ship's deck with an impatient expression. He wore a large hat over his greasy, shoulder-length light hair, and had frilly lace at his throat.

Gius turned and gave Alycia and Tahira hands up onto the plank, where they somehow kept their balance and stepped onto the deck of the ship.

"Welcome to *The Nantes*," the barrel-shaped man said. "I am your captain, Robert Mills."

Alycia dipped into an elegant curtsy and Tahira lowered her head, as usual. "Pleasure," Alycia said. "Thank you for taking us on your ship. My father speaks very highly of you."

Captain Mills nodded, then turned and barked orders to his men. Immediately the sailors jumped into action, pulling up the plank, climbing up the masts, loosing the sails. Tahira gasped as the full size of the canvas was unveiled to her; they, too, were even bigger than she'd imagined. She stared at everything around her until Captain Mills's voice interrupted her thoughts.

"Your room will be the fo'c'sle deck," he said. He pointed to a raised deck at the front of the ship. Four poles had been set up at the four corners of the deck, and had been draped in lightweight white fabric, creating a tent. "We don't want you fine ladies to be soiled by the sailors on this ship. Should a storm come up, we'll take you below to the galley."

"What's the galley?" Alycia asked. She and Tahira grabbed onto a railing as the ship suddenly rocked. Tahira noticed, however, that none of the sailors lost their footing. She didn't like the feeling of the deck rolling underneath her, and she hoped she would get used to it.

"That's the kitchen of sorts, Ma'am," Captain Mills said. "It will be safe from the storm. While you are here, you are free to roam about the deck as you please. But be careful. You see that grating there?"

He pointed to four places where holes had been bored through the deck against the railings, two at the back of the ship, and two near the middle. The holes had metal bars over them to prevent anyone from falling through, but a leg could still be broken by a wrong step.

"Those lead to the cargo hold," Captain Mills said. "You won't be wanting to go do down there, and you don't want to go near that grating."

"What's in the hold?" Alycia asked. "My father said this was a merchant ship."

"It is, Ma'am," Captain Mills said. "My cargo this voyage is animals, cattle and sheep. The smells are quite overpowering."

Tahira nodded, knowing smells of a similar sort. Alycia audibly grimaced.

Duty called Captain Mills away, leaving Alycia and Tahira to explore their new room. It felt so light and pretty inside the curtains, once they'd all been closed, with the white fabric letting in a great deal of filtered light and some breeze. Their only furniture was two cots and a little table. Their bags had already been placed inside. Standing against the railing was a large, metal, cone-shaped container, just taller than knee-height, three paces wide at the bottom and with a hole three hand-widths across at the top.

"What's that?" Alycia asked, nudging it with her foot.

Tahira peered inside. "It's to relieve ourselves," she said. Alycia wrinkled her nose. "It's better than what we had in the slave compounds," Tahira said. "I think it's shaped like that so it won't tip over."

The ship suddenly lurched again, sending Alycia and Tahira falling to their knees. The metal cone slid a little on the deck but didn't tip.

"This moving is going to take getting used to!" Alycia said, staggering to her feet.

Outside their tent they heard the sailors shouting, Captain Mills bellowing some curses, and some whistles being blown. The ship lurched again, harder this time, and Alycia fell over. Their cots and bags slid halfway across the deck and the table tipped over. Then the ship went up and down and up again in quick succession. Tahira felt a lifting sensation in her stomach with each direction change, a sensation she'd never felt before, but rather liked.

"Oh dear," Alycia said. Her face was starting to turn green.

Tahira reached over and pushed the metal cone toward her. "Use this."

Alycia nodded and huddled next to the cone. The ship continued to rise and lower and pitch from side to side. Tahira heard some of the sailors shouting something about an overfall, but she didn't know what it meant. All she knew was that she and Alycia were quickly getting sicker and sicker.

By nightfall, both of them were taking turns vomiting into the metal cone. Outside the curtains Tahira could hear some sailors mocking them. She couldn't bring herself to care.

***

Two days later Tahira staggered upright and left the little tent. She stepped down off the fo'c'sle deck and looked around.

For the first time she saw the open ocean, and the sight took her breath away: miles upon miles of nothing but flat blue water, sparkling and rippling in the sun. There were so many shades of blue. She had never seen something so large before. Rol had been right to tell Tahira that the ocean was bigger than the temple field.

Tahira looked up at the sky and gasped. It was the first time she'd seen the sky unbroken by buildings or the sides of the fields. It was a perfect dome of blue and white and gray, resting on the outer edges of the ocean's horizon.

She walked to the railing and faced the back of the ship, lifting her face into the wind. The air smelled fresh and clean and tangy with salt. She'd never smelled anything like it before and she immediately loved it. Somehow, it was vaguely familiar.

"Glad to see you've survived the seasickness."

Tahira started as Captain Mills came up to her. Automatically she lowered her head in deference.

"I have, thank you," Tahira said. "But Alycia is still feeling sick."

"She'll probably be well in another day or so," said Captain Mills. "I'm surprised you're up and about. Most greenhorns take longer than three days to get their sea legs."

"Is that what it's called?" Tahira asked. She had noticed she was walking on the deck easier. And though Captain Mills's words sounded complimentary, she couldn't help but feel that he wasn't complimenting her. "Where can I get something to eat?" she asked. "I've had nothing but water for three days."

"That's a good thing," Captain Mills said. "Eating while seasick would make it worse."

"I seem to be over it now," Tahira said. She was surprised by the firmness in her voice, but she was quickly realizing that firmness was the only way to get Captain Mills to do anything. "Show me where the galley is."

Captain Mills lead Tahira down the hatchway. It was then she noticed there were two hatchways leading below; this one near the front of the ship, and the other in the middle, which had a heavy lock on it.

"Why does that hatch have a lock?" Tahira asked.

"The animals get to roaming around sometimes," Captain Mills said. "That lock keeps them from escaping and getting on deck."

Captain Mills kept explaining, but Tahira didn't hear much of anything else, for the smell belowdecks overpowered her. She thought the smell inside the compound was terrible, but the smell of sailors was worse. But perhaps, she thought, she was smelling the animals too.

A few cabins down the passageway Captain Mills pointed Tahira into the galley. It was about the same size as Old Joche's cook-space.

A one-legged man was sitting on a stool by the stove, whittling. He glared up at Tahira, and she was immediately put in mind of some of the nastier taskmasters.

"I need some food," Tahira said. "What could I have?"

The cook grunted and pointed his whittling knife at a large pot on the stove. Tahira peered inside and saw a grayish-brown mush. She grabbed a small wooden bowl from near the stove and filled it. She sniffed the mush and was surprised it smelled sweeter than it looked.

"What is this?" she asked.

"Oatmeal," the cook grunted. "We still have good food for a while. It'll turn into burgoo soon. There's tins for water in the back. Water barrels are back there too. Take a biscuit." He waved his hand in the direction of a large barrel near him.

Tahira looked inside the barrel and her heart leapt to see little hard round biscuits. She pulled one out and examined it. Her excitement grew.

"I know these!" she said. "These are the biscuits Old Joche made to feed sick slaves."

The cook raised an eyebrow. "You may have one biscuit per meal," he said. "Mind the weevils."

Tahira swallowed her excitement before the cook could get angry at her, looked down, and saw little worms wiggling in the biscuits. She wrinkled her nose and tapped the biscuit against her hand. The worms fell into her palm and she tipped them onto the floor. She put her biscuit in her bowl then gathered two tin cups of water.

She paused at the galley door and faced the cook. "I learned once that if you make these biscuits with orange juice instead of water, the sailors won't get as sick," she said. "At least, it worked for slaves. And I never once saw worms in them."

The cook shrugged and returned to his whittling.

***

The next morning Alycia and Tahira emerged from their tent looking their best. Tahira retrieved their breakfast from the galley and they ate it while taking a few turns around the deck. As Captain Mills had requested, they stayed clear of the gratings along the railing. The ocean was still as smooth and glittering as the day before, and Tahira relished the expression on Alycia's face as she saw it. She knew she would never tire of the sight.

The crew kept their distance from them, parting around them as they walked. Captain Mills spent much of his time standing on the raised deck at the back of the ship, looking out to sea. Next to him stood a man holding onto a giant spoked wheel and staring straight ahead. Most of the crew was up in the ropes and sails of the ship.

"Look how they're walking on those ropes," Tahira said. "And all of them keep their balance." Alycia followed her gaze. "You know, I've heard a lot of stories about ships like this."

"You have?" Alycia asked.

"Some of my friends came to Typeg on pirate ships," Tahira said. "They told me many stories. One even learned how to get up there and work. She said it was called rigging."

"It looks exciting," Alycia said. "But I don't do well in high places."

She paused, watching as one smaller sailor climbed higher and higher up one of the masts. "What was your friend's name? The one who told you about rigging?"

"Her name was Dot."

"What happened to her?" Alycia asked.

"She was sold to another Master years ago," Tahira said.

"Was she your only friend who was sold?" Alycia asked.

Tahira shook her head, frustration starting to bubble low in her chest at Alycia's questions, coupled with what she had recently learned about Alycia's character. Tahira knew that slavery was wrong, no matter how long she'd lived in it, and she couldn't understand how, even now, Alycia could treat it so lightly.

"You should tell me the stories you know about ships," Alycia said. "They're fitting, seeing where we are."

Tahira didn't know what to say. Suddenly all those stories from the Pirate Women were present in her mind, and the remembrance was painful. Their experiences had been painful, and Tahira didn't want to share them just to entertain Alycia. But Alycia took Tahira's silence for assent. She hooked her arm in Tahira's with a smile. "Let's continue our tour."

They took two more turns around the main deck: from their tent in the front of the ship, past the canvas-covered lifeboat hanging over the side, down the side railing, skirting around the group of seedy men huddled in the middle, all the way to the back deck where Captain Mills stood. Then across the back of the ship in front of Captain Mills, up the other side, past the other lifeboat hanging over the side, and back to their tent.

Later on, Tahira suggested that they explore the lower decks of the ship. But the moment Alycia got a whiff of the air coming up from below, she clapped a hand over her mouth and staggered back, shaking her head.

So they stayed on the main deck and in their tent. Only Tahira ventured belowdecks, and only to get food. Every meal was the same, oatmeal and biscuit.

Tahira's favorite pastime was to sit on the stairs to their fo'c'sle deck and watch the sailors in the rigging. And in watching she finally understood what Dot had meant when she said the sails caught the wind; for while the sails didn't grasp the wind like a hand—as she had thought they would—they did prevent the wind from passing the ship by billowing out as the wind blew into them. After a few days of watching, Tahira started to understand the rhythm of the sailors' movements, when they climbed, when they switched. She even began putting officers' words and the sailors' actions together, slowly understanding all the commands and calls. She remembered how Tel used to love working up in the rigging, and now Tahira thought she understood why.

While she watched the sailors, Dot and Tel's stories ran through her head. She started to remember what Dot called the different parts of a ship: the quarterdeck, the helm, hatchways, the mainmast, bow, stern, and lines.

Many times in the first weeks on the ship, Tahira tried to climb up into the rigging, something she had longed to do since Tel had told her about it. She was confident she could keep her balance, and she knew she was strong enough to hold on. But every time she tried, Captain Mills or one of the sailors stopped her, saying they didn't want her to fall. Reluctantly, Tahira obeyed.

Alycia spent most of her time in the tent, either preening or nursing her sun-reddened skin. She liked to be out in the sun, watching the waves and the occasional sea creature that came to the surface. But she was so fair that the sun turned her skin painfully red. Tahira poked through the galley until she found the ingredients for a healing salve.

Chapter Ten

"Sail ho!"

The shout came just after dawn, startling Tahira from sleep. She listened as sailors ran around, some shouting. Then she heard Captain Mills calling up to the lookout,

"What's her colors?"

A pause. Then, "She's a pirate!"

Tahira's breath caught in her chest. She remembered in an instant everything the Pirate Women had told her about pirates. The pirates could sink them, board them, burn the ship, kidnap her and Alycia, kill everyone, whatever they wanted. *The Nantes* and everyone aboard her were in trouble. Trying to control her panic, Tahira shook Alycia awake.

"There's a pirate ship chasing us," she said above the frenzied hubbub the sailors were now making. "We've got to hide below."

"I'm not going down there," Alycia said sleepily.

"You *have* to," Tahira snapped. Alycia opened her eyes and stared at her. She opened her mouth, but at that moment they heard a loud noise, like a crashing boulder. Moments later something hit the top of their tent, collapsing it instantly.

Alycia and Tahira screamed as the fabric and poles clattered on top of them.

"Come on, we've got to get out of here!" Tahira yelled, her panic pouring out.

She grabbed Alycia's hand and, after several frantic attempts, freed them from the entangling fabric and pulled Alycia from the fo'c'sle deck. She had meant to dive down the hatchway, to get away from the pirates, but she couldn't. The entire crew was on the deck now, running around, panicking. Tahira and Alycia were pushed against the railing by the fo'c'sle stairs, unable to get anywhere.

Tahira looked up at the sails and saw that they hung slack; they weren't running from the pirates. She looked across the deck and over the opposite railing to where she could just see the pirate ship through the scurrying sailors. It was smaller than *The Nantes*, but looked threatening all the same. At the top of one of the masts, a black flag fluttered in the wind.

The sailors of *The Nantes* slowed their movements until they all stood still. Tahira heard them whispering that the pirates had lowered a boat and were sending a few men over. Soon it was so quiet on deck that Tahira could hear the pirates' boat rowing over, the splash of the oars, and the slight grunts of the pirates as they worked.

Alycia looked just as scared as Tahira felt. They huddled tightly together as the boat got closer to *The Nantes*. The sailors stayed equally still, as though fearful of what the pirates would do. Captain Mills was shifting his weight far more than was necessary.

Finally, with an audible bump, the boat arrived at the port side ladder. A few moments later a dark head emerged over the side of the ship. As the pirate stepped onto the deck, Tahira bit her tongue to keep from gasping aloud.

The pirate was tall, broad-shouldered, and moved with easy grace. His clothes were dark: black leather pants, a black velvet vest, and a billowy dark blue shirt. His vest was unbuttoned, and the neck of his shirt was open. His boots were partially undone, as though he'd put them on in a hurry, and he carried no weapon but an empty scabbard at his left hip. His hair was almost black, as was his scruffy beard, and he had a scar on one cheek.

But what made Tahira bite back a gasp were his eyes: amidst all the dark colors of his hair and his clothes, his eyes were light blue and piercing, standing out like lights in his tan face.

The pirate paused, his gaze roving lazily over the deck as though it was his ship, and he gave a half smile of pleasure. Captain Mills stepped forward tentatively.

"Captain Haefen, sir, I'm sorry, but we have nothing of monetary value today," he said.

Tahira and Alycia shared a shocked, wide-eyed look. The pirate was surprisingly young to be the captain, only a few years older than they were. Tahira thought he was a crewman. But as she looked at him again, she could easily see why he was the captain.

Captain Haefen's lazy gaze fell on Captain Mills, and his smile faded. "So says the man who has a hold full of slaves," he said.

His voice was deep and smooth, moderately accented with a pleasant lilt. He laughed a little at Captain Mills's apparent discomfort. He took a few steps forward, his left hand resting on his empty scabbard.

"No, that's all right," he said with a wave of his other hand. "I'm not here for them today, that should make you happy."

Captain Mills visibly sighed. "What are you here for, then, sir?"

"Your hats," Captain Haefen said.

Captain Mills looked confused again. "Our—our hats, sir?"

"Yes," Captain Haefen said, his lazy gaze roving again. Twice it passed over Tahira, and she felt a rush of something course through her body, but she didn't know what it was. "We lost all of ours in a recent storm, and we need new ones. You don't mind, do you?"

He fixed Captain Mills with such an intense stare that no one would have dared refuse him.

"No, sir, not at all," Captain Mills said, clearly flustered. He turned to his crew. "Your hats! Give them to the captain!"

The crew scrambled to comply, taking off their hats and dropping them over the side to the waiting boat. No one approached Captain Haefen, not even Captain Mills, who tossed his hat over the rail just like his men.

Captain Haefen turned his head a little and his piercing eyes met Tahira's. Once again, she felt a rush in her body. She sucked in her breath, staring at Captain Haefen. His brows knitted for a moment, his mouth opened a little, and a strange expression crossed his face—surprise, excitement? Then he blinked, his face back to passive laziness. He looked away from her and stared down at the deck, almost like he was calculating something, his eyebrows knit again.

The sailors returned to their stations, leaving the two captains standing alone in the middle of the deck. It appeared that Captain Mills expected the pirates to leave soon, for his restlessness had returned.

Tahira felt a tingling in her hand and looked down to find Alycia uncurling her nails from digging into Tahira's arm; Tahira was surprised she hadn't felt it before.

"Sorry," Alycia whispered.

As quietly as she had spoken, Captain Haefen seemed to have heard her. His intense gaze found Tahira again through a few sailors standing in front of her.

"Tell me," Captain Haefen said, still looking at Tahira. "Is it now standard procedure to have women aboard your slaver? As passengers, I mean?"

Captain Mills glanced at Tahira and Alycia. "No," he said slowly, uncomfortable. "They are part of the slaves."

There was silence for a beat. Tahira felt like something had hit her. She repeated Captain Mills's words in her mind a few more times, shocked, and believed them at once.

"No," Alycia said with a scoff, stepping forward and pushing the sailors out of her way. Tahira followed a couple steps behind. "No, we're not. We're not slaves. We are aboard this merchant ship traveling the world." She looked at Captain Mills, who suddenly seemed unable to meet her eyes. She raised her nose in the air. "You keep us on the deck so that we're not soiled by the crew."

Captain Haefen took a few steps toward Alycia. "I'm afraid that whatever tales you've been told are just that," he said. "This is a slaver. Have you never wondered about the smell?" He faced Captain Mills. "This lady says you are lying," he said. "And I am inclined to believe a woman's word, especially over yours. So tell me, Mills, why are these lovely women on your ship?"

His voice had dropped to a dangerous tone. Captain Mills winced.

"They were misinformed of their purpose here," he said. "They are part of the slaves."

"No!" Alycia shouted.

The sound went through Tahira's stunned mind like pain. She had always known the Master wouldn't keep all his word. But she had not expected this turn of events, not even from him.

"Why would my father do that to me, his own daughter?" Alycia demanded of Captain Mills. She turned around until she found Gius, the Master's servant, and pointed an accusatory finger at him. "Why would he hire you to take us on a slaver?"

She was breathing hard, her eyes bright with fear. Gius stared at Captain Mills, avoiding Alycia's accusation.

Captain Haefen looked back and forth between Gius, Captain Mills, and Alycia a few times. Finally, he shifted his weight and all eyes went to him. "Captain, a word," he said.

He beckoned with his hand toward Gius, a hard look on his face, and Gius joined him. Captain Haefen put his hand on Captain Mills's shoulder and forcibly steered him toward the aft cabin.

"A bit of advice," Captain Haefen said in a carrying voice. "Never lie to a woman. It hurts her far more than the truth will ever hurt you."

The door to the cabin slammed, the three men inside. The crew ground back into action, dispersing into the rigging or down the hatch until the deck was mostly empty. Alycia turned to Tahira.

"Is this really a slave ship?" she asked. "Are we being sold into slavery?"

"I don't know, Alycia," Tahira said. "I never expected your father would do this."

Alycia stared into Tahira's face. "But you're not surprised, are you?"

"I am, but I'm not as surprised as you are," Tahira said.

"You warned me he would keep only part of his word," Alycia said, starting to cry. "I should have listened to you."

A few minutes later the cabin door burst open. The sailors fell silent again. Captain Haefen led the procession out onto the deck, with Captain Mills right behind him, and a cowed-looking Gius coming out last.

Captain Haefen strode across the deck toward Tahira and Alycia until he stopped in front of Tahira and held out his hand. "Tahira, you're coming with me," he said.

Tahira started. "How do you know my name?" she asked, suddenly and horribly reminded of the Master.

Captain Haefen shrugged, a little smile on his face. "I must have overheard it."

"No, you didn't," Tahira said slowly.

Captain Haefen shrugged again. "You're coming with me," he repeated.

Tahira looked quickly between Captain Mills and Alycia.

"Captain Mills has agreed to release you from his slaver and let you come with me," Captain Haefen said.

"And why should I come with you?" Tahira asked, disdain in her voice she hadn't consciously put there.

Captain Haefen dropped his hand. "Because I promise I won't be taking you to slavery," he said. "I have somewhere else in mind to take you."

Tahira studied his handsome face. She had virtually no experience with men. Despite that, however, Tahira couldn't help but feel the sincerity of his words. That realization shocked her; this was a pirate, a hardened thief and brigand, one of the men who had made life so miserable for the Pirate

Women. Where was this sudden trust coming from?

"Do you really promise?" she asked.

Captain Haefen nodded, his expression softening. He looked kind now. "You have my word. I never break a promise."

Tahira looked back and forth between the two Captains, weighing in her mind what she knew of each, and weighing in her heart how she felt when she talked to each. Her gaze finally rested on Captain Haefen.

"Where will you take me?" she asked.

"I'll not tell you now," Captain Haefen said. His returning sternness shook away some of her inexplicable trust in him. But she still felt he was being sincere.

"All right," she said. "I'll come with you."

"I'm coming too," Alycia said. She stepped a little in front of Tahira, but Captain Haefen did not look at her.

He shook his head. "No. I made the deal only for you," he said to Tahira.

"She doesn't go anywhere without me, she's my sla—" Alycia brought herself up short. She glanced at Tahira. "She's my friend."

But Tahira heard the word. She understood the intent. Despite everything she and Alycia had shared, despite Alycia wanting a friend more than a slave, despite Tahira showing Alycia the truth of slavery, Tahira was still nothing but a slave to her. Nothing in the last year together had changed that. And Tahira realized that nothing ever would change that; Tahira would always be a slave.

Tears sprang to her eyes, tears she did not want Captain Haefen to see. She looked down, blinking furiously.

"Alycia is my friend," she said, and she was glad there wasn't much of a waver in her voice. "She and I go together."

"I don't want to be sold into slavery," Alycia said in a coquettish tone that grated against Tahira, completely oblivious to the pain she'd just caused. She took a step closer to Captain Haefen, but he still did not look at her.

Instead, he stared at Tahira for a few moments. Then he turned to Captain Mills. "It seems I'll be taking them both," he said. "Captain, our business is done. Ladies, come with me."

He walked to the opposite railing, where he turned and waited. Tahira, suddenly desiring to be away from Alycia, made to follow.

"I need my things," Alycia said, pulling on Tahira's arm.

Captain Haefen finally looked at Alycia. "You do not," he said, so severely that Alycia gasped.

Tahira stepped toward him and Alycia slowly followed. Tahira didn't want to go aboard a pirate ship. But she also didn't want to stay on the slaver. Besides, there was something about this Captain Haefen, something she couldn't quite define—almost a nobility—that she had thought would be missing from all pirates, especially captains.

Captain Haefen helped them climb over the railing and down into the boat, where they found seats on the hats. He sat at the back of the boat and two pirates rowed back to their ship.

Chapter Eleven

With dread, Tahira mounted the ladder to the deck of the pirate ship. Alycia joined her, and the two stood with their backs to the railing. The deck was full of pirates, more than twice the amount of the sailors on *The Nantes*. Most of them were dressed like the slaver sailors, though one or two wore velvet or silk or other fine clothing. Many of them looked drunk.

Almost immediately the pirates noticed the two women, and a group of them started toward them, their expressions greedy. Alycia gasped and ducked behind Tahira, pushing her forward. The pirates extended their hands toward her as they advanced. Tahira closed her eyes and turned to the side.

She started at the sound of metal scraping by her ear. She opened her eyes just in time to see Captain Haefen swinging a sword at the advancing pirates. He didn't say anything, but his expression was terrible and angry. The advancing pirates froze, unsure, then scurried away as fast as the crowded deck allowed.

Captain Haefen stared after them for a moment or two, then sheathed the sword in his empty scabbard. He took Tahira's elbow. "Come with me," he said.

Tahira tugged her elbow away. "What are you going to do with us?" She felt all too aware of the dozens of eyes on her, none of them with Captain Haefen's noble aura. She suddenly knew what the Pirate Women had felt, being brought to Typeg by pirates, and she felt more compassion for them than ever before.

"I'm going to take you in your cabin," Captain Haefen said. "You'll live there for the duration of your stay."

Alycia took a step closer to him. "And how long will that be?"

Captain Haefen tipped his head to one side then the other. "It depends on what my crew says. Despite being captain, I don't have complete control of this ship. The crew decides whether or not you stay."

"What if they say no?" Alycia asked, her voice shaking.

"Then I will find you a passing ship and put you on it," Captain Haefen said.

"Do you really think we trust you?" Tahira asked, hiding in her heart that she somehow did.

Captain Haefen shook his head. "I know you don't, and you don't have to," he said. "But I am trustworthy. If my crew won't have you then I will put you on another ship. But if my crew will have you, then I promise you will be safe."

He bent and opened the hatchway.

"Wait, I'm not going down there," Alycia said. "Can't we have a tent on the foxhole, like on the other ship?"

Captain Haefen slowly straightened to look at her, his expression annoyed. "Let me guess. You're the daughter of a Master, aren't you?" he said, and Alycia nodded proudly. Captain Haefen scowled, his expression dark now. "No wonder you think all your requests must be obeyed. No, you shall not have a room on the 'foxhole', as you call it, nor on the fo'c'sle. You shall go where I tell you to go. If you don't want to obey, you are welcome to return to *The Nantes*." He raised a long arm and pointed over the railing to the retreating slaver. "I hope you can swim, because I'm not taking you back there."

Without another word he stepped down the hatchway, Tahira behind him. Reluctantly, Alycia followed.

Belowdecks smelled terribly of salt and rot and men, though surprisingly better than *The Nantes*. Alycia squealed and cupped her hands over her nose. Tahira looked around the deck and saw it was full of long metal tubes mounted on wooden wheels.

"Captain, what are these?" Tahira asked, pointing.

Captain Haefen paused and looked at Tahira. "Those are cannons," he said. He pointed to large round balls stacked in neat piles by the cannons. "And those are the cannonballs. We load the balls into the cannons and fire them at ships. Follow me."

Tahira looked around the deck. So these were the cannons that Dot and Tel had talked to her about. Tahira started counting them, but lost her count at eight as she turned to follow.

Captain Haefen, meanwhile, picked his way through the men and hammocks and extra ropes to the front of the ship where there was a door. He opened it and stepped back to show a small bare cabin, square at this end and pointed at the far end, lit by two single-candle lanterns swinging from the ceiling.

"This is the orlop," Captain Haefen said, lighting the lanterns. "We don't have a surgeon, so this room is yours. I'll have beds brought in soon, just as soon as my crew accepts you." He seemed confident with that outcome. He pulled a key from his pocket, then closed the door behind Alycia and locked it.

Alycia slowly lowered her hands and tested the air. "At least it doesn't smell bad in here."

Tahira sighed and sat on the floor, leaning against the door. She suddenly felt drained after all the events of the morning.

Alycia sat next to her, her legs extended. "You agreed to come over here. Do you think the captain can be trusted?" she asked.

Tahira closed her eyes, the sting of Alycia's hurt still present. "I don't know," she said.

Alycia was silent for a while. "Why do you think my father sold us?" she asked at last.

Tahira opened her eyes and tipped her head down. "In my experience, when a slave disobeys or does something the Masters don't expect, they're considered dangerous. You saw what your father did to me. And you became dangerous to him when you thought about freeing the slaves. Do you understand?"

Tahira's voice had a snap to it that had never been there with Alycia before. Alycia didn't seem to notice.

"I don't know what Captain Haefen intends to do with us, Alycia, or where he's taking us," Tahira said. She paused. "For some reason I do trust him when he says that we will be safe."

Alycia shifted away a little but said nothing. They fell silent but Tahira's thoughts kept running. Tears came to her eyes and rolled down her cheeks. She started as she felt Alycia's finger wiping them away.

"What is it?" Alycia asked.

Tahira took a deep breath. "Am I just a slave to you?" The question came out before she could think about it.

Alycia scoffed a little, but Tahira didn't look at her. "Of course not. You're my friend," she said.

"And yet you called me your slave on *The Nantes*," Tahira said. The sting of the hurt faded; she wasn't angry. "I understand. It's what I've been my whole life, it's what you're used to. But if that's all I am to you, Alycia,

I would prefer you treat me like your personal slave again. It isn't right to lie."

Alycia huffed, her nose in the air. "Is that all that's bothering you?" she asked, seeming to take Tahira's words right to heart and returning to Mistress Alycia once again.

Tahira ducked her head in her old deferent way, and answered her Mistress's question, "We may have been rescued from slavery, but that was a slaver. That's why belowdecks on *The Nantes* smelled so bad, why Captain Mills never let us go down there, why he told us to stay away from those gratings on the deck. The entire hold was full of slaves, and Captain Mills didn't want us to see them. I might have known some of them. We were rescued, but they weren't."

Alycia made no attempt to answer. It saddened Tahira even more that Alycia knew so little about comforting someone. She closed her eyes again.

After what felt like a long time, they heard heavy footfalls coming toward their little cabin. Alycia had fallen asleep, but Tahira shook her awake and they moved away from the door. The key turned in the lock and Captain Haefen stepped inside. He closed the door behind him and leaned against it.

"Good news," he said. "My crew has agreed to let you stay aboard."

"So, that means we are your prisoners?" Tahira asked, standing up.

Captain Haefen narrowed his eyes. "If you choose to see it that way, Tahira, yes. But I see you as passengers. You will be well taken care of, I assure you."

"We still don't believe you," Alycia said, standing.

"I don't blame you," Captain Haefen said, still looking at Tahira. "Being captured by pirates is no small matter." He smiled a little. "I have discussed your treatment with my crew. They are not to touch you or talk to you. But my crew is prone to drinking and are generally not the most obedient lot, and those rules may be broken. If they are, find me in my cabin." He pointed over his shoulder toward the back of the ship. "It's aft on the weather deck. You can get to it by a ladder on the quarterdeck. Come to me for help. There are consequences for those who break the rules, and my crew knows that."

"Captain, what are we to do aboard this ship?" Alycia asked.

"Enjoy the cruise," Captain Haefen said, opening his arms. "I do not want to burden you with the hard work of this ship. I hope that you will see that I just rescued you from slavery."

"You have, but we don't know where *you're* taking us, Captain," Tahira said, gratitude for him stirring in her heart, but not wanting him to see it. "You could be taking us to a pirate port to… ruin us."

"That's all pirates do, after all," Alycia said.

Captain Haefen shrugged away from the door, anger in his face. "Madam, I do hope you have a better opinion of pirates than that."

"I don't," Alycia said, her voice shrill with fear.

"We've heard many stories of pirates that are not flattering," Tahira said, somehow finding it hard to think of Captain Haefen as doing any of the terrible things the Pirate Women had told her about.

"You're all horrible people!" Alycia shouted.

"Perhaps I have a worse opinion of Masters," he said to Alycia, the venom in his voice startling Tahira so much that she stepped back. His eyes snapped to her and his breath caught a little. He shifted his weight back. "I myself do not like pirate ports," he said after a pause, his voice soft and venom-less, something like regret in his face. "So no, I will not be taking you there."

He nodded once and left the cabin, locking the door.

Tahira sighed and sat down again. Alycia paced around the little room.

"I don't see why he got so angry," she muttered. "I was only telling him what I think of him. It's always worked when I wanted a man to go away. Why didn't it work on him?" She threw a hand toward Tahira as she paced by. "And why will he only talk to you?"

Tahira bit her lip to keep herself both from smiling and answering rudely; Alycia certainly was better at having a slave than a friend.

"Now what do you think of him, Tahira?" Alycia asked. "Will he really help us if we get into trouble?"

Tahira nodded against the wall. "Yes, I do believe he will," she said. She paused. "Did you see how he looked at me after he snapped at you?" she muttered, more to herself than to Alycia.

Thankfully, Alycia wasn't listening. Her hands started shaking as she paced, and tears came into her eyes, her expression wild like it always was after her nightmares. Tahira stayed seated. Experience had taught her that when Alycia wanted comfort, she would ask for it. Eventually, Alycia settled herself on the floor on the other side of the cabin without another word.

A while later they heard someone unlocking their door. Alycia, who had been fidgeting uncomfortably, wrenched the door open and ran out.

"Be careful," Tahira started, but Alycia had already run straight into Captain Haefen.

He pushed her back at arm's length as she caught her footing, looking annoyed.

"Captain, may we have a bucket to relieve ourselves?" Alycia asked.

Captain Haefen let go of Alycia and signaled to a pirate who appeared to have followed him; he nodded and ran off, returning moments later with a metal bucket. Alycia snatched it from his hand, pushed Tahira out of the cabin, then shut herself inside.

"Why a bucket, Captain?" Tahira asked. "Why not a metal cone, like on *The Nantes*? It never tipped over."

"Only slavers have those," Captain Haefen said. "But you make a good point. I'll send the carpenter in later to put a hook on the wall." He raised his eyebrows at her. "Are you sure you want a bucket? You could use the head."

"No, thank you. That's where the men go," Tahira said, grateful that Tel had told her about the head all those years ago. "A bucket is what I used when I was—" She broke off. She didn't want him to know anything more about her than he absolutely had to. "Where we came from," she finished. "It will do fine."

But Captain Haefen had noticed her hesitation. "Where *did* you two come from?" he asked.

Tahira raised her eyebrows at him now. "If you're not going to tell me where you're taking us, then I don't think I have to tell you where we came from."

Captain Haefen nodded, his mouth twitching as though trying not to smile. "Fair enough. I came down to tell you how this ship runs."

"I'll get Alycia," Tahira said. She knocked on the door and slipped inside the cabin when Alycia called to her.

"I heard the whole thing," Alycia said before Tahira could say anything.

Tahira knelt over the bucket to take her turn.

"That's smart, to kneel," Alycia said. "I was sitting on it."

"This is how we did it in the compounds," Tahira said.

Alycia started combing through her hair with her fingers, her expression frustrated. "I wish he would have let us take our bags," she said.

Tahira stayed silent, not wanting to pet Alycia's vanity just then.

Captain Haefen was waiting for them outside their cabin. He ducked his head so he wouldn't hit it on the low ceiling and led them up the hatchway ladder. Tahira and Alycia blinked in the bright afternoon sun, and saw that the pirates on deck were milling around with no discernable order. Captain Haefen took Tahira's elbow, she grabbed Alycia's hand, and they followed Captain Haefen through the crew.

Captain Haefen released Tahira once they gained the quarterdeck. In front of the wheel was a hatchway which opened to a ladder. Captain Haefen led the way down, then opened the door at the bottom.

"This is my cabin," he said. "Now you know where it is."

The cabin was a little more than twice the size of their orlop. Against the left wall was a bed, neatly made, with drawers built in underneath the mattress. Tahira doubted very much that Captain Haefen wanted anyone snooping, but the drawers did intrigue her. In the center of the cabin was his desk, littered with papers and maps and a few small boxes. Behind the desk, the wall was mostly made of windows, looking out the stern, with a seat underneath them. And along the righthand wall were shelves, each with weapons or trinkets that obviously held some meaning to the captain.

"Why are we here?" Alycia asked.

"I wanted you to meet the other officers in a private place," said Captain Haefen.

He gestured behind Tahira. She turned and started at the sight of the two large pirates that had silently entered the cabin behind her.

If Captain Haefen noticed her nervousness, he didn't comment. He sat down at his desk, leaned back in his chair, and put his boots on the desk.

"These are my second and third in command," he said. "First is my quartermaster, Peter Scudamore."

The larger of the two pirates stepped forward and nodded. He wore a striped bandana over his bald head and had a gold hoop in one ear.

"He's in charge of doling out discipline on my ship," Captain Haefen said. "When we take a prize, he divides up the spoils evenly. There're many things he does on this ship."

Scudamore moved behind Captain Haefen's chair and crossed his arms over his broad chest. The other man was big and muscular, his skin almost as dark as his curly black hair. He wore an open shirt of indeterminate color and pants that were once tan. He had an ugly scar running down his chest, and an ugly expression on his face.

"And this is my bosun, Andrew Rance," Captain Haefen said. "He's in charge of maintaining the sails, rigging, and the crew."

Rance glowered at Tahira and Alycia then left the cabin, undoubtedly to resume his duties. Tahira thought with bitterness that Rance looked more like the pirate captain she had expected.

"Scudamore and Rance are my most trusted men," Captain Haefen said. "If you can't find me, find one of them. They will protect you."

"Protect us?" Alycia repeated. "Forgive me if I don't feel protected."

Captain Haefen stood up. "You said that you have a low opinion of pirates," he said, anger mounting in his voice. "Why don't you tell me now?"

Alycia looked back and forth between Captain Haefen and Scudamore a few times. "Tahira knows the stories better than I do," she said, looking down her nose at Captain Haefen, though Tahira could tell she was terrified.

Captain Haefen looked at Tahira.

"Where we came from, many of my friends had been brought by pirates," she said when Alycia pinched her unnecessarily. "They told me what it's like aboard your ships. My friends were captured, humiliated, abused, and sold."

"And that's why you want nothing to do with me," Captain Haefen said.

"I never said that," Tahira said.

"You didn't, but she did," Captain Haefen said, jerking his head at Alycia but not looking at her. He sat down again and glanced at Scudamore, who nodded and left the cabin. "But let me ask you something, Tahira. In your brief time on this ship, have I treated you as your friends were?"

"No," Tahira said.

She would have said more; she would have told Captain Haefen how utterly different he was from what she'd thought pirates were. But she held her tongue as she felt Alycia's annoyed gaze boring into her. Alycia was used to being the center of attention, the one men talked to, and she was not going to give up that attention to a mere slave.

"You could start mistreating us any time," Alycia said, stepping in front of Tahira.

"But I won't," Captain Haefen said to Tahira as though Alycia hadn't spoken. He leaned forward on his desk and clasped his hands together. "I don't know what ships your friends were on, but I can promise that they were not on my ship. I will not abuse you, so I wouldn't have done it to your friends. Nor would I take a woman captive."

"And what do you call this then?" Alycia asked, stepping forward again. "You took us off that slaver."

"He rescued us, Alycia," Tahira said softly.

"I asked you to come, and you agreed," Captain Haefen said, a dangerous edge to his voice now. He stood up again. "That's hardly capturing you."

"You more told me to come than asked me," Tahira said.

"You're holding us here against our will," Alycia said.

"And where would you go if not for me?" Captain Haefen asked.

"I don't know," Tahira said. "I don't want to go back to where I came from, though Alycia might want to. And I don't know if I want to go where you're taking us." She paused, wondering if Captain Haefen would answer her. "You might tell me where we're going, and then I'd know for sure."

Captain Haefen gave her a one-sided smile. "No, Tahira, I won't be telling you."

"Why not?" Tahira asked, taking a step forward.

"I have my reasons," Captain Haefen said. The dangerous edge returned to his voice. "And any one of my crew will tell you it's best not to question my reasons."

"Is that a threat?" she asked. She had no idea where her courage was coming from, for she had never spoken to anyone like this before.

"It could be," he said, shifting his weight back again. "Like everything, it depends on how you take it." He and Tahira stared at one another for a few moments. Captain Haefen broke the silence first, "While you're both here, I'd like to tell you how this ship works."

Tahira nodded. Alycia, who had been staring at Tahira, shook herself, diplomatic once again.

"First, you are welcome to any part of this ship," Captain Haefen said. "Explore as you will. My crew is allowed to answer your questions, but don't expect an answer. I do have one request, though. If you go into the powder room, do not bring an open flame with you, or this ship will blow up."

Alycia nodded.

"Second, your meals will be brought to you, and will consist of the same thing. Meat and biscuit are what we all eat. Sometimes we get something better, if we catch a merchant. Pirates don't sail into port often, so we resupply on islands."

"Why don't you sail into port?" Alycia asked. She raised her nose in the air, a pout on her face. Tahira guessed she was objecting to the food choice.

But at Alycia's question Tahira wondered how possible it would be for them to escape. Though she inexplicably felt safer on this pirate ship than she ever had on the slaver, she did not really want to stay here.

Captain Haefen gave a wry smile. "Because there are many people in this world who want all pirates dead. I'd rather not meet them."

Tahira's heart sank a little and Alycia scoffed.

"Third, we will be running gun practice every day," Captain Haefen said, talking over Alycia's interruption. "The cannons are loud, so hide down in the bilges if you don't want to watch. But if you do want to watch, I have no objections."

"*Do* you have any objections?" Alycia asked.

Captain Haefen shook his head. "Not many. I would object to stealing anything. I would also object to you jumping ship. You would drown. And of course I object to you setting fire to the magazine."

"What's that?" Alycia asked.

"The powder room," Tahira said.

"Very good," Captain Haefen said, inclining his head.

Tahira lifted her chin a little. "I'm a quick learner."

Captain Haefen smiled. It was the first real smile she'd seen on him. His eyes crinkled, making him look younger and even more handsome. Tahira smiled back in spite of herself.

"Will you be taking prizes?" Alycia asked.

His smile faded. "If they present themselves, yes," he said. "But I won't be actively looking for any."

"Why not?" Alycia asked.

"I don't want to risk hurting you," Captain Haefen said to Tahira. She was about to question him further, but something in his tone discouraged her. "Lastly, for your own safety, I will be locking you in your cabin every night. Someone will unlock the door and bring you food in the morning."

He paused, then strode to the door. "If you'll excuse me," he said, and left his cabin.

Alycia looked at Tahira. "What do you think of him?" she asked.

"I'm not sure," Tahira said. "Part of me likes him and part of me doesn't."

Her mind was buzzing, but with more than that day's experiences. For the first time in her life, she'd really talked to a man. And he hadn't been afraid or angry or condescending, like other men she'd spoken to. He was intelligent, and he valued and truly asked for her opinion. The way he spoke to her, answered her, looked at her, felt so very different from everything else in her life. She didn't know what to do with that, nor with how it made her feel.

"I have never heard you speak so forcefully before," Alycia said, pulling Tahira out of her reverie. "It was wonderful to hear." She pushed Tahira's hair back from her face, and for a moment Tahira felt the same friendship from her that they used to have.

But then Alycia dropped her hands and her pout returned. "He won't even look at me," she said. "He only answers me when I ask a direct question. He only talks to you. Why is that?"

Tahira sighed and sat on the edge of the desk. Her confusing feelings about Captain Haefen faded as she remembered that she was still Alycia's slave, and was expected to be deferential to her Mistress.

"Let's go back to our cabin," Alycia said.

Captain Haefen met them on the quarterdeck and led them back down to the orlop. Scudamore followed and handed them bowls of food before Captain Haefen locked their door.

After the brightness of the deck, their cabin was very dark, but by the time they finished eating their eyes had adjusted to the lantern light, and they saw that their bucket was now hanging on a wooden peg on the wall. Tahira lay down on the floor and closed her eyes. Alycia said something to her but she was too asleep to hear.

It felt like moments later when she woke up. She realized at once that she wasn't on the floor anymore; someone was holding her in his arms. The realization startled her completely awake and she struggled to get away. But the pirate holding her spoke at once.

"It's all right, Tahira, we're getting your bed ready."

It was Captain Haefen. Tahira stopped struggling and sleepiness started coming in again as her heart calmed down.

"Please put me down, Captain," she said.

Captain Haefen obliged immediately. Tahira stood on her unsteady, sleep-weary feet. The pitching of the ship made it even harder to get her balance and she staggered into the captain, who steadied her.

They were outside her cabin. Three pirates were inside, setting up beds a little bigger than cots on either side of the room. A fourth pirate was holding a sleeping Alycia. Tahira looked up at Captain Haefen, her eyebrows raised in a question.

"We didn't want to wake you," he said. "But we wanted you to be comfortable. My apologies for not coming earlier in the day."

He turned his focus to his crewmen and didn't look at Tahira again. When the pirates had finished, Captain Haefen guided Tahira inside and sat her on one of the beds. Sleep was already overtaking her when she lay down on the surprisingly soft bed and closed her eyes.

Chapter Twelve

Tahira and Alycia spent the next several days exploring the pirate ship.

They went through the cargo hold, finding barrels of water and salt meat, chests full of clothes, kegs and bottles of amber-colored liquid that smelled awful. There were dozens of canvas bags containing dried yellow leaves, sugar, soft white tufts, and soap bars. Several boxes held things like needles and thread and fabric. They found a few chests and bags full of gold, silver, and jewels. Tahira had an urge to run her hands through the jewels.

On the gun deck, one below, they found the magazine, the pirates' personal belongings, the armory, where the other officers bunked, and the carpenter's store room. Tahira counted twelve cannons on the gun deck, and three on the main deck. She shuddered at the sight of them, for she knew from Tel and Dot the damage they could do.

The galley was located at the front of the gun deck, tucked between the foremast and the side of the ship; Tahira and Alycia had to walk to the side of it to get to their cabin. A metal pipe ran from the galley up to the main deck, and there was almost always food smells, coming from it. Tahira tried to go inside the galley, but the cook growled her out.

The main deck was almost always teeming with pirates. Many were on watch duty but the rest lazed around, lounging on the railings, up in the rigging, all over the deck, playing cards, throwing daggers, drinking, or singing. Tahira and Alycia were always on the lookout for grasping hands that might stray toward them as they walked across the deck, but for the most part the pirates kept their hands to themselves, as Captain Haefen had promised.

When the pirates sang, Tahira hummed along with them, for she knew most of the shanties. But these pirates had different words than she had learned, words that were dirty and demeaning. Tahira hummed louder to drown them out a little.

The pirates ran gunnery practice every day. Tahira sat in the bow and watched as the pirates fired on and destroyed, empty barrels they'd set afloat on the ocean. The entire ship rocked and bucked with each cannon fire, especially when all the cannons on one side were set off at once. Tahira soon learned that was called a broadside. She couldn't help but admire the pirates' aim as one by one all the barrels were reduced to floating splinters.

Gunnery practice was Tahira's favorite time, for then all the pirates but the helmsman were manning the guns, leaving the main deck empty. It was the only time she didn't feel like she and Alycia were being constantly stared at, one of the only times she felt like she had space around her.

One morning Tahira and Alycia were standing by the helmsman. Tahira was watching the topmen working the sails when Alycia turned around.

"There's someone back there," she whispered. "Come on."

Sitting against the taffrail behind the helmsman was a sad heap of a man, hunched over a lyre. Next to him were a fiddle case and a drum.

"Hello," Alycia said, kneeling down in front of him. The man roused himself as if from a deep sleep. With a huge effort he sat up and blinked at Alycia. "You don't look like a regular pirate."

"That's because I'm not," he growled. His expression was defensive, like he'd never been shown a moment of human decency, and perhaps he hadn't.

"Who are you?"

"I'm a musician," the man said, a glint of interest in his face.

"What are you doing on this ship?" Alycia asked.

"I was taken right off my ship, wasn't I?" the musician said. He looked almost bored as he stretched his legs in front of him.

"Why?" Alycia asked.

"Because they wanted music." The musician's voice had an edge to it now, like he was challenging them to ask him more questions.

"How often do you play?" Tahira asked.

"Whenever the pirates want me to," the musician said. "Which, in a calm like this, usually is all the time."

"But I've never heard you play," Alycia said.

"I did say usually," the musician said. He shifted his position and laid his lyre gently on the deck next to him.

"Oh, may I?" Alycia asked, pointing to it.

The musician sat up a little, suddenly interested. "Do you play?"

"Yes," Alycia said. "And it's been so long since I have."

The musician actually smiled, then. He picked up the lyre and handed it to Alycia. "Be my guest, my Lady," he said.

"Thank you." Alycia looked pleased that the musician had addressed her as such. She shifted her position and rested the butt of the lyre on one leg, bracing the frame against her shoulder. She stretched her fingers, tuned the instrument, then began stroking the light strings. As Alycia played, some of the crew stopped to listen. One bad-tempered man shouted, "Stow it, musician!"

Alycia finished warming up and stroked the instrument's frame fondly.

"Tahira, let's sing something," she said.

"Very well," Tahira said. She glanced around at the pirate crew, some of whom were still looking at them. "Do you remember the slave song I taught you?"

"Oh, yes, I love that one." Alycia plucked a couple strings, making sure the lyre was tuned right.

With a synchronized breath they began the soft, lilting, song. Tahira's voice carried more of the tune than the instrument, and she smiled at Alycia as Alycia struggled through, being out of practice. As they played, the crew stopped what they were doing and slowly came towards the quarterdeck, listening. They were silent, their expressions far away, as though each one of them was reliving memories while Tahira sang,

Set me free, set me free to the life where I may breathe,
    Set me free to pursue my own goals.
    Set me free, set me free from the life of this oppression,
    Tuned by hardship and omission, with a creed of no compassion.
    Set me free

When the last note on the lyre rang still there was a quiet hush on the ship; even the waves seem to have stilled to listen.

After a moment or two a soft voice broke the silence, "That was the most beautiful thing I have ever heard."

The crew collectively started and moved away. Captain Haefen was leaning against the railing at the bottom of the steps.

"I've never heard such a beautiful voice, Tahira," he said, stepping slowly up the stairs. "When you sing, it's like all of our troubles and cares have disappeared. I hope you will share again."

His light-blue gaze bore into Tahira's. He looked at her with something like longing, but she wasn't sure. She blushed and looked down.

Alycia handed the lyre back to the musician and stood up. "I think there is a possibility for that, Captain," she said. "I love to play."

Captain Haefen inclined his head to Alycia, taking his eyes off Tahira for the first time.

***

A scream filled the cabin. Tahira started awake, her dreams still lingering confusingly in her mind. She finally woke up enough to realize Alycia was screaming in her sleep again, the third time in four nights. Tahira lurched across the cabin, groping for Alycia in the dark.

"Alycia!" she shouted over the screaming. "Alycia! It's all right, it's just a nightmare."

Alycia stopped screaming and clung to Tahira in the dark. "It was horrible," she said, still panting. Tahira could feel her shaking and sweating. "I don't even want to describe it."

"Then don't," Tahira said. She stroked Alycia's hair and rocked her lightly. Alycia was still breathing hard. "Here, lie back down," Tahira said. Alycia obeyed her pressure but continued to whimper.

Tahira lit one lantern, casting a shadow into the cabin. Alycia looked ill, and Tahira instinctively knew she needed a change of air. She tried the door of their cabin, but it was of course locked. She pounded on it with her fist until she heard a voice outside.

"Shut up!" a pirate yelled. "Do ye want to wake up the captain?"

"Yes!" Tahira shouted back.

"Yer mad," the pirate said.

"Please, go get Captain Haefen," Tahira said. "We need him."

"I'm not gonna risk his wrath by wakin' 'im in the middle of the night," the pirate said. He sounded drunk.

"We are under the captain's care," Tahira said, angry at the man's obstinacy. "And we need him." Without waiting for a reply she reached up and hit the ceiling of their cabin with her fist. "Captain Haefen, help!" she shouted.

She knew there was little chance Captain Haefen would hear her, his cabin being on the deck above and on the opposite end of the ship. But she had to try.

"Shut up!" the pirate said again. He sounded panicked.

Tahira stopped and listened with her ear to the door. Outside the cabin she could hear the pirates shifting around, talking in low voices, mostly complaining. But suddenly they all quieted.

"What's going on here?" Captain Haefen's voice asked.

"The wench wanted ye, Captain," the pirate said. "I didn't want to wake ye."

"She is a woman, not a wench," Captain Haefen said. His voice was dangerous. "And do you mean to tell me you were going to let her suffer?"

The pirate stammered. Tahira heard what sounded like a fist hitting flesh and the stammering stopped. Moments later she heard the key in the lock and the door opened. Captain Haefen stood in the doorway, shirtless, his hair tousled, and an annoyed expression on his face.

"I'm sorry to wake you, Captain," Tahira said, gathering Alycia off the bed. "But Alycia needs some air. We're going out on deck."

Captain Haefen stood back. As Tahira stepped out, she saw pirates scurrying back to their hammocks, which were strung all over the deck. One pirate stood nearby, his hands over a bleeding nose. He looked daggers at Tahira as she passed and she looked away from him.

Alycia took a deep breath as soon as her head cleared the hatchway. She stood there for a few moments, breathing, the terror of her nightmare slowly leaving her face. She finished her ascent, moved to the railing and leaned on it. Tahira followed.

Alycia stared out at the moonlit sea for a few silent minutes, a wild look in her face. "I dreamed I died out here, Tahira," she whispered. "I died at sea. And I was alone. It was awful. I don't want to die at sea. I don't want to die alone."

Tahira touched Alycia's arm. "You have me, you're not alone," she said. "And you won't die at sea. When we get where Captain Haefen takes us you will live to be a very old woman."

Alycia turned her face slowly to Tahira. "I've been hearing the pirates talking," she said. "They say that if you have a dream of yourself dying, you will die soon."

The fear in Alycia's face suddenly reminded Tahira of Mary, and that long-ago night when Tahira had helped her through a nightmare. "I've heard that pirates are very superstitious," she said. "Don't worry, most of what they believe is false."

Alycia looked out at the water again. Tahira leaned on the railing and closed her eyes, her face turned up, the breeze soft and soothing. Behind them the pirates were going about their usual nightly watch, thankfully paying them no mind, though a few were drinking and swearing as they wove around the deck.

Finally, Alycia took a deep breath. "I'm all right now. We can go back to bed."

Tahira nodded, suddenly reluctant to return to the stuffy cabin. She turned around and saw Captain Haefen leaning against the mainmast behind them, wearing a shirt now, and staring up at the stars. At Tahira's movement, however, he looked down at her. He raised his eyebrows in a question and she nodded. Silently, he followed them belowdecks.

"Thank you," Tahira said as Captain Haefen made to close their door. "I'm sorry to wake you."

Captain Haefen glanced at Alycia. "I know about nightmares," he said. "The sea air seems to be the only thing to get rid of them."

Tahira nodded, not sure how to respond.

***

As far as Tahira could tell, she and Alycia had been on the pirate ship for a couple weeks. Tahira spent most of her time watching the pirates, seeing how they swung between the masts, how they floated down from the rigging, as they called it. She listened to the pirates talking and learned many of their names. She listened to their commands and shouts, and gradually learned nearly every part of the rigging and sails by name.

Finally, she wanted to try climbing.

She went to one of the rope ladders on the side of the ship that went up a mast, called the ratlines, put her hand on it, and swung herself up like she'd seen the pirates do.

"Wait," Captain Haefen said, appearing out of nowhere. He put a hand on her ankle and Tahira looked down at him. Captain Haefen was staring at her ankle. She followed his gaze and realized he was staring at the iron band. She had grown so used to it that she had forgotten about it. But with Captain Haefen's hand and gaze on it, she was embarrassingly aware of it.

She shook her ankle lightly so he let her go. "What is it, Captain?" she asked.

"I wouldn't climb into the rigging in a dress," Captain Haefen said. His gaze lingered a second longer on her iron band before he looked up at her. He held out his hand and she took it to hop down onto the deck.

"Is that your only objection to me being up there?" she asked.

Captain Haefen knitted his eyebrows, confused. "Yes," he said slowly. "Why else would I object?"

Tahira shrugged. "The sailors on *The Nantes* never let me climb," she said. "They always stopped me, said they didn't want me to fall."

Captain Haefen nodded once. "Ah. I think it was because your price for them would diminish if you were injured." He looked up at the mast. "Do you really want to climb?"

Tahira nodded. Captain Haefen turned around. "Ransome!" he barked.

Moments later, the cabin boy ran up. He was about fifteen years old, skinny and dirty and no taller than Tahira. He seemed both terrified and awed to be in Captain Haefen's presence, and he gave a salute as he stumbled to a stop in front of his Captain.

"Aye, sir?" he said.

"Fetch your extra breeches," Captain Haefen said.

Ransome's salute faltered. "Sir?"

"Now," Captain Haefen snapped.

Ransome flinched and ran off. Tahira stared at Captain Haefen, wondering why he was so mean to such a young boy. Ransome was back in moments, holding his breeches in a brown bundle. He held it out to Captain Haefen then darted away as fast as he could.

"You'll have to forgive Ransome," Captain Haefen said, handing the breeches to Tahira.

"Why is he here?" Tahira asked. "He's so young."

Captain Haefen shrugged. "Every Captain needs a cabin boy." He tapped the breeches in her hand. "Now, whenever you want to climb in the rigging, wear these under your dress."

"Why are you helping me?" Tahira asked.

"Because I can only image how uncomfortable it would be to climb the rigging in a dress," he said. "Also, my ship is full of men who'd... like a peek."

"Oh." Tahira looked down at the breeches, her cheeks reddening, silently berating herself for not thinking of that.

"A word of advice," Captain Haefen said. Tahira swallowed and looked up at him. "It's harder than it looks getting your balance up there. Hold on tight."

"Why are you helping me?" Tahira repeated.

"I want you to enjoy your time here," Captain Haefen said.

He gave a little nod and walked away. Tahira looked after him for a moment, wondering what to think of him. Then she made her way to the fo'c'sle and peeked over the bulkhead toward the bowsprit, making sure no one was using the head. Once she was sure it was empty, she climbed down onto the bowsprit walkway, quickly worked Ransome's breeches over her iron bands and pulled them on. They fit perfectly.

Excitement began bubbling in her chest as she made her way back to the ratlines of the foremast. She swung herself up again and started to climb. Captain Haefen had been right; it was difficult to keep her balance. Though it was a clear day, the ship still rocked, swinging her far out over the ocean. But she held on and made it to the futtock shrouds.

She paused, for there were two ways to get to the foretop, the platform halfway up the mast. One was the sailors' way, straight up the futtock shrouds that were anchored to the outer edge of the foretop. The other was the way the pirates never took, but which looked easier: to go around the futtock shrouds and up through a hole in the bottom of the foretop, right along the mast.

Tahira decided to go through the hole this first time, and in moments she was pulling herself up onto the foretop. She leaned against the mast and looked around.

The view of the sea was beautiful. Tahira could see so much farther than she could down on the deck, and the glittering expanse of water dazzled her. The pirates below her looked small, as did the whole ship. She scooted around to the back of the mast so she faced into the wind, pausing a few times on her way as a pirate climbed past her. She closed her eyes and breathed in the fresh salty air. She braced her hands against the foretop, for she wasn't used to this much movement. After a few minutes she opened her eyes to avoid getting motion sick.

Tahira leaned forward until she could see Alycia waving up at her from the deck. She waved back.

"You came up through the lubber's hole," said a mocking voice behind her.

Tahira started so badly she nearly tipped forward. She whipped around and saw Ransome's head poking over the side of the foretop. He hauled himself up and sat on the edge, one leg dangling off.

"I thought the captain said you weren't allowed to talk to me," Tahira said.

Fear flickered over his face for a moment. Then he shrugged. "Normally, but he's not up here," he said. "And besides, you're in my spot."

Tahira looked at him. Ransome was looking down at his hands in his lap, his dangling leg swinging. He looked like a little boy.

"Do you hide from the others up here?" Tahira asked.

Ransome looked at her sharply. "No," he said. "I just like it."

He didn't look like a little boy any more, but hard and unyielding like the rest of the crew. Tahira scooted a little away from him.

"So that's called a lubber's hole?" she asked.

"Aye, and it's not the seaman's way of getting up here," Ransome said. He glanced at her. "I hope you enjoy my breeches. Captain is the only reason you're wearing them. Otherwise, I'd still have them."

Tahira was stunned by the venom in his voice. She scooted all the way to the other side of the foretop and slid her legs through the lubber's hole to the ratlines.

"I'll use the other top next time. And thank you for the breeches," she said. "But you know, Ransome, you could be a little nicer."

Ransome turned his head to look at her. She held his gaze until he looked away.

Getting back down to the deck was harder than going up, for her dress kept getting in the way. But she was grateful for the breeches when the wind caught her dress and blew it up almost around her shoulders. She heard some pirates howling at the sight. Alycia was waiting for her when she swung off the ratlines.

"Never go up there again!" Alycia said with a squeal, shaking Tahira by the arms. "It terrified me to see you up so high."

"Oh, it was so exhilarating," Tahira said. "I've never been up so high before. It was so beautiful! You should climb up there." She'd never said so much to Alycia about her feelings before.

"No," Alycia said. "You won't get me up in that rigging. It's far too terrifying."

Tahira sighed, her euphoria calming down now.

"Where did you get those breeches?" Alycia asked, touching Tahira's hip where the waistband was.

"From the cabin boy, Ransome," Tahira said. She pointed up at the foretop. "He's up there now. He's a bit nasty."

"He's a pirate," Alycia said, rolling her eyes. "They're *all* nasty."

Tahira might have agreed, except for one pirate. "I'm going to take these breeches off in our cabin."

"Shouldn't you give them back to Ransome?" Alycia whispered as they moved through the pirates.

"Captain Haefen told me to wear these when I want to climb," Tahira said, dodging a groping hand as it reached for her hip. "I assume that means I can keep them. At least for now."

They made their way down to their cabin and closed the door. Tahira pulled the breeches off and folded them at the foot of her bed.

"I wish there was something to do," Alycia said, stretching out on her bed. "You never seem bored, but I always am. What do you do?"

"I'm been thinking of starting a healing box," Tahira said. The thought had been building in her mind for the last few days. "We haven't bathed in weeks. You're going to get sores because you're not used to not washing, and having the proper supplies would help heal those so you don't get sick."

Alycia wrinkled her nose. "Where would you get the supplies?" she asked.

"I'll start in the galley," Tahira said.

"Doesn't this ship have a healer?" Alycia asked.

Tahira shook her head. "Captain Haefen said this ship doesn't have a surgeon. That's ship-talk for a healer."

"What happens if they get sick or hurt?" Alycia asked.

Tahira shrugged. "I guess they die. Or Mr. Ravon takes care of them."

"Who's that?"

"The carpenter." Tahira sat on her bed, trying not to think of how a carpenter would tend to wounds. Now she was thinking about it, getting a box of healing supplies was sounding better and better. But perhaps she'd better talk to the cook in the morning, before he'd had a chance to get drunk.

"Well, maybe after you get your supplies, you can figure out how we can play Jack Dogs," Alycia said. She crossed her hands on her stomach and closed her eyes. "I'm tired of being bored."

***

Just as Tahira hoped, the cook, James Copper, was in a better mood the next morning than he usually was in the evenings. He pointed Tahira to his spice stores and let her look around. When she asked if she could take some, he grunted and pointed her to a metal box full of little compartments. Tahira put a few pinches of each spice and herb in each compartment.

"Thank you," she said and left the galley. For now these supplies would do. She closed the metal box tightly and put it under her bed. She was surprised how much more like herself she felt, just having taken one small step toward healing.

She was still smiling to herself as she made her way up to the main deck. But her smile vanished almost immediately.

She heard Alycia scream.

Tahira pushed her way through about half the crew of pirates crowding the deck to the bow, where Alycia's scream had come from. She stopped in her tracks.

Two pirates, Wilkid and Richardson, were standing in a cleared space, shouting drunkenly at each other and waving their pistols. This wasn't an uncommon occurrence on the ship. But Richardson had his arm around Alycia's neck. Alycia's hair had been pulled out of the bun Tahira had painstakingly placed it in, and her dress was torn in places. The sight sickened Tahira.

"I say she's mine!" Richardson shouted. "She came over to me!"

"Aye, but she was lookin' at me!" Wilkid shouted. He darted forward, but Richardson yanked Alycia out of his reach. Alycia let out a cry.

Tahira darted forward. "Let her go!" she shouted.

Wilkid turned drunkenly toward her. He drew back his fist and threw it at her just as she reached him. Unprepared, Tahira staggered back and fell to the deck. She heard the pirates behind her laughing as her head spun. Her cheek stung. She touched it with a finger and drew away a little blood. She looked up at the leering Wilkid. He turned his attention back to Richardson and Alycia.

Tahira turned and looked at the other pirates. None of them were going to help; their faces were alive with the sport of violence.

She needed Captain Haefen.

With an effort Tahira pulled herself to her feet and pushed her way back through the drunken crush of pirates, more than a few hands touching her as she went. She feared someone would grab her to stop her progress, and her fears were not unfounded. Just as she pushed through the last man, she felt an arm go around her waist, and she screamed as it hauled her off her feet and against the pirate's chest.

Three or four of his mates stood in front of her, trying to grab her feet. Though her head still spun, she kicked and flailed with all four limbs so that more than once a pirate stumbled back, holding some part of himself.

"Captain Haefen!" she screamed toward the quarterdeck, hoping her voice wouldn't be snatched by the wind.

"The captain ain't here ter spare ya," a pirate nearby leered.

Tahira shuddered. "Captain Haefen, help!" she screamed, kicking both feet at once. "Captain Haefen!"

Distantly she thought she heard a door slam, and moments later Captain Haefen's dark head appeared in front of the wheel. Though his hair was tousled and his shirt hung open and his expression was faintly annoyed, Tahira had never been so glad to see him. She screamed in pain as one of the pirates finally managed to grab her ankle, her iron band pinching her skin.

"Captain Haefen!" she yelled again.

His light eyes locked onto hers instantly. He bared his teeth, and faster than she thought possible he was by her side.

"Belay!" he shouted, hitting the pirate holding her so hard that he fell backward onto the deck. He grabbed her elbows to steady her as she fell, the jolt of landing on the deck jarring her entire body.

"Are you—" he started.

"Alycia! They're going to hurt Alycia," she said, frantically pointing to the bow, just as Alycia screamed again.

Captain Haefen glanced at the cut on her cheek, then shoved his way thought the crew to the bow, pulling her after him. She staggered along as best she could, her head still spinning from the punch.

But Tahira could see he was too late.

It all happened in a second. Wilkid raised his pistol and fired. Richardson moved and the bullet hit Alycia squarely in the chest.

Alycia gasped. Richardson yelled and slumped backward. Alycia fell to the deck.

Tahira screamed. Captain Haefen swore.

A hush fell over the deck. Captain Haefen strode toward Wilkid and

Richardson, who both dropped their pistols and stared in horror at their Captain. Tahira ran to where Alycia lay gasping for breath. She couldn't see Captain Haefen's expression, but his voice was terrible,

"Mr. Ransome, take the ladies below. If you harm either one of them you will earn the same fate as this man." He turned to face his crew and raised his voice. "And that goes for all of you! I hope you're not too far gone in rum and sport to hear me. I gave orders, and you all have disobeyed me! For that every man jack of you deserves twelve lashes. As it is, I'll be stopping your grog for a week, to sober you up to what you've just done. If any man here has aught against me, let him speak."

The deck remained silent. Tahira took Alycia's cold hand and rubbed it between hers. She tried to smile as Alycia's breathing turned shallow. She started when Ransome crouched next to her.

"What are you doing?" she asked.

"I'm going to carry her," Ransome said softly, his rudeness of yesterday gone. Very gently he picked Alycia up in his arms. With Tahira walking behind him he went belowdecks and into their cabin. He laid Alycia on her bed and left without a word.

The front of Alycia's dress was turning red. Tahira thought of her small store of spices and herbs, even though she knew nothing of healing a bullet wound. She was just reaching for her metal box when she looked back at Alycia.

Even with a glance she could see Alycia was already dead.

Tahira lurched away, her old fear of watching people die rising within her. Pain and loneliness suddenly flew into her, harder and faster than she would ever have thought possible, harder than when Lores died, harder than when Aney was banished, and she wept. Everyone in her life had left. Now Alycia was gone too.

She was alone again.

After a time, Tahira's cries softened to gasps until she yawned. Exhausted, she laid down on her bed.

She heard the door open and close. Startled, she sat up to see who had invaded her privacy. Captain Haefen stood with his back against the closed door, his hair still tousled and his shirt still open. Tahira wiped the back of her hand over her face, her heart rate returning to normal.

"Tahira, I am so sorry," he said. His voice was softer than she'd ever heard it. "I have dealt with Wilkid for his disobedience."

"What have you done with him?" she asked.

"I keelhauled him."

"I don't know what that means."

"Keelhauling is the worst punishment that I could have given," he said.

"Is he dead?"

Captain Haefen knitted his eyebrows, like her question wasn't what he was expecting, and his harshness came back. "He killed your friend. Didn't you want revenge?"

"No, I didn't want revenge!" Tahira cried.

"Not even for the life of your friend?" he asked, his voice rising. "He killed her. He deserved to die."

"I don't think so."

"What would you have done?" he asked. "Forgiven him and gone as if nothing had happened?"

"Forgiven him, yes, eventually," she said. "I don't want revenge."

He shifted his weight back a little. "When a man murders, he must pay for the life he took with his own."

Tahira stood and faced Captain Haefen. "If you really follow that rule, don't you deserve to die too?" she asked. "Wilkid killed my friend and you have killed him."

Captain Haefen raised his eyebrows. "You do have a point," he said. "But what's done is done. He is gone."

She sat on her bed again. From the moment she boarded the pirate ship she had wanted nothing to do with the pirates and their customs, even this strange captain who didn't seem a pirate like the rest. But she suddenly needed someone to talk to, someone to comfort her.

"Captain, what is keelhauling?" she asked.

"Dragging someone under the ship from one side to the other," he said, his soft tone mostly returned. "Considering Wilkid's crime and disobedience I dragged him from stem to stern."

Tahira's stomach curdled a little. "You mean he was dragged along the bottom of the whole boat?"

"Ship," Captain Haefen said. "And aye, he was." Tahira looked up at last and saw no remorse in his face.

Her curdled stomach tightened in anger. "I am ashamed that you would stoop to such things, Captain," she said, standing up. "What a terrible way to die!"

"He was a terrible man, Tahira," he said, his anger matching hers. In that moment she felt incredibly intimidated by him. "Don't all terrible men deserve to die?"

Tahira stopped herself from scoffing with difficulty. Her anger died and she sat down again. "You are a pirate, Captain," she said. "I don't think you can judge him." She rubbed her forehead. "What will become of Alycia?"

For the first time, he ducked his head with an expression like remorse, and he shifted his weight back again. "She shall be given a proper sea burial," he said. "That is the best I can do for her."

Tahira looked up at him, pleased to see that his humbled expression was still there. "And what will become of me?" she asked. "What have you intended to do with us all this time?"

"You know that I will not answer that," he said, his face hardening. "So why ask it of me now?"

Tahira pulled herself to her feet once again, suddenly feeling very old and tired. "Because I am alone," she said, her voice breaking a little. "My friend is dead. The least you can do is tell me my own fate."

Captain Haefen took a deep breath as though steadying himself. "Your fate, for now, will be to remain on this ship under my protection."

"Alycia was under your protection," she said softly, though she wasn't accusing him.

"Aye, she was," he said just as softly.

She remained silent. Tears started to sting the edges of her eyes again.

"I'm sorry, Tahira, I didn't come in here to argue with you," he whispered. Slowly, as though scared of frightening her, he leaned away from the door, his hand extended towards her as though he wanted to take her hand. After a few moments of staring at it she slowly raised her hand. She did not know what he intended to do, and she didn't know if she wanted to still trust him. But as soon as her hand brushed his fingers, he took her hand.

At his touch another sob broke from her chest. She closed her eyes against her tears and felt Captain Haefen move closer until her cheek was resting against his bare chest. He put his arms gently around her. She took a deep breath and held it while her sobs silently racked her body.

Tahira had been hugged before, but never like this. Captain Haefen held her, gently, as though instinctively knowing this was what she had wanted, what she needed, but didn't know how to ask for. It felt wonderful, but she didn't really know what to do with it.

"Tahira, I am truly sorry for Alycia's death," he said. The tone of his voice made her look up at him, spreading one hand open on his chest. He looked kinder than she'd ever seen him, and she felt comforted. "I am sorry that you are now alone. But it was never my intention to take on Alycia. I did not want her."

This stung Tahira, yet she did not pull away. "Are you saying that her death is my fault?"

"Of course not," he said, tightening his arms around her briefly. "It is Wilkid's fault. And mine for not protecting her. I agreed to bring her along. But I only wanted you."

After another silent moment Captain Haefen let go of Tahira and left the cabin without another word.

Chapter Thirteen

Tahira stood at the rail after Alycia's sea burial, looking out at the ocean. The mood of the ship was very subdued. She heard no music, no singing, and surprisingly no complaining for the remainder of the day. Hardly anyone spoke, and no one tried to touch her. Tahira suspected that Captain Haefen had disciplined more than Wilkid that afternoon. She watched the sun as it set into the ocean, a ball of fire disappearing into the blue, bright in the face of her sorrow.

Her mind was blank, numb. Of all her friends she'd lost, Alycia's death seemed to hurt the most, though she couldn't understand why. She had been closer to Old Joche, and she and Lores had understood each other better, while Alycia had treated her more as a slave than a friend. Why would Alycia's death affect her worse than any of the others?

After staring at the ocean for hours, she came upon a possible reason: no matter who she had lost, she had always had other people around her. Now, instead of being surrounded by fellow slaves—surrounded by women—she was surrounded by dangerous men, led by a mysterious captain.

She truly was alone on this pirate ship.

The sun had barely set when the weather started changing. The breeze turned colder and the waves started moving quicker. White caps appeared on the tops of the waves, and the space between them deepened. Soon the wind increased so much that Tahira had a hard time keeping her dress down.

Captain Haefen put his hand on her shoulder. "I'm sorry, but you need to go below!" he shouted over the howling wind. "This is a bad storm. You'll be safe in your cabin."

Tahira pushed her hair out of her face and nodded. She followed him down to the orlop, where he locked the door behind her. Tahira looked around the cabin three times before it really settled in her that she was alone.

The ship started jumping violently. The motion threw her to the floor more times than she could stand up, until she managed to pull herself onto her bed. She curled up under her blankets, her body being crushed into or lifted off the bed harder and harder as the storm increased.

The numbness that had enveloped her after the burial melted away and she started to cry again. But suddenly she felt water splash on her face. She sat up, confused. In the dim light of the lanterns, she could see a little puddle on the floor. As she watched, the puddle got bigger, accompanied by another splash. Tahira stood up and crossed to the front of the cabin, looking for the source of the water. A few more splashes later, she found it: there was a crack in the boards.

"Help!" Tahira shouted, running to the door and pounding on it with both fists. "There's a leak!"

The ship suddenly fell several feet. When it landed in the waves Tahira was jarred to the floor, hard. She heard a snap and knew the crack had opened wider. Every few seconds more water came in as wave after wave beat against the bow of the ship. Tahira kept pounding on the door and shouting. But if any pirates heard they weren't heeding her call.

Gradually the water got deeper. The box under her bed started floating around the cabin, bumping between the walls and her ankles. Several times she had to hold onto the doorknob for support as the ship battled through the storm.

Soon the water was to her knees. The sides of her hands were bleeding but she kept pounding on the door. Her shoulders seized up every time she lifted her arms. If the cabin filled with water, not only would she drown, but the ship could sink. The water rose higher.

Tahira's voice was now hoarse and her hands and shoulders ached. She was cold from the sea water. Abandoning the door for the moment she climbed up on the bed and pounded on the ceiling, screaming even as her shoulders did.

The ship bucked, knocking Tahira over. Her head hit the cabin wall and she fell into the water. She was now exhausted enough that it was difficult to stand up. When she finally staggered to her feet, she leaned against one of the beds, coughing. The water was now to her chest.

"Please, someone help," she said. She was fast losing strength, fast losing the will to keep going. Her head was pounding and spinning, making it difficult to stand. She leaned her forehead against the door, feeling the water rising ever higher.

Her knees buckled and she slipped underwater. It reminded her of her first bath, only no one was holding her down. Her chest constricted and she could hear her heart pounding in her ears as her body ached for the air she had no strength to find. Her limbs twitched and she listened as her heartbeat started to slow…

Suddenly she felt the water moving forward, fast. She felt herself hit the deck. She felt someone dragging her before laying her gently down. She felt her arms moving up and down.

Tahira started coughing. Someone turned her onto her side and pressed on her ribs. She coughed until all the water left her body. She rolled onto her back and opened her eyes.

Captain Haefen was kneeling over her, his dripping hair falling into his face. His wet coat was open to his dry shirt underneath, and Tahira could feel his body heat pouring onto her. As she opened her eyes his expression changed from anger to relief, and something of a smile came to his face. He put his hands under her arms and lifted her to her feet in one easy, fluid motion.

"Are you all right?" he asked.

Tahira tried to nod but instead her knees gave out. Captain Haefen held her upright against his chest. The heat from his body seeped into hers and she shivered. She resisted the urge to wrap her arms around him.

"No one saw the water coming under your door until now," Captain Haefen said. "Come." He scooped her up in his arms and carried her to the hammock furthest from her cabin. As he placed her inside, she heard the pirates shouting and the sloshing of the pumps.

Captain Haefen snapped his fingers with a barked order and a wet pirate appeared at his side with a dry blanket. He tucked it over Tahira and put his hand on her head.

"Captain!" someone shouted.

"I have to go," Captain Haefen said.

Tahira closed her eyes. Within moments she felt herself drifting off to sleep.

***

Sometime later Tahira felt the hammock being opened. Fear shot through her and she sat up so fast her head spun. Scudamore stood next to her.

"Captain wants you in his cabin, Miss," he said.

"What does he want?" Tahira asked.

"He wants you in his cabin," Scudamore repeated with a slight growl.

He held out his hand. Reluctantly Tahira took it and he pulled her out of the hammock with surprising quickness. Pain shot through her shoulder at the movement, but she bit off her gasp of pain, concentrating instead on following Scudamore's long strides up to the main deck.

She was surprised to see it was almost midday, and the sky was clear and blue. Scudamore opened the grating on the quarterdeck for her but didn't follow.

"Come in," Captain Haefen called at her knock. He was sitting on the edge of his desk with his arms folded, waiting for her.

"Captain," she said, automatically ducking her head.

"I'm sorry for last night," Captain Haefen said. "Are you all right?"

"What happened?" Tahira asked, nodding. "Why was there a hole?"

Captain Haefen shook his head once. "Some of the tar binding came undone," he said. "Mr. Ravon did what he could last night. We're going to need to refit, but your cabin will be ready for you by nightfall."

Tahira nodded. She suddenly felt judged under his intense gaze. She felt exposed. And now that the horror of the night was past, the sadness of the day before started to come back. She wanted nothing more than to get away from the crush of pirates and hide up in the rigging.

She took a step back. Captain Haefen stood up.

"Actually, I called you here for more than an apology," he said.

"What is it?" Even to her own ears she sounded tired.

Captain Haefen stepped to the side and pointed to a large basin of water standing between his desk and the stern windows. "I thought after last night you would like a chance to bathe."

He sounded embarrassed. Tahira barely held back a smile at watching him. But then she realized something and gave a little gasp.

"Captain, that's a huge amount of water," she said, pointing at the basin. She knew by now how limited the stores of water were on a ship, and she couldn't imagine such a precious thing being wasted on her. "I can't take it from the ship's stores."

Captain Haefen shrugged one shoulder. "We put barrels up in the tops during storms," he said. "We got six barrels last night, and my crew doesn't like drinking water. This is for you."

"But you took the crew off of rum yesterday," she said. "They'll need water."

"This is for you," he repeated.

He said it with such certainty that Tahira knew there would be no use arguing. But his tone removed any guilt she felt, replacing it with something like awe. This water was for her. She had never been given anything before.

He dropped his gaze and pointed to a wooden chest at his feet. "My crew assures me there's women's clothing in there," he said. "When you're done you can give your clothes to Mr. Copper to clean, if you want to keep them." He stepped around Tahira to the door and opened it. "Take as long as you like. You won't be bothered."

Just as the door was closing, it occurred to Tahira that she hadn't heard her name since the day before. She couldn't have explained it, but hearing her name suddenly seemed important.

"Wait," she said. The door paused. She looked up at Captain Haefen's blue eyes. "How did you know my name?"

Captain Haefen stepped back into the cabin. "I told you, I must have overheard it on *The Nantes*," he said.

"From Captain Mills?" Tahira asked.

"Perhaps."

"But no one knew my name but Alycia."

There was something in his expression that she couldn't read, but she could feel he was keeping something from her. It seemed for a moment that he was going to explain, but then he shrugged.

"I must have overheard it from her, then," he said.

Tahira sighed and nodded, not in the habit of pushing for information. Captain Haefen still hadn't said her name, and now there was something else mysterious about him. She turned toward the stern windows, her iron bands clinking together as she moved her feet.

"Wait, Tahira," Captain Haefen said.

She smiled at the sound of her name.

"Those iron bands on your ankles," he said. "Do they come off?"

She turned and lifted the hem of her tattered dress so the bands were visible. "They do," she said. "But I don't have the key."

Captain Haefen grunted, clearly upset. He knelt in front of her and pulled out his dagger.

"What are you doing?" Tahira asked, taking a step back.

He pointed at her ankle. "I'm going to take those bands off," he said. "Could I have your foot?"

Tahira stared at him. He was almost the only person in her life who asked her to do something; mostly everyone just demanded. Captain Haefen raised his eyebrows expectantly. Tahira leaned against the desk and raised one foot.

He pulled off her thin slipper—frayed from rough decks—and rested her foot on his knee. He turned the band around until the lock was facing him, then inserted his dagger inside and started jiggling it. After a few seconds the band unlocked and fell to the floor with a thud.

Tahira gasped. She hadn't realized how much the bands were holding her down. Nor how much they hurt. Captain Haefen ran one finger gently on her ankle where the skin was rubbed raw.

"Did you ever take these off?" he asked.

"Only when I bathed," Tahira said. She removed her foot from his knee and extended the other one.

"How long have you been wearing these?" he asked, unlocking the second band.

"A little over a year," she said.

He sheathed his dagger and picked up the bands. He stood up, his expression somewhere between annoyance and sympathy. He sighed, balancing the heavy bands in his hand. "If you don't mind, I'm going to throw these overboard," he said. "You are never wearing these again."

Tahira stared at him again, marveling; even with her limited knowledge of men Tahira knew that Captain Haefen was very different from others of his kind. He inclined his head and left the cabin.

Tahira moved around the desk and stared out of the stern cabin windows. After the storm, the sea was calm and glittering once again. It was hard to believe that that same sea had nearly killed her the night before.

With some difficulty Tahira peeled off her salt-encrusted clothes and piled them next to the basin. She was surprised to find the water was warm; all her baths had been cold. She had never known until now just how good a warm bath felt; she felt her sore muscles, relaxing. She wetted her long hair and massaged it, watching the salt and grime float away.

After soaking in the warm water for a while, she cleaned herself with a bar of soap she found on seats under the windows, noticing there were sweet-smelling herbs in the bar. The sides of her hands were full of splinters, but she could tell they would work themselves out.

Once she was clean, Tahira climbed out of the basin and wrapped herself in the towel that was draped over the back of the captain's chair.

"Let's see what's inside you," she said, moving to the wooden chest. It was indeed full of women's clothing, and she found the necessary undergarments as she picked through the chest. She pulled out all the dresses inside, trying to find the plainest one, but all the dresses were almost as nice as Alycia's. Tahira felt out of place. She finally settled on the blue and green one. She dried herself off and dressed. The dress fitted her perfectly, and she twirled a little in pleasure.

But then she was reminded of Alycia, and how Alycia loved to do that very thing when she got a new dress.

Thinking of Alycia reminded her again that she was alone on the ship. Suddenly loneliness or grief or fear slammed into Tahira again, so hard she staggered back. The cabin was too confined. All she wanted was to get away, to be free, to feel safe.

She left the cabin and ran up to the mainmast. But there were dozens of pirates to push through, each one capable of hurting her, and most of them looking like they wanted to. Dimly she heard a few of them muttering about an unlucky woman bringing the storm. It took all her willpower to not scream as she pushed through the crush of them, her breath coming in gasps.

It was only when she reached the mainmast that she realized she'd left the breeches in her cabin. She didn't want to go get them, not now. She bent over and bundled the dress together before wedging it between her legs. Then she jumped, higher than she ever had before, and she quickly realized why: the iron bands had strengthened her legs this past year, and without their weight she could jump higher, move faster. She suddenly felt so free.

She jumped up and caught the underside of the ratlines. With the dress pinched tightly in her legs she used her arms to climb hand over hand up the underside of the ratlines, her body dangling over the deck. She kept her elbows bent as she climbed, relishing in the pain and tightness in her arms, ignoring the searing pains in her shoulders. Pirates climbing the ratlines stepped on her hands but she kept ahold of the ropes, climbing ever higher.

When she reached the futtock shrouds, she reached up and grabbed hold of them, pulling herself up until she reached the edge of the maintop platform. With one last burst of strength, she pulled herself onto the maintop, where she relaxed her legs and let the dress blow freely.

Tahira closed her eyes and faced into the wind, feeling it blow her hair dry as she sat still. The salty air stung her raw ankles. She shuddered as some pirates moved past her on the maintop, but none of them bothered her. Below her on the deck she could hear pirates singing shanties and bullying the musician into playing for them.

Tears leaked out of her eyes and her chest shuddered with the effort of not crying.

More than ever before, she longed to be free. Truly free, like Rol, Lores, Dot, and Tel had described to her all those years ago, when her dream of freedom had begun. She had thought she was going to freedom when the Master sent her away, but like much of her life, it had been a disappointment, yet another loss.

Tahira realized as she sat there that the ache in her was for more than losing Alycia, and for more than being alone. It was for losing more of what she had hoped to have, of a promise yet again revoked, of freedom still denied.

After a while Tahira scooted back and leaned against the mast, her legs straight in front of her and her feet just dangling over the edge of the top. She folded her hands in her lap and stared at the sea. It was, she noticed, the same color as her new dress.

She heard a grunt beside her and Captain Haefen's dark head appeared through the lubber's hole. One corner of his mouth lifted as he saw her alarmed expression. He brought one arm up and put a wooden bowl next to her.

"I just thought you hadn't eaten today," he said.

Tahira looked at the bowl of meat and biscuit he'd left, realizing she hadn't eaten since breakfast the day before. She opened her mouth to thank him, but he was already floating down to the deck.

***

Tahira couldn't understand it, but she felt less afraid of being alone when she was around Captain Haefen. There was something indefinable about him, something that comforted her, like when he'd held her in her cabin.

She tried not to follow him, but she was irresistibly drawn to him. She sat on the quarterdeck when he was in his cabin. She stayed on the main deck when he was, and climbed to the maintop when he was in the rigging with his crew. When he paced the deck, she walked half the ship behind him.

Finally, he caught up with her as she stood at the quarterdeck railing, facing the sea.

"Tahira, do you wish to speak to me?" he asked.

She started and turned around. Captain Haefen was standing almost uncomfortably close, his thumbs tucked into his belt. Tahira felt herself flush.

"No, Captain," she said. "Why do you ask?"

"Because you've been following me around for two days," he said. He paused, his eyebrows raised. "What is it?"

Though his voice was rough, his face was kind and invited confidence. Tahira opened her mouth to explain, but found that she couldn't.

"Captain, could you tell me about this ship?" she asked instead.

"Hmm," he said. He leaned his back against the railing next to her. "My ship is a brigantine. She has two masts, fore and main. The foremast is square rigged, while the main has a fore-and-aft mainsail and a square-rigged topsail and topgallant. She has square-rigged trysails and flying staysails between the masts, which makes her go faster, and also support the masts. I've gotten her up to twelve knots. She carries twelve guns on the gun deck, two swivel guns at the stern and a Long Tom at the bow. Her crew is ninety-nine pirates and one passenger. She's a combat vessel sure enough, light and fast."

"What is the name of your ship?" Tahira asked. She understood what he'd said, but she wasn't really listening to his words. It was his voice she wanted to hear. Somehow it calmed her.

"I call her the *Royal Conlan*," Captain Haefen said.

Tahira nodded, not knowing what else to say. She stared out at the sea, at the sun reflecting off the waves. She thought she saw sea creatures just below the surface of the water.

She felt Captain Haefen shift next to her and turned her head to see him looking at her, mirroring her position with his elbows resting on the rail. His expression was kind again.

"When I was a boy, first at sea, I had what sailors call a 'sea dad'," he said, looking out at the waves. "My sea dad taught me everything he knew about sailing. And he was there when I witnessed my first death."

"Alycia wasn't my first death," Tahira said softly, wiping her eyes on her sleeve. Captain Haefen turned his head to look at her, something like pity on his face. She shook her head, indicating she wasn't going to elaborate.

"He helped me through it, my sea dad did," he said. "I would have gone to pieces if not for him. He didn't know he was helping me, or maybe he did. He just let me follow him around and he talked to me."

"Are you saying that you're my sea dad?" she asked, embarrassed at how much his story mirrored her own actions.

He shook his head. "No, Tahira, I'm simply saying that I know something of what you're feeling."

She let out her breath slowly. "Was that when you first became a pirate?" she asked.

Captain Haefen looked at her, and for a moment she didn't think he'd answer. But then he shook his head, a little smile on his face. "No, that was when I was in the Navy," he said. "I didn't become a pirate until later."

"How did that happen?"

He pursed his lips.

"Never mind," she said. "It's none of my business."

"I am the only pirate I know who doesn't want to tell that story," he said.

"Was it embarrassing?" she asked.

He paused again. "No. It was painful."

Tahira looked at him, and for the first time, the Captain had disappeared, leaving the man behind. He looked different, younger, kinder. His face had adopted the faraway look she'd seen when she had sung. She wondered what he was remembering.

"That first death was my best mate," he said. "He was killed during a battle. My sea dad taught me that you grieve for a while, and then you move on." He looked at Tahira again. "If Alycia's death is not the first you've witnessed, I take it you know how to move on?"

"Is this your way of asking me to stop following you?" Tahira asked. She asked it meekly, hoping he wouldn't harden against her.

To her relief, he smiled, his eyes lighting up. "This is my way of asking if you're all right."

Tears came to her eyes again and she gave a watery laugh. "I will be," she said, resisting the unexpected urge to rest her head against his shoulder. "It's more than Alycia. I've never been alone before. Other people who've died, there's always been someone else. But now I'm alone. And I think you'll agree that it's dangerous for me here." She looked at him and what had been unknowingly bothering her came spilling out, "Captain, I'm afraid."

Captain Haefen raised his hand, hesitated, then rested it on her shoulder. He opened his mouth to say something, but at that moment they both heard a noise up in the rigging.

"Ransome!" Captain Haefen roared. Tahira started at the violence in his voice. "Down here double quick, or it'll be twelve lashes across the cannon!"

Captain Haefen stepped down onto the main deck and met Ransome as he fell more than climbed down from the maintop above them where he'd been hiding.

"What have I told you about eavesdropping?" Captain Haefen asked, his voice quiet but palpably dangerous. Every pirate around the captain moved quickly away, leaving him and Ransome in a semicircle of cleared deck.

Ransome shrank. "That I shouldn't do it, especially with you."

Scudamore stepped out of the mass of pirates and stood shoulder-to-shoulder with the captain, glaring down at Ransome.

"Report to Mr. Copper," Captain Haefen said. "You'll remain there as punishment until I release you."

Captain Haefen nodded to Scudamore, who pushed and kicked Ransome down the main hatchway, the cabin boy wailing and pleading for an easier sentence as he went. Captain Haefen turned to face Tahira, anger still in his face. But it faded as he saw her expression, and he shifted his weight back.

"I'm sorry I startled you, Tahira," he said. "But if I do not uphold even the smallest of laws on this lawless ship, then we would all die."

Tahira turned away and sat with her back against the railing. Their moment was gone, and whatever he'd been about to say was lost forever.

Chapter Fourteen

"Land ho!"

The lookout above Tahira was pointing off the port bow. Tahira grabbed the shrouds leading up from the maintop where she'd been sitting and climbed higher until she could see the small island ahead of them.

"Is that our final destination?" she shouted up to the lookout. He looked down at her and shrugged.

"No, it's not," Captain Haefen said, stepping onto the maintop. "We're careening here for a few days to refit the hull."

He flashed Tahira a glance that felt like a smile and floated down to the deck again. He sent someone out to the bowsprit to spot the shallows.

Tahira kept climbing up the shrouds until she reached the highest sail, the topgallant. Above that, under the lookout's perch, was a line, called the topgallant brace, which ran between the masts. Tahira had seen Ransome and some of the smaller pirates running on this brace, and she'd always wanted to try it. But it looked more daunting now she was at the top of the swaying mast.

"Here, Miss," the lookout said. He had grabbed a loose line and was holding it out to her. "Swing across to the foremast. It's safer than running along the brace. Don't want to anger the captain by letting you get hurt."

"Thank you," Tahira said. The lookout nodded once and returned to his post.

Tahira swung across to the foremast as the lookout said and settled in the crosstrees above the fore topgallant, her arm looped around the topgallant shrouds.

From her position high on the mast, Tahira watched the lookout on the bowsprit, sounding out the reefs and rocks he saw as they came into the shallows around the island. But she was thinking about what the lookout had said. To her, Captain Haefen had been reserved and even kind at times, and he had never acted like the rest of his crew did. But it seemed his crew saw him almost as a terror, someone to tread carefully around.

She looked down at the deck until she saw the captain. "What kind of man are you?" she whispered.

As though he'd heard her, he looked up. "Clear the rigging, Tahira!" he shouted, pointing toward the bow. "The ship's about to heel over."

Tahira followed his pointing finger and saw they were very close to the island. She suddenly remembered that careening meant to run the ship up onto the beach so that the bottom—the hull—could be scraped and cleaned. Quickly she grabbed a shroud and started to climb down. She had almost reached the deck when the ship shuddered and scraped onto the beach. She let go of the shroud and landed on the deck. But the ship was listing so much to port that she staggered several steps. Before she fell over, Captain Haefen grabbed her arm and steadied her.

"Why don't you go down onto the beach," he said. "We'll be setting up camp soon."

Tahira nodded, made her way to the port rail, and climbed down the ladder. The moment her feet touched the beach she almost fell; the sand was unnervingly solid.

She looked up at the ship, at the pirates swarming the deck, gathering ropes and throwing them over the yards. Some pirates were already swinging down to the beach, including Captain Haefen. Tahira retreated from them, uneasy on her feet, and found a large rock to sit on.

The pirates seemed to be anchoring the ship onto the beach, running lines out and securing them with blocks and tackles to the sand and nearby trees. Captain Haefen walked away from the ship, a roll of papers in his hand, leaving Rance, the bosun, to direct the careening. Rance shouted through the speaking trumpet and directed the pirates into six groups—three on each side—which took hold of lines.

Tahira looked at the sand around her feet, and marveled how different it was from the sand in Typeg. The sand there was one color, coarse, and irritating. But the sand here was multicolored and soft with bits of stuff in it, shells and other things she couldn't name. She swiveled around so her feet were in the waves of the high tide. The wet sand sucked her feet down and it took a few tries to pull them out.

Then Tahira heard a crack and her head snapped up to see what was going on. Rance was still shouting orders and hadn't yet noticed that the crew was not pulling evenly. Tahira's heart paused, the familiar scene flashing before her eyes.

"Stop!" she shouted, jumping up and running over to Rance. "Stop!

You're going to kill someone!" Surprisingly the pirates stopped and looked at her. She pointed toward the men at the bow. "You men, you're pulling too hard. You're going to snap the jib. You men," she pointed at the men at the stern, "you're not pulling hard enough. The ship will shift, and crush the men on the starboard side."

Silence greeted her words. Rance sauntered toward her, tapping the speaking trumpet against his knee.

"Oh, and you think you can do this better than us?" he sneered.

"Easy, lad," Captain Haefen said, suddenly walking up. His face was borderline dangerous. "Speak kindly to the Lady."

"Aye, sir, apologies," Rance said, saluting and stepping back clumsily.

Captain Haefen glared at Rance. "What is it, Tahira?" he asked, the danger gone from his expression as he faced her.

"Captain, I saw this same thing when I was a—" Tahira stopped herself just in time. Captain Haefen raised his eyebrows at her hesitation. "Some men were lifting stone statues off the ground," she said. "Some were pulling too hard, some weren't pulling hard enough and the statues started to twist. The taskmaster didn't see the problem, but I did. I figured out what they should do instead and they got the statues standing."

She glanced around at the pirates staring at her. She felt uncomfortable.

Captain Haefen nodded, his eyebrows still raised slightly. "Well then, Tahira, since you know more about this than I do, please continue."

Tahira looked at Captain Haefen, trying to read his expression. He seemed sincere, even impressed. She took a deep breath and turned to the crew again. She looked the ship up and down, then the crew, trying to gauge where best to move them. Thankfully, it was only the three groups on the port side that needed correcting.

"You two switch places," she said, pointing to two men standing at the stern. They obeyed, the stronger one now further back. Tahira jogged to the bow and pointed to the strongest man there. "You, let go of your rope." Finally, she stepped to the center of the ship and pointed to four of the men. "And you four, step away."

"Are you sure?" one of the pirates, Samson, asked, stepping away.

"Yes, I'm sure," Tahira said.

"You don't even know what we're doing," Rance said.

"I think you're trying to rotate the ship from to port side to starboard. That's why you have men on both sides," Tahira said, refusing to be cowed by his anger. "All I could see is that you were pulling it wrong." She looked over the ship again. "You should be evenly spaced."

She stepped away from Rance and walked back toward her rock, passing Captain Haefen.

"I'm sorry for my bosun's rudeness," he said. "My men don't trust you yet."

Tahira stopped and looked up at him. "Do you?"

Captain Haefen folded his arms. "I am letting you direct the careening of my ship."

"Yes, you are," Tahira said. She watched the crew for a while; with their new instructions they were successfully heeling the ship over on her starboard side and securing her.

"Tahira, I am pleased you are helping me," Captain Haefen said.

"I didn't do it for you," Tahira said.

"I know that," he said. "But you still did it. You could have left Rance to it."

"But the ship would have broken and you might have lost some of your crew," she said, turning to look at him. She waved a hand at the ship. "You're the captain, you should know how to do this. Why didn't *you* say anything?"

"I was looking at my charts," he said, scuffing his foot in the sand and looking down at it. "I was not noticing what my men were doing."

"But when you did, why did you let me do it?" she asked, stepping in front of him so he'd look at her.

He did, his light eyes piercing right through her. Her breath involuntarily caught in her chest.

"Maybe I wanted to give you the chance to do something," he said. "Doing something helped me move past my grief when I was a boy."

Tahira fought back a smile mostly unsuccessfully. It pleased her, somehow, to hear that Captain Haefen had thought of her. She turned around to look at the ship. "I should thank you, then."

Captain Haefen stepped to her side, his thumbs in his belt. "You don't owe me any thanks," he said. He paused for a moment, then touched Tahira's shoulder. "I'm sorry that you were a slave."

Tahira looked up at him sharply. "How did you know that?"

"Your story," he said. "There's only one place for taskmasters. That, and the bands around your ankles, and Alycia's comment on *The Nantes*."

Tahira nodded, silent. She'd hoped to keep that a secret, but she somehow wasn't as upset as she thought she'd be that he knew.

"Why would you feel sorry for me?" she asked.

"Because I have seen enough of slavery," he said. "Among men, mostly, but it saddens me that women are also subject to it."

"I was on my way to it again when you intercepted that ship," she said.

"Aye, I know."

Tahira stepped in front of him again and poked a finger into his chest, suddenly feeling the need to make herself clear. "I won't be made a slave again, Captain."

He put his hand on top of hers, pressing it into his chest. She could feel his heart beating. "I promised you that I would not take you to slavery. I stand by my word."

Tahira nodded. She extricated her hand from under his and faced the ship again. The pirates were now swarming around the hull of the ship, scraping it off and shouting for the carpenter, Ravon, to come inspect little holes. Ravon himself stood at the bow, inspecting the patch he'd made in the orlop following the storm.

"I would like to hear more of your life," Captain Haefen said.

"Why?" Tahira asked, confused; no one had wanted to hear about her life before.

"I'm not sure," he said. Someone called his name, and he turned to see Scudamore waving at him. Captain Haefen waved back. He started to step away, but then stopped and faced Tahira again. "But I'd like to hear about it."

**

While the crew worked all day on the hull, a few pirates spared some time to set up tents on the beach: one for the captain, one for the quartermaster, one for Ravon, one for the galley, and one tent set apart from the rest for Tahira. Copper stayed inside his tent, with Ransome sitting sullenly in the entrance.

Later in the day Ravon approached Captain Haefen.

"We'll be ready in two days, Captain," he said. "The crew's nearly done with the starboard side. We'll heel her over in the morning and clean the larboard."

Captain Haefen nodded. "Very good, Mr. Ravon, see to it. Mr. Copper!" he shouted over his shoulder. Copper staggered out of his tent, red-faced. "Tomorrow at first light take a party into the jungle. Forage for what you can find, especially fresh water."

Copper saluted clumsily and disappeared back into his tent, kicking Ransome on his way by. Ravon saluted and went back to his duties, leaving the captain standing alone.

Tahira looked down at her ankles, still raw from the iron bands. She'd started healing them with the supplies from the galley, but she didn't really have what she needed. She approached Captain Haefen from behind.

"Could I go with Copper tomorrow?" she asked.

Captain Haefen turned. "Of course, Tahira, if you wish."

"You're not worried I'll run away?"

He smirked slightly. "This is an island. There's nowhere to run."

"I could hide," she said. She was considering it. She may not know how to survive on an island, but at least she would be free from the pirates.

Captain Haefen opened his mouth, a threat in his face. He paused, then closed his mouth, shook his head, and shifted his weight back.

"What purpose do you have in going with Copper?" he asked instead. "He's not a very amiable fellow."

"I know," she said. "I just want to see what the island has."

"And I'm sure you'll want to venture out alone," he said. He rubbed his hands together and squinted at the sky. "Just be careful."

***

The next morning Copper gathered a foraging party. As far as Tahira could tell, it was comprised of those pirates who'd either grown up on islands or had been marooned before. She walked closer to Copper than to the others, even though Copper was irritable.

"I don't know why you wanted to come," he growled at her.

"Remember that case of herbs you helped me start?" Tahira asked. "I want to add to it."

Copper grunted.

"I don't know what these plants are or what they do," Tahira said. "Perhaps you could help me?"

Copper grunted again and glared sideways at her, but he didn't decline.

As they walked through the dense, lush jungle he pointed out plants.

"There's noni for gettin' rid of lice," he said. "That cerasee there cures most everythin'. Shatterstone is good for after a drinking spell. Helps the liver, see? See those long thin leaves? That's gavilana. It's good for the gut and for infections, so I've been told. This is dormilona. It's shy, but it helps sleep and calms muscles. This here has two names, the easier one's leaf of life. It helps with breathing. If you've got worms take that soursop over there. And this one's my favorite. Cacoa. Chew enough and it's like a whole bottle of rum. But one leaf is good for pain or for missin' a meal."

"How do you know all this?" Tahira asked, taking a handful of each plant and putting them in the satchel she'd brought with her. She hadn't had these plants in Typeg, but these were perhaps better suited to a life at sea.

Copper shrugged. He had something of an interested expression, but his face fell back into its usual surliness as they kept walking.

Tahira stepped over a fallen tree. "You know, Copper, I think you're a happier man than you let on. Smarter too."

Copper grunted again. His face had been growing redder as they walked, and now it was as red as his handkerchief. He didn't look well. Tahira quietly thanked him and stepped away on her own.

The jungle teemed with life, loud and mobile. She pushed through a thick tangle of bushes and emerged in a large clearing full of flowers. She gasped at the sight, and a smile came to her face. She'd never seen so many colors, smelled so many scents, never knew there were so many flowers.

She walked around the clearing slowly, feeling every flower, breathing in their scents. It was the first time in a very long time that she felt happy. As she stroked velvety petals she felt as though the last bit of her grief at Alycia's death had drained away, though some of her fear remained.

Almost without planning to, she started to sing: slave songs, sea shanties, folksongs, other ditties her friends had hummed while working. It felt like it had been so long since she last sung. It felt good to stretch her vocal cords, to sing as loud or as soft as she liked, something she'd never been allowed to do before.

Finally, her voice grew hoarse. She sat down and closed her eyes, the sunlight brushing her face. For a long time she sat in silence. She still wanted to be free and away from the pirates, but not with the intensity of a few days before. Patience had replaced desperation.

"Tahira? Where are you?"

Captain Haefen's voice broke through her meditation. She started and her eyes flew open. The sun was starting to get low. She hadn't realized how late it was.

"I'm here, Captain," she called, standing up. Moments later Captain Haefen pushed out of the undergrowth and stood on the edge of the clearing. He looked relieved. Behind him, Tahira could see Scudamore and Rance, cutlasses drawn, fighting through the vegetation.

"When Copper came back without you, I wondered if you had hidden," Captain Haefen said. "I just had to see if you were all right."

"I'm sorry to have worried you," Tahira said. She picked her way carefully through the flowers toward him. "I wasn't hiding."

"You don't have to come back to camp now," Captain Haefen said, holding up a hand.

Tahira shook her head. "No, it's time."

She tripped over a hidden root and pitched forward. Captain Haefen caught her arms and stood her up.

"Thank you," she said, her face flushing.

"There's been a change of plans," Captain Haefen said. With Scudamore and Rance behind them they started back toward the beach. "We cleaned the hull and got repairs done quicker than expected. The crew wants to leave in the morning."

"To our destination?" Tahira asked.

"No. This island didn't have enough food, and no fresh water that we could find."

"None?" Tahira asked, looking at the lushness around her. "How is that possible?"

Captain Haefen shrugged, looking annoyed. "I'm sorry, but we have to go into a pirate port."

Tahira gasped involuntarily. "You said we wouldn't be going there."

Captain Haefen took her hand and helped her step over a fallen log. "I know," he said. "But we don't have enough provisions to get us where we're going. We have to go into port."

Tahira clutched the strap of her satchel with both hands. "I don't want to go to a pirate port."

"Neither do I," he said softly. "But my crew is getting restless. They've been dueling all evening. A brief stay in a pirate port will calm them down again. Besides, they don't like being sober."

Tahira looked sideways at Captain Haefen. His expression looked as wary as she felt. He glanced down at her and pulled one corner of his mouth down. In that moment Tahira felt like she had something of a friend in him.

But then they broke through the jungle and were accosted by shouts and clangs of metal; the pirates on the beach were engaged in a full-out brawl.

Without hesitation, Captain Haefen pulled out his pistol and shot up it into the air. Tahira screamed at the bang and stepped away from him.

"Avast there!" he shouted, running toward his crew.

Scudamore took Tahira's elbow and hurried her to her tent. "I'll send Ransome with your dinner," he said. "It'll be safer if you stay here." He pushed her roughly into her tent and ran off toward the brawl.

Tahira curled up on her cot, listening as the shouts and shots and clashes gradually receded into angry murmuring. It hadn't taken Captain Haefen long to restore order. That was something about him she knew with certainty.

But she still didn't know if he was a kind man masquerading as a pirate, or if he was a hardened pirate pretending to be kind.

Most of all, she couldn't explain why she cared to riddle him out.

***

It was a disciplined, sore, and bruised crew that set sail the next morning. It would be several days before they reached port. Due to the lack of food on the island, rations were down to one bowl of meat per day, instead of the usual two, and the second meal would be two hardtack biscuits and a tin of water. The more days passed the louder the pirates grumbled at staying sober. Tahira was wakened several times during the night to the sound of one or more of the pirates screaming in his sleep about the horrors.

Tahira thought it would be safest if she stayed in her cabin until they reached port. The first thing she did was work on her ankles, and to her delight the plants Copper had showed her healed them. Afterward she asked for paper and a charcoal pencil from the captain and spent her time labeling the herbs and plants with crude drawings depicting what they healed. She dried them like Old Joche taught her and added them to her metal box. Once her herbs were accounted for, she paid a visit to Ravon in the carpenter's store room when most of the crew was piped to dinner.

"What do you want?" he asked.

"You've been the ship's doctor, haven't you?" she asked. Ravon nodded stiffly. "I was wondering if I could have some of your supplies."

"What for?" Ravon asked.

"I was a healer once. I'd like to put together some supplies, just in case," Tahira said.

"Are you saying you're a better doctor than me?" Ravon demanded, testy. He picked up his awl and dug it into his worktable. Tahira took a half step back.

"I'm merely asking a favor," Tahira said, raising her chin and surprising herself with the confidence she heard. "I said it was just in case."

Ravon considered her, his jaw working. Finally, he nodded. He reached under his worktable and pulled out an open box full of bandages, a bottle of spirits, and tools more delicate than his carpentry trade. Tahira picked through it quickly, taking the cleanest-looking bandages, and left the store room.

Her days were unmarked and lonely. She only knew the time of day when she went topside, and she was often surprised how much time had passed. But though she knew it was wiser to stay in her cabin, she longed to talk to someone.

Finally, the *Royal Conlan* reached the pirate port on Turtle Island. She listened as the pirates loudly left the ship. Her ears almost hurt in the silence left behind. She didn't even hear a watch pacing the deck.

"Is anyone here?" she whispered aloud.

Tahira made her way up to the main deck. There was plenty of noise up here, but it was all in the town. From the deck she could see rows of wooden stalls, each covered with brightly-colored fabric. She guessed they were for selling goods, but they were now closed and empty. Several buildings near the docks were alive with lights and music and the sounds of breaking glass. Smells she'd never encountered before wafted up to her from the town and she breathed them in. The smell of the wharf was there too, rotting seaweed and stale salt. Around the *Royal Conlan* were several other pirate ships, all empty; it seemed that all the pirates were in the buildings.

Tahira turned and faced the empty ship. No one was watching her. No one would stop her from leaving. But something was stopping her.

She looked toward the quarterdeck and saw that the hatchway down to the captain's cabin was open. She could see a light, so she assumed Captain Haefen was still aboard. Tahira made her way down the hatchway ladder and knocked on the partially-open door.

"Come in, Tahira," he said.

She pushed the door open, but didn't enter. "How did you know it was me?"

Captain Haefen was sitting at his desk, reading over something. "Because you're the only one who knocks like that." He sounded tired. "What can I do for you?"

"Captain, what is keeping me on this ship?" Tahira asked, leaning against the door.

Captain Haefen looked up. "What do you mean?"

"Your crew is gone," she said. "You are the only person here. There is no one on the docks. What is keeping me from leaving?"

He leaned his elbows on his desk, his hands clasped. "Nothing."

She hadn't expected that answer. "I'm serious, Captain. What if I leave? Would you stop me?"

"I don't think I would, Tahira," he said.

"Would you recapture me if I ran?" she asked.

"Do you want to?" he asked, leaning back.

"Would you blame me if I did?" she asked, taking a step inside.

He leaned forward again, his eyebrows knitted in something like concern. "Tahira, why are you here? You could have left this ship. You could have walked away. I am not keeping you here, you could go any time. Yet here you are, asking if you can go. Are you really still a slave?"

She took a step back. He was right; she felt like a slave in that moment, asking for permission. "I wanted to make sure that I *could* go, that I would be safe once I left," she said.

"Of course you won't be safe," he said with a slight scoff in his voice. "This is a pirate port. You're only safe on this ship because you have me to protect you."

"Why should I believe you?" she asked, though a part of her always had.

"You shouldn't, because you have no reason to," he said with a wry smile. "And yet I'm asking you to. I am also asking you—not telling you—to stay on this ship."

"Would you recapture me if I ran?" she asked again.

"I never captured you," he said softly.

Tahira realized that he was right. She felt a little guilty for pushing him so hard. "It's just that I don't want to have a taste of freedom and then be dragged back here," she said. The words came almost against her will, giving voice to thoughts that had been in her mind for days. "If I am free to go then I want to go. I don't want to stay here anymore."

"Even if I tell you that I am the only one who can give you what you want?" he asked, intent.

"And what do I want?" she asked. She wondered if Captain Haefen noticed her enough to understand her.

"You want your freedom," he said. "My guess is that you have been a slave your whole life. It chafes you that you are trapped on this ship. You still see it as a prison, which you have a right to. Yet you stay. Why? Maybe it's because you want to be the one who tells yourself where to go and what to do, just like in that song you sang. You don't like being told what to do, and you don't like the idea of being owned."

"How do you know that?" she asked, surprised.

His expression softened until he looked wistful. He opened his mouth like he wanted to say something but didn't dare. "I know slaves, Tahira," he said at last, his voice soft. "And you have been one. You are not a slave here, you are a guest. And I ask you to stay."

"Give me a reason to, Captain," she said.

"I'm afraid I can't," he said, standing up. "Not without saying too much. I can only ask. It's up to you." He paused. "Tahira, you told me some time ago that you were afraid. What are you afraid of?"

She looked up at him and studied his face. "I'm afraid of being alone on this ship. I'm afraid of what will happen to me. Though most of that fear has gone away now."

He smiled a little. "Please try to believe me—if not to trust me—that when we get to our destination you will be free," he said. "You will have no Masters, and no captains over you."

Tahira stared at him. Though she had tried and tried, she still failed to understand Captain Haefen. From the very beginning he wasn't at all what she thought a pirate captain would be. And he seemed to have changed since she first met him, though she couldn't define how. And though she had tried to keep her secrets to herself, he had learned them.

He reached into his desk drawer and pulled something out, then paced out from behind his desk. "Tahira, before you leave I have something for you."

"What is it?" she asked.

He held out his hand, palm up. "Here," he said. She peered into his palm and saw a silver key. "This is to your cabin."

She glanced up into his face. "Are you not going to lock me in at night anymore?" Gingerly she reached out and took the key from his palm, half expecting him to close his fist again.

"No," he said. "I may not be able to give you the freedom that you want right now. But I can give you this freedom. You are now in charge of your cabin door."

She looked at the key in her palm for what felt like a long time. "Why would you give me this freedom?" she asked. "Why now?"

He paused long enough that she looked up at him. His mouth was open a little, like he was thinking about what to say. He closed it when he saw she looking. "I don't think you're ready to hear the answer yet," he said.

"I don't think you're willing to tell me," she said, narrowing her eyes.

"Perhaps," he said with a smile.

She smiled back despite herself. "I don't think I will ever understand you, Captain," she said.

"It astonishes me that you are trying," he said, his smile turning sad.

"I have little else to do," she said. "If I can unravel your mystery then I won't feel like I might go mad from isolation. I won't feel so afraid."

"Would you like me to tell my crew that they can talk to you?" he asked.

She thought for a moment. "No," she said, looking down. "They are so hardened and harsh."

He tipped his head. "And what about me, their captain? Am I hardened and harsh too?"

"I don't know," she said. "That's why I can't figure you out."

She clenched her fist around the key and turned to leave the cabin. But she stopped and faced him again.

"Captain, this is very long overdue," she said. "Thank you. For everything."

He bowed his head. "You are welcome. Go where you will."

Chapter Fifteen

Tahira still hadn't decided by the next morning whether she was going to stay or leave. But she knew she had time to decide, for she had overheard Captain Haefen telling Scudamore that they would stay at Turtle Island for two or three days. The possibility of being truly free for the first time in her life both terrified and excited her. But she remembered Captain Haefen's words from the night before, and knew he meant to keep his promise.

She stood on the main deck in the early afternoon, looking over the rail at the town. Now that it was day, it was alive with a market, and she even saw children running amongst the adults.

"A far cry from last night," she said softly.

"Have you made your decision?" Captain Haefen asked, stepping up to her.

"No," Tahira said. "But I would like to go out and look around. May I?"

"Of course," Captain Haefen said. "But I have a warning." Tahira raised her eyebrows. "A woman alone is not very safe on Turtle Island, even during the day. There are too many men who would take advantage of you, though I have no doubt you could hold your own. I've seen how strong you are."

"Would you go with me?" Tahira asked. The question surprised him, but it surprised her more, and they stared at each other for a moment. He recovered first.

"I would be honored," he said.

"Thank you," Tahira said. She stepped toward the gangway.

"I have one more warning," Captain Haefen said, following. "Pirate ports are full of rules and secret codes. How you touch someone, for instance, means a lot. And there's a certain way that we need to touch, if you don't mind, in order for you to be safe and not mistaken for a brothel woman."

Tahira nodded, interested in avoiding that fate. "How do I touch you, then?"

"We will have to hold hands," Captain Haefen said.

Tahira raised her eyebrows. "Really? That simple?"

"Yes," he said. He clenched his hand in a fist, looking nervous. "But holding my hand means that we are more or less betrothed."

"But we're not," she said, shifting away slightly.

"No," he said, still nervous. "But it will ensure your safety. No one will bother you, not even the drunkest pirate. Do you still want me to go with you?"

"If you would." She didn't know exactly why, but she did want him with her.

Captain Haefen nodded. He shed the long leather coat he sometimes wore on board and tossed it to Scudamore. "Make sure at least one of you stays," he said.

He held out his hand to Tahira, like he'd done on *The Nantes*. But this time she took it without hesitation. His rough, calloused hand dwarfed hers.

"Shouldn't you have more than one guard on the ship?" she asked as they walked down the gangway.

Captain Haefen gave a little chuckle. "Usually yes. But like I said, pirate ports have certain rules. More than one guard is not needed here because we all have each other's word that we won't try to steal each other's ships."

"So why the one guard, then?" Tahira asked. "If you all agree to not steal ships?"

"Just in case a drunk idiot decides to torch a ship," Captain Haefen said. He looked down at her and smiled. "But these rules only apply here on Turtle Island. Other ports have other rules."

As they walked closer to the town Tahira began to see some pirates walking with women on their arms, some with one woman, some with two, and one with three.

"What does that mean?" Tahira asked, pointing to their looped arms.

"That means she's chosen him for this evening," he said.

"Captain, why did you warn me?" she asked. "Why didn't you just let me make a fool of myself?"

Captain Haefen pursed his lips. Tahira looked up at him, but he didn't answer. By then they had reached the first of the wooden stalls that Tahira had seen from the ship the night before.

In the daytime the stalls were open for business, selling clothing, food, and trinkets from all around the world. While still holding Captain Haefen's hand she looked at each stall, running her fingers through the hanging strings of beads, feeling fabrics she never knew existed, smelling exotic spices on foreign foods, counting how many different kinds of shoes there were. This was a class of people that had not existed in her corner of Typeg.

She and Captain Haefen were engulfed in a crush of people as they kept walking. Everyone was jostling everyone else, but there wasn't anyone telling them they were wrong, no one ordering them around. People pushed and hugged, smiled and pulled. The women selling wares looked happy, and many of them had broods of laughing children clinging to their skirts. The men selling wares were excitedly shouting out the contents of their stalls. Almost everywhere she could hear singing.

So this is what free people are like, she thought to herself.

"Do these people live here on the island?" she asked.

"Aye, someone has to run the taverns and the shops to keep this island going," Captain Haefen said. He shouted to an old man sitting back in the shade of his stall. The old man smiled toothlessly and Captain Haefen and Tahira passed by. "A few of the old men were once pirates, retired here now."

"Was that man one of them?"

"Aye," Captain Haefen said. He smiled again, the smile that lit up his whole face. Tahira noticed, too, that the set of his shoulders was relaxed. "He was my captain once."

Tahira looked over her shoulder at the old man now quickly disappearing behind the crowd. "Don't you want to talk with him?" she asked.

Captain Haefen shook his head, the smile still there. "He and I have a deep understanding. We don't need to talk anymore."

Tahira squeezed his hand. She watched him out of the corner of her eye as they penetrated further into the town. She had never seen him like this. No longer was he the strict, brooding captain. Nor, even, was he the tender man who'd held her while she tried not to cry. Here in this town he was a man willing to smile and relax and even laugh. She liked this side of him.

Behind the stalls were the taverns, already overflowing with pirates, and even from the street Tahira could smell the drink and hear the bawdy music. But the town wasn't just full of taverns. As they moved away from the market Tahira saw the shops Captain Haefen had mentioned. Like the stalls they sold goods, but these shops were in buildings, and sold things much more professionally-made than what she had seen in the stalls: clothing, food, paper, books, jewelry, flowers, house-building materials, and farming equipment.

It was far less crowded here than down by the stalls. Because of that Tahira could see more of the island itself. From the port the island sloped upward into several wooded hills that comprised the center of the island. Houses dotted the forested area, and near the top of one hill was a fort-like building, partially hidden by trees. Somehow, it all seemed vaguely familiar.

"What is that?" she asked, pointing up to the fort-like building.

Captain Haefen stooped a little to follow her finger. "That's the Governor's mansion," he said. "He was supposedly in charge of this island. But when he didn't do his job, he was removed. There hasn't been a Governor here since then. That's why Turtle Island is now a pirate port."

"But families still live here?" Tahira asked. Captain Haefen nodded. "I don't mean to be rude, but why would they stay here if there are pirates everywhere?"

"You do make a good point, but it's not easy to move to a different place," he said with an amused expression. "In order to leave Turtle Island, you'd have to find a ship to take you. And only pirate ships come here. Can you imagine what would happen if a family with children were on a pirate ship?"

Tahira tried not to. "They'd be safe if they were on your ship."

Captain Haefen stopped walking. The crowd around them was now sparse, and they could talk at a normal volume again. His thumb worried hers for a few seconds, then he turned to look at her.

"That may be your experience," he said. "But that wasn't always the case on my ship."

She knitted her eyebrows. "Why tell me that?"

"There's something you need to know about me," he said. "I have a reputation among all pirates. I'm not the worst, but I am considered one of the more ruthless captains on the seas. Perhaps you have seen something of that."

She nodded. "You killed Wilkid."

"Aye, I did," he said. His face held something of remorse. "And while I did not mean to kill him, you were right. I meant for his punishment to be painful and cruel. But I did something else that day, something I don't think you've noticed."

"What?" she asked. She felt suddenly cold, though their clasped hands were hot.

"Have you seen Richardson lately?" he asked. She thought for a moment, then shook her head. "That's because after I keelhauled Wilkid, I lashed Richardson to the grating and gave him forty lashes with the cat. He's been with Ravon ever since, healing."

Her mouth fell open.

"I will not have disobedience on my ship," he said. "I told you that here on Turtle Island we all have a rule of not stealing ships. And while that works only on this island, it always works for me, no matter where I am. No one would dare steal my ship."

"Why not?" Tahira's voice came out a near whisper. For nearly the first time since she'd met Captain Haefen, she felt afraid of him. She started to pull away, but he grasped her hand tighter.

"Because everyone knows the consequences of stealing my ship," he said. "And that's probably all you want to know."

She opened her mouth for a moment before anything came out. She looked down at their hands. "If you have such a fierce reputation, why the charade of holding hands?" she asked. "What are you going to do to me?"

His expression cleared. "Nothing," he said, shaking his head once. "I won't hurt you. We are doing this charade because that's unfortunately the only thing my reputation can't stop."

"But why tell me how ruthless you are?" she asked. She still felt a little afraid of him.

He smiled sadly. His shoulders relaxed. "For some reason you're still trying to riddle me out," he said. "I'm trying to help you."

"Do you *want* me to figure you out?" she asked.

He shrugged carelessly. "As you said last night, I'm the only one you talk to. We may as well get to know each other. And as for my reputation, not all the stories told about me are true." He looked away from her, back toward the market in the town, out to sea, up at the sky.

Tahira stared at him. It was easy to see him as the ruthless pirate captain he was claiming to be, the one she had seen. But other than his treatment of Wilkid and Richardson, and his threat to Ransome, he hadn't been a ruthless man. His treatment of her had been nothing short of kind. And he was telling her who he was, almost forcing it on her. Couldn't that be an indication of something? Once again, she was left to wonder what kind of man he was.

He squeezed her fingers. "We should be heading back to the ship." He looked down at her and noticed her hesitation. He started pulling his hand away. "Unless you don't want to return?"

"No, it's not that," she said. Now it was her turn to grasp his hand tighter. "Believe it or not, Captain, you are the first man I've really talked to. Certainly, the first person who hasn't treated me like a slave. I'm still not used to that. And you are the most puzzling human being I have ever met."

Captain Haefen looked a little embarrassed. Tahira liked it on him. She nodded and started back toward the town. He followed.

The street was even more crowded than before. Tahira was jostled and pushed by passersby until someone walked between her and Captain Haefen, causing them to let go of each other. Tahira stopped walking and turned toward him, but she had already lost sight of him in the crowd. She stayed where she was, turning on the spot, trying to find him.

A clammy hand closed on her elbow. She whipped her head around to see a heavily intoxicated pirate leering at her.

"Well, 'ello dearie," he said. "Fancy some comp'ny?"

"No. Let go of me," Tahira said.

She yanked her arm easily out of his grip. He lunged for her again, but she drew back her fist and hit him in the face. She had never done that before, and was surprised and slightly horrified at how naturally she had done it. The pirate stood a moment, dazed, but then his expression turned murderous. Tahira took a few steps away from him while he considered what to do. He lunged at her again, this time his hand going for a weapon.

Tahira opened her mouth to scream, but at that moment she felt Captain Haefen take her hand. He pulled her a little behind him so he blocked her from the other pirate and raised their clasped hands to his chest.

The other pirate sheathed his weapon immediately and bowed his head.

"Captain Haefen, sir, I'm sorry, I didn't realize," he stammered.

"Shove off, mate," Captain Haefen said, his voice dangerous.

The pirate scurried off faster than Tahira would have thought possible in the crowd.

"I see what you mean," she said, looking up at Captain Haefen. He raised his eyebrows. "The rule and your reputation."

"Ah," Captain Haefen said. "Let's get back to the ship. Do you still want to go?"

Tahira hid a smile; his constant checking with her charmed her.

She still looked around her in wonder at everything to see as they made their way to the docks. If she chose to stay, she felt sure she would have a good life on this island. She had learned two trades, and with them she could stay away from the pirates and the taverns.

When they got to the docks Tahira returned her mind to the present, weaving with the captain through the pirates, crates, bales of rope, and animals that littered the docks. As they approached the *Royal Conlan* she looked up. Rance was standing at the rail, watching them. Tahira didn't like the look in his eye. She let go of Captain Haefen's hand.

"Here," he said when they gained the deck. He put his hand in his pocket and pulled out a handful of flat, round golden discs.

"What are these?" she asked, taking his one handful in both of her hands.

"This is money," Captain Haefen said. "Tomorrow we'll be restocking the ship. If you want, you can go back into town and buy something."

"Buy?" Tahira asked.

"Trade," Captain Haefen explained in a way that didn't make her feel foolish. "You tell the vendor what you want and he will tell you how many coins it is worth."

"Oh."

"And if you want to slip away, you can."

Tahira closed her fingers over the coins and shifted her weight to one hip. "Captain, do you *want* me to leave?"

"No, of course I don't," he said. "I want you to stay. But I also want you to have the choice. You didn't have a choice before. I have seen what happens when someone has no choice for too long."

Tahira nodded, knowing well that feeling. She bounced her hands, feeling the weight of the coins. "Will you go with me again tomorrow?"

"I don't think that will be necessary," he said.

"But what about the rules?"

Captain Haefen gave her a crooked grin that for some reason made her heart skip a beat. "I think if you stay closer to the docks you will be fine. Perhaps enough people saw us together. And no doubt that drunk will pass the word along as fast as he can that you are not to be trifled with. And if not, well, you have a good punch."

"I didn't take pleasure in it," Tahira said softly.

Captain Haefen didn't answer. He nodded to her and joined Rance on the quarterdeck.

***

The next morning Tahira watched as the wooden stalls in the town set up for the day. The money Captain Haefen had given her hung in a bag on her belt.

"Have a wonderful time," he said, coming up behind her. "We'll set sail by sundown."

"If I want to come back," Tahira said.

He paused. "Aye."

"Captain, what would happen with your crew if I didn't come back?" she asked, turning to look up at him. "They agreed to take me. I assume it was for some kind of incentive."

"Don't worry about them," he said.

Rance called Captain Haefen and he stepped away, leaving Tahira standing alone. Without a backward glance she walked down the gangway and into the town.

Once again, Tahira was jostled by huge crowds as she walked up the street by the stalls, looking at the things for sale. She listened to the vendors shouting their wares and prices, most of which were the same from the day before. She drifted through the crowds toward a stall filled with women's clothing. She stopped and stared at the beautiful clothes.

"You've just come from a pirate ship, haven't you?" The woman behind the stall stood up, startling Tahira. She was very tall with long, graying black hair. She was wearing a dress very similar to the ones she was selling: colorful, loose-fitting, and with many layers of fabric. She was smiling, which made Tahira comfortable enough to take a step closer.

"How did you know?" she asked.

The woman reached out and touched Tahira's sleeve. "You smell like rum," she said.

"Oh," Tahira said, blushing.

The woman's smile widened. "My name is Jaazah."

"Tahira."

Jaazah's face blanked for a moment, as though remembering something. "Tahira," she said slowly. "Your name sounds familiar." She knitted her eyebrows, then shook her head, a polite smile on her face once more. She stepped away from her stall and reached out to put her arm around Tahira's shoulders. "You look like you would like a wash," she said. "Come up to my house, I'll set you with a bath and a new dress."

Tahira looked down at her dress and suddenly realized how filthy she was: her dress was torn in several places, full of splinters and dirt, and stained with tar. She knew the rest of her looked no better.

She looked into Jaazah's face, at her graying hair, which reminded her of Shipra and Pula. There was kindness in every wrinkle, just like her mother's face had been. Something about Jaazah's eyes reminded Tahira of Old Joche. Jaazah's face reminded her of someone else, but she couldn't quite place the resemblance.

"All right," Tahira said. "Thank you."

Jaazah led the way across the road and between two noisy taverns, behind which was another, quieter, street with smaller stores. Jaazah led the way between them, and they left the buildings of the town behind them. They walked on a gently-winding dirt road leading up the hill toward the houses. Almost at once the smell of the sea was left behind them, and the birds changed from screaming gulls to singing warblers. Tahira had never heard birds like this before. She stopped and gazed around her, taking in all the green and noises of life. She turned toward the sea, just a shining mass of blue under the burning sky, the ships at the dock bobbing like large flies on the water.

Jaazah stood silently by until Tahira was ready to keep going. "Who is your captain?" she asked after a while.

Tahira glanced at her. "Captain Haefen."

Jaazah raised her chin and sighed, "Ah."

"You smile," Tahira said, confused.

"Well, don't you?" Jaazah asked, her face lined with matronly intrigue. "He's such a handsome young man."

"He is," Tahira said, nodding a little. "But I don't know what to make of him. One moment he's kind, and the next he's yelling at his crew. He has promised me that I will be safe on his ship, and I have been. But I had a friend with me when I boarded, and she was killed by the crew. He couldn't protect her. He killed a man, nearly killed two, for what they did to her."

Tahira lapsed into silence, wondering if she'd said too much. But Jaazah was the first woman she'd been with since Alycia died, and she hadn't realized just how starved she was for feminine company.

Jaazah didn't answer, but continued leading the way up the dirt road. The houses were coming into view, picturesquely hidden among the dense jungle trees, their roofs and doors cheerfully colored.

"This one is mine," Jaazah said, pointing to the first house they encountered. It was little and brown with a bed of purple flowers by the door.

"These are beautiful," Tahira said, pointing.

"They're gilboa irises," Jaazah said. "Come in, I'll have a bath drawn up in no time."

Jaazah was true to her word, and soon Tahira was stepping behind a screen and into a basin full of warm water.

"Hand me your dress and I'll wash it," Jaazah said. "Oh, and here." Her arm appeared around the screen, holding a jar. "This is sand. Rub it on your skin to get all the dirt out."

"Thank you," Tahira said, taking the jar and handing over the tattered dress. "You really didn't have to do this for me."

"I'm glad you came," Jaazah said. "Most girls around here have no business with kindness. Their lives are full of violence and lust and greed. It's refreshing to meet someone like you."

"What will happen to your stall while you're away?" Tahira asked, scrubbing sand into her arms. It stung her skin as she worked it in, but the tar and dirt were coming out immediately.

"It'll be there when we get back," Jaazah said.

"The dresses were lovely," Tahira said. "Do you make them all?"

"Some," Jaazah said. "Others I've bought or traded."

They fell silent, each absorbed with her own cleaning. Jaazah finished first. Tahira heard her wring out the dress one last time and hang it up to dry. Tahira climbed out of the basin and wrapped a towel around herself. She wrung her hair out over the basin and let it hang loose where it covered most of her back and her right shoulder.

"It feels good to be clean," Tahira said, stepping around the screen.

Jaazah stood up from her chair and smiled. She went to a brown chest on the floor and opened it. "Come choose something to wear," she said.

Tahira knelt by the chest and sifted through the dresses, careful to keep her towel around her. "I don't know where to begin to choose one," she said. "I'm no Lady. I only picked that dress because I liked its colors."

"Well, it all depends on what you're going to be doing," Jaazah said. "What do you do on the ship?"

"I love to climb in the rigging," Tahira said. "Captain Haefen gave me the cabin boy's breeches to wear under my dress."

Jaazah raised her eyebrows in surprise. "Well then. I have the perfect dress for you."

She dug through the chest until she extracted a dress from the bottom. She stood up and unfolded it to show Tahira. Most of it was dusty blue, but the bodice was lined with white fabric, and the long, light sleeves were white as well. The skirt was long in the back and just longer than knee-length in the front. Underneath the dress were black leather breeches.

"I've never seen anything like that before," Tahira said, fingering it with one hand.

"I traded for this dress years ago," Jaazah said, looking down at it.

"I love it," Tahira said.

"Then it's yours," Jaazah said. She put the dress in Tahira's hand and pushed her behind the screen again.

"It fits perfectly," Tahira said once she had navigated it on over her underthings. She was surprised at how comfortable it felt, how soft the breeches were. She ran her hands over the dress and for almost the first time in her life she felt pretty. When she stepped around the screen Jaazah gasped.

"You look so beautiful," she said. She waved her hands, beckoning Tahira to her chair. "Come, let me comb your hair."

Jaazah sat down in her chair and Tahira knelt on the floor in front of her. Carefully, Jaazah started combing through Tahira's golden-brown tangles.

"You remind me of my daughter," she said after a while.

"You have a daughter?"

"I did." Jaazah's voice turned sad. "She died a year ago."

"I'm so sorry," Tahira said. "Would you tell me about her?"

"She always wanted adventure," Jaazah said. "You'd think she'd get plenty of adventure living on a pirate island, but she wanted more. So she paid for passage on a pirate ship and left here. But the pirates sold her into slavery."

Tahira's breath caught in her chest. This story sounded familiar.

"She endured terrible things at the hands of her Master," Jaazah said. "I won't go into details, but she suffered much. That man even carved his initial into her shoulder to show she was his property. Imagine that! Eventually she was sold to another Master. A kinder Master, even though he put a huge hoop through her ear. And when he heard she wanted to go home, he arranged passage on a ship to bring her back here. She was changed, yet she was still my little girl." She paused to sigh in reminiscence. "But she got sick on her journey home and never recovered. She died last year."

"I'm so sorry," Tahira said again. "I imagine she's why you want to help the pirate girls who come here?"

"She is," Jaazah said.

Tahira thought over the story, rolling it around in her mind. When she was sure of herself, she said, "Jaazah, was your daughter's name Rol?"

Jaazah's combing hands stopped. "Yes," she said slowly. "How did you know that?"

Tahira turned around on her knees and grabbed Jaazah's hands. Her resemblance to Rol was unmistakable now; how hadn't she seen it immediately? "Jaazah, I knew her! I knew Rol."

"What?"

"I was a slave, too. Look, I have the same scar Rol did," Tahira said, pulling down the neck of her dress to show Jaazah the mark from Master Gall. "Rol was my friend, and I loved her. I cried when she was sold and sent away. I always wondered what happened to her. I'm so glad she returned home to you. She wanted nothing more than to come home."

"You knew my daughter?" Jaazah whispered. She stroked Tahira's face, tears in her eyes. "No wonder I felt something when you walked by my stall. I just knew I had to talk to you. You were kind to my daughter. Oh! Tahira. She told me about you. That's why your name sounded familiar. You were the girl who was always happy, and always wanted to hear the stories, and had a beautiful singing voice."

Tahira smiled, pleased with Rol's description. "She told me about you too, Jaazah," she said. "She told me about this island, this house. She told me about your stall. She told me she wished she had stayed here with you instead of leaving the island."

She paused, and Jaazah stared at her. Tahira could tell she wanted to say more, to ask more questions, but she didn't. Both women felt pain at this connection, at this knowledge, but also relief as Jaazah's pain finally began to heal. They both smiled, each knowing what the other was feeling.

But after a few moments something closed behind Jaazah's eyes, like the door that Tahira remembered closing between her and Old Joche, when Old Joche didn't want to talk any more. Jaazah pulled away, sniffing, and wiped her eyes on her sleeve.

"I don't owe Captain Haefen anything," she said. "But I do feel grateful to him for bringing you here."

Tahira wiped her own eyes. The moment had passed. They were acquaintances again.

"Do you know him?" she asked.

"Not personally, no," Jaazah said. "I've only seen him a few times. He doesn't come into town hardly at all. But I know of him."

Tahira turned around again and settled between Jaazah's feet. Jaazah resumed combing her hair.

"Can you tell me what you know of him?" Tahira asked.

"Well, I can only tell you what I've heard," Jaazah said. "The other pirates say he is a very fair man. But he values discipline on his ship. I have also heard that he is a man of his word."

Tahira knew as much. "He made a promise to protect my friend and me."

"But she died," Jaazah said. "Tell me how that happened."

Tahira took a breath and told Jaazah the facts of that morning.

"Ah," Jaazah said when she was done. "My guess is those pirates waited until they knew the captain was unable to stop them. And they probably had their friends gathered around, friends who wouldn't stop them. You say that he killed one of them? The captain, I mean."

"He did," Tahira said. "He's told me that he didn't mean to kill him, just punish him."

"Well, that is a strict disciplinarian," Jaazah said. She put her hands on Tahira's shoulders. "There, your hair is done. Why don't you stand up and show me yourself."

Tahira stood up carefully on numb feet and turned around. Jaazah clapped her hands together once.

"You look so beautiful," she said again.

"Thank you," Tahira said.

"Come on, let's get something for you to eat," Jaazah said, leading the way into the cook-space. "You must be hungry."

"For more than meat and biscuits, yes," Tahira said. "After a while they wear on you."

"Luckily, this island is abundant with fruits," Jaazah said. She worked quickly, cutting up fruits and putting them on a large plate.

Tahira sat at the table and lapsed into a thoughtful silence. She still didn't know what she was going to do, where she was going to stay. All that Jaazah had told her about Captain Haefen were things she already knew.

Tahira longed to know the kinds of fruits she was eating. But one look at Jaazah's far-off expression told her that Jaazah wouldn't hear her. She guessed that Jaazah was thinking about Rol again.

"Let's get you back into town. Thank you," Jaazah said as Tahira cleaned up their meal. She took down Tahira's damp dress and draped it over her arm. "Tahira, I have heard that Captain Haefen doesn't like violence that much. But if someone crosses him, if someone breaks a promise with him, he will do what is necessary."

Tahira opened the door. "Is he a kind man?"

"Kindness does not describe any pirate, especially a captain," Jaazah said, locking the door behind them. "But I think that if any pirate possessed kindness, it would be Captain Haefen." She pointed down the hill toward the port. "Why are you on the ship? And why have you been allowed to roam around alone?"

"Captain Haefen is taking me somewhere," Tahira said as they started walking. "He brought me out here yesterday to show me the town. He held my hand to keep me safe."

Jaazah stopped walking. "He did?" she asked.

"Yes."

"I did not expect that."

"Why not?"

"In all my time in that stall, I have only seen Captain Haefen a few times. I said that before," Jaazah said. "And I never saw him with a woman. Ever. Some say that he hates women. But if he's been so kind to you, I don't think that's true."

"He was protecting me, remember," Tahira said. "But what do you think that means?"

"I don't know," Jaazah said. "I can see why he's such an enigma to you."

"Captain Haefen has told me I could stay on this island, if I wanted," Tahira said. "But I don't know what to do. I would ask your advice, Jaazah, but I don't know you very well. But you've been most kind, thank you for everything." She pulled out her money bag. "Can I pay you for this dress?"

Jaazah smiled and draped the damp blue and green dress over Tahira's arm. "No, keep it as a gift," she said. "I've long wanted to help one of the pirate girls I see around this town. And in you I finally found one who would appreciate a little feminine company. And in you I found a little more of my daughter."

Tahira nodded. "Thank you."

They walked in silence for a while. Tahira lifted her face to feel the sun as it started to set toward the ocean. She hadn't realized how late it was; she had even less time than she'd thought to make her decision. Though she couldn't quite pick out the *Royal Conlan*, she imagined Captain Haefen busy with re-provisioning. Perhaps he was even waiting for her.

Just before the noise of the town reached them, Jaazah stopped walking again.

"You didn't ask my advice, Tahira, but I'll give it anyway," she said. "This island is beautiful. It's plentiful, and it has charms. But it's also a terrible place to make a life. I was born here because my parents couldn't buy a passage off before the pirates came. Rol left with a hope for a better life. I've been around pirates my whole life and I wouldn't trust even the soberist one."

Tahira nodded. "So your praise of Captain Haefen means something," she said.

"You are correct," Jaazah said. "To have *anything* good to say about a pirate is significant. Wherever he's taking you, it's got to be a better life than here. There was a time that if I could have, I would have left, gone somewhere far away where they've never heard of pirates. But now, my place is here. I want to be buried with my daughter. If you stayed here, you would be stuck here. You don't look like the kind of person who likes to be trapped."

"You're right, I'm not," Tahira said. She looked around, taking in the beautiful island again.

Jaazah grabbed Tahira's arm and shook her gently. "Then don't stay here. You would be here for the rest of your life. You'll never find another captain kind enough to take you, and none who would keep his hands off you."

Tahira felt herself blush. When they reached Jaazah's stall, a line of people formed almost at once to examine her wares. Tahira stepped closer to Jaazah.

"You've been most kind," she said.

Jaazah smiled, her mind already on her business. "You were kind to my daughter," she said again. "You've earned every bit of it."

She stepped away from Tahira to tend to her customers. Tahira pulled a few coins out of her money bag and put them on Jaazah's stall before stepping away. Her steps wandered back down towards the dock.

She looked around her, trying to imagine herself staying on this island. She had her two trades, midwifing and healing. But could she stay here, where there was a constant flow of pirates? Would life be full of dangers? Would life be dull? Jaazah's life seemed aimless and alone, with only her business in her stall by the docks.

Tahira sat on a coil of rope and stared up the hill toward the houses. All her life she'd been stuck in one place, never progressing, always doing the same thing. Just thinking about doing it again made her shudder. Though she didn't like being on a pirate ship, it was the first time in her life that she had been free. And for the first time in her life, she had a choice. Captain Haefen had given her that.

Tahira closed her eyes and felt inside her for what she wanted to do. She sat for a long time, weighing everything she had heard and seen and felt. Finally, she opened her eyes and climbed off the coil.

She reached the *Royal Conlan* just as the sun was setting. She could see pirates crowding the shrouds and yards like birds, waiting the order to weigh anchor and set sail. She wondered that they hadn't already left.

But then she saw Captain Haefen. He was standing at the starboard rail, looking toward the town. He had his telescope in his hand, unused at his side, his eyes searching the market behind her. Rance stood a few paces behind him, his whistle in his teeth, his whip tapping against his leg. The quartermaster, Scudamore, stood by Captain Haefen's side, rocking on his heels with impatient glances at the captain. Something about the whole scene brought a smile to Tahira's lips.

"Ahoy the ship!" she called, stepping to the bottom of the gangway.

Captain Haefen started and looked down at her. He stared at her for a few seconds before his face cleared and he hid a smile. "Ahoy the dock!" he said, stepping to the head of the gangway.

He held his hand out to her. Tahira quickly walked up the gangway and took it. The moment her foot touched the deck, Scudamore and Rance shouted orders to get the ship under way. Pirates ran around the deck, securing lines as the sails bellied out in the fresh strong breeze. Captain Haefen led Tahira to the quarterdeck.

"You got a new dress," he said.

"I did," Tahira said. "A woman invited me to her home to clean up." She pulled her money bag off her belt and held it out. "Here is the rest of the money.

Captain Haefen shook his head and leaned his elbow against the axle of the helm, looking as relaxed as he had the day before. "It's for you, Tahira. Keep it."

She put the money bag back on her belt. When she looked up again, he was staring intently at her face.

"Why did you come back?" he asked. He said it softly, as though he didn't want to be overheard, looking surprised but relieved.

"The woman I met told me what life on this island would be like," she said. "I realized I couldn't be trapped in another place again."

"You're trapped on this ship," he said.

She looked up into the rigging. "But we are going somewhere," she said. "It's away from the life I had before, and away from an island I would be trapped on for the rest of my life, and a pirate port at that. And you promised me I would be free. So I came back to you."

Her last words surprised her, and she hoped he hadn't heard them. Before he could see her blushing, she turned away and went to the hatchway. But she glanced back at him before she stepped down, and she thought she saw him smiling.

Chapter Sixteen

Tahira woke very early, at three bells in the morning watch. She unlocked her door and made her way through the snoring hammocks up to the main deck, passing several bleary-eyed pirates as they made their rounds on watch. She nearly bumped into Scudamore by the main hatchway.

"Sorry," she said, moving around him.

"Apologies," Scudamore said, tipping his head so his gold earhoop swung.

Tahira stepped over some pirates scrubbing the deck with holystones and went to the rail. She swung herself up on the shrouds then ran up the ratlines, marking with a level of pride how good she was getting at it, and thinking about how Tel could beat everyone in her pirate crew. Jaazah had been right about the dress; it made the climbing much easier. Tahira would have to remember to give Ransome his breeches back.

She gained the main top from the futtock shrouds and stood holding onto a backstay, looking over the starboard side.

The night before, when Captain Haefen had brought her her meal, he'd told her that he loved watching sunrises from the maintop. He'd said it casually, but the idea took hold of her, and she wanted to see it for herself.

"Just in time," she whispered. The sun was just barely peeking out of the ocean, a sliver of gold above the nearly black water. The sky above it was a dark green, slowly darkening upwards to the dark blue of night. Tahira breathed in the early morning air, a little sharp from coolness, and thought back to all the years of waking up before dawn in the slave compounds and watching the sky lightening while eating her morning meal.

Pirates moved past her on the top and shrouds as they set the sails per Scudamore's orders. They were acclimated to her presence on the maintop now, and no one bothered her.

Tahira shielded her eyes as the sun lifted fully out of the sea. Its warmth seemed to travel over the miles to hit her first and she breathed in the light. For all her years of rising with the sun, she had never seen a sunrise before. She could not imagine a more glorious sight. She would have to do this every morning from now on.

After a while, far below her on the deck, she heard the ship's bell ringing eight bells—the end of the morning watch. Pirates came falling out of the rigging all around her, running for the hatchway as soon as their feet hit the deck. Though she had always been in her cabin at this time, she knew that this morning watch was going to breakfast and then to bed, while the forenoon watch ate breakfast before coming out on deck. For a few minutes, the deck would be empty except for the helmsman and either Scudamore, Rance, or Captain Haefen, the three captains of the watches.

She lay on her stomach and watched Scudamore step onto the quarterdeck. He stared out over the port aft rail, standing very still. Then he ran to the rail and jumped onto the shrouds, still looking aft. Tahira was confused until she followed his gaze and saw a ship. Even from this distance she could see it was much bigger than the *Royal Conlan*. All the sails were bent and she was gaining fast.

Tahira looked down at Scudamore again, wondering if this ship was to be a prize; Captain Haefen had said he would take prizes if they presented themselves.

Scudamore ran to the hatchway in front of the helm. "Captain!" he shouted. "I think it's the *Menace*."

Moments later Captain Haefen came running up the hatchway, pulling his shirt on as he ran. He met Scudamore at the port rail and put his glass to his eye, staring at the ship gaining on them. It was now close enough that Tahira could just see a man standing at the forward rail, looking at them through his own glass.

"Orders, sir?" Scudamore asked.

"Beat to quarters," Captain Haefen said.

Scudamore turned and gave several sharp blasts on his whistle. A roar came from belowdecks as the entire crew of pirates spilled up like ants.

"Topmen aloft to make sail!" Scudamore shouted. "Crowd as many as she'll carry. Man your stations, load the cannons, cutlasses at the ready!"

Tahira stood up and threw her back against the mast to keep from being thrown off the top as the pirates ran up to loosen all sails. She looked down at Captain Haefen, who hadn't moved.

With a great flapping all the sails of the *Royal Conlan* were loosed. But though the ship heeled to starboard, caught the wind, and leapt forward with a hum, Tahira could tell the *Menace* would catch them; it was close enough now that Tahira could clearly see the flag flying from the mainmast: black with a white skull. As the flag whipped in the wind Tahira caught glimpses of other white shapes on the flag below the skull.

Fear gripped her heart as she looked between the gaining ship and the pirates below her. There was a desperation in their movements that she'd never seen before.

"Sir?" Scudamore asked. Even with the melee of pirates around her she could still hear them. Captain Haefen finally lowered the glass. "Why is he doing this? He gave his word he would never attack you."

"This must be about Wilkid," Captain Haefen said.

"How?" Scudamore asked. "There's no way he could possibly know what happened."

Captain Haefen faced Scudamore slowly. "We were just in port. Perhaps someone there talked."

"I didn't see the *Menace*."

"That doesn't mean she wasn't there," Captain Haefen said. "He has spies everywhere. Wilkid is the only reason he would be chasing us. Because you're right, he gave his word."

He raised the glass again. *Menace* was even closer. Captain Haefen turned and looked at his own crew, making as much sail as the ship could carry. There came a shout from below of "Cannons ready, sir!"

"Where's Tahira?" Captain Haefen asked. He looked up at the maintop. "Tahira, are you up there?"

"Yes," Tahira said, stepping forward so Captain Haefen could see her.

"Get below!" Captain Haefen said.

"Why?" Tahira asked. "Aren't you friends with that other captain?"

"Far from it," Captain Haefen said. He handed the glass to Scudamore. "Now get below quick! You need to be safe."

"I think I'll be safe up here," Tahira said. "I'm pretty well hidden." She did not want to wait in her small, dark cabin. She wanted to be out in the fresh air as much as she could.

But just then, with two huge blasts, the *Menace* fired its bow cannons. One cannonball landed harmlessly in the water off their port bow. But the other sailed into the rigging, passing so close to Tahira that she saw the heavy black ball rocket past her. She froze, fear now coursing through her.

"Samson!" she heard Captain Haefen shout. "Get her down!"

Through her shock she felt the enormous black pirate throw her over his shoulder and climb down the ratlines. Captain Haefen grabbed her shoulders and shook her.

"Are you all right?" he asked. "Get below, they're going to board us."

Behind him Tahira heard Scudamore shouting orders to heave to and strike their colors. At once she felt the rocking of the ship decrease as it slowed down.

Captain Haefen released her and ran off to attend to his ship. The enemy pirates must already be on their way over, for the crew was staring over the port rail.

Still in shock, Tahira sank down on a rope coil in the waist of the ship. This was her first experience in real pirating, and she suddenly regretted her decision to stay. She looked toward the hatchway, but already she knew it was too late to get safely down.

Whoever this other pirate captain was, whatever deal he had made with Captain Haefen, however he was connected to Wilkid, he was coming.

Captain Haefen, his hand on his sheathed cutlass, stood at the rail by the ladder, watching as boats from the *Menace* rowed steadily closer. Up in the rigging Tahira could see the topmen reefing the sails. The ship bobbed gently in the water, but was otherwise completely still. With a bump the boats arrived at the *Royal Conlan*.

First on board was a woman, which surprised Tahira. She had an unruly mane of greasy red hair and wore men's clothes. The naked cutlass in her belt clattered against the railing as she climbed over it. A swarm of pirates followed her, surrounding the crew of the *Royal Conlan*. Thankfully, the new pirates didn't notice Tahira.

"Killian!" the woman said, stepping over to Captain Haefen.

He shifted his weight onto one foot. "Maryanne," he said.

"It's good to see you," the woman Maryanne said. Keeping her hands at her belt she stepped up to Captain Haefen and kissed him. Tahira couldn't tell if he kissed her back. But as Maryanne pulled away Captain Haefen grabbed her hands.

"It would be better to see you, Maryanne, if you weren't trying to kill me," he said, and pulled a dirty dagger from her hand.

Maryanne tisked. "Oh, come on, it's just a little, dull dagger," she said. She leaned forward again and put her hands on Captain Haefen's chest. "Just a friendly hello between former lovers."

Captain Haefen took a step back. "I take it you're still angry with me."

"No," Maryanne said with a false sweetness that made Tahira's skin prickle. "What makes you say that?"

Captain Haefen raised an eyebrow but didn't answer. He looked down at the dagger he still had in his hand. "Hang on," he said. "This is the dagger you were going to use to kill James. Did you get your revenge?"

"Oh, I did," Maryanne said with a leering smile. She sauntered closer to Captain Haefen again. "So tell me, Killian, how has it been since we parted ways? Have you missed me?"

"No, Maryanne," Captain Haefen said in a hard voice. "I haven't."

Maryanne looked shocked. "You haven't? Have you moved on, then?"

"No," Captain Haefen said. "And no, before you ask, I'll not take you back on my crew."

Anger covered Maryanne's face. In a swift motion she grabbed her dagger from Captain Haefen. "Then perhaps it's time I sharpen this dagger again!" she shouted.

She swung the dagger toward Captain Haefen's heart. Tahira gasped.

"Avast!"

Tahira started at the rough shout. So did Maryanne; she spun around, and all eyes followed hers to the railing. The pirate who'd just stepped on deck had to be the captain of the *Menace*. He was wearing three belts of pistols, a felt tricorne hat, and a dull scarlet fearnought coat. His face was full of anger, but as he looked at Maryanne it softened a little.

"Maryanne, we discussed this," he said.

Maryanne took a few steps back, still angry.

"Charles Nave," Captain Haefen said. His hand was still on his cutlass. "I wish I could say it's a pleasure to see you. But it never is."

"Cut the games, Haefen," Captain Nave snapped. "You know why I'm here."

"Actually, I don't," Captain Haefen said. A flicker of worry crossed his face. "If it was your wish to pawn Maryanne back onto my ship, I will not have her."

"No, Maryanne is mine now," Nave said, his gaze hardening again as he looked at Maryanne. "And she would do well to remember it." He stared at her until she turned as red as her hair and looked down. Nave raised his chin, satisfied, and turned his attention back to Captain Haefen. "No, this is about my son."

Captain Haefen raised his eyebrows. Tahira thought she still saw the worry in his face.

Nave cast his gaze around the ship. "Where is my son, Haefen?"

"He's not here," Captain Haefen said. "He died in a duel."

"A duel?" Nave said. He strode casually toward Captain Haefen. The entire ship tensed. "No, I don't think that's it at all."

Captain Haefen didn't reply. Nave paced in a complete circle around Captain Haefen before speaking again. "You see, one of my spies heard you talking to your wench," he said. "You admitted to her that you killed my son."

Tahira almost couldn't hold in her gasp. She remembered the conversation. She could see that Captain Haefen did too. He opened his mouth to answer, but Nave held up a hand. His other hand was gripping his sword hilt.

"No, Haefen, you don't get to speak," he said, his voice a dangerous growl. "I allowed my son to come aboard your vessel, and in exchange, I would leave you alone. But now that you've killed my son, that deal is broken."

In a sudden flurry of movement and sound, every pirate in Nave's crew drew their cutlasses and attacked the crew of the *Royal Conlan*.

Tahira fell off the coil onto the deck. Above her head she heard shouts, clangs, and shots being fired. Screams at different pitches shattered the air. The sounds were deafening, and she clapped her hands over her ears, trying to deaden the sound.

But she could still see the battle. Blood was flying almost as fast as the weapons. She felt drops splatter on her. Several pirates hit the deck, but only a few got up again. Pistol smoke hung over the deck. She'd never seen anything so violent, not even when the taskmasters got carried away, not even when Master Gall had whipped her. The sight made her stomach turn, and she was suddenly glad she hadn't eaten that morning.

She pulled herself to her feet but kept bent double. She staggered along the starboard railing toward the quarterdeck, dodging weapons, shrapnel, and pirates stumbling and staggering over each other. She thought if she could make it she'd be safe. But just as she reached the hatchway down to the captain's cabin, an iron-strong arm slipped around her waist.

"Let me go!" Tahira screamed, struggling.

"You're Haefen's wench, aren't you? You're coming with me," said a gravelly voice in her ear, and Tahira realized with a jolt of terror that it was

Captain Nave.

Nave started dragging her backwards across the quarterdeck toward the port rail. She gathered all the strength she had to fight back. She threw her elbows back but met nothing but air. She stomped her feet, but never hit his. His grip around her waist was too strong for even her to break. She pushed up with her feet, launching her weight backwards, but all she accomplished was a few moments with her feet in the air.

"Stop fighting," Nave shouted in her ear.

But Tahira kept fighting, even when Nave pressed the sharp, sticky blade of his cutlass against her throat.

"Help!" Tahira screamed, but her voice was snatched away almost at once by battle noises.

Nave pressed his cutlass harder against her neck, cutting off her airway a little, and Tahira felt blood dripping down to her collarbone. Closer and closer Nave dragged her toward the railing. She knew that once he got her into the boat it would be almost impossible to get back. She didn't want to think about what would happen to her then. But no matter how hard she fought, Nave was stronger.

Terrified, Tahira threw her gaze around the deck, her breath coming in gasps against the cutlass blade. The deck was awash in blood, smoke, and screams. Pirates from both crews were scattered around, lying on the deck, swinging limply from the rigging, or still battling.

No one had noticed her. No one had heard her. In one last effort to break free from Nave, Tahira let her knees go slack and dropped her weight. But it was no use; Nave kept a firm hold on both her and his cutlass.

Suddenly Tahira saw Captain Haefen. He was only a short way away from her, battling two enemy pirates at once. His expression was fierce and frightening, so unlike anything she had seen from him before.

But somehow, she knew that he would hear her.

"Captain Haefen!" she screamed, the cutlass painful at her throat.

With one final stab, Captain Haefen ran his two opponents through. They fell to the deck, grasping their middles. He turned his head. He saw Tahira.

"Captain, help!" she yelled.

Captain Haefen's expression turned to rage. The sight of it scared her, and she almost didn't want him to rescue her. He raised his cutlass above his head and charged. She closed her eyes as he got closer, not wanting to see the murder in his eyes. Nave's cutlass scraped against her throat as it was pulled away. Above her she heard Nave's grunt punctuated with a clash of metal. His hold on her waist slackened at last and she opened her eyes.

Captain Haefen grabbed her and pulled her under his left arm. She clung to him, feeling his heart pounding against her jaw. Nave was leaning against the railing, breathing heavily, a fresh cut on his cheek. Tahira hadn't realized how close she'd come to being captured.

"It's true then," Nave shouted, touching the cut with a finger. "You have gone soft."

Captain Haefen swung his cutlass up to Nave's chest, pressing the point into his skin. "Say what you will about me," he said, his dangerous voice echoing in Tahira's head. "I will not allow you to do to her what you do to other women."

Nave straightened up, his face ugly with hate. He batted away Captain Haefen's cutlass with the back of his hand. "This isn't over, Haefen," he growled. "You killed my son, and you shall pay for it."

"You know full well there was no love lost between you," Captain Haefen shouted, raising his cutlass again. "And I didn't mean to kill him."

"Of course you did," Nave said, suddenly swaggering. He pushed Captain Haefen's cutlass away again. "You never do anything you don't mean to. You will pay. Perhaps Captain Jean or Captain Soto will help me destroy you. I will see you soon!"

Nave put his fingers in his mouth and whistled. Somehow over the sounds of battle his crew heard him. They stopped fighting immediately and launched themselves over the port railing into the waiting boats.

Captain Haefen backed up to let Nave's crew pass, pulling Tahira with him. His cutlass remained raised, ready. But no one attacked. The crew of the *Menace* manned their oars and pulled off toward their ship.

Captain Haefen dropped his cutlass and wrapped both arms tightly around Tahira.

She had meant to be brave. But in that moment, the trauma of the battle and the fear of near-kidnap overpowered her. She buried her face in Captain Haefen's shoulder and wept. She clung to him tighter and tighter, gripping the back of his sweat-dampened shirt with both fists. He gently rocked her, one hand on the back of her head, the other hand around her back. After seeing him so fierce in battle, she was surprised at how tender he was. But she now understood why he had a reputation of being a ruthless Captain.

Finally, she felt the terror drain out of her body and she pulled away. Captain Haefen let her go and take a step back from him. She swiped the backs of her hands over her face.

"I'm sorry," she said.

"For what?" he asked, wiping fresh tears off her cheeks with his rough thumbs. "You didn't do anything wrong. *I'm* sorry. He almost got away with you."

Tahira hiccupped a little and looked up at him. None of the fierceness from the battle was on his face now. In its absence he looked almost scared. The sight made her uncomfortable and happy at the same time.

She sniffed. "You have a cut on your neck," she said. Tentatively she reached up and touched it. He didn't pull away.

"It doesn't hurt," he said.

She dropped her hand. "Let's get something on that so that it doesn't get infected."

Surprisingly, he nodded. He put his arm around her shoulders and turned toward the hatchway below.

"Mr. Rance!" he called. "Are you still alive?"

"Aye, sir!" Rance said, standing up and saluting with his left hand; Tahira saw a gash in his upper right arm.

"I want a full report when I get back," Captain Haefen said. "I want to know how many of my men are dead. Throw Nave's dead overboard. Find Mr. Ravon and get him to work immediately."

"Aye, sir!" Rance said again.

Tahira climbed down the hatchway first, Captain Haefen right behind her. She led him to her cabin and closed the door behind them. Her candle was nearly out, but Captain Haefen replaced it while she sat on her bed, suddenly shivering.

He turned to face her. "Are you all right?" he asked.

"Captain, what did he mean that he was going to destroy you?" she asked.

Captain Haefen shrugged. "It's a threat all pirates tell one another."

"But does he mean to kill you?"

He took a deep breath and sat down next to her. "I believe you wanted to look at my cut?"

Tahira started like she'd heard another gun. She felt distracted and flustered, and all she wanted to do was bury her face in his shoulder again.

"Yes," she said. She knelt on the floor and pulled out her box of healing supplies.

"Where did you get that?" he asked.

She froze for a moment, wondering what to say. "I was taught to heal," she said. "I wanted to get some supplies together. Copper helped me get some from the galley, then from the island where we careened, and I thought—"

She hadn't realized how frantic she sounded until he put his hand on her wrist. "Tahira," he said softly. "You don't answer to me. I'm not a taskmaster."

She let out the deep breath she didn't know she was holding. "I'm sorry," she said. "I don't know where that came from. I know you're not a taskmaster."

"I'd guess that came from long habits and a terrifying experience," he said.

She nodded and placed the box on the floor. She removed a few herbs and ground them between her hands, hoping he wouldn't see that they were shaking.

She dumped the herbs into one hand, grabbed a couple bandages with the other, and stood up. In this light he looked years younger. He was almost smiling as she approached him and bent over his neck. She forced herself to focus on his cut.

She used one of the bandages to wipe away the spattered blood and grime from his face and neck, making sure his wound was clean. Then gently she tipped her herb-filled hand until it was resting against his neck. He grunted softly as the herbs touched his cut, but he bit his lip against it. She held the herbs there for a few more moments, then carefully pulled her hand away; some of the herbs stuck to the wound, but the remainder stayed in her hand. She placed the bandage against his neck and held it there, dabbing every now and then, until the bleeding stopped.

"There, you're finished," she said.

"Wait." He grabbed her wrist as she turned away. "You have a cut too," he said, pointing a finger to the side of her neck. "It's deeper and bigger than mine."

"Oh, yes," she said, remembering Nave's cutlass digging into her neck.

Captain Haefen retrieved another bandage from the box. Clumsily he wiped off her face and neck too. He bit his lip as he worked, concentrating. Tahira had to hold back a smile at his expression. She felt something fluttering in her stomach at his touch.

But then he wiped the bandage right through her wound, and she gasped and grabbed his wrist.

"Sorry," he said. "I'm not as good as you."

She nodded. She let go of his wrist and put the herbs against her neck. She closed her eyes against the stinging pain.

He put his hands on her shoulders and her eyes shot open.

"Sorry," he said. "You were swaying. I thought you were going to faint."

"I'm all right," she said, but she let him guide her to sit next to him.

"Captain, who was that woman?" she asked, removing the herbs and putting the clean side of a bandage on the cut.

"Maryanne Ronny," he said. "She was on my ship for a time. She dressed herself as a man to get aboard."

"Why did she do that?"

He shrugged. "She went to sea because she didn't like her situation. But no captain would take on a woman, so she disguised herself as a man."

"Did you know she was a woman?"

He nodded. "I wanted to give her a chance to find herself, rid herself of her demons."

"I take it she didn't," Tahira said, and he shook his head, a rueful expression on his face. "What happened? You don't mind me asking, do you?"

"I don't," he said, and she believed he meant it. "When she came aboard, she was a sad thing. But she wasn't cruel yet. I thought she would improve, but something happened while she sailed with me that hardened her. I didn't want to be around her anymore."

"Did she fall in love with another while she was with you?" Tahira asked. "She did say you were lovers."

"Aye, that we were, for a short time," he said, but he didn't look proud of it. "And she fell for many other men. But no, it was her bloodlust that had me leave her in port. I hadn't seen her since. Until today."

"I'm glad she's not on this ship," Tahira said. She removed the bandage from her neck and put both hands in her lap. She shuddered involuntarily and looked at him. "I have never seen you so fierce. I understand your ruthless reputation now."

Captain Haefen leaned forward, his elbows on his knees, and looked over his shoulder at her. "I'm sorry I frightened you," he said. "But I hope you know that I wanted to protect you from all of that. I didn't want to have you on deck when Nave came."

"No, you're not to blame," she said, shaking her head. "I should have gone below when you told me to." She paused. "Thank you for saving my life," she whispered.

He stood up and faced her. "Of course," he whispered.

He left her cabin, pulling the door almost closed behind him. She listened quietly to the pirates on the deck above her. She heard moans and grunts and knew that many of them were injured. She heard faint splashes as Nave's dead crewmen were thrown overboard. The ship remained still.

"This is my fault," she whispered to the ceiling.

Tahira closed her metal case and made her way up to the main deck. She mentally prepared herself for the carnage, but it was more than she had anticipated. She hadn't noticed how many dead bodies there were, pressed against the scuppers, draped over the railings, propped up against the capstan. She gritted her teeth.

"What have I told you, Robbie?" Captain Haefen said behind her. She turned to see him supporting Ransome across the quarterdeck. Ransome was limping but otherwise looked unhurt. "You need more experience before you should be in a fight."

"I'm sorry, Cap'n," Ransome said. His voice was shaking.

A group of pirates was crowded in the fo'c'sle. Tahira approached them from behind, carefully stepping over blood on the deck, and they parted to let her through. Against the bowsprit bulkhead, Ravon sat on a barrel, receiving each injured pirate as he came. Tahira arrived in time to see Ravon cut off a pirate's broken finger and wrap it in a dirty bandage. The pirate stepped away, whimpering. Ravon glared at her.

"What do you want, wench?"

"I have a name, Pierre Ravon," Tahira said, tired of his surliness. "I suggest you learn it." She held up her box. "I told you I was a healer once. I've come to help you."

Ravon's expression didn't change. "Don't help me, help them," he growled. "I have yards to fix." He stood and stalked away.

Tahira put her box on the barrel he left and turned to face the wounded pirates. "I will need lots of seawater and all of your neckerchiefs to clean you off."

The less injured pirates complied, bringing her several buckets of sea water. She turned to the first pirate in line. He was so bloodied she couldn't see where the wound originated.

He handed over his neckerchief and she wet it down before mopping up his face. "What is your name?" she asked.

"Goss," the pirate said. "Me mates call me Gossy."

"Well, Goss, it looks like you're more blood than injury," she said. "However, you do have a cut on your forehead." She opened her box and pulled out needle and thread. Goss held still while she sewed his wound, though he winced as she bathed it again in seawater.

Some wounded pirates she sewed up, others she gave herbs and bandages. A few required a tonic, for their wounds were deep enough that Tahira feared sickness. One needed a salve for powder burns to his face when he'd stepped in front of a pistol to help his mate.

She asked all their names as they came, though she knew most of them: Birdson, Withstandenot (called "Withy"), Gittin, Glassy Harry (with a glass eye that unnerved her at first), Hincher, Shurin, Williams, and Hynde. Some of the pirates already tended to by Ravon came to her for help. One of them was Sam Morwell.

"Ravon says he'll chop it," Morwell said, tears in his eyes. Tahira had never seen a pirate cry before. "I shoulda listened to me dad, he told me not to go to sea. One injury and the carpenter'll chop ye up fer parts and send the rest down to Davy Jones. That's wha' 'e told me."

He held out his arm, still rambling. A lump by his elbow told Tahira that the bone had been pushed out of place, but was still sound. She put her hand gently on his wrist and he winced away, which made him cry out in pain.

"It will take some time, but I can heal it," she said. "You won't lose your arm."

Morwell looked ready to hug her, but she was grateful he didn't.

"I am going to have to pull this back in place," Tahira said. "Have your mates hold you. Brace yourself, it's going to hurt."

Tahira waited until Morwell was braced before taking his hand. She felt his arm for a moment, making sure all his bones were in the right place, then yanked hard in one sharp motion. The bone popped back into place, but the sound was drowned out by Morwell screaming and swearing.

"Now I need a splint," Tahira said. She bent down and picked up a piece of a broken spar. "Can I have your knife?" She carved the broken wood, shaving off the rough edges until it was the perfect size. She placed it along Morwell's arm and wrapped it in a bandage. "Here's your knife. Do your work as normally as you can, but don't strain your arm. In a few weeks you'll be able to take it off."

Morwell nodded his thanks, his face still streaked with pained tears. He staggered away, leaving his mates to stare at Tahira with a mixture of distrust and awe.

When the last pirate stumped away, Tahira sat on the barrel and sighed. By the sun she could tell it was midafternoon; she'd spent half a day tending to the pirates. She looked in her silver box, unsurprised to see how depleted her stores were. She hoped there wouldn't be another large need again soon.

"Thank you for healing them," Captain Haefen said, coming up to her. Behind him the crew was pumping water onto the deck and scrubbing it with holystones. Blood and white holystone water ran out of the scuppers and into the sea.

"How many men did you lose?" Tahira asked.

His expression darkened. "Ten. And eighteen wounded, as you know. Thankfully, a low number."

Tahira felt drained. She stood up and started to gather her things. She felt rather than heard Captain Haefen approaching her from behind. She turned around and found him standing a few steps away with his hands at his sides and his head down. She left her box and faced him.

"Are you all right, Captain?" she asked.

In a quick motion, as though frightened of losing his nerve if he hesitated, he closed the gap between them and hugged her. She hugged him back, knowing he needed this, just as she had when Alycia died, just as she had earlier that day. He rested his cheek against the side of her head and let out several long, slow breaths that warmed her shoulder. She gently rubbed his back. She felt so comfortable here.

"I'm sorry," he said at last, pulling back.

"Don't be," she said. "I could be your sea dad now, if you wanted."

He looked up at her and gave a sad chuckle.

"I think I need to apologize, Captain," she said. "You were talking to me when you admitted you killed Wilkid. It's my fault Nave found out."

He shook his head. "No. It's not your fault at all."

She put her hand on his shoulder. "I'm still sorry."

He put his hand on top of hers. His expression was hard to read, but she thought she saw a lot of pain. He nodded once and returned to his crew.

Chapter Seventeen

Ravon's repairs took a short amount of time, and the ship got under way again the next day. For the first time, the pirates were sober, somber, and did their work with hardly any encouragement or complaints. Everyone had lost someone in the battle; Tahira saw several of them crying when Captain Haefen held the sea burials.

Over the next few days Tahira kept busy with seventeen of the wounded pirates (Rance refused to come near her). Luckily, the crew was still large enough that they could be on the sick list and the working of the ship wouldn't suffer.

But the seventeen wounded were needier than anyone Tahira had ever dealt with. The pirate with the amputated finger got an infection, Sam Morwell constantly complained about his arm, and three of them claimed stomach pains that had nothing to do with their injuries to the same area. Most of them were crude, but when she didn't rise to their baits and comments they settled down into sullen silence. Tahira imposed greatly on Copper in the galley to make tonics and salves for them all. Her supplies were dwindling fast, but thankfully she had plenty of salt water with which to keep wounds clean.

Nearly a week after the battle, an island came into sight. Captain Haefen sailed the *Royal Conlan* into the shallows and sent several pirates ashore in two of the boats. Tahira stayed in the fo'c'sle with her remaining charges; those who had healed enough had returned to their duties a few days before.

She took the bandage off the amputated finger and checked it. "You're doing much better," she said. "The infection should be cleared up in a few more days, and then the finger can heal."

The pirate grunted. His was the only name of the seventeen she didn't know, as he rarely talked to anyone. Sam Morwell sidled up and proffered his arm. Tahira held in a sigh.

"Morwell, I've already told you," she said. "If I keep unwrapping your arm, it'll never be still enough to heal. It's only been a few days. It will be fine, trust me."

Morwell's face fell and he stepped back.

"Tahira?" The group started at finding Captain Haefen standing behind them. The pirates parted, giving their Captain an unimpeded view of Tahira. She looked up at him. "I need to talk to you," he said.

She followed behind him as he walked slowly toward the quarterdeck. Once there he leaned on the starboard rail and looked toward the island. "I'm sorry, Tahira, but I have to let you off here."

She was startled. "Why?"

"For your protection." He wouldn't look at her.

She put a hand on his arm. "I don't understand."

"Nave. He's coming for me. You were right. He means to kill me." His staccato tone told her more than his words did.

"Then why did he leave?" she asked.

Captain Haefen looked down at the rail for a moment, then back up at the island. "Because Nave usually only goes to battle when he knows he will win," he said. "He was losing the battle before he grabbed you, and he knew it. But with a second or even a third pirate ship he will win."

"Why don't you get away?" she asked. "You don't have to fight him, do you?"

"No, I do," he said. "There's nowhere I can hide where he and his allies won't find me. He will hunt me down if I don't fight him. Besides, I don't run and hide. I need to go and get allies of my own." He gripped the railing for a moment then turned to face her at last, looking as though he was steeling himself. "But I need to know that you are safe. If you are on my ship during a battle there is every chance you will be killed. I cannot let that happen."

The passion in his voice surprised her. "But Captain, if you die—"

She paused and sighed, not sure how to continue. She was feeling something deep inside her at the thought of him being in a battle, something she'd felt many times before, especially when he touched her. She didn't know what it was, but this didn't seem the moment to explore it.

Instead, she asked, "Will I be trapped on that island if you don't come back?"

"No," he said, nodding over the railing. "I picked that island for a reason. Ships pass by here often. They'll pick you up. You can begin a life. Tell them who you are and what happened, and they will take care of you.

You don't have to wait for me."

She opened her mouth but no sound came out; her mind and heart had suddenly reached a decision that surprised her. She opened her mouth again and pushed out what she was going to say, "But I think I want to."

He smiled. "And once again you choose to stay."

She felt herself blushing. "What if I want to stay on the ship, and not go to the island?" she asked.

"Is that a declaration of trust or distrust?" he asked.

"I don't know," she said, though she knew that the inexplicable trust she had felt in him from the first had only grown in strength. "It just seems like you're ordering me to stay on the island. You know I don't like that."

He sighed and ran his hand through his hair. "It does seem that way, doesn't it?" he said. "And maybe I am forcing you off my ship. But it's because I don't trust other pirates. Nave didn't know you were here until he saw you. I'm sure he'll tell everyone about you. You would become an instant target, and no matter where you hid, you would be found and undoubtedly killed."

"Oh," she said, shivering a little.

"I'll take you ashore," he said. He stepped away, calling for Rance to ready the last boat.

Tahira leaned on the rail and stared at the island. Like Turtle Island it looked so picturesque. It was long and almost rectangular, its center filled with tall leafy trees, and its edges lined with white sand. The waters surrounding the island were an unusual, tantalizing blue color. The sight of it made Tahira want to jump directly into the water.

On the beach she could see pirates milling around, some of them in the water, some further in the island, some climbing back into a boat. She felt Captain Haefen walk up to her again.

"Captain, what are they doing?" she asked, pointing.

"They're getting things ready for you," he said. "You've never survived alone on an island before, but they have."

Tahira turned to face him. "Why are you really doing this, Captain?"

Captain Haefen paused, still looking out over the railing. "I'll tell you when we get to the island," he said quietly.

"Boat ready, sir!" Rance called. Captain Haefen nodded and Tahira followed him over the port rail and down into the boat. Two pirates manned the oars and Rance sat at the tiller, guiding the boat under the bow of the ship and toward the island.

Tahira sat in the bows of the boat, rising and falling with jerks as the boat made its way through the waves and breakers to the beach. She reached down and trailed her hand in that blue water, surprised by how warm it was. Once the boat landed the pirates tumbled out onto the sand and Captain Haefen lifted her out.

A pirate from the first landing party ran up and saluted. "Sir, everything is ready," he said.

"Very good, Mr. Stretton," Captain Haefen said. "Show Tahira what you have prepared for her."

Stretton nodded, then turned to Tahira. "If you please, Miss, come with me," he said.

His politeness surprised Tahira, but then she remembered that most of the crew feared Captain Haefen, and so Stretton would speak respectfully to her in front of him. Tahira followed him across the sand, hearing the sound of chopping as a couple pirates downed a tree for her use.

Stretton led the way to a large ring of stones in the sand right up against the edge of the trees. As they entered the ring, the breeze died; this was the lee side of the island, and thus a perfect place to build a camp. Just outside the stone circle, at the point furthest from the trees, was a large piece of thick canvas, painted with tar to keep the water out.

"There be dry wood under that canvas to light a signal fire," Stretton said, pointing. "D'ye know how to light a fire?"

"I do," Tahira said.

"Start with the little wood, and gradually get bigger pieces," Stretton said. "Add wet stuff and seaweed when the fire is good 'n' big, and the smoke'll turn black. Easy to spot for miles. Build it here, on the lee side, and it'll burn strong. Put it out with sand so's ye can light it next day. And here's wood fer yer cookin' fire." Stretton pointed to a pile of wood up the beach, just under the trees. "It won' stay dry, so if there's a storm comin', put it with the dry wood." Next, he pointed to a grouping of canvas bags huddled next to a familiar-looking chest. "Over here's yer cookin' utensils. Plates and forks and pans and the like. They'll be just fine over an open fire. There's hardtack in one of 'em, and soap in another."

He stepped over the stones and into the tree line, walking a few paces before stopping and pointing up at a very large tree. "We've rigged ye a cot up there," he said. "It'll keep the bugs outa yer ears."

Tahira looked up and saw an intricately webbed net braced between three large branches. The pirates had thrown a few blankets up there, and had nailed wood into the trunk of the tree so she could climb up.

"Are there any animals on this island?" Tahira asked.

"None but birds an' bugs an' fish," Stretton said. He pointed further into the trees, then drew a line with his finger toward the beach. "That way is a freshwater stream, endin' in a fresh pool. There's buckets in yer camp fer catching rainwater. It rains hard here. Bury the buckets in the sand when it rains and they won' tip over."

He led the way back out of the trees, through the camp, and past some rocks to the shore. Half a dozen pirates stood thigh-deep in the water, placing nets and baskets.

"Check those every day," Stretton said. "Ye should have plenty to eat. We've gathered some pigweed, and some fruits from the jungle, and some clams and oysters. They're in yer camp. And watch for turtles layin' eggs. If ye dig up the eggs right after they've been laid, they make good eatin'."

Tahira nodded, looking at everything Stretton had showed her. Her eye caught on the chest in her camp, and she finally recognized it as being the one that had been in Captain Haefen's cabin, the one full of women's clothes. "Why is that here?" she asked.

"Those are your personal effects," Captain Haefen said, striding over to it and giving it a little kick. "There's a telescope inside for watching for ships, as well as all the women's clothing I had on my ship. And I took the liberty of getting everything out of your cabin for you, your other clothes and your silver box."

He glanced at her, then looked down. Tahira opened her mouth, suddenly realizing what he was really saying. Stretton cleared his throat and walked away.

"You're not planning on coming back, are you?" she said slowly, walking closer to him so they wouldn't be overheard.

He gave a halfhearted shrug. The sight of his resignation worried her a little. "Just a precaution," he said. "And you might change your mind and leave."

"No, that's not it," she said. "Could you really lose this battle with Nave?"

He didn't answer. His expression wasn't impassive, but it was so conflicted she couldn't tell what she saw there. She put her hand on his shoulder.

"We're on the island now," she said. "You promised to tell me. Why are you really letting me go?"

He bit the inside of his cheek; he didn't look ready to answer. "You've asked me several times now why I have done what I have done," he said at last. "And I've never given you a satisfactory answer."

She dropped her hand. "As I recall, you didn't give me any answer."

His mouth twisted as though he was trying not to smile. "Aye, that's true." His expression turned serious again. "Why did I give you your key, why did I warn you about Turtle Island, why have I given you so many opportunities to leave, and why am I now marooning you here?"

He paused, biting the inside of his cheek again. She didn't know what to say, but the fluttering inside her had returned, stronger than ever.

"I still can't tell you, I'm sorry," he said. "But I can tell you this. I'm letting you go because I don't want to see you die. Not after everything you've been through."

They stared at each other for a few moments, and she suddenly realized just how much he had protected her these last months. She'd never been protected by anyone before, and she supposed that's why she hadn't recognized it right away. But he had taken her under his protection before they even left *The Nantes*, he'd rescued her from the slaver, stopped his crewmen from hurting her, comforted her, saved her from drowning, given her choices. And after all his care and attention, he was letting her go so that she wouldn't be killed.

The pirates by the boats called and Tahira started; she had forgotten they were there. Two of the boats were shoving off from the shore. Captain Haefen waved to the remaining boat.

He looked back down at her and put his hands on her shoulders. He looked so sad at that moment that she wanted to say something comforting to him. But she had no idea what to say. He smiled a little and moved his hands up her shoulders to cup her neck. Then, very gently, he kissed her forehead.

"Goodbye, Tahira. I love you," he whispered, and stepped away.

She gasped and tears sprang to her eyes. For she suddenly realized what her own feelings meant, the fluttering in her stomach, the blushing, feeling drawn to him.

She turned around just in time to see the boat shove off from the shore,

Captain Haefen sitting in the middle, his head bowed. She watched the boat, shading her eyes against the sun as it approached the ship. And finally, Captain Haefen looked up. He raised his arm and waved. She waved back.

She stood on the beach and watched the *Royal Conlan* sail away, tears running down her cheeks. She stood there until she could no longer see the ship. She stood there until her legs grew too tired to stand and she sat down in the sand.

Captain Haefen loved her. Though she had been loved in her life, he was the first person to say those words. The knowledge felt strange though exciting.

But he was gone, gone to fight a battle he may not survive. Would she lose him too? She shuddered at the thought. For she loved him, so very much.

She felt as though something was caught in her chest, and after a while it came bubbling out of her in the first laugh she'd had in a long time. She felt free and happy, despite the fact that Captain Haefen was gone. For he loved her, and she loved him, and that made her feel wonderfully vulnerable. Her laugh turned into a cry of happiness as the sun set into the ocean.

Chapter Eighteen

Tahira lost count of the days after a few sunrises. But time didn't matter here. She enjoyed the freedom and the space. For the first time in her life she was completely alone, though the aloneness didn't press on her. Not at first.

Though she'd always hated the work of slavery, she liked to keep busy, and so she spent a few days cleaning her clothes. She scrubbed each garment with the soap from the canvas bags, then rinsed them off in the freshwater pool and hung them on trees to dry. Like Stretton had said, the freshwater stream emptied into a large pool, but there was another stream leading out again, so the water always stayed clear.

She bathed in the ocean, scrubbing herself with sand and soap and letting the seawater rinse her. Then she soaked in the pool while the seawater drifted away.

A while later the rains Stretton mentioned hit the island. Tahira had never known such rains before; they came out of a clear blue sky, and the drops fell so thick and fast that when she cupped her hands together, they filled in a matter of seconds. She got soaked to the skin putting her water buckets out in the sand, and by the next morning the storm had moved on. Tahira found the windward side of the island and stood turning in the wind while her hair and dress dried.

She had never eaten from the sea before, despite being on a ship for a very long time, and she found she liked what the sea offered. The fish were sweet and very moist, and while the clams were chewy, they had a pleasant flavor. The pigweed from the island she didn't like, but something about it told her it would be beneficial to her body.

She spent several days exploring the island, finding herbs and plants. She compared them with those she already had in her silver box, and was delighted to find that many were the same. She spent a large amount of time drying these plants and replenishing her stores. But she found several new plants, and she would have liked to ask Copper about them.

Every day she climbed to the top of a tree with the telescope and scanned the horizon for ships. Every day a ship passed by the island, sometimes one, sometimes two, sometimes three a day. Each flew a different flag, and she wondered what far-off countries these ships were coming from or going to.

But though she had plenty of opportunity, she never built the signal fire. The wood remained under the tarred canvas, unused.

From time to time, she sat on the sand looking out to the horizon where the *Royal Conlan* had vanished. She wondered what was happening with Captain Haefen. She wondered if he would come back for her.

Even after days apart, she still felt a bubbling happiness every time she thought of him. She wanted to tell him about eating fish for the first time, and how terrified she'd been the first night when the jungle came alive with animal night-sounds, and to ask him about the flags she saw. She wanted to tell him she loved him. After a while she began to long for human company, especially his.

She knew she loved him, and had for a while. But did she love him enough to wait for him? She laughed to herself whenever she asked herself this question, for she knew the answer.

Tahira had always been a loving person, accepting everyone who came within her circle. Her parents, Shipra and Pula, Old Joche and Amra, then Mary and the other Pirate Women, and then Aney. But when Aney was taken away, some part of Tahira had closed off, and she had spent the next nearly two years in a self-contained darkness. Only when Tahira had heard the hope of slave songs again did her broken heart start to heal, and her loving nature to come back again. Tahira loved again, first Neph, and then Alycia, as much as Alycia had allowed.

But now, for the first time in her life, Tahira hungered for a different kind of love; she hungered for someone to love her back, to want her and care for her. Not a woman's love, as she had only known before, but the kind of love that a man has, a love she didn't know existed until she met Captain Haefen, the kind of love that protected and provided, the kind of love that would be steadfast and strong. She didn't know how much Captain Haefen loved her, but it was enough for now to know that he did.

As more time passed, and aloneness started pressing on her, she looked for the *Royal Conlan* to return.

***

Tahira was startled awake one morning by the boom of a ship's cannon. She flattened herself on her roped cot to see under the tree's canopy. There, bobbing like a cork in the sea, was a ship. Her heart leapt as she recognized the familiar lines of the *Royal Conlan*. The pirates on deck were moving slowly and lazily. She knew every pirate by his gait, but she couldn't see the captain.

"Where are you?" she whispered aloud.

Then, from around the stern of the ship, she saw a boat. Even from this distance, there was no mistaking Captain Haefen sitting hunched in the bows. Tahira's heart and smile rose so quickly she almost cried aloud.

She climbed down from the tree quickly and ran to the freshwater pool to clean herself up. By the time she finished and was coming back to the beach, the boat had arrived, but none of the pirates inside were disembarking. Goss and Stretton stayed at the oars, and Scudamore still sat behind Captain Haefen, one hand on the captain's shoulder, looking around impatiently. Captain Haefen, meanwhile, was still sitting hunched in the bows of the boat. He looked sad and despondent, and Tahira's heart reached out to him.

But she felt suddenly embarrassed to see him right then, though she couldn't really explain why. Maybe she wanted to meet him alone. Maybe she wasn't sure how much he loved her, and she wanted to watch him. Conflicted, Tahira sat down behind large rocks, where she couldn't be seen.

"Captain, you realize she might not be here," Scudamore said after another minute or two of silence, his voice carried to her by the wind.

"I know." Captain Haefen was looking down at his hands.

"Then why are we here?"

Captain Haefen didn't answer. Scudamore looked frustrated, as if expecting an explanation. He shifted his position. "What is it about her, sir?" he asked. "I've never seen you like this before. Some of the men are wondering what it is."

Captain Haefen finally looked up, toward the trees. "I don't know. But they are right that something's different."

"What if she's not here, sir, what if she's gone?" Scudamore asked. Tahira could hear the mounting frustration in his voice.

"Then we will return to pirating," Captain Haefen said. "But if she is here, we will resume our voyage." For the first time, his voice had the usual

Captain's ring to it.

"Is that really wise, sir?" Scudamore asked, sitting back a little. "You know the men don't really like what that means for you."

Captain Haefen turned his head to look at Scudamore, his jaw set. "That is not my concern. I have my reasons, and you know not to question them." Scudamore ducked his head, and even Goss and Stretton shrank back. Captain Haefen noticed and his expression turned to interest. "Gentlemen, I put the question to you. If Tahira is still here, do we continue with our voyage?"

Goss and Stretton looked at each other, and Stretton said, "Aye, sir."

Captain Haefen gave him a small smile. "You're only saying that for the pardon you might get."

"Aye," said Goss, who looked drunk. "But I won't refuse it."

Captain Haefen made an amused sound and put one hand on the gunwale to hoist himself out of the boat. It was only then that Tahira realized he was injured; the effort to stand up nearly had him toppling over, and he breathed hard as he held the gunwale with both hands now. Immediately Scudamore launched out of the boat and offered his hand. Captain Haefen took it and let Scudamore half-carry him out of the boat. He straightened up, his right arm around his ribs.

"What is your plan, sir?" Scudamore asked, steading Captain Haefen as he staggered a little. "Shouldn't she have come out by now?"

"I don't know," Captain Haefen said, casting his gaze around the island. "She might be waiting to see what I do." He turned toward the boat. "Cast off, stay in the shallows. I will wave when I need you."

Captain Haefen walked along the beach, watching the boat recede from the shoreline. Tahira watched him for another minute. She smiled as his expression turned to longing as he looked at her camp. Deciding to not make him wait any longer, she stood up and started across the rocks and sand toward him. He had his back to her now, his broad shoulders squared against the breeze and his head back. Her heart was pounding in her chest, but this didn't seem a moment for effusiveness. Slowly she reached out a hand and put it on his shoulder. His whole body seemed to let out a breath.

"You stayed," he said.

"You came back for me," she said.

"Of course I did." He turned around and looked at her, taking her in. "If there was even the slightest chance that you were still here, I couldn't abandon you. But why did you stay? I was gone long enough you could have flagged down a half-dozen ships."

"Twenty-eight, actually," she said.

He knitted his eyebrows. "You could have gotten away."

Tahira felt the color rising in her cheeks at the thought of her response. But she couldn't brush it away or lie to him, not now. Yet she didn't know how to tell him she loved him.

He seemed to realize she was struggling, for he changed the subject.

"So, do I take you back onto my ship?" he asked. "Or do I leave you here to light your signal fire after all?"

She scoffed. She reached forward and took one of his hands. "I appreciate you giving me the choice to leave, but I think you and I both know what choice I will make," she said quietly.

He looked surprised, then he knitted his brows. Then he closed the gap between them and kissed her.

Tahira had seen a few slaves kiss each other before, but she had never done it. She was unsure at first what to do, but she soon stopped worrying. Captain Haefen cupped her jaw in one of his big rough hands and put his other hand at the small of her back, pulling her closer. She ran her hands up his arms and clasped them behind his neck, her fingers in his hair. She felt like something was bubbling in her stomach. She liked the feeling. She liked his touch.

She was the first to break away. She looked up into his face, her arms still around his neck and smiled at the look on his face, like he couldn't quite believe what had just happened.

"I'm glad you came back," she said.

He smiled and rested his scruffy chin on her forehead. She moved her hands down his chest to hug him very gently around his ribs.

"Are you all right?" she asked. "What happened in the battle?"

He grimaced, lowering his chin again. "It wasn't pleasant," he said. "I lost many men, as did the other ships."

"Did you find an ally?" she asked.

"Aye, I did," he said, a look of pride coming into his face. "And they fought just as valiantly as my own crew."

"Did you win?"

"Aye, we did," he said. "I killed Nave."

"Does that mean it's over now?" she asked. "Are you safe?"

He ran a thumb over her cheek. "I doubt it," he said. "Nave had many friends. One of them will come for me one day. For revenge, you know." He paused and fixed her with an intense stare. "Really, Tahira, why did you stay?"

She laughed a little and moved one hand from his ribs up to his chest, over his heart, and she felt it speed up. "When you told me you loved me, I realized something," she said. "I love you too."

He stopped breathing for a moment, his expression hard to read. "Why?"

"It's difficult to explain," she said with another laugh. "I think I started falling in love with you from the moment I saw you. You're not a ruthless pirate any more. Maybe you never were. You treat me like no one else has before. You gave me a choice. You've kind and you've protected me. I've never had that before."

He took a deep breath and put one hand over hers. With his other hand he tucked a strand of hair behind her ear. "I treat you as you should be treated," he said. "But I am still taking you to an unknown destination.

She smiled and shifted closer to him. "I trust you, Captain, I always have," she whispered. "I love you. So I will go with you to wherever you're taking me."

He smiled a bittersweet smile that made him look younger. He squeezed her hand on his chest. "You have no idea how happy that makes me. I love you, Tahira."

She laughed again, feeling warm inside. She rested her forehead on his chest. He kissed the top of her head.

"I suppose we should get back to your ship now," she said, after a few moments. She looked out to where the boat waited beyond the breakers. "Your men are staring at us."

"Aye, that they are," he said. He raised one arm and waved, grunting in pain.

"Really, what is wrong?" she asked, her gaze snapping to his face. "I can help you. What happened during the battle?"

"There are many reasons I didn't want you to see it, and injuries is one of them," he said. "But thankfully, we borrowed a surgeon from a passing ship and he stitched us all back up."

"Does that mean you captured him?" she asked, half-exasperated.

"No, it means we borrowed him," he said with a crooked smile. "Once his work was done, we let them go."

"I'll bet that surprised them more than anything," she said.

He looked out to sea to check on the progress of his boat as it battled through the breakers of the tide going out. He shook his head. "Some of my men weren't happy with it," he said. "They seemed to feel that letting a ship go unscathed could send a message of weakness." He smiled as the boat finally got through the breakers and started coasting to the beach. "Many harder captains than I would have sacked and burned that ship, even while injured."

Scudamore ran over before she could answer. "Come, sir, let's away," he said. "There's a storm coming."

Captain Haefen looked up at the sky, which Tahira just noticed was starting to gray. "Aye, let's away."

***

The storm raged all night, heavier and harder than the last storm. But Captain Haefen ordered *Royal Conlan* to remain at anchor, with a skeleton watch on deck to mind the storm and the reefed sails. The rest of the crew battened down the hatches and retreated belowdecks.

Most turned into their hammocks and swung in time with the storm. Some were seasick for the first time in years. Tahira sat outside the galley with Copper, learning about the new plants and herbs she'd acquired on the island. Gradually, the more injured pirates gravitated to sitting around her, including Captain Haefen. Tahira smiled inwardly at their boy-like eagerness.

Captain Haefen's ribs were nearly broken and very bruised, and he had a deep cut on his ankle. Goss had reopened his forehead wound. Sam Morwell's wrapped arm was now full of splinters, and Tahira set Ransome the task of picking them out by the light of a lantern. Rance's arm gash from the first battle was starting to fester, but he refused to let her touch it. Haak, Dugan, and Ardeon had broken fingers, which Tahira splinted so delicately they didn't even feel pain.

Cosins was completely black and blue with bruises. Tahira thought his injuries were merely from the battle, but his mouth was also bleeding, something she hadn't seen in a long time. Even as he explained all the pains in his body, a tooth fell out and he spit it across the deck. Tahira handed him one of the fruits from the island and told him to eat it right away.

"Too little food," she whispered to herself. After Cosins, she kept her eye on the other pirates, looking for signs of the same illness, but none of the others had it. Not yet, at least.

Cromby, James, Nositer, Huggit, Mundon, and High all had cutlass injuries. Tahira bathed their wounds in salt water—ignoring their choices of words—before smearing them with a salve and wrapping them up. Ashplant had lost an eye and kept bumping into things until Captain Haefen took pity on him and ordered him to the sick list until he got his balance back. Tahira cleaned the bloody socket and wrapped him back up.

As the night wore on, the air grew so thick and rank and hot that Tahira begged to open the gun ports to let in fresh air.

Finally, all the pirates were in their hammocks. The cacophony of snoring nearly drowned out the storm. Tahira sat down next to Captain Haefen, their backs against the galley bulkhead, with wind and water blowing across them from the open gun ports.

She was exhausted. She put her head on his shoulder and closed her eyes. It felt good to be close to him. It felt good to love him. It felt good to be loved by him.

Just as sleep was starting to cement her eyes and sound was starting to crowd out of her ears, he put his hand on her knee. She started and grabbed his wrist. He chuckled and she looked at him, blinking.

"Sorry to wake you," he said. "Why don't you go into your cabin? It's almost dawn, and the storm is over."

"All right," she said.

He pulled her to her feet and she rubbed one eye with the heel of her hand. "Thank you for healing my crew again," he said.

"Of course," she said. "Are we setting sail?"

"Aye, as soon as I have enough of the crew awake," he said. "And then I'll take you where we're going." He kissed her once then climbed the hatchway ladder. She entered her cabin and locked the door. She was asleep almost before she lay down.

Chapter Nineteen

Sometime later that day, Tahira was wakened by cannon fire. She thought at first that the pirates were doing gunnery practice. But no subsequent volleys followed. And instead of hearing commands she heard running, shouting, panicked voices. She sat up just as the ship heeled over and she fell against the wall.

Something was wrong.

Tahira changed into her dress from Jaazah, unlocked her cabin, and ran to the hatchway ladder. Afternoon sun was streaming down onto her, but it was partially blocked by shadows. Tahira looked up with her hand on the ladder and saw Scudamore standing next to the hatch. Her movements caught his eye and he looked down at her.

His eyes widened and Tahira noticed that his gold hoop had been ripped out of his ear. Blood ran down the side of his neck onto his shoulder. He held up a finger, indicating that she should remain where she was, then turned his attention, like the rest of the pirates she could see, to the port rail. She listened.

"Don't tell me the captain is still abed," said an unfamiliar voice. Tahira shuddered at the sound; it was grating and harsh, reminiscent of Master Gall.

"No, sir," said Captain Haefen. His voice was distant, as if he was near the bow. "He's just disinclined to face you when you come with such hostilities."

"Where are ye?" the unfamiliar voice shouted. Tahira heard a blade being unsheathed. "Show yerself, Haefen, or this seaman dies!"

Tahira heard a grunt, and then a terrible scream. The crew of the *Royal Conlan* shouted, but none of them moved. The shouts died out all at once, and then she heard a heavy thud on the deck. Complete silence followed.

She couldn't bear it. She silently climbed the hatchway ladder until her head just cleared the deck and she could see through the sea of legs in front of her.

Standing against the port rail was a pirate captain so large he comically dwarfed the men standing nearest him. All his clothing, weapons, and his hair were black, except for his coat, which was so red it dazzled in the sun. In one hand he held a black dagger, dripping blood from its blade. In the other hand he held what looked like a bleeding human heart. At his feet lay a dead pirate.

Tahira's empty stomach heaved and she clapped a hand over her mouth. She looked up at Scudamore, who motioned with his hand that she should go back down.

"You didn't need to do that, Soto," Captain Haefen said, his voice choked. Tahira saw his legs moving out of the crowd of his crew toward the other captain, Soto. "Have you never heard of giving a man a chance?"

"Not since I was a child," Soto said. Tahira saw his hand raise the heart to his mouth and looked away before she saw what he was going to do. The crew cringed but remained still and silent.

Why had no one rushed forward to save the pirate? Why were they standing still now? Tahira looked more carefully around her, and soon identified why; it seemed all of Soto's crew had boarded the *Royal Conlan*, effectively surrounding her crew with weapons and teeth and drunken rage. Tahira shrunk down a step.

"Now that I've got your attention, we can get to business," Soto said. Someone in front of Tahira shifted and she saw Soto, his mouth ringed in red, toss the heart over his shoulder into the sea.

"What do you want, Soto?" Captain Haefen asked. Unlike when Nave came onto the ship, there was no swagger in Captain Haefen, no commanding presence in his stance. He looked afraid. But then Soto took a step toward Captain Haefen and rage replaced his fear.

"I want to avenge Nave," Soto said.

Captain Haefen's commanding presence returned in full. "Nave has no need to be avenged," he said. "He attacked me to avenge his son, which he accomplished with his death. You have no business here."

"I think you'll find I do," Soto said. "Nave told me about a wench that you have. She wasn't on your ship during the battle. Nave tasked me to find her."

Tahira heard Scudamore suck in his breath.

"I have no woman aboard my ship," Captain Haefen said with such conviction that even Tahira believed him.

Soto seemed to believe him too, for he took a step back. "What have ye done with her?"

"I marooned her," Captain Haefen said. "She's probably dead by now. I'm sorry you went to all this trouble."

"That wench and avenging Nave were not my only reasons for coming," Soto said, stepping forward again, his voice harsher than before. "I want to prove that you're still a pirate captain."

"I think letting me captain my ship will prove that," Captain Haefen said, his jaw clenched. "But since you've been following me since dawn I take it that's not enough for you."

"It isn't," Soto said.

He moved so fast Tahira almost missed it. Soto darted forward, seized Captain Haefen and threw him over the railing. There was a sickening thud as he landed in a waiting boat. Tahira's hands flew over her mouth, barely in time to muffle her scream.

Soto signaled to his crew, who swarmed like beetles over the port rail. Finally, there was only Soto left. He gave the *Royal Conlan* one last sneer and turned to follow his crew.

Tahira didn't know when she had climbed all the way up the hatchway ladder. She pushed past Scudamore, heading for Soto.

"Wait!" she called. She hadn't gotten far when Scudamore grabbed her from behind. He pinned her arms to her sides and hauled her back.

"Quiet, if you want to live," he hissed in her ear.

Soto stopped and slowly turned around. "Did I just hear a woman?"

Scudamore let go of Tahira and pushed through the pirates to face Soto. "No sir," he said without a hint of panic in his voice. "That was our cabin boy."

"And was he defying me?"

"No sir, he was asking *me* to wait," Scudamore said. "You see, I was taking him below. He didn't want to leave before he saw such a magnificent captain as yourself leaving this ship."

Captain Soto straightened up in pride. He leaned over a little to see around Scudamore to where Tahira stood hidden among the pirates.

"Well lad, choose your captains better in future," he said. He passed his gaze over the rest of the crew. "And don't worry, men, I will release your captain soon enough."

Soto climbed over the rail into the waiting boat. Tahira and the rest of the crew waited in silence while Soto's men re-boarded their ship. Her heart caught in her chest as she watched Captain Haefen's unconscious body being dragged aboard. Distantly they heard Soto shouting orders. Suddenly the pirates around her were ablaze with movement.

"All hands down!" Scudamore shouted. He darted back to her, grabbed her, and threw her down on the deck.

Cannon fire suddenly erupted from Soto's ship and *Royal Conlan* shuddered. Tahira screamed and covered her head with an arm. Above her through the thundering and whistling of cannonballs she heard Scudamore grunt, then felt him fall half on top of her.

Just as suddenly as it started, Soto's broadside stopped. Scudamore pulled Tahira to her feet and shoved her toward the hatch.

"Get below!" he said, following behind her. Pirates were running around the gun deck. Somewhere Tahira heard running water and saw light coming from somewhere near the stern. Scudamore pushed Tahira from behind, guiding her through the confusion. "Get in your cabin, and do not come out until I come for you."

"You can't order me!" Tahira said, shaking his hand off.

"Yes, I can," Scudamore said. He opened the door of Tahira's cabin and pushed her inside. "Because I am the captain now. And if something happens to you under my watch, it will not go well for me. Now stay there."

"Wait," Tahira said, grabbing his arm as he made to leave. "Why did you tell me to be quiet?"

Scudamore turned back to her, impatient. "Because Captain Soto hates women," he said. "If he knew that you were on board, if he saw you, he would have killed you. That's why he asked for you. And I spared you because Haefen would kill *me* if you died."

Tahira couldn't help but smile a little. "I understand," she said. "And I will stay here."

Scudamore's expression softened and he gave her a terse nod. Tahira closed and locked her cabin door. She sat cross-legged on her bed and put her head in her hands.

After the action of the upper deck, she felt ablaze with emotions: terror at listening to Soto brutally murdering a man; shaken from the broadside; and most of all, bereavement at losing Captain Haefen again. She did not know Soto, but her brief encounter of him showed her that he might just kill her Captain.

Tears came to her eyes and she leaned back against the wall, her legs stretched out in front of her. She was alone again. Alone, and unprotected. She shuddered at the thought.

She decided she'd go see Scudamore when things quieted down, but it seemed like the ship wouldn't quiet down. After what felt like hours of hearing the pumps and hammers, she left her cabin. There were several holes in the starboard side of the gun deck, and Ravon was directing the repairs. The running water she'd heard earlier had slowed, but the pumps were still working. She guessed they'd been hit at or below the waterline.

She found Scudamore at the helm.

"Where are we going?" she asked.

"After Soto," Scudamore said. He looked up at the sails; Tahira noticed that all of them were bellied out. "We won't be able to catch up quickly, though, even though we're crowding sail. He's had too much of a head start."

"He probably planned it that way," Tahira said. Her eyes traveled down onto the deck where the murdered pirate still lay. "Who was it?"

"Richardson."

Tahira gasped. Without planning to she walked over to him. Someone had brought his hammock up, but he hadn't been sewn up in it yet. This was the first time she'd seen him since Alycia died. She touched his cold forehead with her fingertips, trying not to look at the gaping hole in his chest where Soto had carved out his heart. His blood had coagulated on and around him.

"I'm sorry you had to die like that, Richardson," she whispered.

She looked around her. All the pirates were busy handling or repairing the ship. There was no one to attend to Richardson.

Tahira made her way down to the sailmaker's storeroom and found a bone needle and thick black thread. She tucked them into her pocket, then collected a cannonball from the powder room. No one paid her any mind. Not until she'd wrapped Richardson into his hammock, placed the cannonball at his feet, and started sewing. She was aware of pirates coming to stand around her to watch, but no one made a sound. She stopped sewing once she'd reached Richardson's collarbone and sat back on her heels, looking up at last.

Scudamore stood closest to her, almost smiling. But Rance, behind him, was glaring with open hatred. Scudamore held down his hand to her and she allowed him to stand her up. Still no one spoke, but a quick glance showed Tahira that the pirates around her had been friends of Richardson.

"I'm sorry," she said. "It wasn't fair for him to die this way."

"Big words coming from you," Rance growled. "Are you trying to get back at him for your friend?"

Tahira looked at Rance, at a loss for why he was showing her so much hatred. "I did this to help him and you," she said. "But if my help is not appreciated, I'll not burden you with it."

She was now getting more than one hateful glance. She suddenly didn't feel safe, even standing close to Scudamore. As quickly as she could without running, she went down the hatchway and into her cabin.

***

The noises from the crew gradually moved from those of repairing to those of normal work. But later that evening, Tahira heard someone down in the hold beneath her cabin. Moments later came exulting shouts. Soon, above her head and outside her door the pirates became louder and louder. She heard the clinks of glass bottles, poorly-sung sea shanties, shots, and stomping.

In moments she deduced what was going on: the pirates had broken into the rum and were getting roaring drunk.

She gritted her teeth, all the terrible stories she'd heard from the Pirate Women about drunken pirates coming to her mind. She unlocked her door and dashed into the galley for something to eat before it was too dangerous for her, relaxing only when she'd locked her door again.

The longer the drinking went on, the louder the pirates got. Tahira could hear every word, every curse, and every challenge quite clearly. Then she heard their plans:

"We've got a woman aboard!"

"She'll make excellent sport." That sounded like Rance.

"Haefen's not here!"

"Get Haefen's woman!" That was definitely the bosun.

Tahira gasped, fear momentarily gripping her heart. She didn't know what they would do to her, but she wasn't going to give them the chance to do it. She moved her bed to block the door; the pirates could only come in one at a time, and after years of lifting boulders, she was sure she could fight them off, drunk as they sounded.

Dimly, she wondered where Scudamore was.

Almost before she was ready, the pirates started pounding on her door. They shouted to her, entreating her to open her door like a good girl, and when she didn't respond their pounding increased. The door started to give.

Tahira took a deep steadying breath as it burst open.

The first pirate into her cabin was Rance. He kicked her bed aside as easily as if it were an empty barrel and came at her. Tahira gave him a good kick with her heel, causing him to scream and fall to his knees, holding himself. But she only had a moment to celebrate. The next pirate launched himself over the incapacitated bosun and came at her from above.

She turned to the side so that he landed across her shoulders. She grabbed his breeches and one arm and turned around so that his head was now toward the door, hearing his limbs and head hitting the walls and other pirates. With a yell she launched him off her shoulders and out the door. He landed on his head with a sickening thud.

She kicked the next two pirates as they came through the door, and they were pulled away by the others.

The pirate with the amputated finger came in teeth and fists first. She dodged his fists easily, bringing her own up into his nose as he staggered. While he yelled and covered his face with his hands, Tahira hooked one elbow around his neck from behind and flexed her arm. The pirate moved his hands from his nose to her arm, trying to free his neck. He fell to his knees as Tahira squeezed tighter.

She heard angry shouts from the other pirates waiting to enter. One more bold pirate, Withy, flew through the door. But he was slow. As he came at her, Tahira raised her other hand and caught him tight around the throat.

As soon as the pirates saw she had two of the crew tight by the necks, their drunken lust turned to worry.

"Leave me alone," Tahira said while the two men gasped for breath. "I don't want to hurt you, but I *will* defend myself."

She looked at all the faces she could see. Some looked murderous, and some looked serious. She released the pirate in her elbow. He fell forward, coughing, then slowly crawled out of her cabin. Withy was looking close to unconsciousness. She shoved him out of her cabin, where he tripped over someone and fell to the deck.

Tahira closed the splintered and battered door and relocked it as best she could, knowing it wouldn't hold against another attack. She rested her forehead against the wood, breathing hard.

She had injured six pirates, and she dismayed that she'd had to fight at all.

Hadn't Captain Haefen's orders been enough? But perhaps drunken pirates didn't remember orders very well. She'd never seen the crew so lawless as now; *this* was how she thought *Royal Conlan* would be when she boarded. A big part of her feared for her safety. She hadn't seen Scudamore, and could only hope he was incapacitated somewhere and couldn't come to her rescue, for she had thought he, at least, could be trusted.

Tahira repositioned her bed and fell onto it, curled up into a ball. She suddenly felt small and weak. She missed Captain Haefen more than ever. Her arms and hands were shaking. Around her the drunken party raged on. Perhaps their attack on her cabin had already been washed away in rum. Despite the noise, she fell asleep.

Chapter Twenty

Tahira started awake when she heard hammering on the door. Her heart jumped as she remembered the night before.

"Who is it?" she called.

"Scudamore," came the answer.

In that one word, Tahira couldn't hear much of his tone. "Are you drunk?" she asked, her heart calming; it was good to know Scudamore was alive.

"No."

"What do you want?" She sat up and put her head in her hands, her arms sore.

"I came to tell you that the crew has had a vote," Scudamore said. "They have voted you as Captain."

Tahira straightened up. "Captain of what?"

"Of this ship," Scudamore said. He sounded irritated. "Since Haefen's been taken the crew voted you in."

"Scudamore, I am not a candidate." Tahira slid off the bed and stepped toward the door. "Tell them I decline. You should be the captain. You're the quartermaster."

"Aye, I am, but the crew wants you."

"And why would they want me?"

Scudamore paused for a moment, and Tahira wondered if any other pirates were there, listening. "Because they seem to think you can lead them," he said. "The crew votes in who they want, no matter who was second in command."

"Go back to the crew, talk them into making you Captain," Tahira said.

"I tried," Scudamore said. Tahira thought she heard him shuffling his feet. "They nearly hanged me for mutiny."

Tahira had no answer for that. She rested her forehead against the door, not knowing what to say. It made no sense for them to want her as Captain. She did not want that responsibility.

"Please come out, Miss," Scudamore said, startling her slightly. "The crew is waiting for you."

"I don't want to talk to them," Tahira said. "I don't want to be their captain."

"They will force you, if necessary," Scudamore said. His voice carried a hint of a threat.

Tahira thought about what they could do. Unreasonable though pirates were, they could be convincing in mean ways. "Very well," she said. "I'll come out."

The entire crew was congregated in the aft part of the gun deck, clustered closer than was probably comfortable. Scudamore, sporting a brilliant black eye and a clean but earhoop-less ear, pointed to a small barrel in front of the pirates then held out his hand to her. She took it and stepped up onto the barrel, her other hand gripping the beams above her head to keep her balance.

"As many of you might remember, you attacked me last night," she said, her voice carrying around the deck. "And today you made me your Captain. I don't understand why. But I warn you, if what happened last night happens again, I will throw every drop of rum overboard. You had no right to disobey Captain Haefen's orders, and you had no right to attack me."

She paused to let her words sink in, surprised at the authority in her voice. After a life of doing only what she was told, and keeping forcibly silent, she was now speaking her mind. There was a time she would have been punished for it, but now, she knew it was the right thing to do.

"As of yesterday, we were sailing after Soto," she said. "I don't know what plans you've made as a crew. But I say we should rescue Captain Haefen, or at least be nearby when he is released."

She heard murmurs among the crew but none spoke up, even when she asked them to.

"That's all I have to say," she said. "Please return to your work."

The crew pushed each other to the ladder. Tahira saw a few disgruntled faces, but most of them looked pleased. Scudamore, who had been standing by her this whole time, started to step away, but she grabbed his arm and he stopped.

"What are my duties?" she asked.

Scudamore raised his eyebrows. "Don't you know? You've been watching us for months."

"I'm not a sailor," she said. "If you want me to be Captain, you're going to have to tell me how."

"You'll do it, then?" Scudamore asked.

Tahira stepped down from the barrel. "Not that I have much of a choice, but yes," she said. "Will you help me?"

Scudamore straightened up, his chin raised. "Aye."

He led the way up the hatchway and down to the captain's cabin. He pointed to Captain Haefen's desk, littered with papers, a leather folder, and a few maps.

"Start by familiarizing yourself with the inventory and the charts and logs," he said, turning to leave the cabin. "Once you've done that come out and I'll show you the rigging."

"What are the charts and logs?" Tahira asked, her hands fluttering between the leather folder and a map.

"The charts tell us where we are and where we've been, and the log details what has been done every day," Scudamore said. "The captain is in charge of keeping those."

Tahira gaped at him for a moment. "I can't, Scudamore. I don't know how to read. Could you keep it?"

Scudamore stared at her with an impassive face. Then he shrugged. "I can't either," he said. "We'll leave it for Haefen."

"Is Captain Haefen unusual for being able to read?" Tahira asked, running her hand down one paper, admiring the captain's handwriting.

Scudamore nodded.

Tahira considered him for a few moments. "Scudamore, why did the crew vote me in as Captain, really?"

The quartermaster stared at her again. "I think most of the crew is afraid of you."

That surprised her. "Why would they be afraid of me? What have I done?"

Scudamore looked down at his feet, shifting them, his hands clasped behind his back. "We're not used to meeting women like you," he said, looking up at her. "The women we know are not strong, not smart, and never fight back. Most of the crew thinks that having you as Captain is safer than angering you."

Tahira sat down at the desk. "And what about you? Do you fear me?"

Scudamore looked for a moment like he was going to smile. "I respect you," he said. "Captain," he added.

Tahira shook her head. "That doesn't sound right."

Scudamore considered her for several long moments. Tahira considered asking him about the night before.

"Come up to the quarterdeck," he said before she could speak. "It's easier to show you the rigging from there." He led the way up to the quarterdeck where he stood behind the helmsman, his feet spread apart. Tahira stood next to him, her feet also spread, but she was having a harder time keeping her balance than he was.

Scudamore pointed to the mainmast in front of them. "The mainmast has two different sails."

"Yes," Tahira said. "Fore-and-aft mainsail and a square-rigged topsail and topgallant. The foremast is all square-rigged. The sails, from bottom to top, are the foresail, then the fore topsail, then the foretopgallant."

"Aye," Scudamore said, looking at her, impressed. "You've picked this up."

"I have been here a while," Tahira said. "But I haven't figured out why you're not struggling with your balance."

"It's because I'm on the centerline," Scudamore said. He stepped to the side and gestured for Tahira to take his place. At once she felt her balance settle as she found the center of the ship. It almost felt like she was standing on a heartbeat.

"Oh, that's better," she said.

"Tell me about the staysails," Scudamore said.

"They're the triangular sails between the masts," Tahira said, pointing them out. "They help hold up the masts, and are attached to the yards by rings so they slide for repositioning."

She and Scudamore stood on the quarterdeck for quite some time, Scudamore testing her knowledge of the rigging. Just as they finished, the crew was piped to dinner and Scudamore hurried off.

"Where to, Captain?" the helmsman, Peter la Fever, asked.

Tahira stared at him. "Stay your course," she said. "Go after Captain Haefen."

"Aye, ma'am," la Fever said, returning his gaze to his duty.

Scudamore came back onto the quarterdeck, holding a bowl of meat and biscuit in his hand. "Here you are," he said, handing it to her.

"Thank you," Tahira said slowly. "You've never done that before."

"I always bring the captain his dinner," Scudamore said.

He stood next to her while she ate, then took her bowl away. It was strange to be served like that.

But though Scudamore talked to her while doing his duty to her as quartermaster, none of the rest of the crew did. They looked at her when she spoke to them, they obeyed her orders, and thankfully they did not try to attack or even touch her; even Rance was keeping his distance. But still the crew would not speak to her. Tahira suddenly realized just how valuable the sparse conversations with Captain Haefen were to her, for though she was surrounded by seventy-four men, she felt alone.

***

The next afternoon, Tahira found Copper in the galley with his feet on the table, drinking from a glass bottle. His gaze was more or less focused as she closed the door behind her, but he sprang drunkenly to his feet when he finally noticed her.

"Captain," he said, setting his bottle on the table.

"Mr. Copper," Tahira said, glancing around the galley. "How is our food supply?"

"Our food stores are good," Copper said.

"But the men are getting sick," Tahira said. She had noticed more and more men becoming sick with too little food in just the last few days. "What can you do?"

Copper cocked his head to the side, blinking back the rum. "What illness is it?"

"The men aren't getting enough," Tahira said.

"Enough to eat, ma'am?"

"No," Tahira said, not sure how to explain it, for Old Joche hadn't been able to explain it either. "Enough of something different from meat and biscuit." She looked down at a plate of biscuits on the table. She reached out to touch one but pulled back her hand when she looked closer. "These biscuits are full of bugs." She looked up at Copper. "I've never seen biscuits this bad. Show me what you have."

Copper saluted clumsily and stumped around the galley, showing Tahira all the barrels of salt meat, flour, water, molasses, hardtack, and a small assortment of fresh vegetables and fruits.

"This isn't all the food on the ship, is it?" she asked.

Copper shook his head. "No, ma'am, there's more stores down in the hold."

"What are these for?" Tahira asked, pointing at the fruits and vegetables.

Copper peered into the barrel. "Oh, that's for making salmagundi."

"What?" Tahira wrinkled her nose at the sound of the dish.

"I assure you, it tastes better than it sounds," Copper said.

"Why haven't I eaten it?"

"Because it can only be made when we have fresh food," Copper said.

"Which we have had since Turtle Island," Tahira said. "Let's make it, the men need these foods. They're getting sick because they're not eating them."

In the deepest corner of the galley, she found a wardrobe full of more fruits and vegetables, spices, fancy dried meats, sugar, and even some fresh meat. But her attention was drawn to a barrel of orange orbs.

"Oranges," she said, holding one in her hand. Memories of Old Joche's cook-space in the healer's house flooded her mind. She held out the orange to Copper. "You have oranges," she said. "Why aren't the men eating them?"

"This is the steward's cupboard," Copper said. "The oranges and everything else in there, is for the captain—for you."

Tahira huffed. She turned to look at the contents of the wardrobe again. All that food for one person, all the food that could help the crew stay healthy. She suddenly got an idea. She replaced the orange in its barrel and marched out the galley door.

"Ransome!" she shouted up the hatchway. "Ransome, come to the galley!"

Somewhere above her head she heard running footsteps. She returned to the galley, and a few moments later Ransome entered, breathless and nervous-looking. He straightened his clothes and pulled off his hat, looking at Tahira warily. The sight made Tahira's heart hurt, but she pushed that away for now.

"Gentlemen, we are going to improve our food," she said, spreading her hands on the table and looking back and forth between Ransome and Copper. "We are going to make sure that the men don't continue getting sick."

Copper looked somewhere between offended and intrigued. "How are we going to do that, Captain?" he asked.

"Ransome, you see those oranges?" Tahira asked.

Ransome leaned around her to look, then straightened and nodded. "Yes, ma'am."

"Get your knife and cut all of them in half," Tahira said. She reached under the table and grabbed two of the buckets that Copper kept there. She placed both on the table and pushed one toward Ransome. "Put them in this bucket. Mr. Copper," she said, pushing the other bucket toward him. "You and I are going to juice them."

"And then what, ma'am?" Copper asked, still blinking away the drink. "I doubt you can get the men to drink juice instead of rum."

"No, we're going to throw out all the old biscuits and make new ones," Tahira said, with a little smile. "But we're going to use the juice instead of water."

Ransome and Copper looked at each other. "Captain, do you think that will work?" Copper asked at last.

"I do," Tahira said. "Trust me."

Surprisingly, Copper straightened up and saluted, his gaze intent on her face. "Of course, ma'am."

Tahira smiled. "Then let's get to work."

Ransome cut the oranges in half and pushed them down the table for Copper and Tahira to squeeze. Soon the galley was awash in the sweet smell of the oranges. Tahira bit her lip against the sting as orange juice found minute cuts on her hands.

"Captain, how are we going to cook the biscuits?" Ransome asked. "We've never made hardtack on board ship before."

Tahira looked at him; his gaze was still intent on his work, as though frightened of looking away. She wanted to tell him not to be so afraid of her.

"On the wood stove," Tahira said, pointing with a dripping finger. "I learned how to cook on one."

She glanced at Copper just in time to see a relieved expression fade. For all his title as the cook, Tahira began to wonder how much cooking Copper actually did, and how much of his job was rationing what they already had.

Once the oranges had been juiced, Tahira set about making the biscuits. She had Ransome and Copper bring her the flour and salt and a large bowl to mix it all up in. She poured the orange juice into the bowl first, and then added the flour until the ratio was correct. She threw in a few pinches of salt and started mixing with her hands, watching with pleasure as the lumpy dough turned orange. In her mind's eye she saw Old Joche's gnarled hands showing her this technique, patiently teaching a stubborn girl to make food.

"Now I'll need something to roll out the dough thin, and then something to cut the dough into biscuits," Tahira said.

Copper stepped away from the table and returned with a long smooth wood stick about the length of Tahira's forearm, and a piece of metal that had been pounded thin and formed into a circle. Tahira paused in her mixing to pick it up and inspect it.

"It cuts the biscuits," Copper said.

"Oh. We used a knife," Tahira said.

"That would take a long time," Copper said slowly.

"It did." Tahira finished mixing and wiped the dough off her hands. "Ransome, will you roll the dough out on the table?" she said, handing the cabin boy the smooth stick.

Ransome nodded and got to work. Tahira turned to the stove. She showed Copper how many logs to add, and how hot the fire should be. Copper brought out his biscuit pans and set them on the table.

"Could you show me how to cut these?" she asked Copper, holding up the metal circle. He nodded and switched places with Ransome. He pushed the metal circle into the dough, then picked it up, with the dough nestled inside. Copper held out the circle over Tahira's hand and the dough fell into her palm.

"I've never seen anything like that," Tahira said, placing the biscuit on the pan and watching Copper cut out three more in quick succession. "I wish I'd had something like that."

"Where did you learn how to do this?" Ransome asked, scooting closer to watch her.

Tahira smiled a little. "I learned in the life I had before I came to sea," she said. "A kind woman taught me how to cook biscuits, and to use orange juice in them. They saved my life on a number of occasions."

For the next several minutes Tahira and Ransome worked together, rolling out the dough, cutting biscuits, until the two pans were full. Then she and Copper placed the pans over the fire with Ransome to watch over them.

"Now what?" Ransome asked when the biscuits were done.

"We let them cool, and then we eat them," Tahira said. "Ransome, I'm leaving you in charge of cooking the rest of the biscuits."

The cabin boy nodded and got to work. Tahira turned to Copper.

"This salmagundi you mentioned," she said. "We should make it now."

Copper opened his mouth to argue but then thought better of it. He stumped over to the barrels of fresh foods and carried them to the table. Ransome moved over to make room for them.

"What is salmagundi?" Tahira asked, grabbing some knives.

"It's a dish made from what we have on hand," Copper said. He reached under the table and pulled out another large bowl. He placed it on the table and started dicing up the fresh meats from the steward's cupboard. "It tastes different every time because of that." Tahira had never seen someone cut meat so quickly, and she stood mesmerized while Copper cut, startling when his hand suddenly pointed across her face. "Get that bottle of wine."

Tahira tore her attention from his hands and found the wine. Copper directed her to open it and pour most of its contents on top of the meat.

"What are all these?" Tahira asked, pointing to the meats piling up in the bowl.

"This is chicken, and this is turtle meat," Copper said, pointing. He glanced up and saw Tahira's nose starting to wrinkle in distaste. "How 'bout I stop telling you what you'll be eating? It'll taste better that way."

"All right," Tahira said. Copper finished cutting up the meat and mixed them and the wine together with his hands.

Suddenly the whole galley shifted violently from side to side. The pan Ransome had been filling fell onto his foot with a loud bang and he hopped around yelping and swearing. Copper managed to save the bowl of meat and wine, but everything else tumbled to the floor.

"What's happening?" Tahira shouted above the clanging of pots and pans. One of the logs rolled out of the fire and Tahira ran to put it back in before the galley caught fire.

"Storm!" Copper shouted. "We've got to stop cooking for now, it's too dangerous. Boy, get sand on that fire and help me batten down."

The galley door opened and Scudamore leaned in. "Captain!" he shouted. "We need you on deck!" He held out a tarred-over heavy canvas coat and Tahira took it, pulling it on as she followed Scudamore.

The ship was pitching violently and waves were crashing over the railings. Tahira could see pirates high in the rigging, desperately trying to reef the sails. Scudamore grabbed her arm and dragged her up to the helm.

"Orders!" he shouted at her.

Tahira could feel panic rising inside her. She knew nothing about storms at sea. The sight of it frightened her: the dark sky lit occasionally by lightning, the faint cries of pirates as they clung to the masts and yards, the waves reaching the height of the maintop before crashing onto the deck. But most terrifying was that the entire ship was depending on her. She felt Scudamore hitting her shoulder and shouting at her, but when she turned to him, she had nothing to offer.

"You're the captain now!" Scudamore shouted, angry. "Tell us what to do!"

"I don't know what to do," Tahira said. A white-capped wave washed over the taffrail but lost momentum at her knees. "You know how this ship works."

"But I can do nothing without your authority," Scudamore said.

He reached down and grabbed the speaking trumpet before it rolled onto the lower deck. La Fever was desperately trying to keep the wheel, but was quickly losing to the storm.

"Which way do we need to go?" Tahira asked. Scudamore pointed off the port quarter. "Then go that way!" she said. "We have to get to Captain Haefen."

"We won't get to him if we don't outlive this storm," Scudamore growled, looking out on the deck. Tahira followed his gaze, where she saw a wave crash right through the open hatchway.

She grabbed the trumpet from Scudamore. "Batten down the hatches!" she yelled into it.

Several pirates stepped to immediately, shutting the hatchway and nailing heavy canvas over it. Tahira looked around again. If they needed to go a few points to port, then they needed the ship to hold still in this storm. But she had no idea how to do it. She hit Scudamore on the shoulder until he stopped yelling to the helmsman and looked at her.

"We have to go that way," she said, pointing off the port quarter. "Can't we reef all the sails, turn the ship that way, and ride out the storm?" Scudamore shook his head. "What about dropping the anchor where we are?"

"She'll break free," Scudamore shouted. Lightning flashed overhead and Tahira saw he was looking at her with anger and disappointment.

"If my authority is what you need, then you have it!" she shouted, pushing the trumpet into his chest. "Do what needs to be done."

Scudamore looked hard at her for another moment or two, then stepped around her, raising the trumpet as he went. Another wave washed over the taffrail and hit Tahira, knocking her to her knees against the railing. She watched as Scudamore's unintelligible shouts were carried out. Pirates ran up and down the rigging with more confidence than before, pulling in all sails but the forestaysail.

"Captain!" la Fever shouted. Tahira barely heard him over the storm, but when she turned to face him, he was beckoning to her with jerks of his head. Tahira scrambled to her feet and staggered to him. "I need your strength to hold the helm!"

Tahira nodded and stepped beside him, the thunder loud in her ears. She grabbed two spokes of the helm and prepared herself for a long, hard fight. La Fever kept his eye on the compass, shouting to her whenever a course correction was needed to keep *Royal Conlan*'s head into the wind.

A wet figure crawled up onto the quarterdeck, and headed straight for her. Tahira tore her eyes away from la Fever's instructions and recognized Rance. Her heart froze as she saw him reaching for her, though her body was too numb from cold rain to feel his grasping hands. But by the glances over his shoulder, she knew he intended to throw her overboard. He pulled harder and harder at her, and her hands started to give way. Desperately she threw her elbow toward his face, and felt a stinging pain as it connected.

Lightning flashed in the sky as Rance reeled back a step and then lunged for her again. Tahira screamed.

Beside her she heard la Fever yell; he had finally noticed Rance. La Fever kicked out and Rance flailed backward. The next wave over the taffrail washed Rance down onto the main deck, where he remained. Tahira didn't look toward him again, but she could almost feel the waves of hate coming off him.

It was dawn before the last of the storm's harsh winds finally blew out. Tahira collapsed to the deck against the helm, shaking, as she heard pirates cheering in the upper rigging.

"Now, let's see what Copper has for us," la Fever said.

"Thank you for helping me with Rance, that can't have been easy for you," Tahira said, staggering upright again. "But Copper stopped cooking when the storm hit."

"He's resourceful, that Copper," la Fever said, waving away her thanks.

As Tahira descended the steps, she realized that all the pirates were making their way toward the galley, all of them bedraggled and wet. Tahira darted ahead of them and opened the galley first, somewhat trepidatious at what she might find.

She was greeted by a warm, strong smell that stopped her in her tracks, framed in the galley doorway, the crew mumbling hungrily behind her. She couldn't identify all the smells, but it smelled good in an odd sort of way.

Ransome turned around from the stove, sweating, holding a pan of finished biscuits. Behind him, Copper was holding his deepest pot, full to the brim with the ugliest assortment of colors Tahira had ever seen.

"Salmagundi!" Copper announced.

"Just in time," Tahira said, smiling. She turned around and faced the crew. "Everyone back out on deck," she said. "We'll bring the food up to you."

The pirates looked at one another before complying, and Tahira remembered that this wasn't how food was usually distributed. But she knew this method would work, for it was how meals were served in the slave compounds. She stepped into the galley and helped Copper and Ransome carry the pot and biscuits out onto deck. The crew had gathered around the hatchway with their mess kits, and Tahira, Copper, and Ransome quickly dished out the salmagundi and biscuits.

At first the men were too tired to realize what they were eating. But as the hot food hit their bellies and started pushing back the numbness from the night's storm, their eyebrows raised and they slowed their eating to savor it. Most looked impressed.

Tahira took off her canvas coat and hung it over a shroud. She wrung out her hair over the side then took her bowl and found Scudamore sitting cross-legged on the deck.

"Why did you do that?" she asked him. He looked up at her. "Why did you make me be the captain in the middle of that storm? We all know you're better suited."

Scudamore slowly swallowed his food. "I wanted to see what you were made of."

"I'm not made of Captain material," Tahira said. "I don't want to be the captain." Dimly she was aware that half the crew was listening in. "I don't appreciate what you did to me, Scudamore, and I hope you will never do that again."

Scudamore looked at her long and hard before standing up stiffly. "Are you saying you'll give the captaincy back to Haefen?" he asked, only curiosity in his voice.

"Of course!" Tahira said. "He is the captain of this ship."

She looked around at the crew, grateful that Rance was nowhere to be seen. "But I'd like to be of use while I'm here, if you would all help me," she said.

"You've already been of use in the galley," Copper suddenly said, waving his biscuit. "Men, she's put something in here as will help us not get so sick. And it was her idea to serve up salmagundi."

Cheers rang out and Tahira felt her face reddening.

"And you're right, I was testing you last night," Scudamore said. "I was testing your loyalty. You see, each man here has sworn oaths to Captain Haefen. You have sworn no oaths, and you were only voted in as a temporary measure. I wanted to see if you knew that. And you do. You are loyal to Captain Haefen."

Tahira scoffed a little, shaking her head. "I don't want to be a pirate, so I won't be signing your articles," she said.

Scudamore chuckled. "You already are a pirate. You've been made a Captain, just like Haefen."

"As I hope is obvious by now, I am not Captain Haefen," Tahira said softly. Those who heard her, laughed.

Chapter Twenty-One

Royal Conlan had lost valuable speed because of the storm, and Tahira was eager to crowd sail and catch up. But as Scudamore and other pirates started teaching her to sail, she realized how foolish and dangerous that would be.

In just a few days' time, the pirates taught Tahira nearly everything about sailing. Soon she was beating Ransome in races into the rigging, just like Tel used to do. She learned how to reef sails, splice a line, throw the log, and patch the sails. The old calluses from slavery grew again on her palms and she could slide down shrouds like any of them. She wanted to work and the pirates let her, though she knew that some of them were silently mocking her.

Though she had never been vain, Tahira noticed that her hands were getting rough and cracked again. And as exhilarating as sliding down shrouds was, she wanted to keep her hands nice. And so she started working on a salve that would protect her hands, like she had in Typeg, and after a few trials and errors, she succeeded.

While she worked, she sang shanties along with the crew to get a rhythm to their work. She noted with disappointment how out-of-tune the shanties had become ever since the musician had disappeared on Turtle Island.

While she worked and sang, she kept her eyes on the horizon, always hoping to see Soto's ship. As the days leaked by, she started to lose hope. It was strange to her that Soto's ship had disappeared so completely. But if the *Royal Conlan* was on a different heading it would be impossible to find them; they were only guessing where Soto had gone.

But while she sometimes cried herself to sleep, she kept her face clear for the crew. The thing she feared the most was that the crew would decide to attack again.

And those fears were not unfounded.

One morning Tahira stepped onto the railing, grabbed a shroud and leaned out over the side. The wind blew through her hair and dress and played over her outstretched arm. She felt like she was flying, flying to wherever Captain Haefen was. She'd had a dream about him the night before, and she wanted to see him again more than anything.

She heard someone step to the rail beside her, but before she could turn her head, she felt someone push her, hard. Her feet slipped off the rail and her hand ran painfully down the shroud as she fell. She cried out as her body hit the side of the ship.

She looked up. Rance, Withy, and the pirate with the amputated finger were standing at the rail, leering down at her. Withy raised his hand to show her he was holding an awl. He paused, then hit her hand with the bulbous handle.

Tahira screamed, her hand weakening.

She heard a shot, followed by a shout of "Avast there!"

Her three would-be murderers turned and Tahira grabbed the shroud with her other hand. But she suddenly felt so weak she couldn't pull herself up, and her hand was throbbing painfully.

Immediately, hands reached down and pulled her onto the deck: Stretton and Morwell. Tahira stood gasping against the railing, cradling her injured hand against her chest.

"It's mutiny to kill the captain!" Scudamore shouted. Tahira looked up to see him facing Rance, Withy, and the pirate with the amputated finger. He was holding his still-smoking pistol in his hand, and he looked angrier than she'd ever seen him. "You all know the code, you've got to have more than two on your side before you attempt a mutiny."

"This wasn't a mutiny," Withy growled.

"So it's murder, then?" Scudamore asked. He hit Withy over the head with his pistol; Withy swore and ducked away. "Murder on Haefen's ship? You know what that means for you, Withy! And you, Rance, was this your idea? Haefen wouldn't see her murdered."

"Aye, but Haefen's not here," Rance said. He was swaggering, and Tahira shuddered to see it.

"No, but I am," Scudamore said, his voice lowering as he took a step forward. "If you try to kill her again, I'll string you up on the yardarm myself, and hang the consequences."

Rance stood for a moment before sneering in the quartermaster's face. He gestured to his two companions and they stalked off.

Scudamore put his pistol back in his belt and approached Tahira, waving away Stretton and Morwell, who had remained at her sides.

"How's the hand?" he asked roughly.

Tahira finally looked at it, flexing her fingers. "It'll heal," she said. "Thank you for stopping them."

Scudamore sucked his teeth and looked up at the rigging. "This isn't the first time Rance has tried to kill you, is it?" he asked.

"No, it's the third," Tahira said softly. Scudamore looked down at her in surprise. Tahira opened her mouth to again ask him why he hadn't been there to stop the attack on her cabin, but he interrupted,

"How about you stay away from the railings, unless I'm right there," he said. He pulled his bandana off his bald head and handed it to her. "Wrap your hand in this."

As he walked away, Tahira started shaking. She'd never been in such danger before, and it frightened her. The next time the pirates decided to attack she might not be able to survive. She turned and looked out to sea again.

"Where are you, Captain?" she whispered.

***

The next afternoon Tahira sat on the port rail, one leg dangling over the side. She'd had a nightmare the night before in which they never found Captain Haefen, and despair was threatening to overwhelm her. But looking out at the sea in relative quiet was helping.

"I thought we discussed you staying away from the rail," Scudamore said with some annoyance, stepping up to her. When she didn't even look at him, his expression changed and he leaned against the rail next to her. "It's not good for the crew to see their Captain so forlorn."

"You and I both know I'm Captain in name only," she said, still staring at the sea. "You're the captain, Scudamore. I'm only a woman alone on this ship."

Scudamore folded his arms. "Why did you agree to come with Haefen, at the beginning?" he asked.

Tahira raised her eyebrows and finally looked at him; Scudamore had never asked a personal question before. "Do you know what ship I was on?"

"Aye, the slaver *Nantes,* Mills's ship."

Tahira nodded and looked out to sea again. "Then you know I had the choice to come with Captain Haefen or go to slavery," she said.

Scudamore scratched his chin and squinted at her. "How did you end up on *The Nantes*?"

Tahira looked up at the masts. Ransome was running across the topgallant brace. "Alycia's father was angry at her and he sent us away on *The Nantes*," she said. "I didn't know until Captain Haefen came that it was a slaver."

"You didn't?" Scudamore asked. Tahira could hear the disbelief in his voice.

She looked down at him. "No," she said. "Alycia's father told us we were to see the world. Mills bunked us on the fo'c'sle, and only I went below, to the galley. We were told there was livestock in the hold. That's why we weren't allowed down there, why there was a lock on the hatch, and why it smelled so horrible."

Scudamore swore and shook his head.

Tahira swung her leg back over so she was sitting sidesaddle on the rail. "Scudamore, how does Captain Haefen know Mills?"

Scudamore glanced at her sideways. He scratched his head, uncomfortable. "Haefen wouldn't want me saying this, but he stops Mills regularly," he said. "He'll take slaves from Mills and set them free."

Tahira was so surprised she gasped. "What?"

Scudamore nodded. "But I'm the only one who knows that," he said, lowering his voice. "The rest of the crew thinks Haefen gets them to be slaves, and when they don't work like they should he maroons them or sells them. But he really takes them where they want to go. Usually back home."

Tahira realized her mouth had fallen open and she closed it. She felt her love and respect for Captain Haefen growing. Then something occurred to her. "Is that what he's doing with me?" she asked. "Taking me home?"

Scudamore shuffled his feet. "No," he said. "Otherwise, we'd have gone back to Typeg."

"Where is he taking me? Do you know?" Tahira blurted it out, her curiosity overcoming everything else.

"I do," Scudamore said, nodding. "But I don't know why. I'm sorry," he added, holding up a hand as Tahira opened her mouth. "I promised Haefen I wouldn't tell you."

Tahira figured as much. She slid off the rail. "Thank you," she said.

She was just turning away to check on la Fever when Scudamore spoke again, "I'm sorry," he said. Tahira turned around. "That you were on *The*

Nantes, sold. That's not right."

Scudamore walked off toward the bowsprit. Tahira stood still, surprised. Besides Captain Haefen, Scudamore was the first pirate to show her compassion. She wondered at it.

***

Just over a week after the storm, Tahira ordered Scudamore up into the lookout on the mainmast, then grabbed holystones with the forenoon watch and got to work scrubbing the deck. In the middle of the watch, she heard Scudamore call.

"On deck there! Captain!"

Tahira heard the urgency in his voice and stood up, the holystone still in her hand. Scudamore was gesturing to her. She handed the holystone to Morwell and ran up to the lookout post. Scudamore handed her his telescope.

"Where away?" she asked, raising it to her eye.

Scudamore pointed. "There's something off our starboard bow. On the horizon." He pushed the telescope a little with his finger. "Just about there. Do you see something?"

Tahira focused the telescope and finally found what Scudamore had been looking at; even with the telescope, it was little more than a black dot on the horizon. But the longer she stared at it, the more it seemed to take shape. Slowly she lowered the telescope, keeping her eyes on the same spot.

"Scudamore, it looks like a boat," she said slowly.

"Aye, that's what I thought," Scudamore said.

Tahira looked up at him to see a small smile on his face. She could feel a similar smile on her own. "Do you think it's Captain Haefen?" she asked.

Scudamore shook his head once. "It might be," he said.

"Then we need to get to him, quickly," Tahira said. "How long will it take?"

Scudamore looked at the sails a moment, his eyes narrowed. "We should reach it in a couple hours."

"Then set course," Tahira said. She looked at the sails and the position of the sun. "That would be two points to the northwest?"

Scudamore smiled a little. "Three."

"Set the topgallants, Scudamore," she said. "I have a feeling we need to hurry."

Scudamore floated down a shroud to the deck. Tahira put the glass to her eye again and trained it on the black dot. Below her she heard Scudamore barking orders and the pirates chanting their responses.

Gradually the *Royal Conlan* sailed closer to the black dot, which proved itself, after an hour or two, to be a drifting longboat. At first it appeared empty. But then she stood up, balancing on the yard, and looked again. She could just make out a prone figure inside the longboat, dressed in black. Her heart skipped a beat.

"Scudamore!" she shouted. She tucked the telescope into her belt and slid down a shroud as fast as she could. "Scudamore!"

Scudamore ran from the stern to meet her in the waist. "What is it?" he asked.

"I think it is Captain Haefen in that boat," Tahira said. "But he's not moving, I don't know if he's alive."

She didn't realize how afraid and agitated she was until Scudamore put his hand on her shoulder. The gesture was so calming she took a deep breath of surprise.

"Keep an eye on him," Scudamore said. "I'll bring us alongside."

Tahira nodded and turned her gaze back out to the longboat, tapping the telescope in one hand. In less than an hour, Scudamore brought the ship alongside.

"Hooks!" Tahira shouted. "Scudamore, Stretton, overboard."

She called the commands, but she never took her eyes from the prone figure in the longboat. Captain Haefen wasn't moving, though he might have been asleep. There were two empty waterskins, a pistol, and a small bag littering the bottom of the boat.

The pirates threw grappling hooks down to the longboat and brought it bumping against the side of the ship. Scudamore threw a ladder over the side and descended. After a brief scuffle, Rance shoved Stretton down the hatch and followed Scudamore into the longboat. Tahira didn't care enough to stop him; she had eyes only for her Captain. She didn't realize she was holding her breath until she started feeling lightheaded.

Scudamore turned Captain Haefen onto his side and bent over him. "He's alive and breathing," he called up to Tahira. "But he's unconscious."

"He's got a fever," Rance said, staring up at her. She wouldn't look at him. "He's probably been drifting for a while." He nudged an empty waterskin with his toe.

"Bring him up," Tahira said. "We'll take him straight to his cabin." She looked over her shoulder. "Ransome!" she called. In moments the cabin boy was by her side. "Open the hatch to the captain's cabin and light some candles. Ask Mr. Copper to heat some water in a bowl and bring it with cloths. Fetch a waterskin also."

Ransome nodded and darted off. Rance and Scudamore carried Captain Haefen up the ladder and Tahira put the telescope down to help them. Rance climbed up first, then leaned over the railing to lift the unconscious Captain from Scudamore. A cheer went up from the pirates at the sight of Captain Haefen on deck, a cheer that petered out quickly when they saw their Captain was in no fit state.

"To the cabin, quickly," Tahira said. Scudamore slung Captain Haefen over his shoulders and Rance cleared a path through the pirates to the cabin. Tahira shooed Ransome out and closed the door behind him.

Scudamore stood Captain Haefen on his feet by his bed. He groaned but stayed upright.

"Is he waking up?" Tahira asked.

"No," Rance shook his head. "It's the fever. He's not well."

"Get his coat and boots off, get him in bed," Scudamore said. Ransome returned with the hot water and waterskin and Tahira set them on the desk. By then Captain Haefen was settled in his bed, where he laid very still.

"He's asleep again," Scudamore said, his hand on Captain Haefen's arm. "He'll need to be looked after."

Tahira nodded. She'd never seen Captain Haefen looking so vulnerable. "I'll do it. Rance, step aside." She waited until the bosun had moved over before approaching the bed, repressing a shudder as she passed him. "Scudamore, I'm turning charge of the ship over to you. I want you to get us to land. Once we get there tell Copper to get as much fresh food and water as he can. For now, I'll need some hot broth."

"Captain, what if we sight an enemy ship?" Rance asked, a sneer in his voice.

"I'm not Captain anymore," Tahira said, still looking at Scudamore. "But if you see an enemy ship, especially Soto, flee. I don't want a fight right now, not while Captain Haefen is so weak. If any of the crew disagrees, tell them to come to me."

Scudamore nodded and left the cabin, taking Rance with him.

Alone with Captain Haefen, Tahira took his warm hand. "Welcome back, Captain," she said. "I've missed you. We found you adrift in that longboat and you're very sick."

A soft knock interrupted her: Copper with the hot broth. "How is he?" he asked, peering around Tahira.

"I don't know yet," she said. "But he's alive."

Copper nodded and left.

Tahira turned her attention back to Captain Haefen, determined to make him well. She kissed his forehead and drew back almost at once, surprised. Rance had said Captain Haefen had a fever, but his forehead was cool. She put her hand on his chest and felt his heart beating weak and fast.

She knew these symptoms. The overseer, Mo, had been like this once, sick with too much sun, and Old Joche had healed him. But another slave, Sesmar, hadn't been so lucky: *His wife had delayed in bringing him to Old Joche, and by then it was too late to save him. He'd shouted and flailed in a crazed delirium, vomited on the floor, then fell backward off the cot and cracked his head open on the stone floor.* The memories of his death rose in Tahira's mind and she fought to tamp them down again.

"We rescued him just in time," she whispered.

Tahira ran around the cabin, opening all the windows she could. At once the cabin felt cooler as sea breezes flew between windows. She grabbed a full keg of rum and used it to prop the cabin door open, then ran up the ladder to open the hatchway. Then she sped around the cabin again, taking stock of what was there, of what could help Captain Haefen. She had to cool him down, and quickly.

The open doors and her movements finally attracted Scudamore, who came in silently with his eyebrows raised.

"How long until we reach land?" she asked without preamble. She was pleased her voice didn't have the note of panic that her thoughts did. Captain Haefen seemed to be getting worse; he started sweating and tossing a little in his sleep. She couldn't let him die like Sesmar had.

Scudamore glanced at Captain Haefen before he answered, "Within a few hours. We were closer to land than we thought."

"Good," Tahira said. She opened the last drawer in Captain Haefen's desk and found a woman's hand fan. "Aha! This is what I need."

"What are you doing?" Scudamore asked, watching Tahira stand by Captain Haefen and start fanning him.

"I've seen this illness before," Tahira said. "He'll die if we don't cool him down. That's why we need to get to land quickly." She paused for a moment, trying to remember what Old Joche had taught her; it had been so long since she'd healed someone with too much sun. "Oh! Scudamore, help me sit him up."

Tahira grabbed the waterskin while Scudamore lifted Captain Haefen into a half-sitting position. Tahira opened his mouth and slowly poured in water, a little at a time. Captain Haefen swallowed. Tahira smiled and gave him more water. The waterskin was half empty before Captain Haefen stopped automatically swallowing. She put the waterskin down and started unbuttoning his shirt.

"Let's get this off before you lay him back down," she said to Scudamore. "I'll need it soaked in sea water and brought back."

"All right," Scudamore said.

"When we get to shore there will be more to do." She finished unbuttoning the shirt and pushed it off his shoulders, maneuvering around Scudamore's supporting arm.

"What now?" Scudamore asked.

"Soak his shirt in seawater and bring it back. If you can't help me, find someone who can."

Tahira didn't like to hear the sharp edge to her voice, but Scudamore didn't comment. He did as she said. Tahira spread the wet shirt over Captain Haefen's bare chest and smoothed the sleeves down his arms.

"Here," Scudamore said, handing her a length of rope. "I need to get back on deck. Tie this rope around the shirt and toss it out the window when you need to. I'll let you know when we're ready to land."

"Thank you," Tahira said. "Oh, and Scudamore?" The quartermaster paused and turned back. "Please make sure Rance doesn't come in here again."

Anger passed over Scudamore's face before he nodded and left the cabin.

Tahira picked up the fan again. Within a few minutes the shirt was nearly dry and warm. Tahira re-wetted it and placed it back over Captain Haefen, trying as she did so to resist the urge to curl up next to him on the bed, for his long, lean, and muscular body looked so comfortable, and she longed to be closer to him. His bruises from the battle stood out against his tan skin, and she could see that most of his ribs were still healing.

Tahira kept a cycle of activity going, wetting his shirt, fanning him, giving him water or now-cold broth, then re-wetting his shirt. While she worked, she talked. She told him everything that had happened since he'd been kidnapped by Soto. She told him her concerns of the ship and all she had tried to do to help. She told him how inexplicably kind Scudamore and Copper and Ransome had been to her. She didn't know if he could hear her, but she talked all the same, which helped keep her worry at bay.

The longer she worked the more tired she became, and her bruised hand ached. But she remembered Old Joche's words from that long-ago day with Mo: *When you're trying to save someone's life you can't think of your own discomfort.* She bit down her fatigue; she couldn't let Captain Haefen down.

Soon Scudamore came back, announcing that they'd arrived at the island. One shore party had already landed and reported a fresh stream. The longboat was ready for Captain Haefen.

"Good," Tahira said, wiping her shaking arm across her forehead. She held up the damp shirt. "Let's put this on him again. We're going to need at least two more strong men to come with us." She paused and looked up at him. "Will you come with me?"

"Aye," he said. Tahira nodded. "What are we doing?" he asked, pulling Captain Haefen up into a half-sitting position again.

Tahira knelt on the bed and supported Captain Haefen from behind. "We're going to put him in the stream," she said. "That will cool his body down."

"And then will he wake up?" Scudamore almost whispered, though they were alone in the cabin.

Tahira sighed. "I hope so. I've never done it this way before."

Scudamore chose Samson and Stretton to come with them to shore, leaving Rance in charge of the ship. The three pirates carefully lowered Captain Haefen into the longboat and Tahira dropped in after them as they cast off. She kept one hand on Captain Haefen's chest to feel his heartbeat as the pirates rowed ashore, her eyes fixed on the island. On the beach she could see the group Copper brought with him milling around, filling their boats with bunches of fruits. Scudamore guided their boat in right beside them.

"The stream's just over there," Copper said, pointing to their right into the dense jungle trees. "We were just going to take the big barrels over."

"Good, we'll join you," Tahira said, vaulting awkwardly out of the boat and staggering a little with fatigue.

Captain Haefen was a little more awake as Scudamore and Samson pulled him from the longboat, and he was able to drag his feet along a little. Copper led the way through the jungle to a stream bubbling with the clearest water Tahira had ever seen. She paused to stare at its beauty, at the way the water glistened in the tiny sunrays peeking through the leaves above them, at the perfect order of the stones on the streambed.

"Miss?" Copper asked, putting his hand on her shoulder.

Tahira started and shook her head. "I'm sorry," she said. She turned to Scudamore and the others. "We need to submerge him. I'll keep his head out of the water, if you men will hold him to make sure he doesn't float away."

Scudamore nodded and mutely pointed to where he wanted the other two to stand. Tahira followed them into the waist-deep cold stream and cradled Captain Haefen's head in her hands. His eyebrows constricted as his body submerged, but he still didn't wake up.

Out of the corner of her eye Tahira saw Copper directing his men to fill the water barrels right next to them.

"Stop!" she said before the first barrel went in the water. The pirates started in surprise, one or two stumbling into the stream. "You need to fill those barrels upstream."

"Why?" Stretton asked.

"Because sickness comes when you drink water that's touched a human body," Tahira said. "The water upstream is clean and will be perfect for drinking."

Copper stared at her a moment before ordering his grumbling men to follow her instructions.

"Where did you learn all these things?" Scudamore asked.

Tahira looked down at Captain Haefen's face and stroked his dark hair off his forehead. "I learned in another life," she said. "One I don't really want to remember any more, even though I still do."

"Was it painful?" Samson asked.

She heard Scudamore hiss at him, but she still answered, "It was."

Silence fell at the stream except for the necessary communication for filling the barrels and making sure Captain Haefen didn't float away. Tahira kept her gaze on Captain Haefen, but she noticed that the pirates were not singing, cursing, bragging, or slurring drunkenly. She wondered what had come over them, and concluded that they were all concerned for their Captain.

But she didn't see them staring at her in wonder as they rolled the barrels back toward the beach. She didn't see the salute Copper gave her as he passed. She didn't see Scudamore, Stretton, and Samson grit their teeth against the cold water rather than disobey her.

Tahira had never healed someone from too much sun with a stream, though she had long ago lost count of how many times Old Joche had wished for one. And Tahira was glad to see that Old Joche's longing for a stream had merit, for gradually Captain Haefen started showing signs of life: his eyes darted under their lids; his heart slowed and beat stronger; and finally, with a little gasp, he opened his eyes. Tahira smiled down at him.

"Tahira?" he whispered.

"Hello, Captain," she said.

"Welcome back, sir," Scudamore said, moving closer.

Captain Haefen startled in the water, splashing everyone, his eyes darting around. The pirates righted him into a standing position in the stream and held him steady as he swayed.

"Why am I here?" he asked, his voice hoarse. "What are you doing here?"

"We rescued you from that lifeboat, Haefen," Scudamore said, putting his hands on his captain's shoulders. "You were in bad shape. If it weren't for Tahira here, you might have died."

Captain Haefen's gaze rested on her with such intensity that she blushed. She suddenly felt the cold of the stream and she rubbed her arms. But she realized that that was the first time Scudamore had called her by her name.

"Back to the ship?" Scudamore asked.

Tahira nodded. She clamored out of the stream with difficulty with her wet dress and shaking legs, while the pirates half-carried Captain Haefen out of the water and supported him back to the boat. Tahira kept silent, torn between relief and exhaustion from the last few hours, and wanting to hold Captain Haefen. She could feel his gaze on her as they rowed back to the ship, but she couldn't bring herself to look at him.

A cheer rang from the crew as Captain Haefen staggered aboard. He raised his hand in acknowledgement, then nearly fell over with dizziness. Scudamore threw Captain Haefen's arm over his shoulder and guided him to his cabin.

Tahira changed into something dry then went down to the galley, where Copper was still finding places for everything he'd gathered.

"How much did you get?" Tahira asked.

Copper turned and swept an arm over the food-laden shelves and wardrobe. "A great deal. We have enough food for several months. And lots of fruits."

"Good," Tahira said. Exhaustion overtook her relief and she sat at the table with her head in her hands. Her body was shaking with more than cold and she felt a little dizzy.

"How is the captain?" Copper asked.

"He's finally awake," Tahira said. "Scudamore is taking him to his cabin. He'll be all right now." Silence fell, and Tahira rested her head on her arms. After a few minutes Copper put a teacup in front of her. "Thank you," she said, sitting up and taking a sip.

Copper sat next to her. "You have no idea how much you have changed things on this ship," he said. "And no one who has been watching you these last few hours could doubt that you care very much for the captain."

Tahira felt her face flush again and took a hasty sip of tea. "I'm just doing what anyone would do."

Copper shook his head. "No one would have done what you did. I had my doubts about you at first. But it wasn't until you became the captain that I began to see what Haefen saw all along."

Tahira felt pleased with the flattery, something she had never received in Typeg. And she too had noticed the change in the crew's behavior. But she couldn't dwell on that now. Captain Haefen was still sick. She touched Copper's arm and stood up.

"I need some things for the captain," she said.

Copper stood up too, businesslike again. As she gathered things the galley door opened and Scudamore peered in.

"The captain wants you," he said.

"I'll be in shortly," she said.

"And who knows, perhaps he cares for you too," Copper said under his breath. Tahira smiled, her relief overcoming her exhaustion.

With her arms laden with fruits and waterskins, and a knife in her belt, Tahira followed Scudamore to the captain's cabin, where he held the door open for her then left.

Captain Haefen was sitting on his bed in dry clothes, his hands braced against the mattress, staring out the still-open windows at the sunset. Tahira's heart fluttered at the sight of him. After over a week of trying to find him, he was finally here. She hurriedly put her armload down on the desk.

"Captain," she said.

Captain Haefen turned his head, a tired smile on his face, and reached one arm out to her. He put it around her waist when she stepped closer to him, using her as an anchor to stay upright. Tahira spread her feet to take his weight and hugged him tight around his shoulders.

"I heard you talking to me," he said.

"Then I don't need to tell you anything," Tahira joked. Captain Haefen chuckled a little. She pulled away and put her hand on his forehead, glad to feel that it was more or less the right temperature. "You're doing better."

Captain Haefen nodded, blinking slowly, his grip on her waist slackening. Tahira let him lean forward until his cheek rested against her chest. She held him to her, rocking him slightly.

"Thank you," Captain Haefen said after a while. "You saved my life. How did you learn all those things?"

"Old Joche taught me," Tahira said, running her fingers through his still-wet hair. "She was a healer, and she taught me everything I know. The illness you have, she called it 'Too Much Sun.' I don't really know what it is, or what causes it, or really how to heal it. But I've done what she taught me to."

Captain Haefen pulled away enough to look up at her. "That's the most you've ever told me about your past," he said. "Tell me more."

Tahira leaned her forehead against his. "Later," she said. "For now, we've got to get you well. You have a ship to run."

Tahira made sure he could sit on his own before stepping away. She grabbed several fruits and a waterskin from the desk then sat next to him.

"Here, eat this." Tahira used the knife from her belt to cut into the yellow-green skin of a soft oval fruit, revealing orange flesh and hundreds of black seeds.

"Where did this come from?" Captain Haefen asked, taking half of the fruit and using his fingernails to dig out the seeds.

"Copper found it on the island," Tahira said, holding out her cupped hands for the seeds. "Captain, what happened?"

"Killian," Captain Haefen said. He glanced at Tahira then back to the fruit.

"What?" Tahira asked.

"Killian," he repeated. "That's my name. When we're in here, alone, you can call me that."

Tahira mouthed the name a few times, remembering Maryanne Ronny saying it. The more she rolled his name around her mouth, the more she liked it. She leaned her head on his shoulder as he started eating the fruit.

"Killian, what happened to you?" she said.

Killian's smile faded. "They court martialed me."

"What's that?"

"It's where a captain is under investigation by a panel of other captains," he said. "He is judged to see if his conduct during a battle or a chase or a raid was right in every respect. He and all his officers are brought to the court martial to tell the panel what happened."

"But your officers weren't there," she said, sitting up and throwing the seeds out the window. "So this wasn't a real court martial."

"That's right," he said. He took another bite and wiped his chin on his sleeve. "But that didn't matter, they were going to kill me no matter what the court martial decided."

"You said there is a panel of captains," she said. "Who else was there? It wasn't just Soto, was it?"

"No, it was Nave's friends," he said. "All of them."

"How could Soto have gathered them all that quickly?"

"I don't think he did," he said. "I think that Nave put this plan into action before the battle, kind of after-death revenge. Even if I won the battle I would still die."

She sighed and leaned her head against his shoulder again. He finished the fruit and took her hand. The juice from the fruit made their hands stick together, and she smiled.

"They found me innocent under the terms of the court martial so they had to kill me in a way that wouldn't violate that," he said. "In other words, they couldn't execute me outright."

"That's why they put you in that longboat," she said.

"With provisions for three days," he said. He leaned his cheek against the top of her head. "I made them last as long as I could, hoping you'd come in time."

"The ship?"

"No."

Tahira smiled. "How long were you out there?"

"I lost count after four days."

She cast her mind back, then sat up. "Did they put you out there after the storm?"

"Aye, they did," he said. He rubbed his forehead with his free hand. "How long ago was that?"

"Just over a week," she said.

He paused. "I thought I had died. And when I heard your voice I thought that meant you were dead too. That's why I was so surprised to see you at the stream. It was like a confirmation that we were both dead, but I couldn't understand how you had died. But then I saw Scudamore and felt the cold, and I knew I wasn't dead after all."

Killian suddenly fell forward. Tahira jumped to her feet and caught him, easing him upright again. He blinked slowly, looking dazed. She grabbed a waterskin from the desk and handed it to him.

"I'm sorry," he said.

"Don't be. We thought you were dead at first," she said while he took a long drink from the waterskin. "And it frightened me. I didn't want to lose you."

His intense blue eyes never left her face. "I didn't want to lose you either. I hung on until you found me." He shivered and put his arm around her waist again.

"I'm cold," he said. "Is that a good thing?"

She smiled and kissed his forehead. "It's much better than it was before," she said. "Come on, you need to sleep now."

Killian shivered more violently as he lay down and Tahira covered him with the sheet. She was worried for a moment, even though a few slaves had had this reaction, but then she realized that Killian was indeed just cold.

"Do you have another blanket?" she asked.

"In one of the lockers beneath me," he said. He gritted his teeth together so they wouldn't chatter. "Am I all right?"

"Yes, you're just cold," she said. "That's what happens, I guess, when you get put in a stream."

She knelt down and opened drawers under the bed. Their contents weren't nearly as interesting as she had imagined on her first visit to the cabin, but at last she found the blankets. She draped a thick one over Killian and closed the drawer again.

He turned onto his side, his eyelids drooping even as he shivered. Tahira leaned over him and rubbed him with her hands, her sore arms starting to shake again. After a few minutes his shivering subsided and he closed his eyes.

"Don't leave me," he said, reaching one hand toward her. Tahira's heart squeezed at how helpless he looked. She pulled the chair over and took his hand as she sat down, stroking his face with her other hand.

Killian's breathing slowed and deepened as he fell asleep.

Chapter Twenty-Two

Tahira was wakened the next morning by a hand on her head. She started, then remembered where she was. She sat up and rested her elbows on the mattress, her neck and shoulders stiff. Killian was propped on one elbow, grinning at her. At noticing her pained expression his hand moved to the back of her neck, his fingers massaging the muscles. She felt years-worth of muscles unknotting under his gentle vice-like grip.

"Hello," she said.

"Good morning," he said. He leaned forward and kissed her. She cupped his scruffy face in one hand and kissed him back. She was a little breathless when she pulled away.

"How are you feeling?" she asked, standing up and putting the chair back.

"Hungry," he said. He pushed back his blankets and sat up. He swayed suddenly and she grabbed his shoulders. "Dizzy."

"Maybe because you're hungry," she said. "Can you stand?"

"I think so," he said. Slowly he slid off the bed and stood up shakily. Tahira supported him to his desk, then started peeling an oval green-red fruit while he drained a waterskin. The fruit inside was orange and released a sweet smell.

A knock sounded at the door.

"Come in," Killian said.

Copper opened the door. "Captain, Miss," he said. "Do you need anything?"

Killian looked at Tahira. "What do you say?"

"Bring a wide array of foods, please, Copper," she said. "But no rum." Copper nodded and closed the door. Tahira sliced some of the sweet orange fruit from the large center pit and handed it to Killian.

"Did Scudamore tell you about anything that happened?" she asked.

"He told me that the crew made you Captain," he said. "That surprised me."

"It did me too," she said, taking a bite of the fruit herself. "This is really good."

"It's called a mango," he said. "They're one of my favorites. Mm, he also told me that the crew has been getting a much better diet under your command." He gave a sideways grin that made her sit on the edge of the desk.

"The men were getting sick, so I made hardtack with orange juice and added fruits with every meal," she said. "It's a sickness Old Joche called 'Not Enough to Eat'."

"At sea we call it scurvy," he said.

"Scurvy," she repeated. She cut another piece of mango for them both. "I think you have better names for things."

Killian leaned back in his chair and smiled at her. Copper knocked and came into the cabin, Ransome right behind him, both laden with food. Tahira made to get off the desk but Killian put his hand on her knee and she stopped. Copper and Ransome deposited the food and left with salutes.

Tahira put one foot on Killian's knee. The movement was so natural it surprised her. "Do any of the crew know things have changed between us?"

"No," Killian said. "Though I think Scudamore suspects."

"Copper definitely does," Tahira said.

Killian picked up a piece of freshly-baked bread and a hunk of salt meat and leaned back in his chair again. "Is that all right with you?"

"It is," she said. She suddenly realized how hungry she was, and she couldn't remember when she last ate. She took some bread and selected a piece of cheese. "I like Copper. He's turned into a friend. And Ransome isn't as rude as he was at first. In fact, he seemed scared of me at times when I was the captain."

"Well, that's trained into every cabin boy, pirate or Navy," Killian said with a little laugh. His hand moved down her leg to her ankle. "What do you think of Scudamore and Rance?"

"Scudamore is an ally. I trust him," she said.

Killian raised an eyebrow. "And Rance?"

Tahira paused. "He hates me, Killian. Did… did Scudamore tell you that the crew attacked me?"

Killian stopped mid-bite. "They did what?" His voice was dangerous.

"It was the night you were taken," she said. She tucked both feet under his leg so she could scoot closer to him. "They got drunk and were making a huge ruckus. And they started talking about me, saying how there was a woman aboard. Rance said they should come get 'Haefen's woman'."

"He did what?"

"Rance was the first one through the door," she said. "Six in all came in."

His hand tightened on her ankle. "Were you hurt?"

"No," she said. "But I hurt all six of them in defending myself. And the next morning they made me Captain."

Killian blinked, his grip relaxing. "Where was Scudamore that night?"

"I don't know," Tahira said. "But he was the one who tutored me in how to be a captain, and he's been with me almost all the time."

"How has Rance been since the attack?"

Tahira paused. She didn't want to complain, but she was so relieved to have Killian back at last, to have someone she knew and trusted, someone who would take care of her and make all the dangers disappear, that the words spilled out, "Oh Killian, he tried to kill me twice since the attack. Once during the storm, but la Fever stopped him, and once a few days ago with two others, but Scudamore stopped them. I don't know how much longer I might have survived if we hadn't found you."

She finished with a gasp, suddenly realizing she was crying. Killian pulled her off the desk and into his arms in one fluid motion.

"Why didn't you tell me sooner?" he asked. He squeezed her tighter, as though holding her would take away the attacks.

Tahira sobbed into his chest a few times, wrapping her arms gently around him. She snuggled deeper into him, tucking her forehead against his neck. It felt so good to be close to him. How she had longed for him! She felt safer now than she ever had before.

Killian held her for a little while longer before relaxing his grip. Tahira pushed herself up, sitting sidesaddle on his knees, and wiped her sleeve across her face.

A knock came at the cabin door.

"Who is it?" Killian called, the captain again.

"Scudamore, sir."

"Come in. You're just the man I wish to see." Killian pressed the small of Tahira's back and she stood up. Killian stood too, leaning forward on the desk for support.

Scudamore entered and nodded. "Sir. Miss."

"You have a report?" Captain Haefen asked.

"Aye, sir," Scudamore said. "According to your charts we'll see land in two days."

"Very good, Scudamore. Set course," Captain Haefen said. The quartermaster hesitated. Captain Haefen's voice was soft as he asked, "Why didn't you tell me about the attacks on Tahira, Peter?"

Scudamore looked up at his name but didn't offer an answer.

"Is it because Rance was here?"

"You let Rance back in the cabin?" Tahira asked.

Scudamore nodded, looking sheepish. "He slipped in before I could stop him."

"Where were you the night of the first attack?" Captain Haefen asked.

Scudamore looked at Tahira. "Rance told me what he was going to do to Tahira, wanted me to join him," he said. "I tried to stop him before he could convince the crew to follow him. But his mates jumped me. I woke up the next morning."

He paused, still staring at Tahira. "I'm sorry I wasn't there."

Tahira nodded. "I knew there was a reason you couldn't come. You've taken care of me, just like you promised. And you saved my life."

Scudamore looked relieved.

"Rance needs to be punished for his disobedience," Captain Haefen said, straightening. "I take it you didn't punish him because you were awaiting my order?"

"Aye, sir," Scudamore said. "I didn't want to risk a mutiny. She would have had no protection otherwise."

Captain Haefen nodded. "What punishment do you see fit?"

"Twelve lashes and then the brig," Scudamore said immediately. "Him and his mates."

Tahira looked at Captain Haefen, whose eyebrows were raised. "Very well, Scudamore, make it so," he said. He looked at Tahira. "You said there were five others in your cabin?"

"Yes," Tahira said. "Though I did more damage to them that night than they did to me."

A corner of Captain Haefen's mouth twitched. "Scudamore, give those five the option of either taking their own punishment or letting Rance bear it all. Carry it out immediately under my order. Oh, and Scudamore, make sure it's on the grating, not the capstan. And make sure the whole crew is there."

A smile of dark pleasure spread across Scudamore's face. "Aye, sir."

Captain Haefen looked at Tahira as the door closed. His face cleared and he gave her a grin. But as sounds of the pirates gathering on the main deck reached them, his grin faded and he sat down again. "I never thought my bosun would turn against me. I chose him to the post."

Tahira ran her hand through his hair. "Don't worry, Killian," she said. "No one stays the same forever. People change, for good or bad. Rance made his choices and made his change. It's not your fault."

He rubbed her back and let out a deep breath.

"Let's have you eat more," she said, turning to the desk. "You're going to need your strength if we're landing in two days."

Killian stood and wrapped his arms around her waist, resting his chin on her shoulder. Tahira's entire body blushed and her insides danced. She handed food to him over her shoulder. "Killian, is our destination the only thing you'll keep from me?"

He unwrapped himself and sat on the desk. "Aye, though it's almost time to tell you," he said. "As you may have noticed, it's not in the nature of a pirate to divulge."

She sat on the desk next to him and took a bite. "But you weren't always a pirate."

He shook his head, his mouth full. Tahira longed to ask him about his past, more than the one story he had told her, about having a sea dad. But since he had given her own past privacy, she thought it best to return the favor.

He took her hand and ran his thumb gently over the bruising there. "Is this from Rance and his mates?" he asked.

She nodded. He let out a frustrated breath. But then his expression changed and he kissed the back of her hand. "Tahira, when we get to our destination, things might change. Things with us. I'm worried about what that will mean."

She studied his face and saw real worry and even insecurity. She squeezed his fingers, her heart expanding even more toward him.

"You know, Killian, in the slave compounds, people were constantly being sold or dying," she said. "It was hard to make friends. It was hard to get close to anyone."

"But did you anyway?" he asked.

"I did," she said. "Even though everyone I loved… left. Even though I was alone a lot of the time. Even though for a while I closed off a part of myself because so many people had been taken. Thinking back on it now, I think I realized I couldn't live closed-off like that. Killian, you are almost the first person I've really been able to get close to. Whatever happens, whatever you're worried about, we will always have that."

He nodded and squeezed her fingers back.

***

That afternoon, Captain Haefen addressed the crew on deck while Tahira returned their empties to the galley. Copper actually smiled at her when she came in.

"I was right," he said. "You both care for each other."

Tahira blushed. "Don't tell anyone?"

Copper tapped the table and nodded. "I may be a drunk pirate, but I'm surprisingly secretive."

Tahira chuckled. "Copper, when we get to our destination, what will you do?"

"Captain told us that once we get there, we're likely to get pardons," he said. "Pardons are valuable to pirates."

Tahira hadn't expected that answer. "Being pardoned for all wrongdoing? I suppose so." She looked at him. "But how many pirates stay pardoned?"

Copper smirked and Tahira had her answer.

The door opened and Ransome tumbled in. "Excuse me, Cap—Miss," he said. "Captain's gone back to his cabin. Said he wasn't feeling well."

"Thank you, Ransome," Tahira said. She grabbed a couple waterskins and left the galley, saying over her shoulder, "Copper, come check on us before you serve dinner."

"Aye," Copper grunted.

She found Killian shivering in his bed. His eyes were closed and he looked pale despite his tan. Tahira put the waterskins on the desk and touched his forehead. His skin felt normal, if just a little warm.

"What's wrong with me?" he asked.

"You're still recovering, you'll be all right," she said in a soothing voice. He nodded and gave a violent shiver. She leaned over him and started rubbing him again. But after a few minutes it seemed Killian was too cold for that to work again.

Tahira slipped off her shoes and slid under the blankets, scooting closer to Killian until their shared body heat filled the space between them. She put her arm over him, her hand flat on his back, and Killian's eyes snapped open.

"This is the fastest way to warm you up," she whispered, resting her head next to his on the pillow. "We did this all the time in the compounds during the Cold Time. There was one year it was so cold even this didn't work. But it will work for you." Killian shivered and closed his eyes again. "Just relax, Killian. You'll warm up soon."

She felt Killian relaxing against her. His breathing slowed and deepened, and in a few minutes he was asleep. She hadn't meant to fall asleep herself, but Copper's knock on the door started her awake. She opened her eyes and saw that Killian was still asleep, and that the sun had set.

Carefully she climbed out of the bed just as Copper opened the door.

"Anything, Miss?" he whispered.

Tahira put her finger to her lips and took the waterskins and mangos Copper had brought. She put them on the desk and pushed Copper ahead of her, closing the door behind them.

"I think we'll let him sleep," she said, following Copper up the hatchway.

"What happened?"

"He'll be all right," Tahira said. Scudamore suddenly appeared and held out a bowl of meat and biscuit. "I'm not the captain anymore," she said.

"I'm aware," Scudamore said, but he smiled.

Tahira smiled back and took the bowl. "I'll be in my cabin," she said. "If Captain Haefen wakes up, come get me."

The two men nodded and Tahira went down to her cabin. She felt a little guilty at leaving Killian alone, but she knew that he needed rest more than anything.

***

The next day Tahira breakfasted with the morning watch, then reported to Scudamore for work with the forenoon watch. Scudamore squinted and scratched his head.

"Shouldn't you be taking care of Haefen?"

"I am," she said. "He needs to rest."

Scudamore gave something of a smile. "Ransome and a few others started tarring yesterday. If you'd like to help, I'm sure Ransome will appreciate it."

"What's tarring?" Tahira asked, following Scudamore to the waist.

Scudamore pointed up into the rigging. "Painting the masts, shrouds, backstays, ties, runners, yard-arms—everything but the sails—with tar. It needs to be done often, and we haven't done it in a while."

"All right," Tahira said.

"Luckily for you, the stays are already done," Scudamore said. "If they weren't, you'd be up there swinging on the gant-line."

"Did Ransome do it?" Tahira asked.

"No." Scudamore chuckled. "He fell the last time he did it, and he won't do it again. Ransome!" he shouted.

"So who did the shrouds?" Tahira asked.

"Morwell," Scudamore said.

Ransome appeared, a bucket of tar in his hand. "Sir?"

"Get Tahira fresh clothes and a bucket," Scudamore said. "She's going to help you on the mainmast."

Ransome smiled at Tahira and ran off. Scudamore left to attend to his duties, and Ransome returned in moments with a bundle of clothes. Tahira changed in her cabin and came on deck sporting Ransome's old breeches and a man's shirt. She felt very self-conscious.

Ransome held back whatever mirth he wanted to show as he handed her a tar bucket and showed her how to climb up to the main look-out post with a bucket crooked in her elbow.

Tahira sat on the crossbeams to catch her breath. "Are there any special instructions?"

"Don't let it drip down onto the deck," Ransome said, swishing his brush around the tar.

They worked in silence, carefully painting every part of the mast and spars, climbing out onto the end of the yards and working inward. When they got to the maintop they were out of both tar and breath.

"Can I ask you something?" Ransome asked.

"Yes," Tahira said, rotating one shoulder.

"Do you and the captain love each other?"

Tahira looked at him and saw his embarrassed expression. She opened her mouth to answer, then—

"Tahira?"

She started and looked over the edge of the maintop to see Captain Haefen climbing the futtock shrouds.

"Ki—Captain!" she said, reaching down to help him up. "You shouldn't be out here. Remember what happened yesterday?"

"It's cloudy today, I'll be fine," Captain Haefen said. He leaned against the mast. "And I wondered where you'd gone."

Tahira touched his face. "How did you sleep?"

"Well," he said. He took her hand. "And to answer your question, Robbie, yes."

Ransome smiled, looking like a little boy.

"You are now sworn to secrecy," Captain Haefen said seriously. Ransome nodded and scurried down the mast.

Killian leaned his head against Tahira's. "Since when do you work on my ship?"

"Since your crew made me Captain," she said. "Turns out I like it. And now I know a lot more about your ship."

"It was a pleasure watching you up here, tarring away," he said. "And you look beautiful."

"Killian, I'm wearing Ransome's clothes," Tahira said, her face warm.

He laughed and put both arms around her. "Don't be embarrassed," he said. "Life at sea was not meant for dresses, and that's hardly your fault." He kissed the side of her head and she closed her eyes at his touch. "Hmm, I almost forgot," he said. "I'm having Copper get a basin ready for you in your cabin. With us making landfall tomorrow, I thought you'd like to clean up."

"Then it's a good thing Scudamore ordered Ravon to fix my door after the attack," Tahira said. She held out her tar-covered hands. "And thank you, I suppose I could use a bath." She dropped her hands and kissed his scruffy cheek. "I'll go get washed up." She scooted out of his arms and sat on the edge of the top, one leg dangling. "Are we landing at another pirate port?"

Killian shook his head. "No. I'll tell you more about it tomorrow."

***

Tahira chose a new dress from the wooden chest when she was clean. This one was several shades of purple, with short sleeves, a ribbon around the waist, and a lower back than the others. She hadn't worn short sleeves since she'd had to wear her slave shift. She slipped the dress on, relishing the light feeling of the fabric, and tied the ribbon behind her back. She combed through her hair and pulled it over one shoulder, then quitted the cabin, making her way up to the quarterdeck to dry her hair. She met Captain Haefen at the helm.

"I was on my way to my cabin," he said. He stopped and stared at her, smiling again. "You look beautiful." He put his hand on her stomach and gently pushed her backward toward the hatchway. "Let's have a better look."

"Captain, you can see me just as well up here," Tahira whispered, her face flushing. But she obeyed his pressure and they entered the cabin.

"Yes, but the crew doesn't know about us," he said, closing the door. "Turn around for me?"

Tahira turned around once. Killian's smile had vanished by the time she faced him again. He looked horrified.

"Tahira, what is that?" He stepped behind her, sitting on the edge of his desk, and touched her upper back, bare in this dress and uncovered by her hair.

She looked over her shoulder and could see a few long, raised bumps on the top of her shoulders. She'd forgotten about those. Perhaps she should change dresses.

"Those are scars, Killian," she said.

"From what?"

"From the taskmasters. And the Master."

His hand hovered over her back. "May I?" he asked. She nodded and his fingers traced over the raised scar lines. But she could not feel his touch; the whips had deadened the feeling in her back. "How could they do this to you?"

"Those are the last reminders I was a slave," she said. "I'd forgotten about them."

He remained silent, his fingers still tracing. When they reached her right shoulder, he gasped. He turned her to the side and pushed the sleeve of her dress up to he could see the letter carved into her shoulder.

"What is that?" he whispered.

"That's the mark of Master Gall," she said. "Each Master had his own mark. My Master personally carved that letter into all his slaves. He did that to me when I was born."

Killian paused, and he looked like he was going to say something. But then he decided against it. His fingers returned to the scars on her back.

Tahira felt it was finally time to ask him, "Killian, you told me once that you knew slaves. How?"

His palm flattened on her back. "Do you remember the old man on Turtle Island?"

"He used to be your Captain, right?"

"Aye. When I sailed under him, he had a deal with the Masters of Typeg and other countries," he said. "He would capture people and bring them as slaves. And in return, they would give him one or two slaves for his own. He always chose the biggest and strongest men. I got to know most of them. I had never encountered slavery before and so I was curious. They showed me what slavery is like, and I wanted to set them free. I talked to the captain and explained my reasons. He agreed, and he never dealt in slaves again."

He pulled her down to sit next to him on the desk. "Most pirate Captains have similar deals with the Masters," he said. "But I never did it. I couldn't. I tried to stop other Captains as well, but it's not my place to interfere with their business. I learned that the hard way." He pointed to the scar on his cheek.

Tahira ran her finger down it. "I already knew you never dealt in slaves," she said. "Scudamore told me that you take slaves from Mills's ship and set them free. So in a way, you do interfere with other Captains' business."

He glanced sideways at her and sighed. "Scudamore wasn't supposed to tell you that."

She laughed once. "He said as much. But I'm glad he did."

He gave an embarrassed smile and looked at her back again. "These are so bad," he said.

"I was in the fields for seven years," she said. "And then the Master whipped me shortly after I became Alycia's personal slave."

Killian kissed the base of her neck and she felt a thrill rush though her. "I'm so sorry," he whispered. His expression was remorseful, much more remorseful than she thought it should be; he looked like he was only just realizing that *he* had given her those scars.

Tahira paused. She turned to face him and took his hand. "Killian, would you tell me how you became a pirate?"

Killian smiled a little. "I guess after all this time you deserve to know."

"You said it was painful."

"Aye, it was." He put his arm around her, drawing her closer. "I was a lieutenant in the Navy at the time. We had orders to find a pirate ship, the worst in the seas. And we did, but he was looking for us too. He happened upon us at night. Navy ships usually win out against pirates, but this time we lost because the pirates sent a fireship during the battle."

"What's a fireship?"

"It's a boat loaded with powder and fuses and set adrift toward an enemy," he said. "It exploded at our waist, crippling the ship and killing half the gun crews on the starboard side. The ship started to sink. The pirates stole what they could and got those of us that survived into boats and took us prisoner."

He paused and she leaned her head against his shoulder. His voice became softer as he continued, "I was the only officer who survived. The pirate Captain gave me a choice: turn pirate or he would kill my crew."

"Did he promise to set your crew free if you did?" she asked.

"Aye, he did," he said, squeezing her shoulder. "To save them I took his oaths. But he had lied. He killed my entire crew in front of me."

"What?" She sat up and stared at him.

"He tortured the boys first. I still have nightmares about their screams."

"Killian."

"He told me that if I had refused, he would have freed us all."

"But that was probably a lie too," she said.

"Nearly everything he said was," he said. He sighed and pulled her closer. She stayed quiet, wondering what else he might tell her.

"I never wanted to be a pirate," he said. "But then I chose to be one because it was easier than facing my grief and pain. The pirate essentially held me prisoner, wearing me down bit by bit. After he killed my crew I wanted to kill him. But I couldn't. And eventually, I gave up. He stopped torturing me, but the torture remained inside me. I couldn't fight it off any more. I was as much a pirate as the next man."

"Why couldn't you fight it?" Tahira asked quietly.

Killian leaned his head against hers. "I had nothing to live for any more, and I was alone. And even if I had made it home, there was a court martial waiting for me for deserting my commission."

"But you didn't desert."

"Aye, but that's the official story," he said. He sounded more despondent than she had ever heard him. "I could plead my case, but I'm a pirate now. My word is no longer good to the Navy."

"But Killian, just tell the truth," she said, looking at him. "It's more powerful than anything."

He shook his head. "I wish I still believed that."

She tapped his arm, hard. "Then do," she said. She paused, dreading the question she wanted to ask. "Who was that pirate?"

"Charles Nave."

Tahira gasped and pulled away. "He turned you—he killed—?" Killian nodded. His resigned expression dampened her shock.

"What deal did you have with him?" she asked.

"When I became a Captain, Nave seemed to feel that I threatened him, and I knew he wanted to kill me," he said. "Wilkid wanted to sail but Nave didn't want him. In order to buy myself some protection, I offered to take Wilkid aboard my ship. In exchange for that, Nave promised to never attack me."

"And for once he told the truth?" Tahira asked.

"That he did," Killian said. He glanced sideways at her, one eyebrow raised. "I'm sorry to turn this somber. We were admiring your new dress." He gathered her hair and let it cascade down her back, covering her scars.

"Thank you for telling me," she said. "After all this time of trying to figure you out, I finally understand you."

Killian smiled and kissed her. She felt his heart expanding toward her, and she knew, then, how much he loved her. She knew he would protect and provide for her, and be steadfast and strong. Finally, her natural hunger and longing for love was being filled.

Chapter Twenty-Three

Tahira was barely awake the next morning when she heard a knock on her door. "Come in," she said sleepily.

"The door's locked," Killian said.

"Oh." Tahira climbed out of her bed and unlocked the door. Killian was standing there, holding a plate of food.

"I brought breakfast," he said. He looked tense.

"Come in," she said, stepping back. He sat on the bed next to her and handed her the plate. "You've never done this before," she said. "And you look worried. Is something wrong?"

He shook his head and shrugged at the same time. He still looked tense, but his voice was calm. "I came to tell you about this country we're stopping at."

"Yes, you promised to," she said, starting to eat.

"I told you yesterday this isn't a pirate port," he said, scooting back to lean against the wall. "It's a country called Raemica. It's beautiful here."

"Have you been here before?" she asked.

He nodded and leaned over on one elbow. "I was born here," he said. She gaped at him for a moment. "Though I left with the Navy when I was a young boy, and I've only been back a few times since."

Tahira pulled her legs under her and Killian rested his head against her knee.

"We're docking in Raemica's main port city, though there are dozens around its coasts," he said. "This port is larger than Turtle Island, and much more beautiful. The city climbs up into hills from there, from the port to stores, and finally to houses that are built right into the hill and cliffs. At the top of the hill is the castle."

"What's a castle?" Tahira asked. She liked the sound of the word.

"It's a huge building with lots of towers and windows," he said. "It's where the King lives."

"Are we going there?" she asked, surprised.

"No," he said. He sat up, his smile gone.

Tahira put her plate aside. "Killian, what's wrong?"

He shook his head. "What makes you think something's wrong?"

She raised her eyebrow. "Because you look worried. It's a rare enough expression that I know something's wrong. Come, tell me."

The corner of his mouth lifted. "You are coming to know me very well," he said. He let out a long breath. "This country, like many, doesn't like pirates. At some point today I will be arrested, and I'll face the justice all pirates must."

Tahira felt like something was crumbling away.

"But before that happens, I need to take you somewhere," Killian said. "And when we get there, you'll be safe, I promise. You'll be free."

She stared at him, unable to read his expression. "Killian, if Raemica doesn't like pirates, why are we stopping here?" she asked.

He took a deep breath. "Tahira, it's time to tell you where I've been bringing you, and why, and I'm not sure how to tell you. It may be hard to believe, but please try."

"Of course," she said, scooting closer to him. "Tell me."

"Raemica is our final destination."

"Oh," she said. "You've been bringing me here all this time? Why?"

He shifted his position to the edge of the bed. "I told you how I became a pirate," he said. "Would you like to hear why I joined the Navy?"

She nodded, though she was unsure how this story would answer her questions.

"When I was a little boy, about six years old, raiders from another country came to Raemica," he said. "They landed all over the country simultaneously, it seemed, and captured hundreds of people. One of their ships came to this city, where I lived. I remember they ran in so quickly and were gone just as quickly. I've never seen ships move that fast. No one had any time to prepare for their attack." He paused and looked at her. "When they came, they stole my best friend."

"What?" Tahira said, and she felt such sympathy for the child Killian used to be, watching his best friend being taken.

Killian nodded. "Just like that—gone." He snapped his fingers. "And the next year I joined the Navy as a ship's boy, in the hopes that I would find that ship and get my best friend back."

"And did you?" she asked.

He nodded again, a small smile on his face now. "Yes. About five months ago, I finally found her."

"Her? Five months ago?" Tahira said. "But Killian, that's—"

She stopped as the full force of what he was telling her settled. Her mouth fell open a little and she stared at him, hardly understanding, yet comprehending everything. Why he knew her name on *The Nantes*. Why he was so protective of her. Why he had been bringing her somewhere—here—all along.

"Killian, five months ago is when you found me," she said slowly, feeling something between anticipation and dread. "Are you telling me…"

Killian took her hand and laced his fingers in hers. "Aye. Tahira, you are from Raemica," he said. "But more than that, we grew up together. We played together. Our parents were friends. You were captured and taken away from us. And I joined the Navy in the hopes of finding you."

Tears sprang to her eyes and she found breathing difficult, feeling agitated. "Why didn't you say anything earlier?" she asked. "Why did you never tell me?"

One corner of his mouth lifted sheepishly. "I didn't think you would believe me," he said, running his thumb under her eyes. "When you didn't recognize me on *The Nantes*, I knew you wouldn't have any memories of Raemica. How could I explain to you that you weren't born in Typeg?"

Tahira closed her eyes and her tears streamed down her cheeks. She leaned forward until her forehead rested against Killian's shoulder. He kissed the top of her head. She remembered the surprise she'd seen on his face when he saw her for the first time on the slaver. "Are you sure? How do you know it's me?"

"Because your name is the same," he said. He sounded like he was smiling. "And because you look like your mother."

Tahira sat up. There were so many questions she wanted to ask. But they all got tangled up in her mouth, all eager to be asked first, and so she couldn't say anything. This all felt like too much. Yet it was easy to believe him.

"You and I were playing in front of your house when the raiders came," he said. "Your mother was sitting right there. You had stepped away from me as part of our game, and in that moment, you were taken. Your mother and I ran after you, but that man ran so fast we couldn't catch him. I remember your mother cried for weeks. When I told her I was joining the Navy to find you she cried all over again. And every time I came back your parents asked about you. I haven't been back here for ten years. But now I can bring you home to them."

Tahira felt shocked, still trying to reconcile her memories. Her mother with the sunset-colored hair, and her strong and quiet father were the only parents she remembered. But Killian was telling her that her real parents were somewhere in this Raemican city. She swayed a little, and Killian scooted closer to her and put his arm around her.

"How old was I?" she whispered.

"You were three," he said.

"Why didn't the King stop the raiders? Protect his people? Come after the ships?" she asked, even though these were lesser concerns.

Killian grimaced. "Because the King is not a good man," he said. "I told you that my ship had been ordered to capture Nave. But that was only because Nave had broken into the castle and stolen the King's clothes. The King doesn't care about pirates or raiders that attack his people. He only cared when he himself was threatened."

He looked at her long and hard, and Tahira guessed he was trying to gauge her reaction to all this news. She didn't know herself. She leaned into Killian and he rocked her gently.

"Where are you taking me?" she asked at last.

"I'm taking you home to your parents," he said. "Hopefully I'll be able to do that before I'm arrested."

"But why would you be arrested if the King doesn't care?" she asked, her eyes closed. She couldn't bear the thought of losing him again.

"The King doesn't care, but the Navy does," he said.

She sat up and took Killian's hand again. She opened her mouth to ask another question, but just then Scudamore fell down the ladder and ran into the cabin.

"Sir, it's the Navy!" he said.

Captain Haefen stood up, still holding Tahira's hand. "So soon? Have they fired?"

"Not yet, sir," Scudamore said. He and Captain Haefen suddenly looked worried.

"Have we struck our colors?" Captain Haefen asked.

"Aye, sir, like you said to. And we're bare poles."

"Good. And the weapons?"

"Locked away." Scudamore handed Captain Haefen a key.

Captain Haefen took it. "Very good. Keep everyone on deck, I'll be up shortly. We knew this might happen."

"Hurry, sir," Scudamore said, and ran back up the ladder.

Killian sighed and faced Tahira again. "It looks like I won't be able to take you home yet," he said. "I'm going to surrender, and the Navy will take us into the city. Please, hurry up as soon as you can."

Killian squeezed her hand and darted out of the cabin. Tahira could almost feel the tension in the ship. She closed the door and changed into her best dress. By the time she joined Captain Haefen on the quarterdeck, three Navy ships were moored near the *Royal Conlan*. Already a boatload of six sailors and officers was on its way over. Tahira felt her stomach clench.

Killian took her hand. "Tahira, when they board us, will you stay with me?"

She looked up at him. He was looking at her with such an intense gaze that she gasped a little. In that moment it wasn't hard to see the little boy who had been her friend, who had set out to search for her. She wondered how much of her trust in him stemmed from long-forgotten memories of their childhood together. She was glad Killian had told her the truth, but even more glad to find that she loved him more than ever.

"I will," she said. With those words she meant more than agreeing to stand by his side while he talked to the Navy officers; she meant that she would stay with him from then on.

Killian seemed to understand her, for he smiled. Something caught in Tahira's throat and tears came to her eyes.

Every pirate on the *Royal Conlan* stood still and quiet, his hands at his sides, and his eyes fixed on the Navy officers as they boarded and surveyed the ship.

"Where is the captain?" asked the officer with the biggest hat, in the same lilting accent as Killian.

Captain Haefen let out a sigh of relief. "Lieutenant Rogers," he said, moving through the pirates to stand in front of the officer, still holding Tahira's hand. "It's good to see you again."

Lieutenant Rogers took a slight step backward and squinted at Captain Haefen. "Do I know you, pirate?"

"Aye, you do," Captain Haefen said.

"Haefen," Lieutenant Rogers said after another beat or two. His expression seemed unsure whether to smile or scowl. "What are you doing here?"

"I've finally come home," Captain Haefen said. He glanced at Tahira. "And I'm bringing someone with me."

Rogers took a step forward, his expression friendly. "But why come home now? You know you're going to be arrested."

"I do," Captain Haefen said shortly. Anger flooded Rogers's face.

"What are you on about?" he asked. "How dare you show your face here again?"

Captain Haefen looked confused. "What does that mean?" he asked.

"It means the whole country knows you betrayed your crew to turn pirate," Rogers said, raising his voice. "Got them killed for your own purposes."

Captain Haefen's confusion mingled with anger and disbelief. "That is not what happened," he said. "Come on, now, Rogers. The Killian Haefen you knew wouldn't have done that."

"I haven't known Killian Haefen for ten years," Rogers spat. "I don't know who you are any more."

Captain Haefen raised his eyebrows, a cool expression on his face. Tahira wondered about his history with Rogers. "We're here to surrender," he said, his Captain's confidence in his voice. "We are unarmed and all our weapons are in my cabin. Here is the key." He held it out and Rogers snatched it from his hand. "I may not be the Killian Haefen you knew ten years ago," he said, his voice soft. "But I'm more him than the pirate you seem to think me." Rogers looked down at the key, glancing up at Captain Haefen from under his brows.

"All right, Captain," he said at last. "Let's to your cabin to discuss the terms of your surrender."

Captain Haefen nodded and led the way to the quarterdeck hatch. He motioned for Tahira to descend first, but the cabin door was still locked.

"I'll need my key," Captain Haefen said once they were crowded by the door. He held out his hand, but Rogers fisted the key.

"I'll unlock it," he said. Captain Haefen sighed.

"Don't you trust me?"

"No," Rogers said. He looked between Captain Haefen and Tahira a few times, then back up the stairs, where Scudamore had just stepped down behind him. "And now perhaps your cabin isn't the best," he said, sounding nervous. Tahira wondered why he hadn't brought some of his men along. "If you weren't lying, all your weapons are in there. This could be a trap."

"Rogers, I would never do that," Captain Haefen said, anger in his voice.

"Rogers, just give me the key," Tahira said, speaking for the first time. She reached around Captain Haefen and took the key from Rogers's astonished fist.

"Oh," Rogers said, seeming to see her for the first time. "I thought she was—"

"Was what?" Captain Haefen said, a challenge in his voice. "My silent whore? That was never me."

"I remember," Rogers said in a small voice.

Tahira unlocked the cabin door and led the way inside. The bed was piled high with all the weapons of the ship, but otherwise looked the same from the day before; there were even waterskins and mangos still on the desk. Rogers looked around the cabin before settling himself in Captain Haefen's chair.

"So, tell me your terms," he said, leaning back.

"Unconditional surrender from me," Captain Haefen said, leaning one hand on his desk. "Conditional from most of my crew. Most of them will want a pardon from King Noah."

"He's no longer our King," Rogers said with a sneer. "You'd know that if you hadn't turned pirate."

Captain Haefen pounded his fist on the desk, frustration coming off him in waves. "Stow it, mate," he shouted. "You don't know what happened."

"Yes, I do," Rogers shouted back, standing up. "You lost the *Silver* to Nave and got your entire crew killed to join him. All those boys—" He broke off, sudden tears in his eyes. Captain Haefen straightened up, staring at Rogers. He knit his brows.

"Is that why you're angry at me?" he asked, his voice quiet. "Because your little brother died? His screams haunt my dreams most nights. There was nothing I wouldn't have done or didn't try to do to save him."

"Screams?" Rogers's voice seemed choked off.

Captain Haefen and Rogers stared at each other, each man warring within himself. Tahira sat on the edge of the desk, watching Killian. Once she glanced at Scudamore, wondering if he had heard this story. But Scudamore's face was impassive as he stood with his hands behind his back in a corner of the cabin.

The anger left Captain Haefen's face. "You see, Rogers, you weren't there. But I was," he said. "I was the only survivor by the time Nave was done. Where did the official story come from, then? From pirates. You want to know what happened, ask me."

"How do I know you're telling the truth?" Rogers asked.

"Because you trusted me once," Captain Haefen said. He tilted his head toward Tahira. "And she has changed me back to who I was then."

"Who is she?" Rogers asked, looking at Tahira with a mixture of awe and curiosity. Captain Haefen shifted closer to Tahira and brushed her knee with his hand.

"She is the reason I joined the Navy." Rogers's face cleared and he looked more ready to smile than shout.

"You found her!" he said, and he actually did smile then.

Captain Haefen returned it, then became serious again. He seemed to be waiting for Rogers to make a decision, and Tahira longed to know how they knew each other so well. After a few moments of silence, Rogers sat down in the chair again.

"Haefen, what happened to the *Silver*?" he asked. He looked up at Captain Haefen like he was looking at an old friend.

The tension in Captain Haefen's shoulders relaxed. He told Rogers the whole story, much more than he had told Tahira. He explained that Rogers's younger brother, Benjamin, had just been promoted to midshipman by the *Silver*'s Captain Nigh. He explained how valiantly Benjamin had fought against the pirates, even when the rest of his gun crew was killed. Benjamin had fought the pirates as they dragged him aboard Nave's ship, and had attacked anyone who tried to touch the ship's boys. Captain Haefen detailed how he had turned pirate to save the remaining crew, and what Nave had done then. He described how Benjamin had been tortured, and how no matter how much pain Benjamin was in, he kept assuring his commanding officer, Lieutenant Haefen, that he was proud to die defying pirates.

By the time Captain Haefen finished, everyone had tears in their eyes, even Scudamore. Rogers was quiet for a time as he processed what he'd heard. Tahira looked up at Captain Haefen. It was as if the years had melted away, and he was Lieutenant Haefen of Majesties' Navy again. She remembered him telling her that the sea air seemed to be the only thing to get rid of nightmares, and she now knew the extent of those nightmares.

Killian swayed a little, his face pale. Tahira jumped up and grabbed him before he fell over. Scudamore stepped over to help sit Killian on his desk. Tahira reached behind him for a waterskin. Killian drained it and ate a hunk of bread Scudamore produced from his pocket. After a few minutes, his color returned to normal. He nodded to Scudamore and kissed Tahira on the forehead. As he stood up again, Rogers looked up from his reverie.

"And you really could not save him?" he asked.

"No," Captain Haefen said quietly. "They tied me to the mast so I could do nothing but shout and spit. But believe me, I did everything I could to save them."

Rogers considered for a moment, then nodded, his expression sad. "Aye, that you did. But you remained a pirate."

"Aye, and that's my own shame," Captain Haefen said. He stood up straighter, and the captain's ring was in his voice again. "But I'm here surrendering now, and will hang up my Jolly Roger."

"Which the crew think you're daft to do," Scudamore muttered.

But Tahira was confused. "What?" she said.

Killian put his hand on her shoulder with a minute shaking of his head. She nodded, hoping he would explain later. "Rogers, only allow me to take Tahira home," he said. "Then you can arrest me and take me to the King."

"I told you, we have a new monarchy," Rogers said, standing up. "You know how corrupt the last one was. This new King and Queen were asked to step in to rule about nine years ago. And they have changed Raemica for the better." He gestured out the stern windows to where they could just see the three Navy ships. "This is now Their Majesties' Navy. And they have no tolerance for pirates. I'm under orders to bring you to them right away. You know how orders are."

"Aye, I know," Captain Haefen said. He looked at Tahira with his intense gaze, but there was sadness there.

"I'm sorry, you can't take her home first," Rogers said, striding around the desk and opening the door. Scudamore left the cabin. "I must take you now."

Captain Haefen ignored him. Tahira stepped closer to him, her hands on his waist.

"Killian," she said, her voice pleading. She felt again like something was crumbling away. She wasn't ready to say goodbye.

Killian tucked her hair behind her ear. "I told you I must be arrested," he said quietly. "But you'll still be safe. I'll ask the King and Queen to take you home." He gave one humorless chuckle. "I guess we are going to the castle after all."

Tahira blinked back her tears and nodded. Killian turned to leave the cabin.

"Rogers, I am sorry about your brother," he said.

"Thank you, Haefen," Rogers said, and led the way up.

Every pirate was kneeling on the deck. More of the Navy sailors and soldiers had come over to the *Royal Conlan*, and surrounded her crew with guns. Most of the pirates looked angry, but a few looked as calm as Killian did.

Rogers stepped to the rail. "Captain, your crew shall remain here, under arrest," he said in a loud, carrying, Navy officer's voice. "They'll be brought to the castle later. I'm to take you to Captain Woodes, captain of the guard at the castle."

He gestured to Captain Haefen to join him at the rail. "Let Tahira come with me," Captain Haefen said, reaching his hand back for Tahira. "Some of my crew have tried to kill her."

Rogers looked annoyed. He glanced down at the boat waiting for them, then nodded. "Fine. Let's go, Haefen."

Once Captain Haefen and Tahira were sitting in the bow of the boat, Rogers barked an order and the sailors started rowing the boat away from the *Royal Conlan*.

Tahira glanced back at Rogers, then looked at Killian's profile for a while. He looked nervous and tense, and she could only imagine what was on his mind; nothing about his return to Raemica had gone as he had wanted, and now he could not even do what he had promised her. He had given himself up for arrest, and must now face Raemica's justice. Tahira shuddered at the thought of what Killian might have to face.

To hopefully distract both of them, she asked, "Does he not remember me?"

Killian glanced at Rogers then looked at her. "He's not from this city," he said. "But we sailed together when we were midshipmen. I told him all about you."

Tahira's heart hurt. She was still reeling from what she had already experienced that day, and Killian was about to be taken from her again. Though they were awkwardly cramped in the bow, she hugged him, her arms wrapped carefully around his ribs and her head resting on his shoulder. He held her tightly to him.

"Thank you for coming to rescue me, Killian," she whispered.

He kissed the top of her head.

Chapter Twenty-Four

Two soldiers in dark blue coats were waiting on the pier. When the boat was docked, Rogers and the two soldiers escorted Killian and Tahira toward the city.

The docks smelled horribly of fish and were full of fishmongers cleaning and selling their catch. But as they moved further into the city, that smell stayed behind. The cobbled street did seem to rise, as Killian had said, and soon the streets were lined with stores, low and tall. Through the windows Tahira caught glimpses of fabric, bread, clothing, tools, and sweet-smelling food she had no name for. People moved in and out of the stores, some carrying baskets, some carrying the wares they bought. There were so many people at times that Tahira had to walk behind Killian instead of next to him.

Still the street climbed. Soon the stores ended, and the street opened up into a main square. She paused slightly as she looked around. There were hundreds of people, and somewhere nearby she could hear music and singing. Colored streamers ran high overhead, strung between buildings across the main square. Children were running through everything, screaming and shouting. Good smells wafted and floated all around her, and Tahira thought she might never get enough of them.

"Come on," Killian whispered, taking her hand.

"But I want to see the city," she said.

Killian smiled a little. "You will."

Finally, through the houses that had now started, Tahira could see the castle at the top of the hill, facing west toward the sea. She'd never seen such a beautiful building, nor so many towers. It was many times the size of the Master's Mansion, but she instinctively knew it held more warmth than the Mansion had ever had.

Rogers led them steadily up the hill until they reached the castle. It was so much bigger up close that Tahira nervously gripped Killian's elbow with her other hand. The front double doors rose in front of them, a tall doorway of dark wood. The two soldiers opened one of the doors and stepped aside.

Rogers led the way inside.

"Stop there," one of the blue-clad soldiers said. He walked away while his companion stayed standing next to Rogers.

Tahira blinked and her eyes adjusted to the darker interior. They were standing in a very large entry hall, the floor a polished tan stone, and the ceiling almost lost in shadow. Hallways extended as far as she could see to her right and left. Down the hallway to her right was a lower doorway than the front door, through which she could see people walking by, some holding things, some running, and some talking to others. The hallway to her left was empty. In front of them was the largest staircase Tahira had ever seen, the banisters polished to a shine. At the top of them she could see another set of double doors.

She wanted to ask Killian if he'd ever been here before, but she didn't dare speak; the entry was so large that the smallest sound echoed.

After a few minutes the blue-clad soldier came back with an older, more decorated soldier behind him.

"Lieutenant Rogers," the newly-arrived soldier said. "Thank you for bringing the pirate captain."

"Sir," Rogers said, saluting. He turned to Killian. "Haefen, this is Captain Woodes. He will deal with you from here."

He gave Killian a dark look and left through the front doors. Tahira looked after him for a few moments. Rogers had her almost as confused as Killian once did. He seemed to be torn between duty to the Navy and either anger or friendship toward Killian. Tahira shook her head and turned her attention to Captain Woodes.

Captain Woodes was eyeing Killian up and down. He was a very thin man, a little shorter than Killian. He had something of a permanent smirk on his face.

"A pirate captain, freely surrendered," he said. "I hope you don't expect a pardon for surrendering?"

"No, simply to fulfill a promise and turn myself in," Captain Haefen said.

"You were an officer in the Navy once, weren't you?" Woodes asked. Killian nodded. "It's a shame you deserted." His smirk deepened and he turned to the two soldiers. "Clap him in irons."

Tahira was pushed out of the way as the soldiers unnecessarily wrestled Killian's hands in front of him and put them into manacles. Killian put up no resistance, and Tahira thought she saw disappointment on Woodes's face.

"Come, pirate, time to face your justice. To the throne room," he said. He seemed to Tahira the kind of man who liked posturing more than doing true work. He gestured with his hand and the soldiers started hauling Killian up the stairs. Tahira made to follow but Woodes put his hand up in front of her. "No, wench, you stay here."

"She comes with me," Captain Haefen said before Tahira could respond, so firmly that Woodes actually startled. Without waiting for a response Tahira stepped around Woodes and followed Killian up the stairs.

The doors she had seen from the bottom of the stairs led into the throne room. They were ornately carved and Tahira could tell that the carvings told stories. She was immediately fascinated, and wondered if she'd ever get a chance to look more closely at them. Woodes opened one door and stepped into the throne room, leaving his two guards with Killian and Tahira.

"Will you wait out here?" he asked. "I'll need to talk to the King and Queen before I can ask them to take you home."

"Why can't I come in with you?" Tahira asked.

Killian glanced into the throne room where they could hear Woodes announcing his arrival. "Because I don't think you'll be allowed in right away," he said.

Tahira took Killian's chained hands in hers and kissed his rough knuckles.

Woodes came out of the throne room and nodded to his guards, who hauled Killian through the door. "You wait here," he said to Tahira, and followed them.

Tahira stood at the doors, looking in through the crack between them. The throne room was the largest room she had ever seen. The vaulted ceiling was lined with hammerhead beams, from which hung many multicolored banners. Along the walls were thin windows filled with stained glass. A few doors were interspersed with the windows, and Tahira saw some robed men and women and a few guards exit through one of the doors. At the far end of the room was a raised dais on which sat two golden thrones. And in the center of the throne room, on the long purple carpet, was a large heavy table, filled with papers. Chairs stood around it, all of which looked like they'd recently been pulled out.

The King and Queen stood at the table, talking in quiet voices. They were both clothed in rich colors, but neither wore a crown. The King looked up as Woodes approached with a click of his heels, Killian and the guards right behind him.

"Your Majesties, here is the pirate I—" Woodes began.

But Killian interrupted, "Delrick?" The King stared at him in surprise and the Queen looked up. "Jazara?"

"Quiet, pirate!" Woodes shouted. He turned around and threw his forearm hard into Killian's still-healing ribs. Killian cried out and doubled over. Tahira gasped, one hand flying over her mouth.

"Killian?" Queen Jazara asked. She stepped around the table and trotted toward Killian as he struggled to an upright position. Her face was full of hope and question. "Killian Haefen, is that you?"

Killian nodded as Queen Jazara smiled and threw her arms around his neck, stroking him like a mother would. King Delrick, smiling just as widely, clapped Killian on the shoulder. The guards stepped away, looking at Woodes, whose expression could not have been more confused.

"I can't believe it's you, after all these years," Queen Jazara said, stepping back and cupping his face in her hands. She kissed both his cheeks.

"Woodes, you and your men may leave us now," King Delrick said.

"If I may, Your Majesty," Woodes said. "Allow me to keep the pirate shackled, for the safety of the Queen."

King Delrick looked at Woodes, some of his smile fading. "Very well, Woodes, though I assure you that's not necessary."

Woodes clicked his heels together and left the throne room through one of the side doors, his guards behind him.

"When Lieutenant Rogers told me the monarchy had changed, I had no idea it would be you," Killian said.

Queen Jazara blushed and looked down and King Delrick gave an apologetic smile. "We didn't expect it ourselves, but we felt it was right to accept."

"I also heard you have changed Raemica," Killian said. "The country could not hope for better monarchs."

"Thank you, Killian, we do our best," Queen Jazara said quietly.

"But what brings you here?" King Delrick asked.

"And a pirate, Killian?" Queen Jazara asked. "Are the stories true?"

Killian shuffled one foot. "Not all of them. But the one about me being a pirate is."

Queen Jazara looked disappointed, but put a hand on his cheek. "Killian, how could you? When we heard the news, we and your parents were devastated."

"Aye, I'm sure they were," Killian said softly.

"You know that you will have to stand trial," King Delrick said. He put his arm around Queen Jazara's shoulders, and she leaned into him. "You must answer for your ten years as a pirate. But your court martial is still pending, and will happen first. You know that the Admiralty will handle that. I will not be allowed to attend."

"So before they take you, will you tell us what happened?" Queen Jazara asked. "What made you turn pirate?" She glanced up at the King. "We could hardly believe the news, and we've been puzzling over it for the last ten years."

Killian nodded and told them the same story he had told Tahira. As he talked, she watched the King and Queen. King Delrick was a little taller than Killian, and his hair was somewhere between light brown and golden. He had broad shoulders, a straight nose, and eyes that sparkled with kindness and intelligence. He exuded a kind of manly confidence that made Tahira sure that all his decisions would be correct.

Queen Jazara was beautiful, with her button nose and curling mouth. She was about Tahira's height, and her rich brown hair fell to mid-back in lazy curls. She seemed to be aware of King Delrick with her whole being, yet she listened to Killian with such attention that Tahira felt immediately that nothing was beneath the Queen's notice. Her maternal instincts were on display as she listened to Killian, and Tahira, watching, felt encompassed by them.

She understood at once why the Raemicans had chosen them as monarchs.

When Killian finished his story, Queen Jazara had a few tears on her cheeks, and King Delrick's expression was grave.

"I see," he said. "We're so sorry, Killian, for what you went through. And I'm sorry that the story has gotten muddled and given you a bad name. Your parents will be glad to hear the truth."

"Have you seen them?" Queen Jazara asked.

"Not yet," Killian said.

"But why are you here?" King Delrick asked. "You knew coming here would mean justice."

"I didn't, I just knew it was the right thing to do," Killian said. "My crew only came because they'd heard about King Noah's pardoning every pirate who sailed in Raemican waters. But I came to hang up my Jolly Roger, and my Navy commission as well."

"Why?" Queen Jazara asked.

Killian paused, but Tahira could tell from his posture that he was smiling. "I found someone, Jazara. I mean, Your Majesty."

"No," she said, putting her hand on his chest. "Here, we are Delrick and Jazara. You've called us that your whole life."

"Who did you find?" King Delrick asked.

"Do you remember why I joined the Navy?" Killian asked.

Queen Jazara nodded. "To find our Tahira."

Tahira gasped. Her knees felt weak for a moment. Her parents were the King and Queen? After all Killian had told her of her true heritage, this seemed too much. She couldn't believe it. And yet, staring at them, she could see it. She had her father's hair and her mother's height. And she had seen her reflection just enough to recognize herself in the Queen. It seemed so improbable, and yet the evidence was standing right there.

Killian paused as though he was going to turn around, and Tahira thought he might have heard her gasp. "Aye," he said. "I found someone, and I want you to see if—"

"Oh, Killian," Queen Jazara interrupted. She sounded impatient for the first time. She took a step back and rested against the table. "I don't want to meet someone that *might* be Tahira. It's too hard."

Killian froze and King Delrick stared at her. "Jazara, have you given up?" Killian asked.

Queen Jazara sighed. "No, of course not," she said, her face sad. "I'll never give up the hope that my child is alive. But Killian, Delrick, it's been twenty-two years. And the chances that Killian would find her were always so slim."

Killian took a step toward her. "Jazara, you must never give up," he said, his voice ringing with Captains' authority. "I did. I gave up any hope of seeing Tahira again. I even forgot for a time she was why I was on the seas in the first place. But five months ago, that hope was restored."

"Was that when you found this young woman you want us to meet?" King Delrick asked.

"Aye," Killian said. Tahira could tell he was smiling again. He turned to Queen Jazara. "I promised you I would find Tahira. But what I didn't tell you is that I made a promise to myself."

"What was it?" Queen Jazara asked, standing again. She didn't look as sad any more.

"That I would stay in the Navy only so long as it took to find her," Killian said. "Once I did, I would give up my commission."

King Delrick gasped as he caught Killian's meaning, his eyes sparkling more.

"Killian, you're sure you really did find her?" Queen Jazara asked, taking a step toward him.

He nodded, then turned around and smiled at Tahira. She realized she had stepped into the throne room, though she didn't know when she had done that. She trotted to his side, looking between him and the King and Queen.

"Tahira, I would like you to meet your parents," he said.

King Delrick and Queen Jazara stared at her for a few moments, both with their mouths slightly open in disbelief. Then they slowly took steps toward her, the Queen's tear-filled eyes searching every part of her face. She reminded Tahira of a bird with her unsurety and gentleness. Queen Jazara smiled tentatively, and Tahira returned it. All at once the Queen let out a sob.

"It's her, Delrick," she said. "Killian really found her."

King Delrick laughed once, tears falling down his face, and Tahira could tell she would like his laugh. He put his arm around Queen Jazara and reached out a hand to cup Tahira's cheek. Tahira took a step forward, and Queen Jazara broke away from the King to hug her.

Something bubbled up in Tahira as her mother held her and her father put his big hand on her head. Just like when she realized she loved Killian, she felt like laughing and crying at the same time, and she did. She felt relief, happiness, but still disbelief that any of this had happened.

In one moment on the *Royal Conlan*, she went from being a freed slave to a young woman with a past and a future. And in this moment in the throne room, she had become a daughter. There were people who had loved her her whole life, and now she was reunited with all of them. She had finally found a home.

As Killian had promised her all those months ago, she, at last, was free.

Queen Jazara finally broke from Tahira to hug and kiss Killian again.

"How did you do it?" King Delrick asked, putting his arm around Tahira.

"Where did you find her?" Queen Jazara asked.

"On a slaver in the Dersea Ocean," Killian said, giving Tahira a sideways smile.

"A slaver?" Queen Jazara's voice came out like a squeak and she grabbed Tahira's hand.

"I was a slave in Typeg," Tahira said.

"A slave? My daughter, a slave?" Queen Jazara whispered.

"That's the worst place in the world for slaves," King Delrick said.

"Do you think that's what those raiders did to all those people?" Queen Jazara asked King Delrick. "Sold them into slavery?"

"It's possible," King Delrick said. He looked at Killian, who shrugged.

"My mistress, Alycia, and I had just been sold by her father and put on that slaver," Tahira said. "I didn't know it was a slaver until Killian hove in sight."

"Why did you stop the slaver?" King Delrick asked.

"Why would a father sell his own daughter?" Queen Jazara asked.

"My crew needed hats," Killian said to King Delrick. "That was the first ship we sighted."

"Alycia had plans to free some slaves," Tahira said to Queen Jazara. "Master Gall didn't like that."

"It's lucky Tahira was on the slaver right then," King Delrick said.

"No," Killian said, fixing Tahira with his intense, light-blue stare. "It was more than that."

Silence fell for a moment and Tahira pulled away from her father to hug Killian. He looped his manacled arms around her and held her tight. For a moment it was as though they were the only two people in the room.

"Oh, I see," Queen Jazara said, a sly smile on her face. "The young romance has been rekindled."

"Rekindled?" Tahira repeated, looking up at Killian.

Killian's tanned face darkened and she realized she was seeing him blush for the first time. "No, Jazara, she didn't know who she was until this morning," he said. "And by then she had somehow decided she loved me."

"Of course I did," Tahira said, leaning her head against his shoulder.

"What do you mean 'somehow'?" Queen Jazara asked, putting a hand on each of them. "You were always so easy to love."

Killian shook his head. "I haven't been easy to love for quite some time."

King Delrick nodded, suddenly appraising Killian. "I'm glad to see that's changing, if not all the way changed."

Killian shuddered slightly at the King's piercing gaze. "Aye, sir, it is."

Tahira looked back and forth between them a few times, confused. But just as she opened her mouth to ask what was going on, the throne room door banged open. Several men in Navy uniforms strode in, the larger man in front carrying a large hat.

"Haefen!" he bellowed, his face not kind. "Unhand that young lady at once. You're in the presence of the King and Queen!"

"Admiral, I take it you've come for Captain Haefen," King Delrick said.

The Admiral scoffed, his face turning red. "*Captain*, is it?" he said. "We'll see about that. You were a Lieutenant when I last clapped eyes on you, before you turned traitor."

"I think you'll find that's not the situation, Admiral," King Delrick said. He now fixed the Admiral with his piercing stare, and after a moment or two the Admiral puffed and some of his agitation melted.

Killian drew in a sharp breath and Tahira realized she was squeezing his ribs. She released her arms a little so she wasn't hurting him anymore, but she did not let him go, not even when the Admiral glared at her. The Admiral seemed an angry, blustering man, though one who could see reason if he allowed it. But his treatment thus far of Killian, she thought, was unnecessary. She did not want to surrender him to such a man.

But Captain Haefen patted her shoulder and withdrew his arms from around her. He clumsily saluted to the Admiral with both hands shackled and stood at attention.

"Admiral Myngs, I believe I have a court martial to attend," he said, his eyes fixed on a spot somewhere over the Admiral's head. "I am ready and willing to give my full and complete testimony, telling no lies. But I am afraid I can produce no one and no evidence to plead my case, as all parties are dead."

"All of the pirates?" Admiral Myngs asked. His expression was somewhere between skepticism and amazement.

"Aye, sir," Captain Haefen said. "I and my crew killed the last of them about a fortnight ago. The pirate Charles Nave is no longer a threat to

Raemica."

"Well," Admiral Myngs said, the red leaving his face as relief replaced it. "That is good news, Haefen. Let's see about this court martial."

Two of the Navy officers grabbed Killian and prepared to pull him from the throne room.

"A moment, please," King Delrick said, holding up his hand.

Killian looked long and hard at Tahira. She suddenly realized she was crying. The ebullience of only moments before was draining out of her. She had her parents and her identity back, but she was losing Killian. Again.

"I'll see you soon, Tahira," he said.

"Come!" Admiral Myngs shouted.

Killian looked over his shoulder as long as he could before the throne room doors closed behind him. Tahira's heart broke as she watched him, and she knew his heart was breaking too. She still wasn't ready for his arrest, even though it had come. Her head was spinning and her knees felt weak for a moment. She felt King Delrick holding her up and Queen Jazara stroking her hair. But for a few minutes she could do nothing but cry.

"I'm sorry," Tahira said finally. "I should be happy, I've found you."

"Do not be sorry," Queen Jazara said, taking Tahira's face in her hands and wiping her tears away with her fingers. "If Delrick were suddenly taken from me, I would be even worse off than you."

She smiled and Tahira gave one watery laugh. Queen Jazara kissed her forehead.

"Court martial trials do not last long," she said. "You will be able to see Killian soon."

"Will they kill him?" Tahira asked.

King Delrick held her tighter. "I don't know," he said. "If they don't, he will stand trial for his piracy. The law will decide then if he lives or dies."

Queen Jazara said something sharp to her husband, but Tahira did not hear it; her knees gave out entirely and King Delrick eased her to the floor. She could not have foreseen the end of Killian's surrender, what all it would mean for him. But he must have, at some point, realized what was coming. It hurt her that she hadn't known, but it hurt her more that Killian had. She could feel him protecting her again, withholding information until she was ready to hear it.

King Delrick knelt by her and put his hand on her shoulder. "I promise you, Tahira, that I will do everything in my power to save Killian," he said.

"It will be all right."

She looked into her father's kind, intelligent eyes, and felt her soul quieting. She took a deep, shuddering breath. Queen Jazara hugged her.

"Come, my daughter," she said at last. "Let us welcome you to your new home."

Chapter Twenty-Five

Captain Haefen's court martial trial lasted several days. Every captain, lieutenant, commodore, and admiral of Their Majesties' Navy wanted to hear his story and ask him questions. It seemed the *Silver* was the only ship Raemica had ever lost, and so the Navy wished to know in detail how that had happened. And as many of the officers were traveling into Raemica from their various stations at that time, the full trial would take time.

So Tahira heard from King Delrick, as he heard it from his aides, as they heard it standing listening at the door.

If Tahira hadn't had her parents and a whole life to learn, she might have felt as if she was going mad. But once her tears in the throne room had subsided, she realized something she hadn't before: she was a Princess.

The day after her arrival, King Delrick and Queen Jazara announced to Raemica that their long-lost daughter had been returned to them, and when the time was right, she would be presented to the people as their Princess.

Queen Jazara took her in hand and started training her. Tahira trembled a little at all the rules and customs she was now expected to learn and perform. That is, until Queen Jazara said softly to her,

"Most of these are very silly, and I don't do all of them. I'm just teaching you all there is to being a Princess. You choose what feels right to do."

Tahira's room in the private wing on the north side of the castle was at least twice the size of Alycia's in the Mansion. She had brought nothing with her but what could easily be kept in the wooden trunk and her silver box. But the Queen soon filled her room with furniture and art, all of which fascinated her.

Commissions for new clothes went out to five different cities throughout the kingdom. As the gowns and dresses slowly came in, Tahira repeatedly ran her hands over them: the yards and yards of rich fabrics that made the many layers of skirts and folds of sleeves, and the shimmering belts that outlined low waists. They made her feel beautiful, but they made her feel guilty. All that wealth.

"When I came here, I was wearing the best dress I'd ever worn," she said to Queen Jazara one evening as they stood in front of her wardrobe. "And now I have these gowns. They are more beautiful than anything I've ever seen, but I'm worried that they're too much."

Queen Jazara took Tahira's hand and kissed it, then traced her finger gently over the lingering bruisings there. "You are a lucky woman," she said. "You are the only one who will not be ruined by wealth. Because you know what it is to have nothing, you appreciate when you have everything. I hope you keep this wonder and this gratitude."

"But is it too much?" Tahira asked.

"Of course not," King Delrick said, coming into the room. "Raemicans are blessed to be one of the wealthiest countries in the world. You will see when you travel through Raemica that many people live almost as well as we do."

"But do we live better?" Tahira asked.

"Yes, but it's not because of us," Queen Jazara said. She pulled Tahira over to the little seating area she had designed: five comfortable chairs surrounding a knee-height table in a shape somewhere between a circle and a square, with smaller side-tables standing between each chair. King Delrick followed and they all sat down.

"Do you know why your father and I are King and Queen?" Queen Jazara asked. Tahira shook her head. "It's because the people have chosen to follow us. We were made royalty because the people deemed us worthy to govern them. We tax the people only enough to feed and protect them. And what we have here at the castle"— she gestured around the room— "we have bought with the royal money."

"How did we get so rich?" Tahira asked.

Queen Jazara's face saddened a little and King Delrick shook his head.

"Centuries of past kings taxed the people horribly and kept the money for himself," he said. "This last King especially. And we inherited that money."

"Your father and I work, and we pay for things," Queen Jazara said. "We are giving the money back to the kingdom, a little at a time. Everything we have, everything we wear, was made in this kingdom. And we only acquire what we need, and no more. You and I, for instance, will only get new gowns on special occasions. And you coming home certainly qualifies."

Tahira ran her hand over her deep purple skirt that seemed to float around her. She smiled. "Killian said you've changed Raemica," she said. "Is this one way?"

"Oh yes," King Delrick said. He reached out and took Queen Jazara's hand. Seeing their affection made Tahira's smile widen. "We feel that a wealthy royal family shows the kingdom that we have enough to take care of them. And if at any time they don't feel we are doing well enough, they can put new rulers in our places."

"Like they did with King Noah," Tahira said.

King Delrick nodded. "Being royal is a privilege and a gift that we do not take lightly. We made it our creed at our coronation that we would never resort to tyranny or excess."

There was a knock at the door, and Queen Jazara called out. The door opened and two girls came in. They bobbed curtsies to the King and Queen, and then took away the dishes Queen Jazara and Tahira had used for their dinner. They wore matching uniforms, kept their eyes on their work, and did not speak. Tahira stared at them in horror until they left the room.

"Tahira? What is it?" King Delrick asked.

She slowly turned her head to look at her parents. "They're not slaves, are they?"

"No, no, no, of course not," Queen Jazara said. She moved to the seat next to Tahira and stroked her face and hands until Tahira's terror started to drain away; somehow, she had seemed to understand exactly what Tahira needed. "They're servants, Tahira. We pay them. They go home when their work is done, they have families, and they can leave here at any time."

"There are no slaves in Raemica," King Delrick said. He seemed to be scrutinizing her reaction. He paused. Tahira looked at him and felt as if he was reaching out to her. "Tahira, could you tell us about Typeg?"

"Delrick, now?" Queen Jazara asked.

King Delrick nodded. "But only if she wants to."

Tahira looked back and forth between them and smiled at their attention. "In a word, it was horrible," she said. "I told one of the pirates once that I'd rather forget my life there. I had parents. My mother had bright hair and my father was quiet but very strong." She stopped and looked between them again. "Perhaps it's because of those memories that I haven't called you Mother and Father yet."

Queen Jazara patted her hand. "You are a grown woman now," she said.

King Delrick's steady gaze turned bittersweet, and Queen Jazara's eyes were just a little sad. Tahira remembered how the King and Queen had looked at her in the throne room—with hope and love—and she suddenly understood something.

While she had been in Typeg, they had missed her life. They had missed her growing up, they had missed being parents. Though she had never missed her slave parents after they'd been sold, she missed Old Joche, and the midwives, and all her friends that she had lost. Now, she missed Killian. Though King Delrick and Queen Jazara had never demanded anything of her, she could see they were asking if she could do something.

"No, I think it's right that I do," she said. "Mother, Father, we have missed so much of each other. It's time we stop that."

Mother gave her a wet smile and Father laughed. They took each other's hands again and held them as Tahira kept talking.

She told them about her parents, about Shipra and Pula and about being trained to be a midwife. She told them about being given to Old Joche and trained to be a healer. She told them of Old Joche's death, and the Master's subsequent test of healing that she failed, sending her to the fields. Tahira told them as little as possible about the fields and the work, but luckily Father had heard stories, so Tahira did not need to explain.

Memories flooded through Tahira while she talked, most of them unpleasant. She was shocked at first; her time in Typeg, while difficult, hadn't seemed as awful as it sounded now. But that was all she had known. She did not have what the other women around her had had: memories of a past life of freedom. Now that Tahira had it herself, she felt even more pity for the slaves. She explained this to her parents as best she could, and Mother nodded sadly.

Tahira kept talking, telling of being made Alycia's personal slave, and how Alycia finally decided to free slaves.

"But she didn't want to do it because she knew slavery was evil," Tahira said. "She did it so the remaining slaves would see her as a kind Mistress when she inherited."

"That's horrible," Father said, wrinkling his nose in disgust exactly like she did.

"That's how she was raised to think," Tahira said, telling them both what she had come to accept, and hiding a smile at Father's expression. "When Master Gall found out, he told her he was sending her away to see the world. And like I've said, I didn't know I was on a slaver until Killian came."

"How did that happen?" Mother asked, a little smile coming onto her face. "Did you recognize him?"

Tahira shook her head, but she couldn't help smiling. "He recognized me. And he bartered with the slaver captain for me. Alycia insisted on coming too, and it was then I learned that she never really saw me as a friend, only as her slave."

"I'm so sorry," Father said, reaching out his hand to her.

"So you went with Killian, not knowing who he was?" Mother asked. "I keep forgetting he's a pirate. Tahira, you agreed to go onto a pirate ship? Did you know how dangerous they are?"

Tahira nodded. "I chose Killian because from the moment I saw him, I trusted him. I don't know why. When I got on his ship, I saw that he was different from the rest of his crew; he was kind, and he treated me better than anyone else did. He always was watching over me. He gave me breeches to wear under my dress so I could climb the rigging. He told his crew to stay away from us. And after Alycia was killed by some crewmen, he comforted me. No one had ever done that before. He was the only one I talked to, and he kept giving me the choice to run away. But he also kept promising that I would be free once we arrived at our destination. There was a battle on his ship, and the other pirate captain nearly kidnapped me. I'd never seen Killian so angry before or since. After that he took me to an island so he could battle that captain again. He didn't want to risk me getting killed. That was when he told me he loved me."

She paused again and smiled. Talking about him lessened the sting of missing him.

"He made you fall in love with him," Mother said. She glanced at Delrick and blushed.

"I don't think he meant to," Tahira said. She wondered if she looked like her mother when she looked at Killian: with brightened eyes, a deep smile, and at the point of giggling. "When he came back for me after the battle, he was shocked when I told him I loved him too. I had for a while, I just hadn't realized that's what it was."

"Love was missing from your life," Mother said. Her expression was devastated.

Tahira nodded, but she didn't feel bitter. She told Mother and Father about Soto kidnapping Killian, how the *Royal Conlan* gave chase for over a week. She told them about the attacks from Rance and others, which caused Mother to cry out in fear.

"We finally found Killian adrift in a longboat," Tahira said. "He was sick, and he almost died."

"But you healed him," Mother said.

"Aye, that I did," Tahira said, mimicking Killian's accent. It was, she realized, Raemica's accent, and she supposed she sounded strange with her Typegian accent. "Though he's still recovering, both from the battle, and from the illness. I worry about him."

Father nodded. "I'll send a doctor to see him."

"It sounds like you and Killian have had great adventures together," Mother said. "Though I still don't like the idea of you being alone on that ship, surrounded by all those murderous pirates. And they did try to kill you!"

"I had some allies on the ship, and they helped me," Tahira said. "Not just when the bosun was trying to kill me, but other times as well."

"Who are they?" Father asked, his scrutinizing expression back.

"Scudamore, Copper, Ransome, Stretton, Morwell, and Samson, mostly," Tahira said. "That's the quartermaster, cook, cabin boy, and three seamen."

"Hmm," Father said. He nodded slowly, then fixed Mother with a significant look.

Something clicked in Tahira's mind. "I'm sorry, you wanted to hear about Typeg, and instead I mostly told you about the *Royal Conlan*."

"You said at the beginning that you wanted to forget your time in Typeg," Mother said. "And though I would like to hear more about how my daughter grew up, if you don't want to talk about it, then don't."

"There were things I loved," Tahira said. Mother nodded, her expression inviting. "I loved the babies. I loved the look on people's faces when they were healed. I loved watching the crops grow. I loved seeing a stone carver work. I loved story evenings in the compound when the women told stories of their lives before slavery. I loved humming slave songs while I worked. I had friends, though all were sold or died."

"I can't imagine how that would be," Father said, looking at Mother, who blushed.

"I could show you my scars," Tahira said. "They are the last reminders

I have that I was a slave. They'll be with me forever."

She stood and her parents came to her. She showed them the Master's mark on her right shoulder, then Mother undid the back of her dress so they could see the scars that ran from the base of her neck to the small of her back. Father looked angry and Mother was in tears as she did up her dress again.

"Killian had the same look on his face when he saw them," Tahira said in an attempt to lighten the mood. But her parents looked grave as they retook their seats.

"That is unforgivable," Father said. "To even think about doing that to someone, you'd have to be in the depths of evil."

"From what I've heard of Typegians, they are," Mother said. "Did your Master do all that to you?"

"Only some," Tahira said. She rubbed his mark through her sleeve. "He did this one to all his slaves personally. And he did the most recent ones on my back. Soon after Alycia wanted me to be her friend, I said things a slave should never say to a Mistress. She told her father, and he whipped me in punishment. Alycia was supposed to stop him when she thought I'd been punished enough, but she froze. He kept whipping me until she finally stopped him. I could barely move for a week after that."

Father let out a frustrated breath. "I'm suddenly very glad I'll never meet Alycia," he said. "Her upbringing would be difficult for her to overcome, and I do not want that in my home. I do not want to break bread with the torturer of my daughter."

"Neither do I," Mother said. She looked hard at Father, and he returned her gaze. To Tahira it was as though they were communicating without speaking. She remained silent, watching them, fascinated.

"How did Alycia die?" Mother asked at last.

"Two pirates disobeyed Captain Haefen's orders," Tahira said. "They were fighting over her, and they both had their pistols out. One shot at the other and Alycia was hit. She died before I could do anything to help her."

"What did Killian do?" Father asked.

"I don't think he would do this now, but he keelhauled one of them, and gave forty lashes to the other," Tahira said. "The one he keelhauled died."

"Oh," Mother said, her nose wrinkling.

"Hmm," Father said. "Well, I would like to agree with you, Tahira,

Killian wouldn't do that now. But did you know that keelhauling is a Navy punishment?"

"It is?"

"Yes, and so is lashes with the cat," Father said. "From the little I know of pirates, they don't often punish each other. You would know better."

"It might be better for me to know the Navy," Tahira said. "Now that you've told me that, I'm not sure what was Navy and what was pirate."

Mother sighed and leaned back into her seat. "Perhaps we could save that for another time," she said.

She reached over to the side table next to her, where a little silver bell sat on a white porcelain plate. She rang it, and a few moments later the door to the room opened. Once more, a uniformed girl came in and curtsied.

"Yes, Your Majesty?" she asked.

"Sia, could you bring us some tea, please?" Mother asked. "Bread and cake, if the cook has it. Princess Tahira needs to practice."

Tahira was studying the girl Sia, trying to see just what a servant was. Sia looked at Tahira without moving her head and smiled, showing dimples in both cheeks.

"Of course," she said. She bobbed another curtsy and left the room with a little spring in her step.

Tahira turned wordlessly to Mother.

"What is it?" Mother asked.

"She's really not a slave," Tahira said. "If she was, she wouldn't have spoken at all. You wouldn't have asked her anything, you would have demanded it. And you wouldn't have explained yourself either. She wouldn't have smiled, and…"

She trailed off, aware that she was rambling. Mother and Father moved closer to her. Tahira put her hand on her forehead. "Killian told me once that I still had the mindset of a slave because I was asking him permission to do something. I've never seen a servant in my life, and I'm having a hard time understanding them."

Mother lowered Tahira's hand and peered into her face. "I'm so sorry that you had the upbringing you did. But do you know something? I'm now glad that you did."

"What?" Tahira asked, shocked.

"Because the woman I see in front of me is so much more than I think I could have made her," Mother said. "The things you have seen and experienced and suffered has shown what you are made of. Despite everything you suffered, you are still kind. You fell in love with a pirate, without having any idea who he really was, because you saw his kind heart."

"Your mother's right. You still have trust in people," Father said. "Look how open you have been with us, and yet you've only known us a short time. You don't expect more than what you think is due, and you are surprised at how much is due to you." He glanced at Mother, who nodded. "I may venture to guess that you wouldn't be the woman you are today if you had grown up in Raemica."

Tahira realized she had tears running down her cheeks, but didn't bother to brush them away. "I never thought of it that way," she said. "I just always tried to do my best, to do what was the right thing to do."

The door behind them opened again and Sia re-entered, bearing a heavy silver tray laden with tea. She placed it on the center table and beamed as Mother smiled at her.

"Thank you, Sia," Tahira said. Sia looked at her, her head cocked to the side. "How old are you?"

"I'm fourteen, Your Highness," Sia said, drawing herself up. "I'll be training for your Lady's Maid soon."

Mother chuckled. Sia curtsied and left the room.

"I like her," Father said.

"So do I," Mother said.

"What's a Lady's Maid?" Tahira asked.

Mother explained, then showed Tahira the rules of tea in the royal circles: how to sit, who should host, which order to serve guests, what to say, how to hold the teacup, and in which order to eat bread and cake. Father leaned back in his chair and watched Mother with a contented half smile on his face. When Mother was done teaching, she too leaned back in her chair, and promptly ate her bread and cake in the wrong order.

"I told you, I think most of these rules are silly," she said in response to Tahira's raised eyebrows. "Here, with us, eat and say whatever you'd like. But other royal families will expect you to do it the way I just taught you."

Tahira tucked one foot up under her voluptuous skirts. "Is that why I have to learn all these rules? Because other royals will expect it?"

"Yes, unfortunately," Father said. He chuckled. "You should see the list of rules for the King. I only follow one or two."

"Hmm, yes, thankfully he doesn't pay any attention to the ones concerning his treatment of the Queen," Mother said, taking a sip of tea. "All of them say that the Queen is nothing more than a figurehead and a way for the King to produce heirs."

"If you ask me," Father said, leaning forward to take another piece of cake, "it's why Raemican Kings have not been good. They don't listen to their wives."

Tahira laughed. She was mesmerized as she watched her parents, how they interacted, how they touched, how they talked, how they relied on each other for everything. She hoped that she and Killian would one day be like that. If Killian lived, that was.

She shook her head. To take her mind off such sobering thoughts, she asked, "Mother, you said something earlier about working. Do you work?"

"Oh, yes," Mother said, setting down her teacup and buttering another slice of bread. "We both had to work for a living before we were chosen to rule, and working is still something I enjoy."

"What did you do?" Tahira asked.

"Your father was a carpenter," Mother said, beaming at him. "He made furniture, signposts, things for children, carts, and even helped build houses. In fact," she said, sweeping her arms out to take in the whole room, "he made most of the furniture in this room."

"You did?" Tahira asked, sitting up straighter and looking around as well.

"The bed, that chest over there, this low table, that side table by the bed, and these chairs," Father said, pointing.

"He started making all this before you were even born," Mother said. "It was all going to be for you. But when you were taken…" She trailed off as sadness entered her face. Tahira couldn't even imagine how that had been for her. "When you were taken, he stopped building. But we kept everything he made. We, like Killian, had hope we would see you again. But until then it was too painful to keep going."

"They're beautiful, Father," Tahira said after a pause. "Thank you."

Father patted her hand. "I don't get as much time now to do carpentry any more. But should I get another chance, would you like to learn?"

"I would!" Tahira said. "What did you do, Mother? What do you do now?"

"I worked in a variety of places," Mother said. "But all of them had to do with sewing. I made quilts, blankets, dresses, hats, even shoes once."

Father laughed and took a sip of tea to hide it. Mother gave him an askance look.

"What happened?" Tahira asked.

Father laughed again and Mother sighed. "The first pair of shoes I made were not the same size, even though they looked it," she said. "The customer tried them on in the store and couldn't get one shoe on."

Father laughed again, and this time Mother joined in. "At any rate, I never made shoes again," she said when they'd subsided.

Tahira smiled as they kept laughing. She suddenly felt so happy.

"But now I help your father rule Raemica," Mother said. "It was never a Queen's prerogative before, but he and I felt right in making it so."

"We had done everything together before, why not this?" Father said. "And like I said, if past Raemican Kings had listened to their Queens, they might not have struggled so much."

Mother put her hand on his knee. "But on days when I'm not needed to be Queen, I go out into the city and find some work to do," she said. "Sometimes I let the shopkeepers pay me, and sometimes I don't."

"Could I go with you the next time?" Tahira asked.

"Of course," Mother said.

"There are many opportunities for you, Tahira," Father said.

There was a single knock at the door and then it opened. A young boy in a uniform ran inside, looking a little frantic. "There you are, Your Majesty," he panted, coming to a halt just outside the circle of chairs. "You're needed in the throne room."

Father nodded once. "Thank you, Wiatt, I'll be there shortly."

He kissed Mother, then stood and kissed Tahira on the head. It was the first time he had done that, and she felt more love from it than from anything else he had done. The gesture had been so natural, she knew he had done it when she was a child. She really began to feel like she was home.

Chapter Twenty-Six

Captain Haefen's court martial finally finished a week later. Every Naval officer who had come to hear him returned to their posts all around Raemica, and the harbor, which had been abnormally busy while all those ships were in port, now felt empty. But it was still another day or two before Tahira finally heard the result of the court martial: Captain Haefen was acquitted of all wrongdoing in the losing of the *Silver*, he would not be held responsible for the deaths of her crew, and he would not be executed for turning traitor.

Tahira nearly wept with gratitude.

But Killian was not free yet. Now he and his crew had to be judged by the laws of Raemica for piracy. Father, Mother, and their Council would hold their trials, and then do to them according to the law, whether it was imprisonment, execution, or freedom.

Tahira shuddered at the thought of those trials; Killian may have been acquitted by the Navy, but he was sure to be found guilty by the Council. The pirates would have to wait for their trials to begin, however, as there were several cases ahead of theirs. In the meantime, they were confined to the castle's dungeon. Tahira wanted to see Killian, but Father asked her to wait.

"If you go see him now, the Council might see that as royal favoritism," he said. "If anyone suspects that Killian is being favored by the Crown, that he might be let go just because of our past history, it will not go well for him. We know that we love him, but I hope we also know that justice must be done."

"Killian said as much," Tahira said, trying not to show her heartbreak. "He said he wanted to face the justice all pirates must, that he chose to be a pirate, and he needed to face those consequences."

Father smiled. "I forgot how much I like that boy," he said, and then he sobered. "And he's right. Will you wait, Tahira, until a safer time for him?"

"Yes," she said. "Though I don't like to."

Father gathered Tahira in his arms and held her tight. "Neither do I, my dear."

While Tahira waited for the pirate trials to begin, she continued learning from Mother all the ways of a Princess. Mother also hired tutors from around the city to teach Tahira every day. They taught her to read and write, and then she learned history, politics, another language, geography, and something they called medicine, much of which she learned from Old Joche. She soaked up every lesson.

A week later Father and Mother felt that Tahira was ready to take her place as Princess. And so, on the large balcony overlooking the courtyard on the east side of the castle, King Delrick and Queen Jazara presented to the gathered kingdom their long-lost daughter, Princess Tahira Kellina Amari Colusafay.

Tahira had never heard a crowd cheer so loud before.

After that, she joined her parents at their royal councils in the throne room. The Council was made up of magistrates from all the governing bodies of Raemica. Once or twice a week they all came together to discuss the affairs and needs of the kingdom. Most times Tahira had nothing to offer, as she felt so lost in their discussions. But when she did have something to contribute, the Council listened and often accepted her views.

In one royal council the next week Tahira learned that the pirate trials would be starting soon. Unlike other pirates, who were tried and sentenced together, Killian's crew would be tried individually, due to the unique circumstance of bringing her home.

At hearing this, Tahira's heart froze and she found it hard to breathe. Everything else the Council said was lost to her ears.

Mother noticed. She took Tahira's cold hand in hers and nudged Father.

"Ladies, gentlemen, if you will excuse us, this council is concluded," he said.

One by one the Council stood and exited the throne room. When the door closed behind the last one, Mother and Father drew their chairs closer to Tahira.

"You knew this was coming," Father said.

"I know," Tahira said. She looked hard at Father. "Is Killian going to die?"

Mother leaned her head on Tahira's shoulder. "There are a lot of factors to be considered in a trial like this," she said. "Killian's case is especially tricky. He's effectively been pardoned by the Navy. But he hasn't been by the laws."

"What would it take to get a pardon?" Tahira asked, leaning her head against Mother's. She remembered that the last King, Noah, had given out pardons freely, and how Copper told her that many of the crew had been pardoned before.

"The most important deciding factor is if he will return to piracy or not," Father said.

"Killian won't," Tahira said.

"We know," Mother said.

"On that basis alone, I would pardon him," Father said. "But the Council might not. Because another factor is how bad his piracy was." His face fell.

Tahira raised her head. "Was Killian's piracy so bad?" she asked.

"I don't know much about it," Father said. "And that's a disadvantage for me."

"How do trials usually go?" Tahira asked.

Mother sat up. "The Council or the King asks questions of the man being judged," she said. "How he answers decides his fate."

Tahira shuddered. "There's got to be a way to save him," she said. "The Council has to see that."

"I will look through all our laws and see what can be done," Father said. "I want to save him almost as much as you do. But at the end of the day, it's the majority of the Council that decides the fate of the condemned man, not me."

"That's something your father and I added to the laws nine years ago," Mother said. "It keeps the King from having too much power."

Tahira took a deep breath. "That's a good law, even though it might hurt us."

Father took Tahira's hand. "The trials are set to start next week," he said. "Killian will be tried last. When a man is tried, he is allowed to bring a witness to help plead his case. You said that you had some allies? Would you like to be that witness for them and for Killian?"

"Will I get to see him then?" Tahira asked, hope rising in her. She missed him so much she felt as if she were sick all the time.

Mother shook her head. "I'm afraid the condemned and the witness are never in the room at the same time," she said. "Doing so could give them a chance to plot something together. An elaborate lie, for example."

Tahira felt a little deflated. She thought for a moment. Scudamore, Ransome, Copper, Stretton, Morwell, Samson. All the pirates who had helped her or been kind. They had shown in their treatment of her that they could be trusted, that they could lead different lives from the ones before, if given the chance. Should she help them, as they had helped her? She mentally shook herself; of course she would.

"I won't be able to say much about all of them, but I could say something for all," she said. "I could be a witness for them. I'll be ready when it's time for me to speak."

Tahira had learned enough of Raemican law by now to know that there was only a small chance Killian wouldn't be hanged. For even if he swore off piracy, even if his crimes weren't so great, as Captain he was responsible for the actions and crimes of his crew. Tahira let out her breath slowly and put her face in her hands.

"What is it?" Mother asked.

"I don't want to lose him," Tahira whispered. "But if I must, could you do something for me? Please don't make me watch him die. And please let me say goodbye first."

She felt a hand caressing her head and guessed it was Father's. "Do you want us to exercise our monarchical power and free him? We can do that for special cases."

A sob escaped her. Even the sound of Father's offer was hopeful. But she knew she couldn't do it. Having to refuse his offer was almost painful.

"No, don't do that," she said, squeezing her eyes against tears. "You told me you changed laws so you won't have too much power. You'd be going against those laws if you did that. We have to uphold the laws, all of them. You can't betray the trust of the people for one life."

"But isn't one life worth it?" Mother asked. "He's the man you love."

"I don't want Killian to die," Tahira said, looking up, her voice louder than she'd intended. "But he came here knowing that he would face justice, knowing that he had to. He isn't trying to run from it. He wouldn't want me to run either. I do think he's worth it, but he may not agree. He would want justice done."

"But there's also mercy," Father said, his voice soft and level. Tahira immediately felt calmer, though her chest hurt from holding in racking sobs. "He's been extended some by the Navy already. Perhaps his trial will lend him more."

Mother pulled her into a hug and Tahira couldn't hold back any more; she cried into Mother's shoulder for what felt like a long time. She felt like someone was squeezing her heart. Though her own words pained her, she knew they were true, and she knew she couldn't retract them.

"You know she's right, Delrick," Mother said. "No matter how much we love him we have to let him come to trial. Killian will answer our questions, Tahira will witness, and the Council will decide. That's all we can do for him."

Tahira heard Father shuffling some papers. "Yes. But I will see if there's more that can be done. Because that boy has proved himself no ordinary pirate. Perhaps the Council will see that."

***

The morning of the first trial, Tahira dressed herself in one of her old dresses from the *Royal Conlan* and breakfasted in her room. She and Mother were going to spend the day working in the city, and Mother had advised her not to wear one of her new gowns. Tahira thought it was just as well; she still didn't feel very comfortable wearing them. She made her way down the main staircase, braiding her long hair down her back as she walked.

The staircase ended in an open inner-courtyard-like atrium that served as the center of the castle, the hub from which all the main castle corridors branched. The furthest corridor on her right was the one that led to the front door and the throne room. As she reached the bottom of the stairs, she saw the procession of the Council in their long robes, making their way from the throne room to the trial room on the other side of the atrium. Father looked up the stairs as he passed and waved to her.

"Are they starting?" Tahira asked.

"Yes," Father said. He pulled her into a hug, and she could feel herself trembling. Father held her tighter for a moment.

"Each crewman will be tried individually, so the trials may take weeks," Father said in a low voice, looking after the Council as they kept walking. "Killian will be tried last, and I think that's when we will ask you to witness for all of them. In the meantime, I would advise you to keep close to your mother."

"But doesn't she judge with you?" Tahira asked.

"She does, usually," Father said. "But she didn't want to this time. She did tell me this morning she's taking you to work in the city?" He looked her up and down, taking in her old dress. Tahira nodded. "Have a wonderful time."

Father paused. He turned and looked toward the corridor he had come from, where there was an old man walking slowly toward them.

"Ezra, you just reminded me," Father said. He put his hand on Tahira's shoulder. "Tahira, this is my valet, Ezra."

"Pleased to meet you," Tahira said.

Ezra bowed his old white head, shaking with age. "My pleasure, Your Highness."

"I just remembered I wanted to ask you a favor, Tahira," Father said. He looked after his Council, his expression a little strained now. "Before you go out with your mother, could you do something for me?"

"Of course," Tahira said. She suddenly felt jittery, like she needed to be doing something or she would fly apart all at once. Killian's trial was that much closer, and she needed a distraction.

"Thank you," Father said. He nodded to Ezra and kissed Tahira's forehead. "I must get to the trial room, they're waiting for me. Go with Ezra, he'll explain what I need."

With a final sad smile, Father swept after his Council. Ezra, smiling nearly toothlessly, offered his arm to Tahira. He led her across the atrium and down the corridor toward the throne room. They passed the front door and kept walking, down the hallway that was usually always deserted. The further along they walked, the colder the hallway became, until they came to a heavy wooden door at the end of the hall.

"What does Father need?" Tahira asked.

"He needs you to do something in there," Ezra said, pointing a finger at the door. "I'll fetch a guard to open it, shall I? It's rather heavy."

"Oh no, I can manage," Tahira said. She pulled the heavy door open. A blast of cold air flew up the stone steps just inside the door and hit her in the face; it smelled as bad as belowdecks after a heavy storm. She'd almost forgotten she used to live in that smell.

"Down here?" Tahira asked. Ezra nodded. He had an easy smile on his face, and though he wasn't very forthcoming with what Father wanted, it didn't bother Tahira.

She stepped carefully down the uneven stone steps, one hand steadying on the wall, Ezra shuffling behind her. At the bottom of the stairs, she found two guards playing cards around a small candle-lit table. They startled to their feet at her approach, clumsily bowing and putting on their helmets.

"Your Highness," one stammered.

"Ezra, where are we?" she asked.

"This is the dungeons, Highness," Ezra said.

Tahira looked around. The dungeon had a lower stone ceiling and was made up of several corridors branching off of each other as far as she could see, creating something of a maze. Everywhere were metal-barred cells of varying sizes. It was warmer than the blast of cold air had suggested, and torches hung every few feet, giving the entire place a flickering, other-worldly feeling.

Something between hope and excitement bubbled in her chest.

"Ezra, is Father letting me see Killian?" she asked quietly.

Ezra knitted his eyebrows. "Now, there *was* someone His Majesty wanted you to see while you were down here for him," he said, his eyes twinkling. "He said you would be doing him a favor by talking to this person. I think it was a pirate, but I can't remember his name, Highness, I'm sorry."

Tahira could have kissed Ezra. She was about to laugh aloud, but Ezra glanced quickly at the guards and winked. Tahira understood: she was not being allowed to see Killian; instead, she was on an errand for the King. She took a deep breath to keep most of the laugh out of her voice and faced the guards.

"I'm here to see Captain Haefen," she said.

"He's that way, Your Highness," one guard said, pointing around the corner to her left.

"Highness, I'll take my leave of you," Ezra said, turning to mount the stairs again. "When you've finished the King's business, I imagine the Queen will be waiting for you by the front door."

Tahira smiled at Ezra, silently conveying her thanks.

She walked around the corner and found Killian immediately, as he was the only prisoner in a cluster of empty cells. She tried not to run.

The cell was small, just big enough for him to lie down on the pebbly floor. At the moment he was sitting up against the bars his cell shared with the one next to it, his head back and eyes closed, his arms dangling over his knees. Around him on the ground were a crumpled-up blanket, a candle in a holder, a bowl, a cup, and a bucket in the corner. He made no sign he heard her approach.

"Killian," she said.

His eyes started open and he stared at her for a few moments before his face lit up. She reached through the bars toward him.

"Tahira," Killian said, his voice a little scratchy. He stood up and lurched toward her, reaching through the bars to hug her as best he could. Tahira held onto him, and neither could stop their tears.

Killian kissed her forehead. "I've missed you," he said. He looked down at her dress and gave her a teasing smile. "Couldn't your mother find you some new clothes? You're a princess now."

Tahira laughed a little. "No, she did. She sent commissions to five cities for me," she said. "It's just that Mother and I are going to work in the city, and I didn't want to get the new gowns dirty."

"Where are you going?" Killian asked, tucking a stray piece of hair behind her ear.

"Mother said it was the bakery," Tahira said.

"Ah, yes," Killian said, smiling with fondness. "I loved the bakery. Ask them if you can have a croissant. They were always my favorite."

"What is it?" she asked.

His smile turned crooked. "You'll see." He stared at her as though trying to memorize her, his smile fading.

She suddenly couldn't take the finality of that action. "How are you?" she asked.

"I have been better."

"Father said he would send a doctor to see you," she said, one hand moving to feel his ribs.

"He did," Killian said. "My ribs and that gash on my ankle are all healed. And I'm in no danger from the sun down here."

He gave a wan smile that made Tahira's heart hurt. She cupped his face in her hands, his scruffy beard rough and oily.

"They're starting the trials today," she said. "Your crew will be tried individually instead of together, and you'll be tried last. Father worked out this way for me to see you."

"To say goodbye?" Killian asked. He didn't try to mask the sadness in his voice.

"I hope not," she said. "Father told me about witnesses during trials, and I've agreed to witness for you."

Killian shook his head, suddenly agitated. "Tahira, don't do that," he said. "I'm not worth that kind of trouble. Witnessing sometimes makes the trial last longer."

"Stop it," she said, tapping him sharply on the chest. "I'm going to witness for you because I think you're worth any kind of trouble."

He looked somewhere between dejected and hopeful. "But I deserve justice," he said.

"What about mercy?" she asked, leaning against the bars. "Father said the Navy has already given you some. Why not Raemica?"

He shook his head, his expression hardening. "You don't know what I've done."

"Maybe not," she said. "But I know what you've done since I met you. Whatever terrible things you did, you're not doing them anymore. You're not even that man any more. Yes," she said when he started interrupting, "you made the decision to be a pirate, but you also made the decision to stop."

She took Killian's hand. "I once asked you if you wanted me to run away, and you didn't. I'm asking you now: do you want to die?"

Killian let out a long breath and looked down. He shook his head. "No, I don't. And I believe you think I'm worth all this trouble."

"Then I'm witnessing for you," Tahira whispered.

He squeezed her hand. "I know you love me, but I don't expect you to keep me with you for the rest of your life," he said. "You could be Queen someday, and I don't think I'll make a very good King. Besides, I could very well be on my way to my death."

"Please don't say that," she said.

"Let me say this, then," he said, the captain's ring in his voice once again. "I set out on the high seas for one reason: to find you. And I did. By then I had become a pirate. But I realized something while sitting in this cell. I might not have found you if I hadn't been a pirate. The Navy would not have had any business or right to stop *The Nantes*, and once you had left the ship, I never would have found you, just like I never found you in Typeg. So, while I regret becoming a pirate, and I regret all the things that I have done under a black flag, for your sake, Tahira, I'm glad that I was a pirate. I would probably have never found you otherwise. And now that I have, I can fulfill the promises I made to your parents and to myself. I still have much to atone for, but in that I can rest at peace."

He took her other hand and gripped it tightly. He leaned closer and lowered his voice. "If I am allowed to live, and if you will have me, I will gladly spend the rest of my life by your side. It's what I want."

Tahira didn't realize she was crying until she felt the tears drip onto her hands. She leaned her forehead against the bars and let out a sob. Killian kissed the top of her head.

"Why wouldn't I have you?" she asked, looking up at him. "And why don't you think you'll make a good King? You were a Captain for years. You're a leader."

Killian shook his head. "I was a tyrant most of the time."

"Yet the men followed you."

"They also didn't have a choice," he said. "It was either follow me or drown. Most didn't make the right decision."

Tahira opened her mouth to contradict him, but thought better of it. She didn't want to argue. She blinked her watery eyes. "I don't want to lose you. I almost lost you three times before. I almost can't bear the thought of losing you again."

Tears were falling down his face too. "I don't want to lose you either," he said.

He leaned forward though the bars and kissed her. Tahira pulled one hand out of his and caressed his face, his stubble poking into her hand. She kissed him harder, knowing it might be for the last time, as his trial might not go well, knowing that she might never see him again. That knowledge brought such pain to her soul.

Tahira heard footsteps around the corner and kissed Killian one last time. She pulled away and stared at his face, memorizing every part of it. He seemed to be doing the same.

The guard cleared his throat. "Your Highness? The Queen is asking for you."

Tahira didn't want to say goodbye. Killian kissed her hand as she turned to follow the guard. She looked back at him until the guard led her around the corner and out of sight.

Chapter Twenty-Seven

Mother had arranged for her and Tahira to work in a different store nearly every day during the pirate trials, so that Tahira could learn a little about many trades. With each new store she felt her mind expanding, taking in everything, seeing just how diverse and large the world was.

At the bakery she learned how to make the croissants Killian loved, and they became her favorites too. At the milliner's she kept her distance from the workers, as they all seemed a little odd, though Mother said they were harmless. At the seamstress's she kept out of Mother's way; this trade had once been Mother's, and her fingers remembered the work so well she got more done than the rest of the workers. One day Tahira visited the carpenter, who helped her carve a tiny ship out of sweet-smelling cedar wood. When she was done the carpenter put it onto a thick black thread so she could wear it around her neck. At the grocer's Tahira learned about all the different kinds of foods that grew in Raemica, many of which she had never seen before. She and the apothecary shared healing remedies for an entire afternoon.

Every day when Mother and Tahira took their midday break, they would purchase croissants and eat them in the main square of the city. It was always busy, full of hundreds of people: laughers, dancers, musicians, shrieking children—some in uniforms, some not—shoppers, tradesmen, and sailors from the docks. One afternoon nearly everyone in the square came together and danced to a song two groups of musicians played together. Everyone knew the song and the steps, and hardly anyone made a mistake.

"It's a folk dance," Mother said, noting Tahira's awe and confusion. "They're dances that have been passed down through the generations, and much of the time tell the stories of the people. This one is the most well-known Raemican folk dance. Come on, I'll show you."

Having never danced before, Tahira would have liked to sit and watch. But like with singing in the slave compounds all those years ago, she found that she could learn the dance steps well. Soon she joined the main body of dancers, singing and laughing along with them.

One morning, nearly two weeks after the beginning of the pirate trials, Mother led Tahira through the main thoroughfare of the city as usual. But instead of going to a store, Mother turned to the left off the main road and wound her way through gradually narrowing roads that were slowly coming closer to the docks.

Houses were built here, some large, some small, some falling apart, some new. They lined the road on either side, and by looking through the gaps between the houses, Tahira could see that more houses were built up the hill to her left, toward the castle, and down the hill to her right, toward the sea. Soon Tahira could no longer hear the city noises from behind her, and she could barely hear the noises from the docks. It was quiet here among the houses, a sanctuary from sound and bustle.

"Where are we going?" Tahira asked at last.

Mother smiled and took her hand. "I thought you might like to see your first home."

Tahira's breath caught a little in her chest. Her first home. The home she was stolen from. If they had lived this close to the sea, she understood how that raider had escaped with her so quickly.

Mother stopped at last, and Tahira faced her first house. It was modest and brown, the front taken up entirely by the front door and a window. Between the house and the little fencing in front of them was a small yard, well-tended and green with flowers. But Tahira's eye was drawn to the window. It was taller than the door and twice as wide. The top was arched, and thin lines of wood or stone or metal crisscrossed and webbed through the entire window, making shapes both large and small through the bubbly panes of glass. The mere sight of the window made her smile.

"You loved that window even when you were a little one," Mother said, watching her. "You used to tell me you could see shapes in the panes, like they were telling stories. You and Killian used to make up stories by the hour."

Tahira looked around, at the neighboring houses, at the view out to the sea. "This is a beautiful home," she said. "Did Father build it?"

Mother nodded. "He did," she said, beaming. "He was so proud of it. He still is."

"Can we go inside?" Tahira asked, laying her hand on the gate.

"Not now," Mother said. "We have a family living here, taking care of the house for us. I would hate to drop in unannounced."

Tahira nodded and returned her gaze to the house. She did not remember it, but she immediately loved it. She wondered if the chair on the porch was the one Mother had been sitting in when she was taken. "Where did Killian live?" she asked at last.

"Right here," Mother said. "Your father built this one too."

She moved to their left, and Tahira saw that Killian's old house looked very much like her own, except that it was painted gray, and its front window was not as grand. It suited him very well.

"Killian said you and his parents were friends," Tahira said. She missed Killian so terribly it almost hurt. She gripped the fence hard with both hands as she struggled not to burst.

"Yes, we are," Mother said, watching her carefully. Gently, she laid a hand on Tahira's wrist. "His mother, Marja, was like a sister to me. We grew up together."

"Are they home?" Tahira asked, slowly releasing her grip on the fence. She was grateful Mother hadn't mentioned her inner turmoil. "I'd like to meet them."

Mother shook her head. "I'd like that too, but they're not home. When they are, Killian's mother puts a candle in that window. She always told me it made her feel terrible to think of someone coming to an empty house, so she makes sure people know when she is home." Mother smiled a little. "She does tend to be a fussy woman."

"Did they like that Killian went to sea?" Tahira asked.

"Oh no," Mother said. "They wanted Killian to follow in his father's footsteps and become a goldsmith. But that was never the life for him. I kept trying to tell Marja that, but she wouldn't listen. Sometimes I got the feeling they never understood their own son." Mother sighed and Tahira put her arm around her mother's shoulders. They stood staring at the house for a few minutes in silence.

"Marja is a cook," Mother said at last. "She works in the home of a member of the Council. She's quite good."

"I learned how to cook a little," Tahira said.

"You'd learn a lot from her, if she'll teach you," Mother said.

Tahira paused. "Do they know Killian is back?" she asked quietly.

Mother's shoulders drooped slightly, telling Tahira more than words could have. "They do," she said. "And they are… well, conflicted. You see, ten years ago, when we received word Killian had turned pirate, Marja was devastated. She didn't sleep or eat, she just laid in bed, staring at nothing. Killian's father, Breen, didn't know what to do. And then one day Marja stood up and continued life as though nothing had happened. She rarely spoke of Killian after that. They heard about Killian coming back with you before I could tell them. But I think Breen and Marja disowned Killian in a way. His becoming a pirate put a black mark on them that only they feel."

"Meaning no one blames them, but they blame themselves?" Tahira asked, removing her arm from around Mother.

Mother nodded. "I want you to meet them, but I don't know if they want to meet you. They might blame you for Killian's piracy as much as they blame themselves." She glanced at Tahira with apology.

"They must know that isn't my fault," Tahira said, feeling a little defensive. "I didn't ask Killian to come after me."

"Maybe they do, maybe they don't," Mother said. "But they're in pain. And they want answers for it, even if it's lies."

Mother took a deep breath and shook her head, her long hair dancing further down her back as she lifted her face to the sky.

"They seem like complicated people," Tahira said, looking at the house again. "Like they can't make up their minds. Is that true?"

"I don't think I could have said it better," Mother said with a little laugh. "They are not the Breen and Marja I knew ten years ago. Their grief has changed them, though I still love them dearly." She put her arm around Tahira's shoulders and led her back to their old house. "Oh Tahira, I meant for this outing to be happy, and it's turned a little sad. I'm sorry."

Tahira patted Mother's hand on her shoulder. "I'm glad you brought me here," she said, staring again at the fascinating window. "And I'm glad you told me about Killian's parents. When I meet them, I won't be surprised, however they treat me."

"That's a good way of seeing it," Mother said. She looked up at the sky again, checking the time by the position of the sun. "Let's get back to the castle to meet your father. Oh, and I needed to tell you." Mother dropped her arm from around Tahira's shoulders and took her hand instead. "Your father told me this morning that the Council would like you to witness tomorrow."

"Tomorrow?" Tahira asked, shocked. "Does that mean Killian's trial is today?" Though she never forgot to think about Killian, she had tried to forget his impending trial.

"I don't think so," Mother said. "I'm not following these trials as closely as I do others. You probably understand that."

Tahira nodded. Mother led her away from the house, and they walked slowly along the roads, back toward the main city thoroughfare. Suddenly from behind them came a call of, "Your Majesty!"

Mother and Tahira turned around to find the road behind them filled with people, women and children mostly, who had come spilling out of their houses as they had passed, and who now crowded behind them. Tahira hadn't heard them gathering. Mother smiled and stepped toward them. She knew them all by name, and treated them all as friends. Perhaps they were. A young mother with a crying new baby stood nearest Tahira. She looked tired and wan, and the baby's expression spoke of pain. Tahira held out her hands to the mother, who timidly handed over the baby.

Tahira felt as if she was transported back to the midwives' house in Typeg, working with Shipra and Pula. They had taught her all the ailments that befall a baby, and how to ease their discomfort.

She turned the baby over onto its belly and slid her arm underneath it, so that her fingers were holding the baby's cheeks and her wrist was against its chest. Gently she rubbed and patted the baby's back with her other hand, and after a few moments the baby let out a huge burp. Several children nearby giggled and Tahira smiled at them. She kept rubbing the baby's back until two more burps followed and the baby finally stopped crying.

Carefully she shifted her arm upwards so that the baby was upright, its little bottom against the crook of her elbow. It looked at her with large blue eyes, then blinked slowly. Tahira quickly handed the upright baby to the mother, resting it against the mother's shoulder and chest. After a few blinks, the baby fell asleep.

"Thank you, Your Highness," the mother said, curtsying deeply.

Tahira nodded with a smile and looked away from the young mother to find her own mother smiling at her.

"My friends, may I introduce my daughter, Princess Tahira Colusafay," Mother said in a carrying voice to the crowd.

As one, the crowd curtsied or bowed to her. Tahira glanced at Mother, who minutely reminded Tahira of the proper protocol to accepting such attention. She did it, and the people came forward to meet her.

Chapter Twenty-Eight

Tahira nervously straightened her sleeves as she looked at her reflection. Her new lady's maid-in-training, Sia, was prattling away, making sure the back of Tahira's skirt lay just right. Tahira tried to concentrate on Sia's stories, but she couldn't bring her mind to focus on anything but what was in front of her: witnessing for the pirates.

She had chosen this dress because its black and deep blue fabrics reminded her of Killian. It made her feel important, like someone worth hearing. Sia had pulled back half of her long hair into an elaborate knot at the back of her head, leaving the rest to cascade down her back. She stood up a little straighter and thought she looked pretty.

A knock announced Mother's arrival; she looked as nervous as Tahira felt. Together, they walked toward the trial room: down the corridor of the royal family's private wing on the north side of the castle, to where it flowed into the main body of the castle. From there they went down the staircase to the atrium. Mother turned left and crossed the atrium to the double doors of the trial room, nearly exactly opposite from the corridor to the throne room. Tahira took a deep breath as Mother opened the door.

The trial room was less than half the size of the throne room, a long, rectangular room that felt tight. The doors opened at a short end of the room, and down both sides of the room were chairs in two or three tiers for any spectators to watch the trial. At the moment, the chairs were empty, except for a few people sitting close together at the other end of the room.

Directly opposite Tahira was where the Council sat in judgment at a long desk that ran nearly the whole width of the room, no man higher than another. The desk was about the height of Tahira's head, so that the accused had to look up at his judges. On either side of the long desk were doors leading out of the trial room. To the Councils' right was the door that led back to the atrium through a twisted hallway. But the other door led out to the Gallows Courtyard on the east side of the castle, where once a week convicted criminals were hanged.

The Council was already sitting at their long desk, Father among them.

Tahira was surprised to see how drawn he looked. But he smiled at seeing her and Mother and stepped down to greet them.

"Tahira, you look beautiful," he said in a low voice, giving her a reassuring hug. "You needn't worry about anything, you are simply answering questions." Tahira nodded, trying to put on a brave face. Father turned to Mother and asked for a private word.

Left alone, Tahira's gaze fell on the people sitting in the spectator seats. One was Admiral Myngs, his red face puffed in what looked like indignation. Next to him was Lieutenant Rogers, who nodded curtly to her.

Tahira's gaze fell on the last two people, a man and a woman. She stared. They saw her and rose to meet her, nodding their heads as they stopped in front of her. Even before they introduced themselves, she knew who they were: Breen and Marja Haefen. Killian was a perfect blend of them both: his father's height, eyes, and nose; his mother's dark hair, mouth, and long hands.

Marja smiled sadly. "I'm so glad you're back," she said, her eyes a little red from crying. "I didn't want Killian to go to sea to find you, but I'm glad he did. Look at the woman you've become."

Tahira felt the blame in Marja's words but refused to take it. And even if Mother hadn't explained Killian's parents, Tahira would still have seen the pain in Marja's face. The pain was less pronounced in Breen's face, but he still bore it as he smiled a smile that almost looked like Killian's.

"Thank you for witnessing for our son," Breen said. "None of his crew would, we're told. They're all angry at him for getting them killed."

Tahira knitted her brows for a moment, confused, but then realized what Breen was talking about.

"Killian didn't know the monarchy had changed," she said. "He thought King Noah was still on the throne and granting pardons to any pirate who asked. The crew wanted pardons, but most, I think, would have gone against it at once. Killian was only concerned with getting me home and giving up piracy. He did not intend for his crew to be facing the gallows."

Marja's eyes filled with tears, but Tahira couldn't tell if they were from gratitude or remorse. "He always loved you, you know, ever since you were born," she said, almost as if Tahira hadn't spoken. "He hardly spoke of anything else. He had to find you."

The blame was thicker in her voice now, and Tahira found it a little harder to ignore.

But then Marja took her hand and squeezed it. "Breen and I may not have always understood Killian," she said, confirming Mother's suspicions from the day before. "But I always wanted for him to find someone who could love him for who he is. And it seems it's you who's done that. I'm very grateful to you, Princess."

Tahira felt a lump in her throat and didn't know what to say, so she nodded.

A few minutes later the Council called the room to order and asked Tahira to witness. Breen and Marja returned to their seats by the Admiral and Lieutenant, with Mother sitting next to them. Father returned to the Council behind the desk, preparing his papers. Tahira stood in the middle of the floor, looking up at the Council with what she hoped was confidence.

The man asking her questions, Boam, had a stern, lined face and silvery-gray hair. She knew him from Royal Council meetings to be the man who always found something to contest, the only Council member who didn't like Father. From the look on Father's face, she gathered that Boam had been difficult during the trials.

At Boam's questioning, Tahira explained in detail about individual pirates: who helped her, who was indifferent, who tried to kill her. But Boam was most interested in Killian's involvement.

"What examples of piracy did *Captain* Haefen exhibit?" Boam asked, derision in his voice.

"I'm not sure what was piracy, and what was Navy," Tahira said, biting back her impatience at his prejudice. "Killian Haefen was not like any of the other pirates on the *Royal Conlan*. It constantly confused me, as I couldn't tell if he was truly kind or just pretending. I first met him when he had stopped the slaver I was on, by shooting across *The Nantes*'s bow. Captain Haefen asked for hats from the crew of *The Nantes*. His quartermaster told me later that Captain Haefen frequently stopped that ship and other slavers and stole slaves."

"Did he?" Boam said, impassive. Tahira heard the Haefens murmuring to each other. "What did he do with these slaves?"

"The quartermaster told me the crew thought Captain Haefen sold them or marooned them when they didn't work well," Tahira said. "But really he took them home, or as close to home as he could."

Impressed murmurs ran around the trial room, even from Boam. But it seemed he wasn't satisfied. His questions became more pointed, harder to understand, almost as though he was trying to catch Tahira lying.

She told everything: Alycia's death, Wilkid's keelhauling and Richardson's whipping, the storm that nearly drowned her, careening the ship, Turtle Island. Here she had to pause and explain the customs of Turtle Island, for only then would her story of Killian holding her hand have significance. She heard Marja sigh.

"On our second day there, I went into the town alone, and I met a woman named Jaazah," Tahira said, smiling a little at the memory. "She had lived on Turtle Island her whole life, and knew all about the pirates that came. She had few praising words to say about any of them. I asked her what she knew about Captain Haefen. She told me that she had only seen him in the town a few times, and he was never with a woman. That was very unusual for Turtle Island. Jaazah said that some believed Captain Haefen hated women, but she didn't think so, since he'd held my hand to protect me. She'd heard that he was a strict disciplinarian, but a man of his word. And she told me that if any pirate possessed kindness, it would have been him. That she had anything good to say about a pirate meant something, and she said it about Captain Haefen."

"And why did you ask Jaazah to tell you what she knew?" Boam asked.

"Because I was trying to figure out what kind of man he is," Tahira said. "From the very beginning I felt there was a nobleness to him. I've already said he was different from his crew. He kept giving me the choice to leave, as I've explained. I finally decided that he was a kind man pretending to be a pirate, because he doesn't have the black heart."

"Yet he keelhauled a man," Boam said in an offhanded tone. He looked down at his papers and lazily flicked through them. Before Tahira could respond, he moved on to his next question.

Through it all, Tahira did her best to answer truthfully about everything, even how she felt about Killian, and she was relieved when Boam never looked triumphant at her expense. Father beamed proudly at her from his seat.

Finally, Boam reached the end of his questions. He gathered his papers and slowly stacked them. "It seems, then, that except for a few instances, Captain Haefen acted like the Navy officer he was trained to be," he said. Admiral Myngs cleared his throat importantly. Boam leaned forward and looked down the desk at Father. "Delrick, I may have to consider what you showed me."

"When will Killian be tried?" Tahira asked.

"Perhaps tomorrow," Boam said, his voice hard as he looked down at her. "But you will not be allowed to attend. I cannot be sure that what you've told me wasn't rehearsed beforehand. If I find you've lied to keep a guilty man alive, then—"

"Boam," Father said sharply, standing up. All eyes flew to him as he suddenly commanded the whole room. "That's no way to speak to your Princess."

Boam's face reddened slightly before he looked down at Tahira. "Of course, Your Majesty. Apologies, Your Highness."

Tahira inclined her head, unoffended, though a little rattled. "What did my father show you?"

"I'll tell you another time, Tahira," Father said. He sounded tired and her heart went out to him. He stepped down from the desk and walked around it toward her. "Come, my dears, you're no longer needed here."

Tahira suddenly realized how tired she felt, and her knees wobbled a little. Father had just reached her and Mother when a woman at the desk stood up. "A moment, please, Princess," she called.

Father turned to face her and smiled a little. So did Mother. Tahira looked up at the middle-aged woman, whose light hair was graying. This woman, Aqila, was usually quiet during Royal Council sessions, yet she was revered for her sense of reason. Her kind eyes smiled at Tahira while her mouth did not, and Tahira could feel a maternal regard coming from her, as Aqila had several children.

"Princess, you have answered about Captain Haefen and the other pirates," Aqila said. "I wish you to answer a question about yourself before you go."

Tahira nodded once, retaking her standing place on the floor. Father took Mother's hand and they stepped back.

Aqila watched her a moment before asking, "How would you feel if, after all our deliberations, Captain Haefen is found guilty and sentenced to hanging?"

The question surprised Tahira and her throat tightened. She glanced at Mother and Father, remembering how they had asked her the very same question before the pirate trials began. She recalled that conversation to answer Aqila's question.

"By law, Captain Haefen is responsible for the actions and crimes of his crew," she said. "And the actions of any one of them could be enough to hang him, even if his personal crimes were not so great. I don't want to lose him. But I also don't want him to be spared just because we love each other. That's not reason enough to ignore the laws. I think that he's worth saving, and I want him to be. I want him to be tried for his own crimes, and not the crimes of his crew. Let them pay their own price. But Killian came here to see justice done. If I or the King and Queen pardoned him without a fair trial, he would see that as having cheated, and he might grow to hate me because of it."

She'd spoken the words before her mind had a chance to realize what she was saying. But she knew she'd spoken the truth. She swallowed hard.

Aqila seemed satisfied. She thanked Tahira and resumed her seat. Tahira stood in the middle of the trial room, rooted to the spot with exhaustion, shock, and a sudden sadness. She started when Father touched her shoulder and held out his arm to her. She looped her arm through his, feeling coming back as he led her and Mother from the room. Her witnessing was over. Killian was in the Council's hands now.

At the door, Tahira looked over her shoulder at Breen and Marja. Though they weren't looking at her, she saw in their faces something she didn't think she would see: hope.

Chapter Twenty-Nine

Nearly a week later, the Royal Councils resumed. Tahira had heard no word about Killian's fate, and she didn't want to ask Father in front of the Council. And as he had always looked so tired at evening meals Tahira hadn't had the heart to ask him.

But that day had been a hanging day. Who knew how many of the *Royal Conlan* crew had died.

Tahira barely listened as the Council members droned about their various assignments and needs. No one mentioned the pirates.

At long last the Council left. Tahira realized she was sitting slumped in her seat, and as she adjusted herself, she found Mother and Father watching her.

"How are you doing?" Father asked.

Tahira had a thousand answers ready on her tongue, but none of them would come out. Father's face was so drawn and tired. She wondered how much sleep he had gotten the night before, or for the weeks of the trials. But she had to know.

"What happened during the trials?" she asked, clasping her hands on the table.

Mother hit Father's arm gently with the back of her hand. "You might have known she'd ask that," she said. "I'd like to know too, since you've told me nothing."

Father lowered his head, deferent. "I did not know the final outcome until early this morning," he said. "As a Council we deliberated through the night. Usually decisions over a prisoner's sentence come much quicker, but this pirate crew had us divided. I want to thank you, Tahira, for witnessing like you did. You helped us make our final decisions."

Something about Father's tone made her feel like her chest was constricting, though she couldn't tell if it came from impending sadness or from building excitement. All along she knew Killian might be hanged for his piracy. Boam had been almost merciless in his questioning of her, she could only imagine how he had been on each pirate, especially Killian.

Not sure how Father's next words would go, she prepared herself for the news.

"I promised you that I would do everything in my power to save Killian," Father said. "It wasn't an easy thing to do, as we all knew what might befall him in his trial."

Tahira closed her eyes and braced herself to hear that Killian was going to die.

Father leaned over and put his hand on her wrist. "Tahira, Killian is going to live."

"What?" Mother said. Tahira heard her laugh, but she hadn't fully processed what Father had said. She squeezed her eyes tight, willing herself not to cry.

"Tahira!" Father said, shaking her wrist a little. She opened her eyes and found Father's shining at her.

"What?" she asked, feeling a little frantic and closer to tears.

"Killian is going to live," Father repeated.

Tahira froze as the words finally penetrated into her mind. Then she pulled her wrist away and fell back into her chair, her hands over her mouth, panting and sobbing by turns, her whole body relieved and spirits hopeful.

"How did you do it?" she asked at last. Mother handed her a handkerchief. "How did you save him? I thought for sure he would die."

"I did too," Father said. "And it took two things to save him. The first thing, it was Killian who gave me the idea."

"Killian?" Mother asked. "But you haven't seen him in weeks, how did he do that?"

Father settled back, his elbows on the arms of his chair and his fingers laced together. His expression was slightly smug, as though extremely proud of himself; he wanted to share his story. Mother and Tahira instinctively leaned forward to hear.

"Remember when Ezra gave you that errand from me? The one to the dungeons?" he asked Tahira. She nodded. "I told you I was on my way to the trial room. But when Ezra left you, he came and got me, and I followed you, and listened to you and Killian talking."

"Delrick!" Mother said, tapping his wrist. "Eavesdropping on your daughter?"

"I'm sorry, it was necessary," Father said, looking apologetic and a little guilty. "Boam and a few others of the Council told me from the very beginning that they would see all the pirates hang, especially Killian."

Mother's face paled. "But some of them knew Killian when he was a boy," she said in a soft voice. "They worked with his father for years. How could they do that?"

Father let out a slow breath through his nose and looked long and hard at Mother. Once again, Tahira got the impression that they were communicating without words. "Perhaps you and I could go over the requirements for being a magistrate," he said in a low voice. "See who the other candidates are, and see if someone needs to be replaced."

"You really think so?" Mother asked, her brow worried.

"They were willing to kill the son of a friend without any reservations," Father said. "That won't be forgotten soon."

Mother nodded.

"I didn't want to see Killian die, not if I could help it," Father said, returning his gaze to Tahira. "And so when I followed you to the dungeons, I brought Boam with me."

"To what purpose?" Mother asked.

"I wanted him to see the real Killian, to hear from his own lips why he did what he did," Father said. "I wanted Boam to see what he would be doing if he pushed for Killian to die. That's when Killian gave me the idea. Without prompting he proved to me, and more importantly to Boam, what his intentions were: that he wanted you and not piracy. Questioning prisoners has never led to that result before. And so I suggested to Boam that instead of questioning each pirate, we let him talk. His own conversation would reveal his intentions."

"Boam said during the witnessing that he might consider what you showed him," Tahira said. "Does that mean he let Killian talk?"

Father nodded with a little grimace. "He only said that to be dramatic," he said. "He had agreed at once, and all had his chance to speak."

Tahira wrinkled her nose. "Is it all right if I don't like Boam very much?"

Mother laughed and stroked her hand once. "I don't much care for him either, dear."

"So Killian is safe," Father said. "Though most of the night was taken up with debating what to do with him." He shook his head and let out a weary sigh, running his hand through his hair. He suddenly looked much older. Tahira could only imagine what the whole trials had been like for him.

"They were that divided?" Mother asked. She looked worried, telling Tahira that there was something deeper going on than a few Council members having differing opinions.

Father nodded. Mother gave an impatient huff and shook her head.

"I should have been there with you," she said.

Father touched the back of her hand with his fingertips. "If you had, you wouldn't have been able to vote, Jazara," he said. "You were not part of the proceedings."

Mother sighed and put the fingers of her other hand to her forehead. "How soon can we look over those magistrate requirements?" she asked softly.

Father patted her hand and faced Tahira again, his weariness cleared. "As soon as I finish my story."

"Yes, what was the second thing that saved Killian?" Tahira asked. She didn't fully understand what had transpired between her parents, but she felt confident they would tell her some time.

Father smiled, his eyes twinkling. "You gave me the idea," he said.

Tahira was shocked. "How?" she asked. "I barely understand Raemican law."

"At the end of your witnessing, you said you wanted Killian to be tried for his crimes only," Father said. "Afterwards I asked the Council if they knew of any such law. Admiral Myngs was still there, and he said he did."

Mother tapped at Father's sleeve, showing her impatience and excitement.

"It's part of maritime law," Father said. "An exception can be made to the captain bearing all the blame if the crew acted of its own volition, and not under direct orders. The Admiral knew it by heart."

"He is a stickler for laws," Mother said. "I'm glad his knowledge has now saved Killian twice."

"So," Tahira said slowly, "Killian was tried for his own crimes, just like the rest of the crew?"

"Yes," Father said, slapping the table with the palm of one hand. He looked as eager as a little boy. "Since we'd already heard from the crew, we knew what each man had done, and why. And it seems that whenever the *Royal Conlan* spotted a ship, Killian gave command to Scudamore or Rance and had stayed in his cabin, not taking part in the action or spoils. He personally never killed an innocent or stole from them."

"But wait," Tahira said, shaking her head. "Killian told me he's done terrible things as a pirate."

"Yes, I remember hearing that," Father said, his enthusiasm uncurbed. "He did participate in overhauling ships and in stealing. But not as a Captain. He told us himself that he didn't fully choose to be a pirate until he became a Captain with his own ship. That was only three years ago. Up until then he was considered a forced man."

"How did Boam take to this maritime law?" Mother asked, rubbing Tahira's arm.

"He only accepted it because it came from Admiral Myngs, and only because the Admiral brought the book and showed him the law," Father said.

"Oh, that Boam," Mother said, rubbing her forehead again.

"So Killian told you all about his piracy days?" Tahira asked, feeling a twinge of jealousy; she would have to ask Killian to share it all with her now.

"He did," Father said, nodding. "While some of it is gruesome, I don't think it's as black as he thinks it is. He was tried for his own crimes and deemed worthy of pardon. Perhaps, Tahira, you could help him."

Tahira nodded, smiling. She was starting to feel jittery again, just like before she saw Killian in the dungeon, but with excitement this time. Father saw her question.

"Killian and the other pardoned pirates are being released now," he said.

"Other pardoned pirates?" Mother asked.

"I want to see him," Tahira said. She stood up, but she was curious.

"Oh no, not like that you're not," Mother said. Her expression looked conspiratorial, though Tahira couldn't figure out why. She pushed Tahira back into her seat as she stood. "Meet me in your room, we're going to make you a little more presentable."

She left the throne room before Tahira could respond.

"I don't care what I look like, I want to see Killian," she muttered.

Father chuckled. "It matters to your mother," he said.

"Who else was pardoned, Father?" Tahira asked, scooting a little closer.

Father pulled a paper toward him from his ever-present pile, a slight smile on his face. "These men were pardoned, not because their crimes were less, but because of their intention to never turn to piracy again."

"But Killian had that, why was his case so hard?" Tahira asked, feeling a little annoyed at the unfairness.

"Because Killian was the captain. Harder punishments for him," Father said, wrinkling one side of his nose just like Tahira did. Father turned back to the paper and read the names, "Peter Scudamore, James Copper, Robbie Ransome, Samson, Tom Stretton, and Sam Morwell."

Tahira gasped a little. "Those were my allies."

Father nodded. He patted her hand. "And now, my beauty, it's time to meet your Captain," he said. "But see your mother first."

Tahira kissed Father on the cheek and seemed to float out of the throne room. Her excitement and joy burst out of her as she started running down the stairs. Halfway down she glanced up and saw a small group of men standing at the base of the stairs, looking up at her. The setting sun coming in through the open front doors lit them from behind, making it impossible for her to identify them until she was closer. The men lined up shoulder-to-shoulder as though waiting for her. Tahira slowed her steps, wary, but still smiling.

"Your Highness," said the man on the far left, and Tahira immediately recognized Scudamore. Next to him were the other five pardoned pirates. Killian wasn't among them.

"You retired," she said, stepping off the last stair.

"Aye, Miss, we did," Copper said, knuckling his brow to her. Ransome was physically beaming.

"But why?" Tahira asked.

"Because of you, Tahira," Scudamore said. "You showed us that there're better things than piracy."

"I don't think I did any such thing," Tahira said.

"But ye did," Stretton said.

Tahira nodded once, not wanting to argue. "What will you do now?"

"Find work," Scudamore said. The others nodded.

Tahira took a step toward them. "I don't know if it's my place to offer, but come back here if you can't find work," she said. "I'll see what can be done for you."

"Why would a Princess trouble 'erself with former pirates?" Stretton asked.

"Because you showed me quarter when you didn't have to," Tahira said. "Thank you for that."

The six pirates bowed, smiles on their faces. Five of them turned and left through the front doors, but Scudamore approached her.

"If you're looking for Haefen, he's already out," he said, answering her unasked question. "He was released just after the hangings finished." His face darkened and Tahira gulped. How many of his friends had died that day? "He said something about wanting to find you."

Tahira's heart pumped faster. "Thank you, Scudamore," she said.

Scudamore inclined his head and Tahira left him in the entrance hall. Once around the corner into the atrium she broke into a run, heading up the stairs and to her room as fast as she could.

Mother was waiting inside with Sia. Together they pulled Tahira out of her gown and over to a basin, where they sponged off any sweat, tears, and snot from her body. Mother brushed out her hair and did it up again while Sia readied a new gown for Tahira to put on.

"But Mother, it's sunset, why am I putting on a new gown now?" Tahira asked.

"Because you're seeing your Captain for the first time in weeks," Mother said, her brow knitted in concentration. "I want you to look presentable. This is not just how a Princess should think, but how a normal woman thinks."

Tahira sighed and let Mother work. And when Mother was done, Tahira had to admit she was right.

"Now, Killian will be in the southern gardens," Mother said, finishing the last touches.

Tahira knitted her eyebrows. "How do you—"

"Never mind, get going!" Mother said, chivvying her out the door.

Tahira quickly made her way back to the atrium, then down the corridor that would lead to the gardens. With each step her heart beat faster, excitement bubbling up so high she could barely contain it. Finally, she reached the glass doors into the garden. She paused for a moment to catch her breath, then opened the doors and stepped outside.

The gardens were large and walled in, a haven of quiet after the bustle of the castle. Tahira stood at the top of the steps, where she could see the entire expanse of the gardens. Neatly-pruned shrubs and hedges of all sizes made mazes here and there, and the beds were overflowing with flowers of dazzling colors that reminded Tahira of the island where they careened.

Little statues stood at the entrances and exits of the hedge mazes. Trees that never dropped their leaves stood sentinel at the corners of the garden, each with benches underneath. A stony pathway led throughout the garden, the only part of the ground that wasn't green. And in the center of the garden was a large circular white fountain. Six dolphins stood around the edges, all spitting glistening water toward a candlestick-shaped dais in the center.

The sun was just setting out of the garden, bathing the greenness with orange. Tahira stood on her toes and looked around, hoping to see her dark-haired, black-cladded pirate amongst the greens and flowers and shrubs. But she could see no one but the gardeners. Tahira gathered her skirt with one hand and descended the stairs.

"Killian?" she called. She walked around the fountain slowly, listening to its glistening water. Part of her still couldn't believe that Killian was alive, after all their doubts.

"Tahira?"

She started at the sound of his voice and turned toward him. She gasped at the sight of him, almost not recognizing him. Killian was clean and clean-shaven and wearing rich clothes that weren't his but suited him well. He looked like a prince.

Killian was staring at her, taking in her princess gown, his light blue gaze seeing through her as it used to when they first met. He seemed stunned.

"Killian," Tahira said.

She ran toward him and threw her arms around his neck. He wrapped his arms around her, holding her close, then lifted her off her feet and spun her around once before setting her on her feet again. Tahira couldn't help herself; she laughed with joy. In the middle of it he kissed her, slowly and sweetly.

"Tahira," he said.

"I thought you would be condemned," she said leaning her forehead against his. "I almost couldn't believe it when Father told me you'd been pardoned."

"I can't believe it myself," Killian said, with a laugh. "How did it happen?"

"You and I unknowingly gave Father the two ideas that saved you," she said, then laughed at Killian's confusion at her words. "I'll explain later. But you were tried for your own crimes, not your entire crew's."

Killian looked surprised, for he knew the law too. He blinked and ducked his head, hiding his tears.

"I deserve much worse," he said. "I don't deserve you."

Tahira took his face and forced him to look at her, his smooth face strange under her hands. A few tears spilled out down his cheeks. She smiled, her own tears blurring her vision.

"Don't you think I should be the one who decides if you deserve me?" she asked. "Because you do."

He opened his mouth but nothing came out.

"I love you," she said.

He smiled his sideways smile and her heart skipped a beat or two. He took her hands tightly in his.

"I love you," he said, serious. "I am tired of being taken from you, and I am tired of you being taken from me. It's happened too many times. So, to ensure it won't happen again, I want to ask you something." He paused and took a deep breath. "Will you marry me?"

The question surprised her, and for a moment she didn't know what to say. But as she stared at Killian's handsome face, she realized that she did want to marry him. She, too, was tired of being separated. She wanted him for the rest of their lives. He smiled shyly at her, and he suddenly looked like the little boy who wanted so desperately to find his lost best friend. She found her voice at last.

"Yes," she said, tears renewing in her eyes. "I will marry you."

His smile widened and he kissed her again, harder this time, his big hands cupping her face. Then one hand moved down her neck and over her scars to the small of her back, pulling her in closer to him. Tahira snaked one arm behind his back and held him tight.

"Now all I have to do is convince your father to let me marry you," Killian said when they broke apart, resting his forehead against Tahira's.

"He will, he loves you," she said.

"And get you a ring," he said. He chuckled. "I see your mother did get you new clothes after all."

"Hmm, I told you she did," Tahira said, shifting her weight so her skirt swiveled. "What about you? Where did you get these?" She tugged on his sleeve.

"Your mother found me," he said, straightening up to look down at himself. "I was barely out of the dungeons when there she was, dragging me off to a bath and a change of clothes. She said that I couldn't see you in the state I was in. These were your father's clothes."

Tahira barely listened to his words, drawn so much by how freely he was talking. He had never talked to her like that before, and she loved him all the more for it.

Killian pulled her against his chest, her head nestled under his chin. She felt so comfortable here, and she remembered that the first time he held her like this was when he had rescued her from Nave. So much had happened between them since then.

The sun set into the sea, leaving them in the darkness of the stars. A chill breeze swept in from the sea and ran around the garden, rustling all the leaves and Tahira's skirts. She shivered in Killian's arms and he rubbed her back with one hand.

"Shall we go inside?" he whispered at last. "Your parents might be waiting for you."

"Oh yes," she said. "And it's dinner time. You're probably hungry for something other than hardtack and meat."

Killian chuckled, the sound reverberating through her head. They finally broke apart, and Tahira immediately felt colder for not being close to him. He took her hand and they walked toward the castle door.

Tahira took a deep breath, taking in the sea's salty tang, the garden's heady musk, and Killian's masculine smell. She'd never felt so happy. With her hand still in Killian's, she stepped back into the castle, ready to begin her new life.

Set Me Free

Nikki Anne Ellison

307

Set Me Free

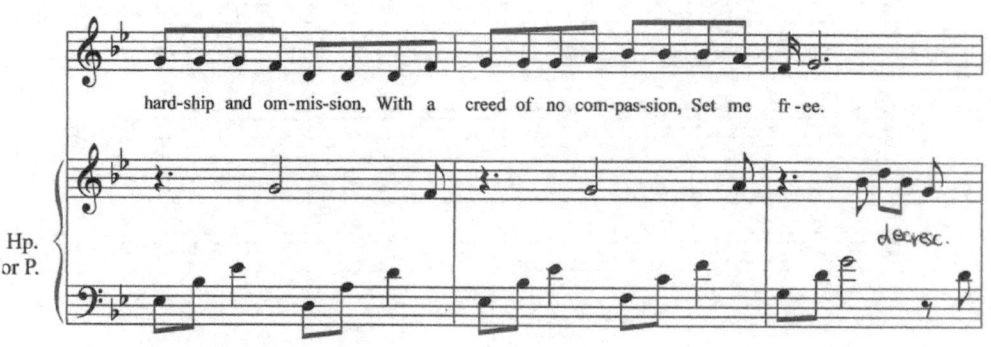

Set Me Free

4   Set Me Free